Black Wolf

Anna Bowman

BLACK WOLF

OUTKAST

BOOK TWO

Anna Bowman

Cover designed by Judah Lamey

This book is a work of fiction. Names, characters, places, and incidents either are products of the author's imagination or are used fictitiously. Any resemblance to actual persons, living or dead, events, or locales is entirely coincidental.

Printed in the United States of America

First Printing: 2021
Kepler Production Studios (KPS)
ISBN: 978-1-7331279-2-9

For everyone who convinced me to see this thing through.

Prologue

STARS BRIGHTENED THE night sky like pearls in a calm, black sea. Flames from the campfire cast long shadows, dancing and twitching across the sand. A man sat cross-legged on the ground. A wide-brimmed hat shadowed his face. Light reflected off the golden edges of playing cards as he shuffled them with nimble fingers. Sharp eyes of dark blue caught Kwyn's gaze. She wouldn't have called him old, but there was nothing young about his appearance either. His long coat fell in folds at his sides, black like his hat.

"What happened?" Kwyn crawled forward from the brush, closer to the fire. "Where am I? And who are you?" The last she remembered, the mark had got the best of her. Scrambling over the dunes, they both tumbled to a rock bed. She touched the knot on her temple. The man must have escaped. Not the best impression for her first job as Esca the Red's would-be apprentice.

"Ah, true to your name." The man knocked the deck of cards against the palm of his hands and swiftly dealt them out into five stacks on the ground in front of him. "Too-many-questions Kwyn." His gaze rose to meet hers again. "That's what they call you."

Scowling, Kwyn reached her hands out to feel the warmth of the flames. "How do you know that?"

"I know lots of things. For instance." He gestured to the cards. "Magic."

"Magic's not real." Kwyn's scowled.

"Care to try it then?" His beard twitched as one corner of his mouth turned up slightly.

Kwyn glanced around, trying to make sense of where she was. A shadowy rise of hills to the west were likely the dunes she'd come across. A stone plateau standing on its own like a misshapen tower in the middle of the endless sand was unfamiliar. She scooted closer as a brisk burst of air whipped through her duster. "Alright." She spread her chilled fingers over the fire, shoving down her unease and unwillingness to completely admit she was lost.

"Pick a stack." His back straight, the man's hand poised over his cards.

"Far left." Kwyn flexed her fingers, wondering if he was the harmless kind of crazy or something more dangerous.

Flipping over the stack, the man spread out five cards. "Pick one. Memorize it. Don't tell me what it is."

"Ok." Kwyn made a mental note of the Jack of spades, edging closer to the warmth while feeling for the knife against her shin.

After shuffling, stacking, and having her select stacks without her card a number of times, he presented her with one remaining card.

"Now. Kwyn. If I'm not mistaken, this is your card." He flipped it over with a flourish.

Her eyes widened as the Jack of Spades with his mischievous black eyes stared back at her, clutching a wooden wand in his hand. For a moment, she thought he pushed back his pointed hat and winked.

She blinked, rubbing her eyes. "How did you…?" Kwyn forgot about her worry for a moment.

The man shrugged, bringing his hands to rest on his knees. "Just a trick. I have a more impressive one." His eyes came to rest behind her.

Sand scraped beneath her boots as Kwyn whirled around to see Zakery Poe, the man she'd been hunting, lying trussed up and unconscious. Her mouth fell open, and she glanced back at the mysterious man with playing cards. "Are you a hunter?"

"A hunter? Hardly." He stood, something of an amused look on his face. "I'm a jack of all trades…" His head tilted back as he looked up to the sky, eyes searching like he expected to find something out of place. "Master of none." He reached a hand into the pocket of his long, black coat. "You can call me Falcon."

Fairly sure Falcon was just a crazy old man, Kwyn limped closer to Poe. He seemed harmless enough, all tied up, but she kept out of reach to be on the safe side. Eyes narrowing suspiciously, she turned back to the man called Falcon. "You're not a hunter?"

He held his hand up like he was swearing an oath. "On my honor." His eyes stabbed through her when he asked, "Are you?"

Kwyn swallowed. "I will be." She did her best to sound threatening. Esca would be forced to take her request of apprenticeship seriously now.

"I see." Sounding satisfied, he tipped his hat. There was the sound of a muffled groan behind her and Kwyn jumped around. Poe struggled, staring at her with bulging eyes. His face went pale when he looked behind her, and he wriggled in the loose soil, pushing away.

Kwyn turned back to the man called Falcon. He was gone—vanished. Frowning at where he had stood, Kwyn crouched down to look for footprints. There were none except for the two where he'd stood. Kwyn was alone with a tied up criminal, a fading campfire, and the sand with its scattered outline of brush stretching beyond the horizon. Shivering in the wind, her words came out as a harsh whisper, "Magic isn't real."

Chapter 1

TRISTAN

WHEN HE FIRST met Tristan, Solomand almost turned away. Let the swank get what he deserved. He wasn't one of them. A Highborn who strayed beyond the protection of the inner gates into the outskirts of the city was free game. What happened to him was not their concern.

Hands in his coat pockets, he paused at the alley's entryway, listening to the angry shouts as burly field workers pelted their target. Scrawny and well dressed, he was no match for the pack of roughnecks—dejected and fed-up with the way things were. No one could blame them for taking out their frustration on the stray. Behind their wall, the Highborn left them all to Slave away in the fields, squandering power for themselves in the shortage, and sparing none for those out here in The Mud district. The scene shouldn't have bothered anyone who fought in secret against the government of Corcyra, but it bothered Solomand.

Solomand cringed as he watched. The idiot wasn't fighting back or pleading for his life, even as his blood splattered on the pavement. Tensions were high these days. It filled the atmosphere like thick fog after a rain. The workers meant to kill him. He exchanged looks with his two friends. Ivan, fresh from the North Continent of Hyperborea, looked menacing as his fists tightened. A head taller than Solomand, the hulking Slav had eyes like gray ice, cropped brown hair. He used to be a member of the Northland's famed assassins; Ice Wolves. Solomand asked about his past once and was met with a hard stare that killed his curiosity forever. It didn't matter, anyway. He was more than willing to fight alongside the rebellion in exchange for room and board.

Solomand was wary of the look in the ex-assassin's eyes now as his glare intensified.

Rayn gave him a sideways look, curling her lip in disgust as the swank's head cracked audibly on the ground. Tucking a loose strand of red hair behind her ear, her green eyes questioned what he wanted to do about the situation.

Shifting uneasily, Solomand sighed. They all knew it wasn't right. But, as usual, they were going to follow his lead; he was the one Rayn's father had put in charge.

"Alright. They've had enough fun," he muttered. Taking his hands from his coat pockets, he motioned to Rayn and Ivan, and they rushed into the alley.

One of the men raised a discarded board bristling with rusted nails. Solomand grabbed it, puncturing his thumb with the splintered wood. "Enough," he snapped, looking at the bloodied ground with distaste. He wrenched the makeshift weapon from the man's hand and threw it aside. "Clear off." His thumb throbbed

The workers' looks transformed from shock to fury at this interruption. Obviously they didn't know Solomand, Rayn and Ivan were members of Black Recluse—a Special Ops insurgent team. The very ones fighting for their freedom.

Puffing his chest out, the oldest one shoved Solomand in the chest. "Don't tell me what to do, half-breed Kree—aghh"

Ivan kicked his legs out from under him. Jerking the man's head back, he pressed the curved blade of his knife against his throat. "He said, clear. Off." He traced the knife against the vein bulging from the man's neck. Slavik words rolled from his mouth as he jerked the man's head back.

Not again. Solomand's heartbeat quickened. Never knowing how Ivan would react was nerve-wracking. Recruiting assassins was always a risky business. You never knew if they would switch sides for a higher amount. Ivan was different. For a hired killer, he had a curious perception of injustice and wanted nothing to do with those dealing it out. When he got his hands on someone, his maliciousness could be startling.

"Alright! Alright! We'll go." The man threw his hands up, trying to shrink away from the knife, to no avail. The others moved forward, but stopped when Rayn drew the pistol holstered at her side, raising their arms defensively.

"Please," the man at Ivan's mercy squeaked.

"I think he gets the hint, Ivan. You can knock it off." Solomand was pleased to note he sounded more in control than he felt. He allowed himself a restrained breath of relief as Ivan released his hold on the man and shoved him away.

Clutching the finger marks imprinted on his neck, the man scrambled to his feet and joined the other four, and they shuffled toward the alley's entrance. One turned back and spit on the ground, giving them all a contemptuous look. At lightning speed, Ivan drew the knife from his boot and lunged forward.

"Don't kill any of them, will you?" Solomand called out with a groan before he and Rayn turned to the man lying in the street. Rayn returned her pistol to her side, and they both kneeled down to roll him over. He was young, as they were; maybe nineteen. Streaks of red stained his blonde hair. One eye already swollen, he coughed as blood dripped from his mouth. Rayn felt his chest, and he yelled in pain. "Probably broken ribs."

Solomand let out a sigh and squatted down. "Well, this is an outstanding mess he's got himself into." He pulled the man's handkerchief from his suit pocket and tied it around the wound on his head. He didn't know if Rayn's father, General Ivers, would like it, but he would not leave this idiot here to die. "You've strayed too far from home, Swank."

The man groaned, gasping as Solomand scooped him up, then muttered, "Tristan."

"What?" Solomand tilted his head to hear better.

"My name. Tristan."

"Whatever you say. Swank."

6

Chapter 2

TRISTAN

"GET HIM ON the table!" A male voice urged; it seemed vaguely familiar to Tristan, from some deep corner of his past. He felt cold metal on his bare back, and the air refused to enter his lungs any longer.

Something I have to do.

He couldn't remember what it was, but it was the only thing that made him fight to stay alive. Arching his back, Tristan focused on the outline of faces covered in surgical masks, framed by bright, blue light.

"Hold him down." The familiar voice said again, and a firm hand pushed his shoulders back on the table. A needle punctured his arm and fire spread through his body. Cries of pain filled the room and before he could realize he was the one making them, he fell into a welcoming sea of blackness. He stayed there for a while, with the strange sense of being both awake and asleep. There was no pain or need to fight; only relief, at last.

Remaining here seemed the right choice. A voice intruded on his peace; brash and easy-going. He knew who it was instantly. "Well, we did it, Tris."

Tristan swallowed, turning to look behind him. Just as he knew he would be, there stood Solomand Black; the airship captain stared back with steel-blue eyes. There was the familiar, determined look about him and a mask of easy confidence.

"Sol?" Tristan looked from the apparition of his best friend to his own hands.

He cannot be here.

Solomand was gone. With any luck, he had escaped the city, and the Continent of Lyonese entirely.

"I'm here as much as you are, Swank." Solomand dragged a hand through his coal-black hair. "You would probably go into some long-winded explanation of the power of the brain. But I'm not going to. Even if I'm only in your head." Solomand lit a cigarette and grinned at him.

Tristan looked down at the scars that lined his chest, recalling the bloody battle years ago where the detonation nearly took his life. "If we are both only in my head, mind giving me a smoke?" He held his hand out.

"Why not?" Solomand shrugged and handed him an already lit cigarette. "Not like it can kill you now."

One can still dream, can't they? Tristan kept the thought to himself. Solomand never did like the way he joked about impending death. Glancing around, he tried to remember what led to this point. Sol's plan had always been to save Tristan's life; break into Corcyra, let him be captured, and the mayor would spare no effort in returning him to full health. Afterwards he would be publicly executed as the city's most-wanted traitor. Unless, of course, Solomand succeeded in an ill-conceived rescue attempt.

He recalled painfully walking across the plains to the main checkpoint of Corcyra's wall, where two guards greeted him at gunpoint. After that, he had collapsed. Whether or not his friends had managed to escape, he could only speculate.

"I feel different. Changed somehow. What happened?" Tristan let the smoke fill his lungs. It felt nothing like he remembered.

"Life. It changes all of us. That's the point of it." Solomand gave him a crooked grin to go with this piece of philosophy that was very uncharacteristic of Solomand.

"Maybe I'm already dead." Tristan stared off into the cool black as flecks of light appeared.

"No." The figment of his imagination who looked like Solomand became stern. "You can't die, Tris. Not yet." He flicked his cigarette away, a swirling ember in the blackness. "You have something to do."

"What do I have to do?" Tristan studied his hand, flexing his fingers, curious at the lack of shaking.

What is wrong with me? Heaviness settled over him, then numbness as his mind went blank.

Empty! His head snapped up.

Solomand grinned at him, nodding in approval. "I knew it'd come to you." His hand clapped Tristan on the back, feeling jarringly real. "Later, Tris." Sol's voice echoed around him. Tristan was alone.

"Sol, wait!" Tristan's heart pounded, a sudden pang in his lungs. He dropped to one knee. Feeling returned to him like waves crashing on a beach. Everything hurt; black sky faded into nothing, dragging with it the memory of what he needed to do.

In and out, in and out; a slow steady pace, the air coursed through his lungs. Tristan's eyes shot open.

I can breathe!

He sat bolt upright and assessed the surroundings. A bulb encased in wires flickered overhead, engulfing the room in soft, yellow light. It was a hospital room—crisp, white and drenched with the scent of antiseptic. In the far corner was a table with staged surgical instruments; bandages, empty vials, trays of pills. Next to his bed, wires ran from a monitor and back to his chest where adhesive strips kept them in place. Blue and red lights alternated back and forth as a needle hovered in the center of an encased dial. A needle attached to his left arm and clear fluid coursed through tubing.

Tristan looked down at the rise and fall of his bandaged chest and worked his fingers between the strips of cotton to see the incisions stitched together with meticulous precision only one person could have managed. Of course it would be *him*.

A storm of mixed feelings swelled inside him. As his pulse quickened, the dial on the monitor jumped sporadically. Tristan yanked the wires from his chest and an alarm buzzed as red lights blinked.

Steps sounded outside the room, and Tristan's hand gripped the cold, silver bed frame, tensing as the door burst open. He let out the breath he didn't realize he was holding as the Chief surgeon stepped inside, holding a clipboard in one hand, the other in the pocket of his white coat. A nurse followed close behind him.

He stopped, brown eyes peering at Tristan over the copper rims of his lightly tinted glasses. "That sedative should have kept you out for another three hours, by my calculation," Galin Highcourt said. "Your guards will want to be notified." His voice was detached as he waved the nurse out of the room.

Tristan felt a lump rising in his throat as Galin walked over to his bedside and pressed a chilly hand on his wrist, checking his pulse. He took the stethoscope from around his neck and held it to Tristan's chest and back, listening as he breathed. Then he slung it over his shoulder, clicked his pen and scribbled on his form. "Your insides were an impossible mess." His eyebrows raised as he spoke. "Why you allowed those primitives to operate on you is beyond me."

Tristan took a breath, finding the courage to speak. "They saved my life."

Galin's brow furrowed and his voice changed from disengaging to angry. "I saved your life, Tristan! Sheer damn luck kept you alive thus far." Tristan opened his mouth to speak, but Galin's voice rose. "I will not have you contradict me. Do you have any idea what I have sacrificed to ensure you weren't sent straight away to some prison cell?" His eyes flashed as he dropped his clipboard onto the table; a glass vial cracked as it fell. "More than you deserve after your disgraceful behavior." The surgeon shook his head and turned to the door.

A flicker of anger cut through the sense of being drowned and Tristan spoke. "You should have let LeFrost take me, Father." He smiled a cold, cheerless smile.

Galin's hand stopped on the door handle, and he paused before stalking away. Tristan's eyes fixed on the door. After all these years, he was still unprepared to meet his father. Galin's indifferent attitude stung more than Tristan imagined it would, but his mind did not stay fixed on the troublesome reunion for long.

Sol.

Solomand's foolhardy plan to get Tristan into Corcyra had worked. The Governor would not miss the opportunity to publicly execute a well-known traitor as Tristan Highcourt. That would only work if Tristan stayed alive and well, something only a surgeon such as Galin could ensure. As he had predicted, LeFrost ordered Galin to return Tristan to health, all for the purpose of executing him in the future. Tristan wondered if Solomand and the others had made it out of Corcyra safely. There was so much that could have gone wrong with their plan.

The door opened. Another visitor stepped into his room; a tall woman wearing a hospital gown, her arm in a sling. Full lips scowled at him"Well, well. You are a difficult man to locate, Tristan Highcourt." Her voice was smooth, if not a bit harsh, just like he remembered it.

"Lady St. Sebastian." Tristan smiled and glanced at her arm. "What happened?"

"Spare me the formalities." She tossed her braided hair from her shoulder and gestured to the sling holding her arm. "This was a present from that uncouth red-headed friend of yours. They escaped, leaving you to face the music, it seems."

They did get out, then!

Tristan leaned back on his pillow, relaxing somewhat. That was the only thing that mattered. He locked his gaze with Minuet's dark eyes, wishing he could thank her out loud for the information. But that would never do. They were no doubt being listened in on.

There was a mist gathering in her eyes. "I'm to be in charge of your interrogation." Her voice was hard.

"I shall count the minutes." Tristan grinned. A flush rose to Minuet's cheeks.

"Captain Black was last seen flying north in an S-class airship. Don't expect anyone to come to your rescue, Highcourt," she snapped, and stormed out of the room.

A grin crossed Tristan's face as he looked after her. After dealing with the war-criminal for so long, she had to know better. Solomand was far too stubborn. Nothing would stop him from trying, even if it meant his own death. But Sol did not know the real reason Tristan agreed to this reckless plan; he was going to fix what he had done and keep the others from trying to rescue him. His eyes closed, and Tristan began to formulate a new plan, one that involved no risk from anyone but himself. This time, Solomand could not stop him.

Chapter 3

RAYN

BRITTLE COLD CHILLED the air, even at the most temperate edge of the Continent Hyperborea. Northpass was the first skyport on the mainland; an isolated outpost nestled in the mountains. Only a few small villages lay beyond its stone walls. Within the skyport, buildings huddled together, their windows already heavily shuttered. Those who were lucky enough to live within the protection of Northpass had sequestered themselves away from the dropping temperatures.

A moonlight shadow slipped up slate-colored walls, darting in to join the darkness that pooled between the ramshackle buildings within. Another shadow stretched above the port. The air filled with the noise of engines. A sleek airship looked out of place as it lowered to the vacant port. Tarnished copper lined the outside deck of flat-black. Propellers slowed on either side of the narrow nose as the hum of the engine purred to a stop. When the aft propellers ceased to spin, the cargo door slid open.

Rayn stepped out of the airship and scowled as a gust of biting air greeted them.

No wonder fugitives run away to the North.

It was the perfect place to hide, which worked in favor of the current situation. Shoving her hands deep in her pockets, she glanced around. Beyond the walls, white-coated hills sharply sloped together. A mist hung overhead as twilight settled over the coast. Orange lamps of the surrounding village homes dotted in a small line leading away from the skyport and deeper into the mountains. Frost coated the metal docks of the outpost and cold seeped into the soles of her lightweight boots. She shrank into her duster as a gust of wind cut across the docks, fighting to keep her teeth from chattering.

The hasty departure from the Fifth Continent prevented them from obtaining clothes more suited to the climate of the Northland. The plains and green valleys of Rayn's home were much more temperate. There were not a lot of happy memories from her childhood, but the weather was much more agreeable.

"What the—" A scraping noise followed. Solomand slammed into her back. Rayn would have lost her footing were it not for the firm hand that seized her bicep. Tall, fierce-looking Ivan steadied both her and Solomand.

"Careful." His deep voice carried a sharp Northern accent.

"A little late for a warning, isn't it?" Solomand let out a yelp as Ivan's grip momentarily tightened.

Giving him an unapologetic look, Ivan released his hold on Sol's injured arm. "Sorry."

Face fixed in a grimace, Solomand's steel-blue eyes narrowed. "I'm not convinced you are." His breath clouded in front of him. Left arm hanging limp at his side. Traces of cuts and bruises still covered his tan face from their run-in with the Governor of Corcyra and his men weeks ago. If she was honest, it gave a certain attractive roguishness to his appearance. Rayn gave him a crooked smile as she folded her arms against the cold.

Taking in the view, Sol scowled. "Is it like this everywhere?"

"No." Ivan raised an eyebrow. "Other places much colder."

"Lovely." Sol's teeth chattered. "Best get some more appropriate clothes before we all freeze to death." He tilted his head upward to look at the burly Northlander, who wore a dark-green uniform coat cut at the waist. "Well, maybe not *all* of us." He turned up his collar and took a few steps toward the dock house, where a light switched on behind the frosted glass of the window.

A man pushed open the iron door, an oil lantern in one hand, a fur cap in the other. He was thin-framed and pale, a lined coat draped over his shoulders, unbuttoned. His shirt was untucked, and he had the look of someone who'd just been awoken and made a half-assed attempt to get dressed.

"I will handle this." Ivan walked ahead.

Rayn felt a quiver run through Solomand as he leaned against her. "Cold?" Her eyes fixed on the Port Master as he and Ivan spoke in Slavik.

"Maybe a little. You?" His hand found hers for an instant, closing around the tips of her icy fingers.

Rayn shrugged, giving him a half-smile. "Only a lot."

"You know, I can help with that, Mrs. Black." His voice lowered to a playful whisper.

Tucking a strand of red hair behind her ear, Rayn rolled her eyes. "Now is not the time."

"I'll rearrange our schedule to make time." He leaned in closer, his breath heating her neck.

A shiver went up her spine, and Rayn shoved him with her shoulder. "Stop."

"Oh, alright." Solomand let out an exaggerated sigh. "But only because I love you." Grimacing, massaged his injured shoulder. "The Ice Man doesn't look too happy, does he?"

Rayn's grin faded as she looked in Ivan's direction. "He'll be much less happy if he hears you call him that." She frowned. Ivan looked increasingly like he was restraining his temper as the Port Master became animated—raising his voice and waving his cap before clapping it on his head. "Can you understand what they're saying?"

"No." Solomand's eyes narrowed. "There's a surprising lack of curses for a conversation involving Ivan, though. Probably not a good sign."

"Are curses all the Slav you speak?" Rayn turned to avoid the wind as it picked up.

"Yes. All I needed until now." Despite his attempt to sound nonchalant, Rayn saw the growing concern in his eyes.

Ivan's voice rose as he exchanged his last few words with the man, pointing back at their airship and throwing his arms in the air. The man then turned, limping back to his small building at the end of the dock. He slammed the door. They stood in darkness once more, cold pressing all around them.

"*Zohpai*," Ivan cursed as he walked back to them.

Giving Rayn a look of satisfaction, Sol said, "Now see, *that* word I know. What's the trouble, Ivan?"

"He say we need passports to dock at this port." Ivan lit a cigarette as he spoke through gritted teeth.

"Passports." Solomand blinked slowly. "Are you… are you serious?"

Ivan glared back, taking a breath of smoke before he spoke again. "And, this is port of entry. So we must submit our intention to enter week in advance."

"A *week* in advance?" Solomand glanced around the port, shrouded with pale moonlight—void of ships and people and any kind of business that warranted such a measure. "Please tell me this is some joke."

"No joke," Ivan grumbled. The smoke from his mouth mixed with the clouds their breath made. "If we do not leave, he intends to call m*ilitsya* to escort us from the skyport."

"What are *militsya*?" Rayn asked. She shifted from one foot to the other as a tingle settled into her toes.

"Northland police. They are corrupt and usually only in bigger cities. But they will probably come to Port of entry."

"Outstanding." Solomand's voice was flat. His fingers drummed against his side. "Well, we obviously cannot comply. We are a week too early to give advance notice to that petty, little port rat. Can't you go Ice Wolf on him?" He made short stabbing motions in the air.

Ivan raised an eyebrow. "I would rather not."

"Can Rayn shoot him, then?" Solomand struggled to light his own cigarette until Rayn took it from him, lit it, and handed it back.

"Not good idea," Ivan said. "If he notified militsya, corpse would not look good."

Cigarette hanging from the corner of his mouth, Sol shoved his hand in his pocket. "What is the point of having an assassin and a sharpshooter around if you can't use either of them?" He sounded grudging as he took a couple drags on his cigarette. "It would probably take Jank over a week to forge the papers and I'm going to go out on a limb here and say that makeshift security guard," he nodded toward the port house, "isn't going to want us sitting around on his dock. Besides that, we'll all freeze to death—well, some of us." He glanced again at Ivan. "So, unless anyone has a better idea, I'm going to go with the 'my passport is a ball of lead' approach."

His glare fixed on Sol, Ivan ran a hand along his neck where a spider tattoo poked up from his collar. "Is not good plan, Sol."

"I didn't say it was good."

Yelling interrupted their conversation. The Port Master stormed back onto the dock, looking more prepared this time. His coat was buttoned up, and he wielded a weapon unlike anything Rayn had ever seen. It was a gun, but what type was unclear. The cylinders were massive. A second barrel was mounted on the top and what looked like a small rocket protruded from the end of it. On the bottom of the weapon, it looked like a flame-thrower. There was another attachment bulging from the side of the machine that's purpose was not immediately recognizable, even for someone well-versed in weaponry.

Rayn exchanged a glance with Solomand. "What the hell is *that?*"

Calmly continuing his cigarette, Sol shook his head. "*You're* the gunsmith. It looks like a mistake best I can tell. Wonder if he knows how to use it."

Ivan spit stray pieces of tobacco onto the dock. "He say militsya has been called. We did not leave fast enough."

"Right." Solomand flicked the remains of his cigarette aside. "He's made our choice for us, hasn't he?"

17

The moment Solomand's hand moved to reach for the revolver concealed in his coat, the port master raised the unusual weapon and fired it. Solomand ducked, dragging Rayn with him as a circular projectile shot out of the gun's attachment, whizzed over their heads and embedded into the doorframe of the airship. "What the…" Sol glanced up at the serrated edges of the small saw-blade. "Talk about excessive."

The man raised the gun, but Rayn was faster than he was. Rising to one knee, she drew her revolver and fired first; he jerked back as the bullet found his shoulder, but he managed to pull the trigger as he fell. A flash of sparks shot out of the muzzle.

Picking up a nearby supply crate, Ivan dashing in front of Rayn to block the bullet as the man struggled to stand. He hurled the crate at him. The man crumpled under its weight, groaning and reaching a shaking hand for the handle of his weapon. Solomand ran forward, kicked it from his reach. Then, for good measure, he punted it off the edge of the dock. Looking down at the man's battered face, he cocked the hammer of his pistol. "Let's do him in."

"No. Will bring too much trouble." Kicking the crate from the man's chest, Ivan seized him by the collar and dragged him back to the port house.

"I think we've already found trouble. But have it your way." Solomand sighed, returning the pistol to his belt.

Rayn glanced off the edge of the dock as she and Solomand followed Ivan. "Did you have to kick it off?"

"What? That bastardized hand missal razor launcher?" his eyes narrowed as understanding registered on his face. "You wanted it, didn't you?"

"Maybe. I would have liked to have a look at it." Rayn shrugged.

"I deeply apologize. Maybe in another place and time when we are not at the receiving end of miniature saw blades or cannonballs, I will think before acting so impulsively."

Rayn rolled her eyes. "Oh, shut up.

Ivan kicked open the door to the port house and hauled the injured man inside. Shoving him into a battered chair, Ivan tore one wire from the radio and used it to lash the man's hands behind his back. Noises crackled over the speaker as lights blinked on the transistor.

Solomand limped over to the man, waving his revolver. "This, you self-important, son of a mountain goat, is all the passport we need." He glanced sideways at Ivan. "How do you say passport?"

Ivan flung open a closet door. Spare coats hung haphazardly among wooden crates and a supply of boots. "*Pazaizyen,*" he said, tossing Rayn a long, white coat.

Sol waved the gun again. "You hear that? *Paz—aiz—yen.*" The man's breathing was shallow; blood soaked the sleeve of his coat.

Rayn slipped the coat on. "Should we do something about his wound before he bleeds out?" She quickly did up the buttons.

Sol scowled. "Surely there is some sort of waiting period for that. It'll be at least a week's wait to remove the lead. If you want something for the pain, that's another week waiting for approval. Three-week minimum for the whole procedure. Ivan, tell him what I said."

Ivan relayed Solomand's words to the man as he rummaged through the closet.

Confusion mingled with fear on the man's face as he looked from Ivan to Sol. "You see my friend over there?" Sol gestured to Ivan. "It's no charge at all for him to cut off your fingers. Getting them put back on? That's an entirely different department."

Ivan stuck his head out, taking longer than usual to translate.

"Did you add to what I said?"

"What if I did?"

"Never mind." Shaking his head, Sol returned his revolver to its holster. "When the hell did the Northland become hung up on idiotic thing like passports? I thought this was the place to go to escape law and order. It's not like there's a waiting list of those wishing to move into a sub-zero meat locker."

Ivan donned a coat before roughly shoving another at Solomand. "I think his attitude has more to do with the fact we look like sky pirates."

"Pirates?" Solomand looked taken aback. "I don't know about *you*, Ivan, but I'm fairly certain I look upstanding."

"I wouldn't be too confident about that." Rayn said. "There is also the fact we are currently robbing him." She took a crate of canned food from Ivan.

"That was his fault!" Solomand glanced unhappily at the man as Ivan hoisted a crate under both his arms and headed for the door. "Pirates. You really think so?"

"I think we need to leave," Rayn said, pushing him toward the door. She turned back for a moment. "Are we just going to leave him like this?"

"*Militstya* will take care of him when they arrive," Ivan said. "We need to be gone before they get here."

Solomand gave the Portmaster a scowl before following behind Ivan and Rayn. "Please tell me this is the worst of this place."

"I tell you but will not make it true," Ivan said.

Chapter 4

TRISTAN

TRISTAN FELT HIS strength returning a little more every day. He breathed deeper, grateful every time the air effortlessly streamed into his lungs. He'd forgotten what it felt like to breathe like this—without a struggle. But there was an emptiness widening in his soul with each passing day, as well. Every time the door opened, he imagined Solomand shoving through it in his brusque manner, wearing a crooked grin and bearing the scent of tobacco on his coat, which he would deny having. Sometimes he thought for an instant it might be Rayn coming to ask him more questions about her past she did not remember—things Sol had wanted so desperately to keep secret; or twelve-year-old Zee popping in to play chess with him.

When meals were delivered on steel trays, he thought of Jank's knack for cooking, and Will's ability to make even toast inedible. Tristan longed for an unsavory meal made by his friend now. He would have given anything to see them—even to put up with Ivan's constant threatening Solomand, which Tristan suspected was not entirely sincere. It was strange how someone's mere presence could lift your spirits and make you enjoy life when every day was a fight to hang on. Going to hell and back with people formed a bond stronger than any blood could hold; his friends were family now, and as much as he longed to see them, he prayed they were far from Corcyra and beyond Governor LeFrost's reach.

As his fortnight in the hospital neared an end, Tristan still had seen no more of Minuet. Her persistent search for him over the past six years had kept his hopes up that she still cared for him. No matter how much Sol insisted she was a deplorable coalition agent, Tristan could not bring himself to stop loving her. During his time in hiding from Corcyra's governor, he had written to her at least once a month and Solomand used the letters as bartering chips to avoid capture.

All of that seemed so displaced from present reality that it might have been an impossible dream. His father came in daily to check his condition, regarding his son like an investment he knew was a mistake but was already committed to. The only words he spoke were that of a physician asking his patient questions. Nurses came and went without making eye contact or saying a word. He couldn't blame them. The penalty for betraying the Coalition of Cities was death, and not a particularly quick one. With such a high-profile case as that of Tristan Highcourt, they likely believed speaking with him would put them at risk for being suspected for collusion.

When Tristan felt well enough to get out of bed, he paced the tiled floor with an endless restlessness, wishing he could ask the guards outside his door for a smoke, or even make a condescending comment to get some kind of reaction other than blank, severe stares. At this point, even interaction with an enemy was better than none.

Scanning the pattern of bolts beneath the white paint on the ceiling, he counted them for the hundredth time, wondering what hour it was. There were no windows to keep track of day and there was always the soft blue from the electric lamp by his bedside.

Seventy-five, seventy-six. A knock on the door interrupted his counting. He turned to see Galin step inside the room, dressed in a drab brown suit and carrying a bundle of clothes under his arm.

Tristan sat up, waiting for his father to speak. Galin adjusted his glasses, finally meeting his son's gaze. "You are being released into my care. Get dressed and come outside. We leave as soon as your case manager arrives." He set the clothes down on the bed.

"What, you mean today? Now?"

"Yes. And be quick about it." Galin hurried from the room.

The clothes his father brought were the drab green uniform of an insurgent fighter. Governor LeFrost always made his captured war criminals wear the uniform they had chosen to defy him with during their trial and execution. Making a quick check of all the pockets, Tristan frowned. He had not really expected them to return his possessions from when he was captured, but he had hoped for his watch; it was harmless enough in appearance. Already his mind threaded alternative possibilities together. He would have to make do without it.

Tossing aside the hospital clothes, Tristan pulled on the undershirt, pants and jacket, slowly buttoning the black buttons. The leather belt stretched across his shoulder and wrapped around his waist. *If he was going for accuracy, he forgot the sidearm.* He thought to himself, tying the red armband around his right bicep. The scuffed boots were a pair of his own. Allowing himself a satisfied grin, he pulled them on.

"Mistake number one." He stood and smoothed the coat down before staring into the mirror over the sink. The man looking back at him had light blonde hair, was clean-shaven and looked strangely assured of his fate. His brow furrowed, recalling faces of those he had known who died wearing these colors. If LeFrost thought this would humiliate him, he was sadly mistaken. Tristan was proud to have taken a stand against the atrocities the Coalition of Cities committed and, if given a second chance, would do it all again. He smoothed his hair back, took a deep breath, and went out to meet his father.

Two guards wearing the gray uniform of the 201st Airborne took hold of his arms, clamping shackles on his wrists and ankles. Tristan gave them a wry smile. "Am I as dangerous as all that? Do tell how you managed to capture me at all."

Galin snapped his pocket watch shut. "Enough." He motioned to the guards, tapping his foot. "See if your commander is here. We're running behind."

"No need, Doctor." Minuet rounded the corner, dressed in her crisp officer's uniform, cap in hand. Her glance passed over Tristan. "The cars are waiting." She paused, then leaned toward Galin. He bent down so she could whisper in his ear. Galin frowned, straightening as he pushed his glasses further onto his nose.

"Lead on." He motioned her ahead of him. Minuet nodded, starting down the corridor.

"Care to let me in on the secret?" Tristan asked in an upbeat tone. The guards shoved him roughly down the hall after Minuet. "No. I suppose that would be too much to ask." He caught the flash in Minuet's eyes as she looked back at him and he smiled at her, rattling the chains on his wrists. Galin was silent as he trailed behind. In contrast to the dour mood of his captors, Tristan felt in good spirits. There was only one thing left to do. That would be easy once he was under house arrest in Highcourt Manor.

Minuet lead them out a side door and down the metal stairs used when the elevator was out of commission. Footsteps on perforated metal echoed endlessly until they finally reached the door marked with a red exit sign. The red light of early dawn streamed through a tall window and Tristan squinted against the brightness of it. As soon as Minuet pushed the door open, camera lights snapped and flashed as a crowd of people pressed in on them. Minuet scowled, pressing her cap in place as she pushed through the mass of newspaper men and women.

There were others there too, a throng of people jeering and throwing insults while the guards shoved them back, forcing their way to the waiting cars. Tristan found it amusing they had nothing better to do then come here. A faint grin spread on his face as he worked his way through the people in between the two guards. A woman reporter stood off to the side, her curled hair uncooperative with the warm breeze tearing through the Plains city.

"I stand outside Copernicus General Hospital, where Tristan Highcourt, the infamous son of Doctor Galin Highcourt, is being released today on house arrest." The two wheels of her handheld recording machine turned as she spoke into it. Tristan cast her a sideways glance, then froze as he saw the boy next to her holding a bundle of newspapers for sale. On the front page, there was the familiar face of a twelve-year-old girl with silky black hair with the bold headline, *Governor LeFrost's long-lost daughter, Sazume found.*

As a wave of horror crashed over Tristan, he heard the reporter speaking again into her recording device. "Three weeks ago, Highcourt was captured attempting to enter the city. At the same time, young Sazume LeFrost, the Governor's daughter, was rescued. While it has been a challenge for her to cope after the trauma she experienced at the hands of these brutal criminals, we are told she will recover in time."

No! His mind raced. The girl being captured was not part of their plan. Tristan stopped, his legs refusing to move. As the crowd pressed in, the guards seized his arms, dragging him forward as he tripped over the chains on his legs, moving in a dazed horror until he found himself shoved into a waiting motorcar where Galin joined him. The doors shut. The car's engine revved, and they moved forward with a jolt as hands slammed against the windows.

Beads of sweat trickled down the sides of Tristan's head, and his hands shook as they rested on his lap. Galin reached across the seat and felt his wrist for a pulse, frowning as he did so.

Tristan couldn't speak. His mind raced as his perfect plan crumbled into thin air. Zee wasn't supposed to be here. It was startling there was no report of Solomand trying to blow up half the city to get the girl back. She may have been LeFrost's daughter by blood, but Solomand had raised her from the time she was six years old. When the other rebels wanted to use her to get back at LeFrost, Solomand protected her. He was more her father than LeFrost ever would be.

The city streets passed by like a blur through the opaque glass; streets Tristan had walked all his life, within the inner circle of Corcyra, manicured and safe from intrusion of the lower class who would eventually rise in protest of their subjugation. When they pulled up to his childhood home, the guards opened the doors. Still in a daze, Tristan did not hear the order to get out until one guard grabbed him by the collar and jerked him from the vehicle. His eyes fell on Minuet.

Why didn't you tell me? That is what he wanted to ask. Could she understand the aching feeling of betrayal by his expression?

She turned away, walking ahead of her men as they entered the gated courtyard surrounded by trees which blocked the city streets from view. Forced along behind them, Tristan's hands clenched at his sides, the contents of his stomach threatening to rise up his throat. Flecks of black blurred his vision as he dragged his feet reluctantly down the familiar garden path, up the stone walkway, and into the foyer of the pillared entrance.

Standing inside, under the vaulted ceiling, he leaned heavily against the wall. Galin's voice was sharp when he spoke to the men that guarded him. "Am I to believe my word is not enough for the Governors' men in my own home?"

There was an uncomfortable silence as they glanced at each other. "N—no, Lord Highcourt," the older one stammered.

"Then kindly remove those archaic chains from my patient before he falls on his face." Galin sounded aloof and threatening at the same time. The guards exchanged a glance, then looked to Minuet.

"Do what the Doctor says" She waved a dismissive hand. The men did what she said and Tristan remained leaning against the wall, pretending her indifferent manner did not feel like a knife sticking into his soul. As Minuet ordered the men outside, Galin told her to bring Tristan into the study, where she could begin her interrogation and disappeared down the hall. After Galin's footsteps faded, Tristan surged forward, taking her by the shoulders.

"Why didn't you tell me?" He searched for any sign of care in her expression.

"Get your hands off of me!" There was the flicker of emotion in her gaze, and he complied, stepping back. She swallowed, switching her cap under her arm. "The recovery of Sazume LeFrost is not something you needed to know about."

"Minuet." He spoke her name in a pleading tone. She looked away, drawing herself up as if heightening her resolve.

"Your physician forbid me from telling you anything that might upset you. He was right, obviously." Arms crossed, she maintained a hard stare. "She wondered off the plains at the same time as you did."

Tristan sank to the floor, burying his head in his hands. "This is all my fault."

"She is back in her father's custody, in no danger. I do not know why you care so much." Annoyance dripped from her words.

Tristan's head snapped up. "Do you honestly believe that? He killed her mother by dropping a bomb on Cierne Island. All he cares about is winning. The soldiers there were already defeated— he had nothing to gain from doing what he did! All she is to him is a political pawn for his public image."

"He had no way of knowing either of them were there, and those were *war criminals*, Tristan."

"Yes." Tristan's voice echoed the hollowness he felt from her words. "And *I* was one of them."

Minuet's light complexion grew paler. Wringing her hands, she did not offer an answer.

Tristan's eyes closed as he rested his head on his knee. A firm hand gripped him under the arm and pulled him to his feet. "Try not to strain yourself worrying about things that do not concern you," Galin said, supporting Tristan as he ushered him down the hall toward his study.

"Yes. I wouldn't want to spoil all the fun of a public execution by dying before it's scheduled." Tristan was so used to joking with Solomand about his impending death that it came out without thinking. He felt his father tense as his grip tightened around Tristan's arm. Once, he would have made a swift apology for being so forward; now, he found it difficult to care.

As Galin pushed him into a high-backed chair, Tristan's gaze fixed first on the polished floor and then to the shelves of leather-bound books lining every wall of the study. In other circumstances, it would have calmed him. Books always did.

Minuet pulled a chair up in front of him and sat down, crossing her legs. "I am going to ask you some questions." Her hair was neatly pleated to the side, lips like red velvet. The ease with which she carried herself in an uncaring and cold manner made his heart feel like molten lead. Head slumping to rest in his hands, he tried not to show how much her indifference affected him.

Her heels clicked on the wooden planks as she paced in front of him. "What was your intention,, coming back here?"

Tristan's fingers rubbed against the wood grain in the chair handle. "You shall have to be more specific."

Minuet scowled. "Solomand Black. Why did he come back here?"

Tristan folded his hands. "I'm afraid you already know the answer to that, Lady. What did he get away with?"

Her cheeks flushed as she ceased pacing to stand in front of him. "You are not the one asking questions."

Tristan raised his head. "Do you mean to ask me then, why would he bring me back here when he knew I was coming to my death? No." He rubbed his chin thoughtfully. "I don't suppose you would ask that. It makes little sense for him to do so. Does it not?"

Struggling to contain the frustration behind her eyes, Minuet gripped the arms of the chair, bringing her face close to his. "I am offering you a chance to cooperate, Tristan. This is not your official interrogation, you know what that will entail."

Inwardly, Tristan cringed. He knew all too well that an interrogation here meant being tortured until you admitted to crimes your ancestors had been accused of committing ten generations past. "Pain." He smiled sadly. "I am familiar with it, My Lady."

Cheeks flushed, Minuet stood stiffly, her shoulders squared. "Very well. Have it your way." She turned to Galin. "I will return tomorrow, Lord Highcourt. Hopefully, your patient will be more... accommodating." Her eyes narrowed as she glared back at him.

Tomorrow. That would give him plenty of time to accomplish the first thing he needed. Then there was the problem of Zee.

Galin bowed and moved to escort her to the door. Minuet held up a hand in protest. "I'll show myself out." She stormed away, her footsteps echoing down the hall.

His father rolled the morning newsprint in his hand, regarding him for what seemed like ages. Tristan's head sank into his hand once more, tired of the disappointed look Galin gave him.

"You are to stay within the Manor. If you go into the garden, you must have guards with you at all times," Galin said at last. When Tristan didn't answer, he spoke again. "Is there anything you wish to have during your confinement?"

Tristan glanced up. "A book of the Old World?" His father would most definitely not approve of him reading such books; this was the reason he asked for it.

Galin scowled, his hands tightening around the newsprint. "Superstitious texts better left on the home our forefathers came from. What other bad habits have you picked up from those dissidents?"

Had it not been for the last seven years he'd spent in the company of those so-called ingrates, Tristan may have had the restraint to keep his comment to himself. "Would you like a list?"

The color in his father's cheeks made him bow his head in shame. This could not be easy for him to be the warden of his traitor son. "I am sorry, Lord Highcourt." His fingers absently moved to the pocket of his coat. "My watch. The one I was captured with. It was a gift. If it is not too much trouble... I would like very much to have it back."

A flicker of suspicion in his eyes, Galin reached into his pocket and produced the brass pocket watch. Tristan did his best to hide his relief as Galin dropped it into his hand. "Open it."

So they could not make it work. He held back a satisfied grin.

"Of course." Tristan pressed the four pressure points. The case sprang open revealing a flurry of gears encased in glass and two hands keeping time with perfect rhythm. On the inside was a photograph of Minuet. Tristan tossed the watch into his father's hand. "You understand, with the company I have been keeping, they may have found this token suspicious. Didn't want to leave it lying around for anyone to see."

Galin tossed the watch back to him and stalked away, frowning. It almost bothered Tristan how easy it was to lie.

Chapter 5

RAYN

THE SMALL SKYPORT village of Ardglass was nestled against the back of a mountain peak. Stone buildings huddled together. A crooked road led down the steep mountain's edge and the ledge of a neighboring cliff was just beyond jumping distance. Leaving Jank on board to watch the airship, Ivan, Solomand, and Rayn ventured into a small inn on the edge of the docks to get information and something to eat.

An old woman dressed in heavy woolen skirts shuffled around the small room with a basket full of roots and small glass jars. She gave them a sharp, disapproving look as they entered, muttering as she jabbed a finger in their direction. Ivan stepped forward, gave her a quick bow, and said something to a man at the bar as he motioned Solomand and Rayn to an empty table in the corner. A few of the other patrons threw suspicious glances their way. With one glare from Ivan, they went back to their business.

A chipped platter slammed down in the center of the table, and the sour-looking waitress refilled their glasses with a dark liquid before shuffling off to tend to the other customers in the cramped bar. A slimy, red eel stared with glazed eyes in a bed of vegetables and stale biscuits.

Solomand jerked back slightly, then leaned forward, inspecting the contents of the dish with an increasingly disturbed look.

"Ivan? What is *that*?" He pointed like he was afraid it might jump up and snap at his finger.

"Smoked enoria eel." Ivan cut off a piece, chewing slowly as his eyes constantly circled the room.

Sol touched a tooth in the eel's fixed-open mouth. It broke off, and the mouth snapped shut, clamping its extended tongue. Solomand's brows knit together as he leaned back in his chair. "I think I'm going to be sick."

Rayn tore off a piece of the eel with her fork and popped it in her mouth. "Not bad." She shrugged and kept eating.

Sol looked increasingly ill. "How can you eat that?"

"I do not wish to starve." Ivan said between bites. "There are much worse things people eat in Northland to survive."

"Please, just... don't tell me." Sol plucked a piece off the eel and closed one eye as he popped it in his mouth and chewed. He grabbed the glass and gulped down the liquid. In the fit of coughing and gasping that ensued, he set down the glass without spilling it all over the table. "What god-awful stuff is that?" he hammered at his chest.

"Beer." Ivan took a sip, eyeing Sol over the top of his glass.

"Beer?" Sol stared at the glass like it had accosted him. "More like engine cleaner! I need a quart of paint thinner to get the taste out of my mouth. No wonder you Northlanders look so pissed off all the time."

The chair legs scraped on the floor as he scooted away from the table.

"Don't be so dramatic." Rayn rolled her eyes. "It's not going to kill you."

"You don't know that." Solomand stood, crumpled up his napkin and threw it on his plate.

"Where are you going?" Ivan asked

"To smoke." Casting another wary look at the platter, he pointed at it, adding, "If I chewed a handful of tobacco, it'd be a better meal than this one. I wouldn't eat too much of it if I were you."

As Solomand squeezed past the tables and maneuvered his way to the door, Rayn watched him leave. Something jarred her mind somewhere else. Frozen, she found herself unable to move or speak as her vision brightened and blurred.

"*Where are you going?*" The words echoed in her mind again, but it was a stranger's voice. A pain stabbed in her temple and the fork fell from her hand, clattering on the table. She was no longer in the cramped bar in the skyport of Ardglass.

"*Where are you going, Ben?*" *The question was directed at a tall man who smelled of sawdust and oil. His smooth face brushed hers as he held her in his arms. No longer grown, Rayn was a child of four.*

"*You sound like my mother, Lemuel.*" *Ben laughed, handing her over to a man with black eyes and tattoos on his arms. "To the mainland. You should go once in a while." Ben winked, bending to kiss Rayn on the forehead. "Have some fun—you know what fun is right?" He ruffled Rayn's hair.*

Lemuel stiffened as he held her. "I do not have that luxury. You should not be so foolish." His voice was steady, though Rayn sensed anger roiling inside him like a storm just below the surface.

Ben shook his head in a chiding way. "It's not like the Morai are going to care much what I do on my off time."

"*As far as they are concerned there is never off time.*" *An edge crept into Lemuel's tone.*

"*Don't worry. I'll be back.*" *Benjamin waved his hand, dismissive of his friend's worries.*

"*See that your fun does not result in another child being dropped on our doorstep.*" *Lemuel turned on his heel, stealing into a sprawl of trees with Rayn on his hip. Overhead a falcon screeched before swooping to land on its master's shoulder as if it wanted the last word in the argument.*

Rayn twisted to look after her father; he stood, looking at her indecisively before shuffling away. Her gaze shifted to Lemuel, her father's friend. Dark eyes, always holding back, always knowing everything, shifted to her. "Don't worry." He offered her a half-hearted smile. "He'll be back."

The vision faded to a white haze as the pain in her head intensified. She could hear herself groaning.

"Rayn!" Ivan was on his knees by her side. He took her by the shoulders when she did not respond.

A woman's voice rose above the noise of the bar. Her Slavik words were brittle and sharp-sounding. Knobby, weathered hand much stronger than it looked, pressed on Rayn's forehead, then onto her stomach. Her long white hair fell over her shoulder as she craned her head up to Ivan, speaking at him in an accusatory tone.

His gray eyes widened as he sat back on his heels. The old woman gasped, her hand moving to her mouth as her eyes fell to where the hilt of Ivan's knife stuck out of his belt. "*Unil di lor!*" Her weathered fingers trembled as she pointed to him.

Ivan slipped his hands under Rayn's arms and pulled her to her feet. "Let's get out of here."

With another groan, Rayn pressed a palm against her throbbing head.

"Are you alright?" Ivan asked, starting for the door.

"I'm fine." Rayn leaned on him, shuffling along. It seemed like everyone was staring as they made their way out the door. The silence accompanying their curious looks made her uncomfortable.

"Come." Ivan's hand was on her back, his arm poised to catch her. He threw a handful of coins on the bar and said something in Slav to the waiter.

Leaning heavily against him, Rayn let him usher her outside.

The Falcon. That was one of the names Lemuel went by. Another, with more sinister undertones, was The Body Snatcher. He was the one responsible for helping them get in to the fortified city of Corcyra and out again. Vaguely, she recalled Solomand telling her Lemuel was her father's partner a long time ago. But Benjamin Ivers and Lemuel Falcon had some kind of falling out. After being struck with the Coalition weapon that wiped her memories, Rayn relied on her friends and fragmented dreams to piece the past together. But in all this time, Lemuel Falcon had never been a part of those clouded memories. Until now.

Chapter 6

SOLOMAND

SOLOMAND LEANED AGAINST the side of a building, cold seeping into his bones, seeking out every past and present injury and locating too damn many. H watched smoke drift toward the sky and took another puff of his cigarette, hoping it would warm his lungs. Clouds roiled below and above like snowcapped mountains that had uprooted to drift across the landscape.

The door to the inn opened and Ivan strode out, his arm around Rayn, who did not look well.

Fear coiled in Solomand's stomach. "What's wrong?" He reached for her, but the pang in his left shoulder caused him to return his arm to his side.

"It's nothing. I'm fine." Rayn allowed him to take her face in his hand. Her green eyes were unblinking until her gaze gave way to a grimace. "Just a headache."

"A headache?" Flicking the remains of his cigarette away, Solomand gave Ivan a questioning glance.

"She passed out." Ivan said, glancing over his shoulder at the closed door. Worried lines formed at the corners of his eyes.

"I'm fine," Rayn insisted. She eased herself away from Ivan, as if to show them both. "What was it that old woman said to you, anyway? Made you look like *you* were going to pass out." She laughed, clearly trying to change the subject.

34

Ivan shifted uncomfortably. "She thought I was your... husband," he muttered, like he didn't want to say it out loud.

"*You*? Her husband?" Solomand felt a stab of irrational jealousy. He moved close to Rayn. "Why would she think that, I wonder?"

Ivan rolled his eyes. "*Valetzyan.*"

Solomand had been called an idiot enough by his friend to recognize the word. "More important—she knows I am Wolf."

"Lose your temper in there or something? Take someone's head off with—owe!" Solomand rolled his shoulder, trying to break free of Ivan's grip as he shoved him down the path where their airship was docked.

"We need to go."

"Alright, alright!" Jerking free of his friend's grip cost him. As his shoulder throbbed and Ivan walked close beside Rayn, Solomand cursed his injury. *He* should be the one protecting her.

As the door shut behind them, Rayn started up the stairs toward the helm. Ivan took hold of Solomand's arm and held him back. "The old woman, she was *kopteilvach.*" His frown was worrying, as was the secretive way in which he spoke.

"Kopta what?"

"Village healer."

"Oh." Solomand paused, guessing this meant something to Ivan.

"She said something else. About Rayn."

"What?"

"She said I should be more careful of her in the condition she was in."

"Condition?"

Ivan looked hesitant, gaze shifting to Rayn as he leaned closer to Solomand. "With child."

For a moment, Solomand felt like something had hit him in the chest. "You can't be serious. I mean, what is a village healer but a crazy old lady with a basket full of roots."

Ivan's face darkened. "My mother was a *kopteilvach.*"

"Oh." Solomand cleared his throat. "Like I said, essential part of a community."

Arms crossed, Ivan stared him down. "What? You're still serious?"

"Yes, *lochek*, I am serious. My mother could always tell."

Solomand's mouth formed a hard line. "I know you must have had a mother, it's just hard for me to picture it." He took a few quick steps back as Ivan looked like he might take a swing at him.

"Be serious, Sol." Ivan's eyes flashed in frustration.

"I *am* being serious. What the hell do you want me to do? Tell Rayn there's a possibility she might be pregnant because some crazy la—er, a revered kopta-I-vak."

"*Kopteilvach.*"

"One of those said so?"

"Maybe not. But if is true?"

Solomand's throat constrained with sudden worry. "I don't know, Ivan." Not having a plan for a significant plot twist was nothing new, but this time it bothered him more than usual. He was aware of the helplessness in his voice. "Can we get the hell out of here, for starters?"

Ivan's expression softened, and he gave Solomand a nod. His grip on Solomand's shoulder was not as oppressing as usual. "Let's go."

Chapter 7

TRISTAN

THE CLOCK ON the bedroom wall chimed every quarter hour. Tristan lay on his bed, staring at the night sky through the third-story window. Sheer curtains played in the breeze like a specter keeping him company. It was a quarter past two and all the noises of life had left the Manor. But even during daylight, it was like death had settled over the mansion. As rain pattered against the window, Tristan threw off the blankets and slipped into his dressing gown, pushing all thoughts of his father aside. Reaching under his bed, he grabbed the boots Galin gave him at the hospital and flipped over the right one. The thick rubber of the heel was worn and faded. He worked his fingers into a crease along the curve and pried it loose. Two steel picks fell into his hand. One was longer on one side than the other; the second was slightly bent on one end. Tossing the boots back under the darkness of his bed, he slipped the tools into his pocket and grabbed his watch.

When he opened the watch this time, he pried the glass free. The encased mechanism fell into his palm, as did the small silver key concealed behind it. Two guards murmured to each other as they kept watch outside his door—ensuring he did not venture where he shouldn't. But there were other ways of getting around the old house.

Tristan put the watch back together and placed it in his pocket. The floorboards were cold on his bare feet as he crept to his closet door and eased it open. A cloud of dust swirled from the disturbed clothing. He pushed suit coats aside, stirring up the stale scent of starch, and felt his hand along the back of the wall until his fingers found the loose panel; behind it was a tiny keyhole. The locking mechanism clicked as he turned the key and the wall eased open, revealing a narrow passage.

Closing the closet door behind him, Tristan slid down the dark hall, breaking streams of cobwebs as he made his way down the passage. His ancestors had a flare for the dramatic, constructing a network of such passages throughout the mansion. When Galin had told him about them, Tristan had to see them for himself. It was easy to pass the time when his father became lost in work, as he often did.

Solomand would have attempted to blow the door off. He laughed to himself, slipping the key safely into his pocket. But there was no one here to diverge from his carefully thought out plan now. Whatever surprises might come up would be his alone to deal with. It was more nerve-wracking than he imagined it would be.

The air was stale, and he fought the urge to cough as he counted in his head the number of steps it took to the turn. Left, twenty more steps, then a right, and here he was at the ladder. Tristan felt for the rungs and climbed to the top in complete blackness. When he reached the top of the tunnel, he lay on his stomach, panting for a moment before turning the codex to the right combination. He could have almost imagined he was twelve again—creeping through the walls to escape the desperate searching of his tutors. But this was not a childish game.

If only those were the worse of my troubles. He stifled the urge to laugh helplessly at the silly things he once thought were problems of any measurable degree. Heart pounding, he eased open the panel. Faint light spilled down the stairs from the fourth floor, where his father's laboratory was evidently in use. Tristan frowned, his hand involuntarily clutching the key in his pocket. What was Galin doing up at this hour?

Glancing down the hall, he considered abandoning his quest for another night.

No. Delay would make no difference. If Galin was working on a project for the government, he would be at it obsessively until it was done. The perfect moment would never come.

Tristan eased the panel back into place and made his way down the abandoned halls to the kitchen. A firebolt lamp emitted a soft-blue glow, seated on the table where the servants ate. A pot of coffee brewed on the stove in a steel percolator while the butler sat, feet propped up on a chair, his nose in a book. Wispy, white hair framed his wrinkled face as eyes squinted over the top of his wide-rimmed spectacles. He looked up, giving Tristan a shrewd look. "If you need something, you can always ring for it, young Highcourt." His brittle voice carried a dignified air. "No need to sneak about your own home like a specter." He licked his index finger and used it to turn a page.

Tristan spread his arms. "Fineas!" He strode up to the counter and plucked an apple from the bowl of fruit. "Aren't you afraid to speak to me? Everyone else seems to think I have the plague." He wiped the apple on his sleeve.

"Hmph." Fineas glanced back at his page. "An amusing suggestion."

"It's good to see you." Tristan took a bite of the apple.

"Yes. Well, pity it were not under better circumstances."

Tristan laughed. "True. Tell me." He sat down across from the butler and eyed the mug waiting to be filled. "What is it that keeps my father up these days?"

Fineas snapped his book shut. "That, Young Tristan, is none of my concern. Your father wants me nowhere near his work. No one goes up there save for the guard at the door." He adjusted his spectacles, locking his eyes with Tristan's for an instant.

"Ah." Tristan grinned. "He always was... careful. Dedicated."

"Hmph." Fineas glanced at the clock on the wall. "He will most likely be down for his last cup of coffee soon."

"You don't say?" Tristan pretended to sound surprised. "He should get more sleep at his age."

Fineas grunted. "I would worry more about your own health at the present moment, young Tristan." He went to the stove and poured coffee into the waiting cup.

Munching on the last bite of apple, Tristan wiped his hand on the back of his dressing gown sleeve. "You're right. I should probably get back to bed myself before anyone notices I'm not where I'm supposed to be. Wouldn't want to cause a panic."

The butler gave him a sideways glare. "I am sure you wouldn't." He muttered to himself, stirring sugar into the cup.

"Thank you, Fineas." Tristan tossed the remains of his apple in the waste bin and started to leave.

Fineas offered him a discontented noise as he returned the sugar bowl to the cupboard and picked up his book from the table. "You should stay out of trouble, Tristan. For your sake, as well as your father's."

Fineas always cared for the well-being of the Highcourt family. The repercussions that would likely befall his father were not something Tristan wanted to think of.

I don't have a choice! There are more important things than either my father or me. He wished he could make them see it was the right thing to do. As much as he hated to admit it, the longing for vindication was still there.

Glancing over his shoulder, he masked his distress with a mischievous grin. "I shall do my best." He winked.

As he made his way through the halls and back up the stairs to the landing below his father's lab, he had far too much time to think. Cool moonlight came and went through the windows of the mansion as fleeting clouds passed. Rain fell in a nagging, persistent spray, much like the worries that plagued his mind. LeFrost would never forgive Galin for allowing his son to destroy certain valuable information. What exactly the repercussions would be was a matter of question, and a hundred gruesome possibilities swirled in Tristan's mind.

Focus!

He forced his mind to only hear the pattering of the rain on shingles. Doubt would not do. Not tonight.

In his dressing gown pockets he found a packet of matches, a cigarette case and a paper clip. He considered his options as he stood outside the secret panel, staring at the light from upstairs that played on the silver-drop leaves of a potted eucalyptus tree. Turning the matchbook over in his hand, the last piece of the plan fell into place. Once he acted, he would have to move quickly.

Sliding the secret door open, he stepped inside the passage and lit a cigarette. A tremor ran through his hand as he allowed the smoke to fill his lungs and contemplated his lack of strength. Calculations leapt to his mind—his chances of being able to climb to the window he needed to.

Enough. Tristan silenced the doubts.

Letting the smoke out in one breath, he carefully inserting the cigarette filter-first into the book of matches and stepped into the hall to position it at the base of the eucalyptus tree where dried leaves curled around the narrow trunk. Smoke curled upward from the glowing tip of the cigarette as it burned its way to the unlit matches. Taking a determined breath, Tristan retreated into the passage.

When the smell of something burning reached upstairs, the guard would leave his post to investigate—as would his father.

Tristan's shoulders grazed the sides of the passage as he rushed through, eyes closed, navigating his way by memory to the room directly beneath the laboratory. Nearly tripping over a chair covered in sheets, Tristan yanked open the window and climbed out onto the ledge.

Rain-soaked brick was easy enough to grip as he maneuvered himself to climb. Tristan pushed up on his toes, his fingertips grazing the windowsill as he reached for it.

Tristan gulped a swallow of heavy air, crouched low and jumped. His fingers barely caught the waterlogged sill.

That wasn't so ba—His right hand slipped before the thought was finished. For a moment he thought this was how it was going to end. Tristan Highcourt, dead from a fall in his own house, lying broken on the garden path below while rain washed blood into the flower beds.

Panic seized his chest. He flailed his legs, searching for a foot-hold, struggling to hold his own weight. Swinging himself, he strained to regain a hold with his other hand.

Almost there. One finger caught. He clawed at the brick, fingers straining to gain a hold. Hooking one elbow onto the edge, he hoisted himself up enough that he could pull his legs up the rest of the way. Tristan paused for a moment to allow himself to breathe. Rain splattered on his face as he looked up at the sky before wedging his fingers beneath the cracked window; Galin always had it open to ventilate the room from his experiments.

Tristan forced it open and rolled through onto the floor. Thankfully, the lab was vacant. At least that much had gone right. Soaked with sweat and rain, his arms aching, he wanted more than anything to rest.

Quickly! He urged himself to stand, and he scanned the room as he leaned against a shelf.

Firebolt lamps flickered overhead. A desk in the corner was covered with a large typewriter and various books opened to charts; DNA strands, anatomy, atoms—none of these were unusual for the doctor to be referencing. A giant copper microscope was mounted to a circular ring in the middle of a workbench. Pages lay scattered around the desk, along with Galin's leather-bound research notebook; it lay open with illegible notes and formulas scrawled over half the page. A collection of glass petri dishes, a circular case with numbered glass vials and a green substance bubbled over a recently lit Bunsen burner.

Tristan made his way to a steel filing cabinet in the corner. Dropping to one knee, he dug the picks out of his pocket. Different locks required different methods of opening. During his lengthy illness, confinement to bed left ample time for practicing such skills. Pulling out his pair of picks, he inserted his tension wrench into the lock with his left hand, applying the slightest pressure while feeling around inside the lock with his other pick. Using the narrow tool he manipulated the internal pins slowly, methodically, just like so and so had taught him. Pin by pin they clicked in. With a snap, the locked opened and Tristan jerked the drawer open, hurriedly rifling through a series of files. They were all classified. The law forbid anyone without clearance to glimpse what they contained.

Galin Highcourt was the only one in possession of the research on how to make the E. X weapon. This was not general knowledge, but his house was well-guarded because of it.

Not well enough, Tristan thought as his hands fell on the file he knew well. It was his work—his weapon. His heartbeat pounding in his ears, he pulled out the file and relocked the drawer. No one would ever use it again.

He hurried to Galin's workbench and turned up the flame of the burner.

Pages curled and twisted on the steel table—words eaten away by hungry flames and reduced to a distorted pile of blackened ash. Relieved, he turned the flame down, fanning smoke from his face. Coughing in his fist, he glanced down at his father's notebook.

"No..." Tristan did not want to believe what he read. Eyes flitting to the petri dishes, then to the window. He needed to go. Now.

Footsteps sounded on the stairs.

Tristan grabbed the handle of the microscope and turned it until the base gears rotated enough for him to look through the viewing glass. Cold chills ran over him as he saw the result of his father's current work.

The lab door swung open. "Tristan?" Galin's eyes, lined with dark circles, widened beneath his glasses as he looked from Tristan to the pile of charred papers on his workbench. "What have you done?"

Tristan raised his head from the microscope. "I took back what was mine." He felt numb.

Galin's face darkened. "I put my head on a chopping block to save you, and this? This is how you repay me?!" He motioned to the wreckage in the room.

Tristan felt planted his hands on the bench to steady himself. "There is nothing you could have done to save me. I was a dead man the instant I stepped foot inside this city."

"You would have had a fair hearing—"

"Would a government seeking fairness enlist you to make such a thing?!" Tristan gestured angrily to the microscope. "You are a doctor. You're supposed to save lives. How many people will die because you engineered an illness?"

Galin's face turned hard. He pointed a finger at Tristan. "Do not lecture me about morals, boy."

"No?" Tristan's mind raced and his eyes shifted to the dull flame of the burner. "You're right, Father. I think the time for lectures is over."

Realization registered on Galin's face, and he rushed forward. Tristan tossed a canister of fuel on Galin's notebook and set it ablaze with the flame from the burner. As the fire consumed his work, Galin turned pale, hurrying to beat the fire out with his coat. By the time the flames subsided there was nothing left of the work but shards of glass and a few fluttering pages in the smoke-filled room.

Coughing into his elbow, he regarded Tristan with a look of stunned horror. "Get out." He pointed to the door.

Anger subsiding, Tristan stormed from the room, unsure of what to think of Galin anymore. No matter their differences, he persisted in the belief his father was a good man. Now he was not so sure.

The scent of smoke and charred eucalyptus wafted through the house. Moonlight filtered through the arched windows that lined the hall, creating shadows on the polished floor. Lights from airships docking at Corcyra's Port looked like stars moving about in the sky. Tristan ran a hand through his hair, wishing he could somehow slip away on one of those airships. But he couldn't leave Zee. LeFrost would soon know of his actions, and everything else would be more complicated.

Chapter 8

Tristan

G UARDS SLUMPED ON either side of Tristan's bedroom door. They jumped to attention, hands moving for their pistols as their prisoner approached. "Good evening." Tristan waved a greeting as he walked between them and turned his doorknob. "Or is it, good morning?"

Exchanging perplexed and fearful glances, the men did not answer. Tristan maintained perfect composure until he shut the door. Out of their view, he changed from his wet clothes and collapsed into bed. If he knew where they were keeping Zee, he may have been able to come up with a plan; sneak out again, find her—run.

He fell asleep, still thinking of a way out.

It was mid-morning when he finally awoke to the sun streaming into his window. Different guards waited outside his door, becoming alert as he exited the room and trailing behind a few paces behind him. Tristan paused, then continued on his way to the study. As much as their presence annoyed him, he was in no mood to play games.

It was quieter than usual. Breakfast was waiting on a trolley and none of the household staff were anywhere to be seen. The sound of birds chirping drifted in through the cracked window. Tristan drank a cup of black coffee and ate a plate of bacon and eggs, wondering about the problem of his father as he watched sparrows search for seed through the rose beds. He had nearly finished when the doorbell rang. Voices carried through the hall as Fineas answered the door. Moments later, Minuet strode hurriedly into the study.

"Good morning." Tristan sat his cup down and stood. There was something in her eyes not normally there. In a plain brown dress, her hair was curled to the side in an unusually carefree way. She looked flustered, like she'd gotten ready in a hurry.

Tristan frowned. He had expected her anger for his actions the previous night, not fear. "What is wrong?"

Minuet wrung her hands, her lips pursing together. "I… there is something I haven't told you." Her eyes darted down the hall nervously.

Tristan took a step toward her. "What is it?"

Minuet did not answer this time, but looked again down the hall as Galin walked in, buttoning up his jacket.

Glaring at Tristan, he turned to Minuet. "May I have a word with you, Lady St. Sebastian?" Minuet nodded, looking reluctant as another man entered the room. Her composure shifted back to coldness as the tall, Slavik figure with broad shoulders sidled in and stared at him with eyes like gray pools of ice; cold and cruel. His clothes were a uniform off-white color. Pure white hair was cut close to his head. Tristan's eyes fell to the curved bone handle sticking from his belt, and his stomach tightened. He had seen that knife before in the hands of his friend. It was the weapon of a Northland assassin; an Ice Wolf.

"This is Aleksei, the governor's personal bodyguard." Hand on her hip, she sounded composed once more. "Governor LeFrost wished for him to assist me today." She turned and followed Galin to the corner where he began speaking to her in a low tone.

Aleksei's head tilted to the side, a grin forming on his face as he sized the prisoner up. An uneasiness settled over Tristan. There was something in that haughty stare that he did not like.

"A pleasure to meet you." Tristan's voice was flat.

Running a finger along his bottom lip, Aleksei laughed. "I do not think it will be *pleasure* for you. I show the lady how to do real interrogation, uh?" Aleksei spoke in a heavily accented voice, grinning as he leaned forward slightly. Tristan could see the pale lines of scars on his face.

"I do not doubt it." Tristan replied without the faintest trace of fear he felt. LeFrost had a history of finding men like this for his dirty work. He took another sip of coffee, regarding this newcomer as if they were simply discussing the weather.

Minuet walked over, looking severe and disappointed. Tristan imagined Galin had told her what he'd done. Smiling regretfully, Tristan returned the empty coffee cup to the trolley and wiped his mouth on the napkin.

"I hope you plan on answering some questions today, Mr. Highcourt." Fingers drummed on her crossed arms and her eyes shifted to LeFrost's bodyguard and back to him.

Aleksei interjected now, looking eager. "Yes. Where has your friend gone, uh? The one with no fear in his eyes?" He threw his head back in laughter. "Soloman..." he snapped his fingers repeatedly until he spoke a gain. "Black, is it not?" Laughing again, he added. "I admit, I admire spirit such as his. Almost like my friend. He is your friend too, I think? Ivan."

Ivan? Tristan could not imagine Ivan having anything to do with this man. Then again, he was an Ice Wolf. Tristan's look of surprise was a mistake.

Aleksei circled Tristan like a wolf might circle a trapped rabbit. "Ah, so he *is* friend of yours. You not know this about Ivan, maybe?" His hand hovered over the handle of his blade. "But he could tell you, we Wolves know how to make men talk."

Tristan's stomach clenched. Minuet's eyes pleaded for him to cooperate. Aleksei motioned to one of the airmen. "Go and tell man outside to come." The Airman hurried away, looking relieved to leave.

Aleksei was circling him again. "Now we see what kind of strength you have, uh?"

There is nothing you can do to me I have not already felt. Tristan thought it best not to say it aloud. Slipping his hands in his pocket, he fixed a stubborn glare on the Northerner.

Aleksei's grin broadened as the familiar voice of a twelve-year-old girl yelled. "No! Let me go!" Her screams became muffled.

Everything in Tristan screamed to hide his emotions, but he could not conceal them well enough—not for this man.

Hands tightening around the watch in his pocket, he shifted his gaze to Minuet, wondering if she could sense his rising dread. Zee was LeFrost's daughter. Surely he would not allow this man to harm her! His heart hammered against his ribs. Nothing prepared him for seeing the familiar Olbian mercenary roughly dragging the girl inside the study.

"Will!" He felt like someone had struck him in the stomach, and his hands gripped the back of the chair to keep himself upright. Will wore an Olbian officer's uniform, like he once had before the insurgents saved his life on the battlefield. His one eye stared, emotionless, nothing like the Will he knew. Tristan jerked his head toward Minuet. There was the faintest glimmer of emotion in her eyes.

Her hand clamped behind Will's brown arm, Zee's golden eyes streaked with tears fixed on Tristan and widened. He could not bring himself to look away.

"Little girl is not like her father." Aleksei was speaking, pacing back and forth between Tristan and Will. "She has spirit! All day yells for you. So I thought I give her what she wants, uh?" He grinned at Tristan, then snapped his fingers.

Will, eye dull and unfocused, jerked the girl's arms behind her and twisted as he forced her to her knees. As she screamed in pain, Aleksei said, "These Olbian soldiers are good to have. Do anything you say, thanks to little dart." He tapped his neck. "Clever trick."

Tristan's hand was on his face as Zee's small voice pleaded, "Will, *stop!*" He had been to her like an older brother, always protecting and looking after her.

Thinking there was nothing they could do to him was a mistake.

"What do you want to know?" Tristan's voice was hollow.

"Ah, you wish to talk now? So soon?" Aleksei looked somewhat disappointed.

"Why did you come back?" Minuet spoke up quickly.

"To destroy the E.X. solution." Tristan's voice shook.

"Really?" Aleksei nodded at Will.

Tristan's fingers tightened on the back of the chair, his horror rising. "I swear it. If I had not come back when I did, I would be dead now." He glanced at his father in the room's corner, unable to articulate an explanation that Galin was the only one who could have saved him in the state he was in. Galin looked pale.

Aleksei chuckled darkly. "And what about this... Soloman Black? Where has he flown to with my comrade?"

Tristan doubted he cared about Solomand at all. Whatever LeFrost's petty quest for revenge may be, this man wanted to find Ivan. He took too long to answer. Aleksei signaled Will with a nod.

As Zee screamed, he took a step forward. The bodyguard seized him. "I swear to you, I do not know where they've gone," Tristan whispered, his gaze falling to the floor.

Aleksei did not tell Will to stop. Zee kept screaming.

"Stop!" Tristan jerked free of Aleksei's grasp and took a step toward Will, searching for any sign the Olbian recognized him. There was nothing in his eye but blank savagery.

"Is that order? My friend only takes order from me—you are only in position to " Aleksei crossed his arms.

Tristan's gaze dropped to the girl, her eyes pleading with him. And he could do nothing. He fell to his knees, unable to stand any longer. "Then I will beg if you like. Stop, please."

Aleksei laughed. "I like how you have caught on so quickly. Just for that, I will, as you say, comply." He snapped his fingers, and Will pulled the crying girl to her feet and away. Tristan could not move. Aleksei grasped him by the shoulder, speaking in his ear. "You did well! Tomorrow maybe I return, uh? See what more you can remember." He chuckled and strode from the room.

Tristan fell forward, the floor rising to meet his head.

Chapter 9

SOLOMAND

SOLOMAND PACED BACK and forth in the helm room of the Dragonfly, periodically dragging a hand down his face as Ivan talked in Slav to the Port Master. Grettos was on the North tip of the Kerrigard Mountain Range; halfway between Grishtanburg, to the North, and Chroburough to the South. They were stopping to resupply. Negotiating with these Slavs was frustrating. Money did them no good. They wanted something more concrete. Solomand agreed to give them 1000 rounds of medved ammunition in exchange for food.

"What the hell's the holdup?" Solomand squinted out the thick, domed windows that encircled the airship's cabin. White fog rolled in from the mountains. If the inevitable storm hit, they'd be grounded here for days. He turned to Ivan. "What's he saying?"

Ivan glanced up with severe gray eyes. "Says problem with trade." His left hand ran across the side of his neck where a black spider tattoo poked above the collar of his olive-green coat.

"What. Problem?" Solomand's jaw clenched as he stopped pacing. These Northlanders had nearly exceeded the limits of his patience.

"He wants tobacco also, or he say anchor will not come off."

The anchor, a massive metal device, was clamped to the airship to prevent it from taking off until the portmaster cleared them for departure.

Solomand stiffened. "What would have given him the idea we even have tobacco to trade?"

"Someone was smoking it when we gave them ammo crates." Ivan shifted an annoyed glance at Jank, who squirmed in his seat.

"How was I to know they'd pull some shit like that?" The engineer threw his hands up defensively. The sketchbook in his lap fell open, and he hastily fumbled to hide its contents.

"This is why is easier for me to deal with them alone," Ivan grumbled. He flipped the toggle on the microphone and spoke a few words in Slav, then flipped it back off. "What is your answer?" He looked pointedly at Solomand.

Sol glowered at the radio as if the man on the other end could see. "You can tell him the Captain says he can go piss up a rope."

Rayn was sitting next to Ivan, a rifle laid across her lap. Her red hair fell in a long braid over her shoulder as she bent forward. "Why don't you just give him some? We have plenty."

Solomand held up his right hand. "I will not. It's the principle of the thing. We made a deal, and I'm not being pushed around by some polar-brained jackass on a mountain."

Ivan rolled his eyes, speaking over the radio again, sounding increasingly agitated. Or it could have just been a normal conversation; it was difficult to tell with the Slav's language. It was coarse, like this god-forsaken continent.

The Port Master's voice crackled through, and Solomand recognized at least three of the words. One of them sounded distinctly like *passport*.

"What did he say?" he snapped.

Ivan looked over his shoulder. "I think you know."

Gritting his teeth, Solomand took the receiver from Ivan's hand and unleased a string of Slav obscenities. Some he didn't know the meaning to, but Ivan had used them on him, so it stood to reason were particularly offensive.

Letting out a frustrated groan, Ivan yanked the headset off his ears and tossed it on top of the radio. "*Krish amada*. Sol. This not Coalition City of Fifth Continent or entry port. They not waste time calling militsya patrol to find you later. They call friends to kill you *now*."

Rayn exhaled, massaging her brow. "Couldn't you at least have waited until we broke their anchor?"

Solomand opened his mouth and paused before finally speaking. "Damn." He turned to Jank, who was bent over his drawings. "Will—I mean, Jank."

There was a lengthy pause that passed as Jank looked up. His brown eyes mirrored the Captain's shock at the slip of Will's name. "Sorry." Solomand felt the emptiness widen. How could he have forgotten? Will was gone.

Silence hung in the air as Jank fought to hide a pained expression. He closed his sketchbook, wiping graphite from his fingers on the side of his jumpsuit. "What you need, Sol?"

Solomand removed the sling and maneuvered his injured arm into the sleeve of his coat. "Pilot the ship, will you?"

"Fine. Doesn't need much piloting, though." Jank scowled at the controls like he had something against their persistence to work like they were meant to. "Where are you going?"

"To get our ammunition back from those jackasses." He checked his revolver.

"You can't be serious." Rayn raised an eyebrow. "Are you giving them back the food?"

"Of course not."

"And you think they're just going to go along with this?"

"Doubtful." Solomand picked up a short-barreled shotgun from the munitions cabinet in the corner. "But I'm not going to stand for anymore of this vast stupidity." He fumbled to open the chamber. "How many could there be?"

Jank tossed his sketchbook aside and strode to the window to get a glimpse of the dock. "Holy…" He let out a whistle.

Ivan stood, looking down on Solomand with a scowl. "Too. Damn. Many." He yanked the shotgun from Solomand, opened the chamber by sliding the pump action, and shoved it back into his hand. "But don't let that stop you." Glowering, he threw a box of shells to Sol, who fumbled before dropping them.

Jank sank into the pilot seat, looking unhappy. "Can't you be less antagonizing for once, Sol?"

"Guess not," Sol replied.

Rayn stood, buttoning the floor-length jacket of white leather. "Let's get it over with." She chambered a round into the rifle and laid it over her shoulders. "I think I'm going to be sick."

Solomand frowned, stopping as he slid two shotgun shells into the chamber. "Still? I told you not to eat that roasted snake." He deposited the rest of the shells in his pocket.

Rayn leaned forward slightly, her gloved fingers coiling around the barrel of the rifle. "Shut up, Sol."

Ivan's head tilted as he looked at her, questioning. "Maybe you stay here this time."

Rayn waved a dismissive hand. "Don't be stupid, Ivan. I'm not going to hide on the airship because of a stomachache."

Ivan gave Solomand a hard stare.

"What?" Sol backed away. "You know I can't *make* her do anything, right?"

Ivan's scowl deepened. "You need better negotiation skills."

"Says the *assassin*. If you haven't noticed, you're short on people skills yourself." Solomand made for the door to put distance between him and Ivan. "Right. Let's go persuade these ice-for-brains Northerners to remove their infernal anchor and give us back our ammo." He drew his revolver.

Ivan and Rayn followed Sol down the spiral staircase to the cargo bay. Rayn was looking paler than usual. Ivan was probably right to want her to stay behind.

Sol frowned. Dismissing Ivan's worries was becoming more difficult. "Sure you don't want to—you know. Stay on the airship?"

Rayn's green eyes shot daggers at him. "Yes. You should have thought of it *before* pissing off the entire Grettos Port."

He turned away quickly. "Never mind." Ivan glared at him as he took the lead down the stairway to the cargo bay, which opened onto the docks.

He muttered in Slavik in an agitated way. "What's that?" Sol asked.

"I say you have death wish—or wish to be cripple." Ivan pulled the knife from his belt, twirling it around his hand.

"That's unaccurate," Solomand said, punching in the code to open the doors.

"Inaccurate," Rayn corrected, dropping to one knee and raising the rifle to her shoulder. "And, he's right. You do."

With a hiss, the door unlocked and cracked open, cold air seeping in. "He is not right—you are not." Sol protested.

Ivan dug his thumb into Solomand's shoulder as he maneuvered himself between Sol and the opening door.

Sucking in a sharp breath, Solomand pulled away. "Damnit, Ice Man!" He rubbed at his wounded shoulder.

Ivan did not reply. His breath was visible as he gave Sol a warning look. "Do not call me that. Or maybe I use you as shield." Arm extended at his side, he shielded Solomand from view of the gathering crowd on the dock.

A sickening guilt settled in Solomand's stomach. "Ivan." He tried to push past. "You don't need to—"

With another glare, Ivan held a finger to his lips.

A group of burly onlookers gathered. Some gripped knives, others tapped clubs against gloved hands. One man carried the crate of ammunition toward the porthouse.

"Plan?" Ivan glanced back at his friend, looking doubtful.

"Right." Solomand swallowed down the rising lump in his throat. "You grab the ammo. Rayn keeps the others busy while I brake the anchor."

"Very strategic." Ivan rolled his eyes.

"No need for that tone." Solomand eyed the muscular portmaster that strode through the crowd to greet them. "You know I'm no good at strategy.

Ivan made an unnecessary scoffing noise. "Oh yes. We know." He edged forward.

The portmaster pulled at his thick mustache and asked Ivan something in Slav.

"He's asking about the tobacco, isn't he?" Solomand scowled at the man.

"Yes." Ivan's hand flexed at his side.

"Sodding blackmailers." The safety of the shotgun clicked as Sol pushed it off. "Time somebody stood up to them." His free hand poised to reach for his revolver.

Taking the three of them into account, the hulking portmaster scowled and barked orders to the others, and they crept toward the Dragonfly.

Ivan twirled the knife around his hand once more. "Try not to kill all of them." He gave Solomand a warning look.

"Again. Says the *assassin*," Solomand muttered as Ivan rushed forward to meet the man head-on.

Rayn's rifle cracked. Blood sprayed on the icy planks as the man fell, yelling and grasping his knee. The others distanced themselves from Ivan as he ran, casting horrified looks at his knife and yelling warnings to each other; *"Leid Valk (Ice Wolf)."* Back on Lyonese, the Fifth Continent, most people looked at Ivan with reservation from his dangerous demeanor and tall, powerful build. Here in the Northland they recognized him for what he once was; one of the Continent's most feared group of elite assassins-for-hire; the Ice Wolves.

The portmaster did not appear to share in his men's reservation. Drawing a pair of pistols from his belt, he fired repeated shots at Ivan, his haphazard aim catching two of his own men as Ivan dashed past.

Reaching for the man with the ammo crate, he kicked his legs from beneath him and yanked it from his hands as he crashed to the ground. As the portmaster fumbled to reload his already spent rounds, Ivan slammed the crate upside his head.

The man staggered for a moment before crashing to the ground.

Solomand skated across the ice-coated steel to where the anchor toward the anchor. Something stuck in his shoulder (it would be the injured one) and he yelled out, cursing. "You bastard frozen-brained—!" He whirled around, jerking the knife from his shoulder and hurling it back. It caught the man in the chest and he fell to his knees before Ivan seized him and flung him over the dock with one hand. His screams faded, then abruptly stopped as he reached the end of the fall.

"Sol, the anchor!" Ivan yelled. His blade caught one of the men's axes as the curved edge swung for his head.

Sol crawled forward, kicking the frozen lever repeatedly. "I'm trying," he yelled.

Two men made it past Ivan and rushed Rayn. As she squeezed the trigger, it clicked. Empty.

Cursing in annoyance, she flung the rifle aside, hurled a knife at one man, and kicked the other in the shin. He cried out as the blade in her boot dug into his flesh.

"Frozen. Piece. Of." Solomand gritted his teeth. With every kick, the ice broke away until the lever finally slammed into place.

The anchor detached, and the massive chain retracted with a loud grating noise as it dragged across the dock. Solomand turned and ran, grabbing Rayn by the arm and pulling her with him back into the airship. Their feet slipped, skating on the blood before they staggered back inside the open bay.

The airship gave a jolt as the engines silently came to life. Solomand fell to the floor. "Not yet, Jank!" he yelled in vain.

Ivan raced toward the open doors and jumped in head first, punching the control panel so the bay doors closed behind him. He lay on the floor, breathing heavily as the Dragonfly lifted and leveled off.

"Well..." Solomand rolled over onto his back. "That wasn't as bad as I thought it'd be."

"No?" Ivan gave him a savage glare, reaching out and pulling him to his feet while simultaneously jerking his coat from his arms as if Sol were a small child. He held up his fingers, wet with blood, for Solomand to see.

Solomand swallowed, looking away.

Ivan forced him to sit. "Owe!" Solomand jumped to his feet. "Look, you son of a bitch, I've had about enough of you shoving me around!"

Grabbing him by the injured shoulder, Ivan's grip tightened like a vice, and he roughly pushed Sol back down. "Take off your shirt," he ordered.

Sol's jaw set in indignation as he did what his friend said. "You know, I think I liked you better when you didn't pretend not to hate me." He pulled his shirt off. "If one more person mentions the word passport or anything similar I'm going to..."

"Curse loudly and throw lead in their general direction?" Rayn offered.

"Close enough."

Rayn shook her head, catching him with a disapproving stare. She left her rifle on the floor, holding onto the wall as she stood. "I'm going to go throw up." Slowly, she made her way up the staircase.

"Maybe not do it on the stairs," Sol called.

"Idiot," muttering to himself, Ivan splashed disinfectant on the fresh wound.

Sucking in a breath, Sol jerked away. "Why?"

Ivan pressed gauze on the deep gash. "Why do you make stupid decisions?"

Solomand fell silent, biting his tongue as Ivan, rougher than necessary, bandaged the knife wound. He sighed. "Sorry. I didn't stop to think."

Ivan handed him back his shirt. "*That* is nothing new."

Solomand felt suddenly tired. Truth be told, he was glad Ivan gave enough of a damn to be pissed at his recklessness. "Thanks, Ice Man. For, you know... keeping me alive."

Ivan's eyes narrowed into an angry stare. "Not push your luck, *Otvali*." Solomand followed him back up the stairs to the helm room, muttering. "Where to next? We're running out of skyports."

"Yes. And when we run out of meat, we just eat tobacco."

Solomand's hand trailed along the railing. "You know what, I'm ok with that."

Chapter 10

IVAN

*I*F YOU LOVE *them, make them disappear.*

Those words of advice held a sinister meaning for Ivan, having come from an unlikely mentor. Aleksei. It was a name that made his blood run cold.

Dawn hailed a break in the heavy fog as the Dragonfly made its way further north toward Grishtanburg. The snow-covered mountain ridge, edged like ever-growing knives, spread out below them and beyond, rising with the slope of the land. Ivan sat cross-legged by a bay window, watching the land pass, marking every port and village far below, and one spot within the black heart of the Chatslow woodland, where a town used to be. That was all a lifetime ago, but it could still enter his mind with unbidden clarity, as if it had been yesterday.

He was fourteen, hiding in the bushes as he watched his sisters walking home from gathering berries in the forest. He meant to jump out and scare them. Nastya was twelve—Lydia, eight. Since his father left, Ivan was the one to make sure they were safe. Still, like all older brothers, he could not resist teasing them. Nastya had dark brown eyes and brown hair like his own. Lydia's eyes were gray, her hair dark.

They laughed as they talked to one another. Laughter turned into screams of terror. Jumping from his hiding place, Ivan saw the men; four of them, trying to drag his sisters away. Blood rising to his vision, he pulled the knife from his boot, a homemade one he'd filed from scrap metal. No one was going to harm his sisters. He charged at the men, furious, shaking. By the time he realized what had happened, three of them lay on the ground in pools of crimson, their throats torn open.

Nastya held Lydia, shielding her eyes from the sight as tears slid down her cheeks. One man got away. He ran back through the forest toward the village. Ivan wiped his knife clean on the snow and took his sister's hands in his. Dread grew with every step back to their cabin, but not regret. Hard choices had to be made to survive here. But Ivan hadn't been given a choice at all.

Their mother was stirring a kettle of soup. Her eyes widened with horror, and she ran to the girls as they entered. She took Ivan's head in her hands. *"What happened?"*

Ivan lay a hand on the pane of the window; it felt cold, like his mother's hands had been that day. He tried to push the look of fear in her slate-colored eyes from his mind. But he could not.

Blood, screams, Aleksei's dark stare all swirled into his head at once. The persistent need stirred within him, hammering at his head to be let in. A hunger for the drug he'd sworn off. It would make him forget. Like it had before.

Ivan sank to the floor, burying his head in his hands as he fought to silence the voices. He was lucky to have survived so many years of taking furi. Most others did not.

"Anything on the radio yet?" Solomand strode into the bay, tinkering with the spherical map he had retrieved from the bell tower of an abandoned chapel on Lyonese. He frowned as Ivan looked at him through spread fingers. "You alright?"

Ivan pinched the bridge of his nose, taking a pronounced breath. "Being here is… difficult." It was not an adequate word, but he knew no better one in their shared language.

He would have preferred Solomand to leave. Instead, he sat down next to him. "Do you want to talk about it? Some people say that helps."

The demand for the drug swelled like a flooding dam. Ivan felt almost as if an invisible force had him in its grip. He shook his head, tightening his fingers into fists to hide the trembling. "I do not wish to speak of it."

What *I want is furi*. The obsessive longing for the poisonous liquid shamed him, and he longed for Solomand to leave him alone.

They sat in silence for a few moments, Ivan with his eyes clamped shut.

"Did I ever tell you about the time we took a smuggling job for some crazy Highborn out of Stonecipher?"

Ivan shook his head, not caring.

"Slick-haired knob. He wanted a pair of Argos desert cats, which aren't strictly legal on this continent because of regulations or some such tripe. Anyway, the damn cage wasn't locked properly. Vicious little shits got out. I found out when one flew onto my bed. Landed on my chest. That was a rude awakening."

Ivan opened one eye, giving Sol a dubious look.

"What? It's true." Sol rolled up his sleeve and pointed at thin scars over his forearm. "This is where the damn thing got me. You can ask Jank if you don't believe me. He nearly got a finger bitten off trying to catch one of them."

"Maybe I will ask." Ivan crossed his arms.

"Do it." Solomand began tossing the sphere in the air and catching it repeatedly. "There was also a merchant who paid good money for us to bring him some rare kind of messenger bird. It got out too, somehow. Jank was positive it had given him rabies. That was the *last* time I ever smuggled an animal for a high-paying moron with more money than brains." He flicked at the craters in the device and sighed, continuing to turn the map over in his hands.

"Sol…" Ivan shook his head. His will was stronger now, and he ordered the hunger for furi away, once again able to master himself. He laughed helplessly, fairly confident not a word of his friend's story was true.

Ivan let out a shaky breath. "Thank you."

A brief look of understanding crossed Sol's face. "You're welcome. It really is true, though."

"Sure it is." Ivan slid up the glass to stand, stretching his arms.

"Hungry?" Sol stood and tossed the sphere in the air again.

"I could eat." He went with Sol to the kitchen.

"Is there anything on the radio from our friends in Corcyra?" Sol asked as they walked.

"Nothing. Is too early," Ivan said. Minuet would be busy trying to conceal her involvement with the Black Recluse. What was more concerning were the complications Aleksei would bring. He kept this to himself. For now. "Where is Rayn?" he asked.

Solomand continued to tinker with the metal sphere. "She said she wasn't hungry. It's probably just this cold getting to her."

Ivan doubted this was the case. "What are you doing with that?" He pointed at the map.

"This?" Sol held it up, looking frustrated. "Kree torture device." He looked like he was about to hurl it out the window. "It's supposed to have maps inside it, but I can't break the code to get to them. All of them, anyway."

"Where did it come from?" Ivan asked.

"Family heirloom." Solomand tossed it aside, dragging a hand through his smoky-black hair as he sighed. "Maps of the stars locked inside it and all I can get it to do is to navigate through a sodding minefield and go from city to city."

"That is all we need to do," Ivan said.

"For now." Sol shrugged and started walking toward the kitchen. Ivan followed him. Rayn was there, her head resting on the table, a plate with a burned piece of toast on it. "Feeling better?" Sol asked, stuffing the sphere in his pocket.

Rayn raised her head, glaring at him. "No," she snapped, pushing hair from her eyes.

Solomand laid a hand on her shoulder, and she shrugged him away. "Just leave me alone, Sol," she mumbled, her head still on the table.

"Coffee?" Sol ventured, keeping his distance. He poured himself a cup of coffee at the stove.

"No." She scooted her chair back, standing. "I'm going back to lie down."

Ivan took a knife from the counter and carved off a slice from the half-eaten loaf of bread. Rayn had been sick like this once before. She brushed it off as she was doing now and refused to stay behind on missions. Ivan had wondered the same thing then that he did now, but he had said nothing. Maybe if he had, things would have ended differently.

"Sol," he started. "Remember what we talked about?"

"What?" Solomand sipped his coffee.

Ivan sat at the table, scowling at his friend. "The old woman."

"Oh. That." Sol wiped his mouth on his shirtsleeve. "No. I don't think so. I don't think she could be after what happened before." Despite a confident tone, his face went an ashy color. Bringing up any part of her past injuries was always a touchy subject.

"Did Tristan say it was impossible?" Ivan took a bite of his bread. Tristan was the one who had patched her up after she was hit by the detonation. He would have known better about the permanent damage it inflicted.

Solomand cringed. "I try not to remember any of that shit, Ivan. Besides, what do you know about it? Midwife as well as an assassin, were you?"

"I helped my mother sometimes. My sisters were too young."

Lines formed around Solomand's eyes as he appeared deep in thought. "I'm trying to picture you as a brother, and my mind is rejecting it."

Ivan slammed a hand on the table. "*For shit's sake*, Sol. Stop being idiot for five minutes." He spread his fingers in Solomand's face to emphasize his point.

"Alright, alright." Solomand eased out of Ivan's reach. His expression turned serious as he sat down and picked his coffee cup back up. "I'm sure it's just the food. Give her another two days and if she doesn't feel better, I'll talk to her."

Ivan nodded, holding up two fingers. "Two days." He repeated, wondering what Solomand planned on doing if he was wrong.

Chapter 11

SOLOMAND

*A*BIRMAIL FIELD WAS *not an agricultural district beyond Corcyra's inner walls anymore. It was a place in time where the world changed, deformed into something new by a fiery blast of gunpowder and blood. While he was awake, Solomand refused to let it enter his mind. But as he slept, things had a way of creeping in.*

A detonation went off when they were on a mission to sabotage a supply train filled with firebolt cores from the Continent Argos. After that, everything was a blur. Ivan carried Rayn back to her father's house, where Tristan did his best to save her. When he came out, he was deathly pale and couldn't talk. Rayn was alright, but...

Solomand sat straight up in bed, shaking, covered in sweat. A hand over his mouth, he glanced at Rayn. Buried under a pile of blankets, he could hear the steady rhythm of her breathing. The strangling feeling around his chest lessened, and he leaned forward, kissing the top of her head. Stirring for a moment, her hand reached for his. Sol squeezed her fingers before slipping out from under the blankets. He grabbed his cigarettes from the bedside table and slid his feet into his boots. Not bothering to put on a shirt, he crept out of the cabin, making his way down to the helm room. He sat there for a long time, unnecessarily adjusting the instruments. The autopilot on this airship operated flawlessly.

Smoke rings drifted to the ceiling, ashes from the burning cigarette in his hand fell to the floor. Had Rayn been sick leading up to that? Sol couldn't remember. He didn't want to. What if Ivan was right? Still bare-chested, Solomand shivered from the chilliness of the helm room. He decided it was best to ask her. What could it hurt?

It turned out to be a lot easier to decide a course of action than executing it. At breakfast would be best, just the two of them. Breakfast faded to lunchtime. By then, Rayn was cursing Slavik food and looking ill again. Ivan gave him a threatening glare and Solomand cleared his throat, tracing the wood grain of the table. "Rayn?" he spoke with hesitation.

"What?" She raised her head and Solomand's courage shrank.

"Ivan's got something to ask you."

Ivan's frame seemed to fill the doorway as he took a step toward Sol. His hands clenched as he uttered in Slavik. Solomand recognized coward and weasel, along with other more generic curse words. Coward was a little unfair.

"What?" Rayn looked annoyed at the two of them. "Just out with it."

Eyes stabbing at Solomand, Ivan stumbled over his words. "Is there possibility you could be..." She gave him a questioning look. "With child." He finished, and her jaw dropped open.

"What? No. And who talks like that, anyway? What would you know about that sort of thing?"

Solomand pointed at Ivan. "That's what I said."

Ivan looked like he might tear Solomand's head off. "My mother was midwife. Besides, you were sick like this before. I remember." There was a heaviness in his eyes as he slid his hands in his pockets. "This is not place for game of chance."

The silence that proceeded Ivan's grim words punctuated the situation. "Ivan's right," Sol mumbled, lighting a cigarette as a familiar aching spread through his chest. "I remember. A little." His eyes locked with Rayn's and he leaned against the wall, dread twisting in his stomach.

Rayn gave him a disbelieving smirk. "You can't be serious." Her fingers tapped nervously on the table, but quickly stopped when she saw Solomand noticed. "I can't be." Her eyes betrayed her uncertainty.

Ivan crossed his arms. "We find out for sure, or I will not let you off airship again."

"But..." Rayn jumped to her feet, giving Sol a look that told him to do something about Ivan. "You can't be serious—Sol!"

Solomand lay a hand on her shoulder. "Maybe he's right," he said quietly.

Rayn turned to Ivan "You're being ridiculous. I don't think I could be after the accident, and, besides, how the hell do you propose finding out? Know a lot of doctors out here?"

Ivan scowled. "We do not need doctor. We have what we need on ship." He stalked away, leaving Rayn and Solomand in a heavy silence.

Rayn sank back into her seat and stared blankly at her cup of coffee. She hadn't actually drank it for at least a week now.

A coincidence. Sol frowned.

⚙

"You want me to make what?!" Jank stared open-mouthed at Ivan.

"Is not difficult. Not for you." Ivan said, dropping a med kit from the supply cabinet on the table with a clang. Jank ran hands through his hair, going every which way, leaving grease stains against the copper-red.

"Who the hell do you think I am, Tristan? I can fix machines, I don't make medical equipment," he continued to protest.

"Test is basically machine—measures hormone in blood. All it does is give reaction."

Jank, eyes bulging, looked at Solomand. "Is no one else disturbed that he knows anything about this?"

Solomand slapped Jank on the back. "Humor the Wolf, will you?" Leaning to his ear, he whispered, "good luck." And then left. Rayn jumped up and followed him out.

"Hey," she caught up, walking alongside him. "Ivan's a little on edge, isn't he?" She let out a nervous laugh. She was frightened. Solomand hooked his arm around her waist.

"Maybe the cold's getting to him, too," he said, trying to sound nonchalant.

Rayn stopped walking. "Sol? What if he's right?"

Solomand pulled her into his chest, wrapping both his arms around her. Resting his head on her neck he whispered, "It will be alright."

It had to be.

Chapter 12

WILL

"*STOP, WILL!*"

The Olbian blinked, piercing blue eyes invading his mind a second time as he escorted the girl back into the Governor's mansion. Names and faces bounced around his head like shards of broken glass. His hand on her shoulder, he pushed the girl up the stone steps, aware of the tears on her streaked face, but not caring about their presence. Following orders was his only purpose in life—the purpose of all Olbian mercenaries.

Inside the foyer, Governor LeFrost waited, a stately-looking gentleman in a pressed gray suit. His hair was a mix of gray and white, as was his beard, and his black shoes had an impressive shine to them. He greeted his bodyguard. Golden eyes that mirrored the girl's looked at her with a sense of discomfort. "How did it go, Aleksei?" he asked, adjusting his tie. "Did you find out where this Solomand Black has gone?"

Solomand Black. There was another name; familiar when it shouldn't be.

"Not yet," the Northerner answered. "But this Tristan will tell me anything I wish to know." He laughed, glancing over his shoulder at the girl.

LeFrost frowned, sparing the girl a quick glance. Her distress made him avert his eyes rather quickly. "Sazume is not to be dragged into this, Aleksei. This was a onetime attempt to garner information."

Aleksei interrupted him. "Do you wish to know where this Soloman is?" Aleksei bent his head, getting close to LeFrost's face as he spoke.

LeFrost cleared his throat, taking a step back. "Well, yes, but—"

"Then let me do things my way, uh?" He looked back at the girl, giving her a broad, toothy grin. "Sazume does not mind, do you, little girl? She gets to see friend, we get information."

Will felt the girl's thin shoulder tense. She jerked her head up. "My name is not Sazume." Her chin stuck out. "It's Zee, you Slavik bootlicker!" This outburst seemed vaguely familiar to Will.

The Governor frowned in a disapproving way. "Now Sazume, you've been through a lot these past years with these… uncouth fugitive scum."

The girl shook with anger. "You'll never find Sol, swank. And *you're* the one who's scum!" She twisted free from her captor's grip, whirled around, and kicked him in the shin. "And *he* is *not* my friend! You've turned him into a monster, like you!" she screamed at LeFrost before dashing down the hallway.

The Olbian stood dutifully, like a soldier, while Aleksei slapped his knee, laughing. "She is like small version of this man you hunt."

LeFrost's face reddened. "You are dismissed, Olbian." He stalked from the room while Aleksei caught up to him.

Solomand Black.

There was a face to go with the name now. The Olbian turned, wondering why the one called Tristan called him Will. Every time he thought about this name, he saw things. He flinched, walking down the street to the barracks. The manicured landscaping and guards faded, replaced by a valley with a curved walkway leading into a vine-covered compound.

His head throbbed as the girl was there once again—laughing—a small for her age, six-year-old with silky black hair falling down her back. Her hands were on his head as he carried her on his shoulders. Another painful throbbing and there she was again, older now, holding his hand as he led her into a thicket, rifle in his other hand, staring down at deer grazing in a wide field.

Now they were on an airship, and the other man was there, the one with the blue eyes; they were playing chess. *Tristan.* That was his name. An airskiff materialized in his mind, and he was carrying someone. It was Solomand Black. His blood soaked through to Will—that was what they called him. A wiry engineer, yelling at Solomand for ruining his engines; a woman with red hair, wielding a long rifle, Rayn; and, finally, a gray-eyed Slav.

Ivan. Will was talking to him, telling him to leave. They were in Corcyra. *"Take care of them."*

He was already inside the barracks and pushing the door to his room open when a hammer of emotion fell with an overwhelming strength that made him stagger toward his bunk.

What have I done?

He had been one of them—a Coalition squad leader, until the day he was hit by one of his own men, firing those cursed memory stealing darts on the battlefield. He was just another casualty. They left him there. It was the insurgents who took him back to their hideout and saved his life, gave him a name, and made him one of their own. But their trust did not come easily, and they never lied to him about who he was. They told him what happened, and he did not care. As Will, he chose his own side. Now he remembered; another dart struck him when they were trying to escape. His memories of being Will dissolved; but they were coming back.

Aleksei's cruel laughter echoed in his mind, his rising an angry storm in Will's chest. The Northlander was going to pay for what he'd done and find out what an Olbian out for vengeance could do.

Chapter 13

Tristan

TRISTAN AWOKE TO Galin loosening his collar. His vision slowly coming into focus, he recognized Minuet standing over him as well. "You!" He sat up, shoving his father's hands away. "Why did you not tell me?" Dizzy and unstable, he fell forward again. Stars swirled, and he was distantly aware of arms taking hold of him before reality faded once more. Voices mumbled to one another, becoming clearer as he followed their words back to consciousness. Rolling to his side, he saw a tree branch tapping against a window, beaten by a relentless breeze.

"Where am I?" His words little more than a whisper, Tristan attempted to get up. Sitting in a chair next to the bed, his father leaned over and pressed a hand against Tristan's head. Shoving his arm aside, Tristan swung one leg over the edge of the bed. "I need to leave."

"Be still." Galin gently took hold of Tristan's arm and prevented him from leaving the bed. "You suffered a severe shock." Placing a cold stethoscope against Tristan's chest, he paused, listening, before slinging the instrument across his shoulder. He took off his glasses and rubbed his eyes tiredly. "You are not healed completely. You need to rest. And eat."

"I'm not hungry." Tristan cringed at the thought of eating anything.

Galin surveyed him tiredly as he picked up a cup from the bedside table and held it out. Tristan looked at the clear broth with disinterest. "Humor me, Tristan. It has been two days."

"Two days?" Surely it had been only moments ago that he... A wave of nausea crashed over him. He met Galin's eyes. This was the first time he had called him by name since his return to Corcyra. His father was wearing the same thing he had two days ago. His suit jacket was hanging on the back of the chair, and the cream-colored sleeves of his shirt were rolled to his elbows. He was unshaven and looked haggard.

"Two days." Tristan gazed at the rain splattering on the window and rolling down the curved edges of tree leaves.

"Yes. And you cannot help the girl if you die of starvation." Galin placed the cup in his hands. Tristan's fingers shook as they clutched it, warm against his chilled skin.

Zee. The tiny flame of hope he had of finding a way for them both to escape darkened to a gasping ember under a harsh wind of despair. "I can do nothing." His eyes clamped shut. The complications were too many and his fatigue too great to see a way out. For either of them.

Unlike his earlier biting manner, Galin's voice was softer when he spoke. "Do not make me beg you, Son. Drink."

Tristan's eyes shot open; the thought of his father begging him for anything made him more nauseous. He choked down the broth, fighting to keep it down, while Galin strode to the window and stared off into the distance. Tristan lay there, breathing in and out slowly, willing the liquid to stay down. He felt the cup removed from his hand.

"Thank you." Galin set it down. "Now get some rest." He pulled out his pocket watch, yawning as he checked the time. "Minuet will be here presently." Tristan assumed his face must have betrayed the horror that shot through him, because Galin's brow furrowed with sympathy. "Just Minuet," he said.

Fixing a stare on the ceiling, Tristan could not evict the image of Zee's terrified face.

"Why would LeFrost allow such a thing?" he was speaking more to himself than anyone else. He'd made such a show of looking for the girl, Tristan assumed she would, at the very least, be physically safe here. He shook his head, hands clutching the blankets. "He is no father."

Ordinarily, Galin would have chastised him for speaking out against the Coalition, and their own governor, no less. This time, he just stared at his son, running a hand along the stubble formed on his chin. "Do not strain yourself." There was a trace of defeat in his tone.

The door opened, and Minuet walked in. Tristan sat up, rigid, eyes locking with hers as the beating of his heart intensified. "Why didn't you tell me?" he burst out, attempting to stand.

Minuet swallowed. "I am sorry. Knowing about Will would have done no good to you. I did not know that he would..." She bit her lower lip and looked at the floor.

"And your noble governor?" Tristan spoke out with indignation, not caring about her tears. "She is his daughter! He lets that... his *bodyguard* use her like a pawn in some cruel game?" His voice trembled. "Minuet, you know what Will was to that girl." His words were bitter, accusing.

"Stop." Minuet snapped, wiping her eyes and attempting to look as proud and controlled as ever. "I have no control over this situation anymore."

"And LeFrost?"

Minuet walked to the window and pulled back the curtain with her hand. "He lost control once he brought that Slavik assassin into the picture." Her eyes flashed as she turned back to Tristan.

"Does he plan to continue to use her to question me for information I do not have?" his voice cracked. "Because if that is the case..." His stomach knotted in terror. Death was far more appealing.

"No, Tristan. But..." Minuet sighed, looking like she did not want to tell him more. "Aleksei has convinced LeFrost to send Sazume to the Northland for the time being. LeFrost believes it will help her... recover." She rolled her eyes, "In other words, make her less like Solomand Black than she is."

Tristan's heart jumped again. "Why would he want to send her there?"

"Truthfully, I believe Aleksei wishes to use her to keep LeFrost in check. I doubt he cares whether Solomand is found. I am rather certain he is more interested in locating your friend, Ivan." Her eyes narrowed, and she shifted her weight to one side. "I do not know what *your* pet Ice Wolf did to Aleksei, but I would not like to be around when the two of them meet."

Tristan felt a chill run up his spine, remembering the way Aleksei had spoken about Ivan. No matter what he said, *his friend* was nothing like this new Ice Wolf. There was nothing cruel about Ivan. A hundred possibilities of how everything could go ran through his mind all at once, making his head throb. Lost in his thoughts, he barely caught the end of what Minuet was saying.

"I have some pull left with LeFrost. I will not allow him to re-move you from Corcyra."

He looked up, the fog beginning to clear. "He wants to send me to the Northland, as well?"

Minuet nodded. "It doesn't matter what he wishes, though." She looked genuinely angry that this newcomer could needle her out of her long-held position with Governor LeFrost so easily.

Who will look after Zee? Tristan jumped to his feet before Galin could stop him. "No. Let them send me to the Northland. You know what will happen to Zee in one of those prisons."

"Out of the question," Minuet snapped.

Tristan turned to his father, eyes pleading. "She is just a child, scared and alone with the one person she thought she was safe around turned against her. Father. Please. Tell them I ruined your research. They won't refuse to send me away then."

Galin looked from Tristan to Minuet. He let out a tired sigh, removed his glasses, and massaged his temple as he sank into a chair. He lifted a hand in resignation. "As you wish."

"Bah!" Minuet gritted her teeth. "Ever noble to the end, Tristan Highcourt." Her voice trembled as she glared at him. Fury dripped from her words, even as a cloud of tears gathered in the darkness of her eyes.

Tristan took her by the shoulders. The scent of summer rose filled his lungs as he pulled her close. "I know you can reach Sol. You know he will never stop trying to set me free. It will be far easier for him to get to me in the Northland than here in Corcyra. Please." his voice dropped to a whisper. "If you ever loved me, do this one thing for me."

Silent tears cut tunnels through her makeup as they streamed down her cheeks. "Alright, Tristan." Her voice cracked. "Have it your way. *Like you always do.*" She started to storm away.

Tristan pulled her into an embrace. She did not resist. He placed his forehead against hers, then leaned in to give her a kiss. Her hands slipped around his neck as she pulled him closer. All the fear and anger and passion shifted to him as she pressed her lips on his. He wanted to tell her she deserved better. Instead, he let his lips linger on hers, trying to drown the aching in his heart—the fear that this was their last goodbye.

Chapter 14

MINUET

*D*AMN HIM. THE thought was involuntary and disingenuous. Why did Tristan have to be so abominably selfless? It was what Minuet hated most about him. Anyone else would have done their job and not cared what the consequences were. Not Tristan Jude Highcourt. He had to get involved and dig deeper instead of taking things at face value. That was what started this entire mess. He got involved with those low-lives from The Mud and then decided his actions were not in alignment with his conscience. Anyone he ever knew (or loved) as a Highborn would turn their back on him forever. Tristan did not care. Right was right.

Minuet realized, somewhat grudgingly, it only made him more endearing. S*he* had no qualms about lying, cheating, stealing or even killing to protect the one person she loved. There were few things she wouldn't have done for Tristan's sake.

When the insurgents fled to Cierne Island, LeFrost ordered the 201st Airborne to wipe them out with bombs. Everyone assumed they killed Tristan, along with the others. Minuet knew better. She'd never stopped searching for him, even making deals with that accursed rebel captain who she would have liked nothing more than to see torn apart. Solomand Black was the reason for Tristan's defection. He'd corrupted him and deserved the worst penalty. It was an impossible situation. Should anything happen to Solomand, she knew Tristan would never forgive her.

As much as she hated all of those mud rats who took Tristan from her, Minuet's idea that he was corrupted to the wrong side was crumbling. A fissure had cracked this notion even more when LeFrost failed to stand up to Aleksei. Tristan had been right yet again.

LeFrost had seemed so determined to find his long-lost daughter. Now that he had her back, his disappointment in the girl's behavior was clear. Still, there was something odd about his fickle attitude toward the girl. Letting Aleksei use her as to extract information from Tristan? Minuet shuddered, trying to force the image from her mind. It was cruel, even by the governor's warped standards.

Solomand Black would never have allowed such a thing. The thought invaded her head, rendering her helpless to argue.

Trying to get information from Tristan this way was fruitless, anyway. He likely knew nothing of where Solomand escaped to. Besides, Minuet already knew, and she had no intention of telling Aleksei. Solomand was the only chance Tristan had left. This was another nail in the coffin of her construct that the notorious war criminal should be brought to justice; he would not leave Tristan to his fate, even if it meant his own death.

Maybe Tristan was right all along. Minuet swallowed hardly. It was not that their ideas of right and wrong were so far apart. Merely their methods of solving the problems. Tristan abhorred politics. She was good at playing the long game of vying for power.

She shook herself of her thoughts and bit back a look of disgust to accommodate a stone-faced appearance as she pushed through the door. No matter what anyone thought of her loyalties, LeFrost had always been a means to an end for Minuet. Her end had always been Tristan.

Aleksei's voice, loud and laughing, carried through the open door. He was no doubt tightening his leash further around the cowardly governor's neck. It was difficult for Minuet to maintain her temper with the Slav standing by LeFrost's side, sharpening his knife and eyeing her with those cold eyes, grinning like this was all some kind of twisted game to him. Then again, she was certain that's what it was. A shiver danced up her spine.

Peeking inside, she wrapped against the doorframe to gain LeFrost's attention. "May I have a word with you, Governor, in private," she added, refusing to even spare the Slav a glance. "It involves top-level clearance information." She felt Aleksei's grin on her. LeFrost gave his bodyguard a questioning glance, as if he were asking for permission. Minuet struggled to stifle her fury at this gesture. What was *wrong* with the blasted man?

"Of course, Commander." LeFrost rose from behind his desk and followed her out into the carpeted hall.

They walked in silence out the back door, in view of a stone pavilion. "What's this all about, Minuet?" Governor LeFrost fidgeted with his watch chain. He looked like he was afraid agreeing to speak with her alone might offend his bodyguard. Minuet smothered the urge to recoil with repulsion at his cowardice; if that was indeed what caused this ridiculous cowing to the Northerner. She wondered if there was more to it.

"It is about Tristan Highcourt, My Lord," she said. "And the *incident* which occurred in Doctor Highcourt's laboratory."

The Governor's face transformed to shock when she told him that Tristan had managed to not only destroy his own research, but the dangerous project his father was near completing. "Can Galin fix it?" his voice raised. "He is supposed to be some kind of genius, and his son did this!" He swung the chain from his watch repeatedly so it coiled around his finger while pacing rapidly on the veranda.

Minuet wondered if it was more a question of whether Galin would fix it. There was a look about him suggesting he was finished playing the puppet. She refrained from saying this to LeFrost. "With time, he believes he can."

LeFrost drew one hand from his pocket, pulling on his beard. "Yes, but how much time? Production on a shipment of E.X. darts is scheduled to begin within the month. And I have diplomats lined up from Hyperborea to see a demonstration of the new project."

Minuet's stomach tightened. But she did not reveal her emotions to him. "If Galin were not occupied with other concerns, he could better focus on those projects." Her words were careful.

"What do you mean?" LeFrost raised one eyebrow.

Casually, Minuet suggested that Tristan be sent to the Northland along with Sazume. "He will be more secure there, and able to fully recover for his trial. Galin would not have to worry about him causing any further delay or damage."

LeFrost's eyes narrowed as he paced again, still pulling on his beard. "Yes. That sounds satisfactory. Alright." He nodded his consent. "Make the arrangements."

"Straight away." Minuet turned on her heel and started down the back path as Governor LeFrost went back to his study. She wondered at the ease at which she wore an emotionless mask when inside a swelling of grief threatened to tear her apart.

⚙

The stone trail led to a brick building on the far side of the Governor's compound. Wire bordered the entire property and guards kept a regular patrol; airmen and hired mercenaries from the neighboring city of Olbia. One of the soldiers was missing and had been for the past two days. She had recommended Will be dismissed back to Olbia. The E.X. formula was used on him before by accident, and who knows what it might do to him a second time around. But LeFrost had listened to Aleksei over her—another injury to her pride.

A highly trained Olbian soldier would never disobey orders. Aleksei did not notice because he lost interest in the mercenary when he had no present use for his skills. Minuet pursed her lips together, wondering if her hunch was right. Instead of going into the red-brick building where her office was, she turned down the path to the barracks.

The polished floor squeaking under her shoes as she passed the empty charge of quarters' desk and climbed up the padded staircase. Minuet didn't bother to knock before twisting the handle and entering.

Will sat at a small table under the window. The lamps were off, and only the shaded light of midday filtered through the window. A bottle of clear liquid sat within arm's reach. Will's thumb moved the cylinder of his revolver in a continuous, mechanical way. His one eye moved to her. There was a frightening depth of emotion that was never there before. Not breaking his gaze from hers, he took a swallow from the bottle and set it carefully back in its place.

Minuet strode to the table and picked up the bottle, raising her eyes as she scanned the label. "Since when does an Olbian drink hundred-proof brew, Soldier?"

Will did not stop toying with his sidearm, answering her in a low, dangerous tone, "My name is Will."

So she was right. Something had broken through to him, and he did not care if she knew it, either. Minuet put the bottle down and took a seat across from him. Her heartbeat quickened.

"Minuet." He said like he was just recalling her name. "I remember. After seeing Tristan." His face darkened. "And Zee." His fingers tightened around the bottle, and Minuet thought he might break it by sheer force.

She straightened, uncomfortable as his thumb absently cocked the hammer of the revolver.

"Will," she began, swallowing. "Whatever you are planning to do with that, don't."

Will sat back in his chair, his finger resting above the trigger well. "I am not on the same side as you. Not anymore." His hand trembled. There was an alarming madness below the surface of his gaze. Minuet fought to maintain her calm display. A trained fighter like Will would be difficult to deal with in this unstable state.

"Don't be too quick to assume that." Emotion entered her voice as she held back tears. "Please, Will. Just hear me out."

Will's face did not change, but his head nodded slightly and he waited.

Minuet breathed out uneasily. "You can still help Tristan and Zee, if you don't take things into your own hands."

"How?" His thumb poised over the hammer.

"I have a plan. But it won't be easy. I have a contact in the Northland—a freelance agent who will help you find Solomand Black. If you agree to help, it will be much easier for them to escape. What do you say? Give this a shot?"

Will let the legs of his chair fall. He nodded, easing the hammer of his revolver back into a safe position. "I will do it."

Minuet let out a relieved sigh. "One more thing, Will." And this would be the hardest part. "Aleksei must not suspect you have changed, or he will not allow this plan to go through."

Will's face clouded. He stood, and Minuet was forced to tilt her head back to meet his gaze. "Fine. But once this is over, *Aleksei* is going to wish he'd never laid eyes on me." He shoved his sidearm back into its holster and downed the rest of the bottle.

Chapter 15

RAYN

THE DRAGONFLY SAILED without noise or effort above the snow-heavy clouds set on a course further inland of Hyperborea's southern coast. Mountaintops jutted from the sea of expanding mist like islands floating in the sky. Glistening light of dawn played across the surface of the rolling vapor in entrancing hues of orange and pale pink.

Making her way from the lower deck up to the helm room, Rayn paused at one of the tall windows, pressing her head against the glass as she allowed herself a moment to rest in the breathtaking view. The continued presence of a queasy stomach nagged at her brain. Laying her hands on either side of the window, she pressed her forehead against the glass, letting the pleasant coolness wash over her. So many questions needed answers. She was afraid to ask them—afraid of the answers. For now they existed as ever-present worries, accumulating and gathering strength; she knew of their existence but refused to acknowledge them.

Rayn broke from her reflection and continued on her path. A pang of hunger quickly shifted to nausea, and she pressed a hand to her stomach, swallowing back a metallic taste. "You. Are. Fine," she muttered in annoyance, quickly drawing her hand away as if ignoring it would make it go away. When she reached the door to the helm room, she took a moment to roll up the sleeves of her shirt. Unnatural heat flooded her cheeks and spread throughout her body, making her curse under her breath. Reluctantly, she went inside.

Lights on the radio flashed green and white and static crackled over the speakers. Ignoring the garbled noise, Jank sat with his feet up on the edge of the control panel, his sketchbook opened in his lap. Bent over the engineer's shoulder, Solomand looked up as Rayn entered and raised an eyebrow.

"What?" she snapped, crossing the room to take a seat on one of the gunner chairs.

"You're not... cold?"

"No." Sweat trickled down the back of her neck as she crossed her arms. "I'm allowed to not be, you know."

Ivan glanced up from sharpening his knife and gave Solomand a look that said, 'I told you so.' Skillfully avoiding his friend's gaze, Sol pulled the orb from his pocket. "Didn't say you weren't allowed. It's just... unusual. Anyway," he quickly changed the subject, producing the spherical map they had both nearly died retrieving from a city on Lyonese. "We were just talking about our plan. We need to find a place to hole up and plan our next move."

Rayn's eyes narrowed. "You mean come up with an actual plan rather than hopping from port to port burning bridges?"

Ivan cracked a grin aimed at Sol, his blade making a grinding noise as he dragged it across the stone in a decisive swipe.

"Yeah, well, I figured it's time to change tactics." Solomand cleared his throat.

"That what you're calling it now?" Jank snorted, shaking his head without looking up from his sketch.

"Moving on." Giving them all a dejected scowl, Sol turned his attention to the map. A series of clicks sounded as he twisted the copper gears and barely visible buttons on the device's surface. There was a flurry of blueish-white light that emitted from the map, forming a moving projection on the metal surface of the ship's hull. The lightning of the display fluctuated until the contrast adjusted to be more visible on its background—a moving picture of the Hyperborea terrain that surrounded them, showing mountains, skyports and villages dotted along their route.

Ivan gestured to the wall with his sharpening stone before slipping it in his back pocket. "How does device track where we are?" he asked.

Solomand shrugged. "I barely know how to work the thing's most basic functions. No thanks to Lemuel." He muttered the last part. Swiping his hand through the air, he looked at Ivan. "Since you're our resident expert, Ivan. Where do you think is the safest place to gather our bearings?"

Ivan shoved the knife into the sheath sticking from his boot and sidled up to the wall. His finger trailed up a line of unnamed dots nestled in the shelter of a mountain, apart from the rest of the range winding up the eastern coast. "Here we should stop for supplies once more." He tapped on a mark that looked like a tower. "Is private dock *Tor Hivyal*. Is used mostly by what you call outlaws. There will be no militsya there. Is dangerous, but we will not attract attention." He gave Sol a sideways glare. "We do not need any more of that." Tapping his index finger on a barren patch marked by a cluster of misshapen black trees, he added. "We go here after." His hand came to rest on the spot and paused. "There is nothing there. Not anymore. It will serve our needs."

"I'll go plot a course." Sol said in a half-hearted way as he pocketed the sphere. "Jank, make a list of what we need for when we get to this Tor Hivyal."

"Like what?" Jank tilted back in his chair.

"The usual."

"The usual would include spare components and engine cores for when you destroy the ones we have with your flying. Those don't seem to be necessary on this ship." Jank scowled.

Solomand let out an exasperated sigh. "Don't play like you're an idiot, Jank. I know you're not a complete one."

Jank slammed his sketchbook shut. "Sod off, Sol. I've got things to do." He stormed from the room.

"Like what? I thought you said there was nothing to fix," Sol called after him. Pressing a hand against his forehead, he muttered in Kree. "*Ise kina'bek.*" It was an insult Rayn heard before, and the memory hit her like a lightning bolt. She toppled forward.

"*Ise kina'bek!*" This came after the punch, which sent her father sprawling across the cabin. Now he rubbed his jaw as blood from a split lip seeped through his fingers. Lamplight showed the stunned look on his face.

"What the hell is wrong with you, Falcon?" He took a step forward, raising his fists until his gaze fell on Rayn. She stood behind Lemuel, clinging to his leg. Benjamin lowered his hands, licking his busted lip.

"Would you like to know what I've been doing while you spend the evening with village whores, Ivers?" Lemuel's voice was a low, threatening rumble.

Her father squared his shoulders. "As judging as ever. Always think you are better than everyone else." He pointed a finger, but kept his distance.

A tremor went through the hand Lemuel had placed on her shoulder. "Rayn was taken."

"That's always been your problem, you know? You regard yourself as some morally superior hero, all while stealing people's lives." The fury on Benjamin's face transformed to shock as he realized what his friend had said. "What?"

"You are compromised." Lemuel spoke with restraint. Rayn could sense his subdued anger. "And I am no hero."

"What happened? How did you…?" Benjamin started to take a step forward, then stopped, thinking better of it.

"Get her back?" Lemuel edged forward, and Benjamin distanced himself. "I used my mark. The one I've been working on for months. The one who took her is no longer a threat, and my mark is no longer viable." Annoyance dripped off The Falcon's words. "Not that you care about another life neutralized."

Benjamin took a knee, motioning Rayn to come to him. She ran forward, throwing her arms around his neck. "I'm such an idiot. I'm sorry, Lem." The warmness of his embrace calmed Rayn, and she buried her head in his neck.

The Falcon's voice softened. "It doesn't matter." He sounded resigned—guarded, even.

Benjamin scooped Rayn into his arms. She could see Lemuel's face now, hard and unforgiving. "No. It does matter," Benjamin said. "I'm always lecturing you about stealing people's lives through sleepwalking, and here I am putting you in a place where you are forced to use that very method to save my daughter."

A faint smile passed over Lemuel's face as he lay a hand on Rayn's head. "I will tell them you're a liability to my work."

Benjamin's hand tightened on Rayn. "You're only doing that to protect me."

"Not only you." His smile faded to hardness when he directed his attention back to Benjamin. "I'll tell them you are more useful as a stationery informant. I know you never liked my methods. This will be for the best." He edged the brim of his hat up.

"Maybe not, but I don't intend to leave you without someone to cover your back."

Lemuel's eyes, black with a shimmer of blue, pierced straight through Benjamin with unspoken accusation. "You have more important things to worry about." His gaze fell to Rayn. Even as a child, she could tell his thoughts were somewhere else entirely. He may not have verbally voiced his feelings, but the message was clear; Benjamin Ivers was doing more harm to him by being around.

"Lemuel, wait!" Pulling Rayn from the ground, Benjamin shifted her to his hip and followed a silhouetted Lemuel Falcon from the room.

⊰✦⊱

"Rayn!" Solomand was kneeling at her side. Behind him, Ivan regarded her with a troubled expression.

"Are you all right?"

"I'm fine, Sol." Rayn let out a frustrated groan. She must have passed out again.

"You keep saying that." He frowned.

Rayn started to shove him aside, but stopped when she saw the worried lines around his eyes.

He took her face in his hand. A pleasant shiver ran up her spine as his fingers trailed down her cheek to curl around her hand. "Can't you see you're scaring the assassin, Mrs. Black?"

Rayn glanced up at Ivan and laughed. Laying her head on Solomand's chest, she relished the way he said Mrs. Black. "If I'm honest, you're scaring me too." His lips brushed her ear as he pulled her deeper into his arms, and Rayn melted into the warmth of his embrace.

Solomand's reassuring presence stilled the confusion and fear marring her thoughts.

With him, she felt at ease enough to swallow back the truth once more.

"Everything is fine, Mr. Black."

Solomand's hands gently laced through her hair, his gaze locking with hers. She knew he saw through her lies. Her breath caught as he leaned in and whispered with a half-hearted grin, "I prefer, Captain."

As his lips pressed against hers, the world faded once more.

Chapter 16

IVAN

IVAN SURVEYED THE dark shape of *Visko Mal*—Bear Mountain—that stood beyond Tor Hivyal. He and Solomand made their way from the ice-covered port and down the winding road that cut through the village. Night air swept across the port, cutting like a sharpened knife. Ivan wore a long coat, pants and boots, all made from a white leather; the garb easily recognizable as that of an Ice Wolf. More importantly, it was effective at warding off the subfreezing temperatures. Even though Solomand wore two layers of clothing, he shivered as he walked alongside Ivan, cursing the cold under his breath.

"Thought you didn't want to attract attention wearing those clothes?" Sol said, grudgingly. He rubbed his gloved hands together.

Ivan hooked a thumb through the belt on the outside of his coat—which made his blade more easily accessible. "Here is better for them to know who they are dealing with." He gave his friend a hard stare. "Willing to take on trouble is not the same as wanting it."

"You make it sound like I go out of my way to get shot at." Solomand's teeth chattered.

Buildings of stone and wood densely crowded together, edging up the sloped edges of a hill on either side of the road that seemed to split the village down the middle and continue on its way, winding up the distant mountain. Smoke curled up from chimneys and lamplight flickered faintly from iron corner posts marking the village edge.

It was harder than Ivan thought it would be to set foot back on this land. Ghosts of the past stirred with every step he took toward Tor Hivyal. Many times he had walked down from Bear Mountain, accompanied by another.

Aleksei. Faces—scream—blood. A plaguing hunger to make the memories go away crashed over him like a sea-wave, hot and cold and unbearable. Ivan almost lost his footing, putting a hand to his head as he stumbled further into the village. For those seeking to banish memories and regrets, this was one such place to go.

Flames flickered from a fire barrel as they neared the village. Men huddled around, warming their hands. Ivan clawed the hood from his head as another wave hit him; voices, a malicious smile, the scent of death. All of it fed that deep-set need Ivan thought he was past.

A man bent over the barrel turned to look at him. A balaclava covered his mouth and nose. A thick woolen hat was pulled down over his head. He called to Ivan, motioning him nearer to the fire. As he dug into his coat pocket, Ivan already knew what he was looking for. It was no surprise when he presented a tiny vial of familiar liquid.

Furi.

Those who dealt in it had a knack for recognizing desperation. Heart pounding in his ears, Ivan could not refuse. *Only a drop.* The voice in his head lied. His hand moved to the pocket, feeling for the last of their coins. One taste is all it would take and its power would consume him. But the *faces* in his mind! Ivan's hand trembled as his spirit battled between resisting and giving in to a moment of peace he knew the drug would give him.

"Ivan!" A rough hand gripped his shoulder, jerking him back. On edge, Ivan drew the curved blade from his belt in an instant and stopped the force of his blow just short of Solomand's throat.

Ivan lowered his knife, his heart hammering wildly. *What did I almost do?*

Solomand used his teeth to pull off the glove on his right hand as he spun to face the unsuspecting furi dealer. "Hey! You!" He stormed forward, unleashing a sling of Slavik obscenities. Before the man could react, Sol's fist cracked into his face.

Hands at his bleeding nose, the man staggered to his feet and disappeared down the street with his two companions. Ivan's hand shook as he tucked the knife back into his belt.

"You alright?" Sol returned, flexing his fingers with a painful grimace.

Ivan steadied himself on a lamppost, bending slightly and muttering in Slav to himself what an impossible idiot he was. "One moment longer and I would have…" He gulped, forcing himself to meet Sol's gaze. "I nearly took off your head."

Sol clapped a hand on his back. "I'm grateful you didn't."

Ivan observed the way Sol's reddened hand was clenched at his side. Giving into a pained expression, Solomand rubbed at his right shoulder. "I think I may have fractured my arm," he groaned. "And before you ask, no. I don't regret it." He breathed out sharply, drawing his arm into his chest. "This damn shoulder will never heal properly."

Ivan laughed, a welcome feeling of relief washing over him. "Probably not. But I have feeling you will not let it stop you from making stupid decisions."

"Damn right I won't." A look of understanding passed between them. "Just… don't tell Rayn, will you? Say I slipped on the ice or something."

Ivan gripped Sol's uninjured shoulder. "This once, I will lie for you." His eyes narrowed. "But do not think I will make it habit."

"Wouldn't dream of asking."

Chapter 17

SOLOMAND

SNOW FLURRIED TO the ground, stinging Solomand as he cast a distasteful look at the night sky. Shivering, he tucked his throbbing hand inside his coat. "How far away is this place, anyway?" The cold air burned as he breathed it in.

"Not far."

"Sodding block of ice—why didn't you talk me out of coming here."

"Don't worry." Ivan grinned back at him as they veered off the main road and down an alley deeper into the village. "I will not let you freeze to death."

Heavy beams ran between the buildings for added bracing. A row of icicles dangled over their head like brittle knives. "Plan on making sure I die before it comes to that, eh?" Solomand shrank into his collar as he glanced up, quickening his steps.

"*Mozyihe.*"

"What?"

"Nothing." Ivan gave him a grim smile as he walked up a set of steps and pounded on the door of a two-story building at the end of the street. Above the heavy door was a single word etched in the pale stonework.

"B-e-o-l-a-n." Sol sounded out the letters. "What the hell does that mean?"

"This is Beolan's residence. A trading post. Sort of." Ivan's gaze changed as it shifted to the mountain in the distance and quickly reverted to the building. He pounded on the door again. Light seeped through cracks in the shutters, and footsteps trailed across the floor inside.

"Looks *very* reputable." Solomand curled his toes as the cold seeped further into his bones.

Ivan raised an eyebrow. "People like us do not go to *reputable* places."

"What do you mean, *like us?*"

Before Ivan could answer, an old man opened the door. Thick white hair was as wildly misplaced as was his lengthy beard. His bare feet and untucked shirt gave Sol the impression their imposing visit roused him from sleep. Muttering angrily, he squinted at Ivan behind thick wire-rimmed glasses. Watery brown eyes widening, he fell silent with unmistakable fear.

As Ivan conversed back and forth with the man, Solomand shivered, eyeing the fireplace behind the cracked door with longing. Beolan at last opened the door wider, and Ivan motioned him inside.

Floor boards creaked under their boots as they walked further toward the comfort of the fire. Boxes and tins were stacked precariously over most of the room. Shelves lined the walls on either side of a padlocked door. There was movement on one shelf and Solomand jumped back. Something large and furry skittered behind a row of canned food. Reddish eyes turned, catching the light, and a can clanged on the floor as a thick hairless tail whipped against it.

Not proudly, Solomand moved behind Ivan. "What in the mutated hell was that thing, Ivan?" He whispered.

"A rat." Ivan did not seem bothered. Nor did Beolan, who glanced at the thing as it crawled down the wall and vanished behind a crate.

"And why the hell does your friend here," Sol nodded at the old man, "seem oblivious to the fact there are twenty pound rats cavorting in his home?"

Beolan was giving them a curious look. He said something to Ivan and motioned to the chairs around the table.

Ivan seized Sol by the arm and dragged him forward. "Remember what I said about not wishing to starve in Northland?" He kept his voice low.

"Oh. Stop—don't say another word." Visions of the disgusting creature served on a plate with roasted vegetables made his stomach clench involuntarily. He took a seat next to Ivan, holding his hands out to reach the warmth of the flames. "I may be sick."

"For someone who grew up with little, you have weak stomach." Ivan sounded annoyed. He said a few words to Beolan.

"You're right. You know that campfire game where you take turns saying things you wouldn't do? Eating rodent on ice was one of those things for me."

"The *list*, Sol." Ivan was holding his hand out, staring at him in a way that was usually accompanied by a threat.

"Oh." Solomand struggled for a moment to remove the crumpled paper from his right pocket, using his left hand. "Be sure and tell him we can't stay for dinner if he offers."

Ivan's jaw tightened, his fingers curling impatiently until Sol finally dropped the list in his hand. He shook his head slightly, then spread the paper out on the rough surface of the table and began speaking with Beolan. Their voices became background noise as Sol fixed his eyes on the dance of the flames over crackling wood. The warmth of it made his eyes feel heavy, and they closed for a moment.

You're running out of time. His own voice chided, causing his eyes to snap back open. How long would it be before they killed Tristan? If they hadn't already. And what of Zee? A pang stabbed at his chest, and Solomand forced his focus back to the throbbing in his hand. *I'm doing what I can.*

Beolan's chair legs scraped on the floor as he scooted back and stood, nodding in a satisfied way. He picked up the bag of coins Ivan gave him and hobbled up to the padlocked door, opened it, and disappeared to another room. Ivan was far too tense for comfort.

"Everything alright?" Sol asked.

"Yes." Ivan's fingers drummed on the table. "He has most of what we need. We have reached agreement. All is left is to seal deal with drink of kurdishin."

Solomand studied his fingers, wondering if any of them were in-fact broken. "What the hell is that?"

"Slavik gin."

"Ha." Solomand snorted in disgust, recalling the last time he dared to drink any liquor brewed in the North. "Well. I suppose it's your stomach."

Ivan shifted in his seat, clearing his throat as he leaned forward onto his forearms. "Sol." There was a disconcerting, guilty look in his eyes. "I told him I was ill. And you would drink with him instead."

"What?" Solomand's eyes widened. The adjacent door opened, and Beolan appeared carrying two glasses and a dusty bottle. "No!" Solomand leaned closer to Ivan, whispering forcefully. "Last time I had Slavik gin it gave me a headache that made me wish I was dead. You damn-well better make a quick recovery of your bullshit illness."

Glasses clinked against each other as Beolan sat them down, exchanging another few words with Ivan before he wrestled to extract the cork from the bottle.

"Sol." There was a hint of desperation in Ivan's whisper. "First time I took furi, I was drunk out of my skull on kurdishin." His gaze shifted back to Beolan, and he spoke in Slav, nodding his approval before giving Sol a pleading look.

Having won his battle with the stopper, the old man shakily poured the liquid into first one glass, then the other.

"Damn." Solomand gritted his teeth, slapping a hand on the table. "Alright."

As Ivan visually relaxed, Beolan laughed, nodding toward Sol as he set the bottle down. "He likes your enthusiasm." Ivan grinned, handing Sol the glass.

"Does he?" Sol held up his glass, making what he thought was an eager expression. "Wait until he sees me enthusiastically vomiting into the snow." A few drops splashed on his fingers as he clinked the glass against Beolan's and took a harrowing swallow. For a moment, his vision blurred as he slammed the glass down, letting the burning sensation slog its way down his throat and into the pit of his stomach. The old man was saying something.

"He wishes you to have one more with him." Ivan smiled sympathetically as he pushed the overflowing glass into Solomand's hand.

"So it's to be death by alcohol poisoning, is it?" Sol threw the glass back once more, slammed it down, and forced himself to stand. "I'll wait outside." Fairly sure he would not make it out the door before the stuff worked its way back up his esophagus, Sol rushed outside.

He wasn't sure how long he waited for Ivan as he gulped in the frigid air, wondering how the temperature had warmed. "Sodding paint thinner." He leaned against the building as the ground spun. Was that the sky spinning? Or were the stars falling? No—snow— that was what they called it. Cold, horrid rain left in the deep-freeze too long. It stung his face as it fell, and his mind traveled back to the valley of his mother's childhood. Green lush meadows, birds diving from the forest and deer drinking from the river that wound from the forest beyond the castle ruins in the hills. It was a place teeming with life. A place he longed to be right at this moment.

"You alright?" Ivan's hands were on him—roughly.

"Yeah. Was just… going to take a nap." Solomand slurred his words, his eyes flickering shut.

"I think not." Ivan jerked him to his feet. Oddly, Solomand's hand didn't hurt so much. "I promised not to let you freeze to death, remember?"

"Maybe… I dunno. I think I've drunk too much of that shit." Solomand stumbled forward, his eyes on the endless stretch of white that stood between them and where they were going. Was it the airship? Yes. That sounded right. Ivan grabbed him by the arm, stopping him from falling on his face.

"I am sorry, Sol." Ivan sounded needlessly sympathetic—guilty even.

"For what?"

Chapter 18

Tristan

IT WAS A grim morning layered in fog. Tristan looked out the shapes of the city below his window, closing his eyes as he remembered it in spring, covered in flowers and streaked with sunshine as he played with the neighborhood children, one of which was a girl with dark curls who kissed him behind the rose bushes. The memory of her smile made him feel warm and sad at the same time; he hadn't seen her smile like that in so long.

His hand went to adjust the red armband as the clock chimed, and he took a last look around his room. No matter if things went well or poorly, this would be the last time he saw Highcourt Manor. If Solomand somehow pulled off a miracle and helped him escape from whatever prison awaited, he could never return. If Solomand failed, well… either way, he wasn't coming back to Corcyra.

As he turned to leave, his father was standing in the doorway, one hand rested against the molding. "Father." Tristan bowed his head slightly. He was grateful Galin did not fight to have him stay in the city. It was a peculiar feeling, knowing they were unlikely to see each other again. Considering their strained relationship, did it even bother Galin?

Eyes squinting behind his glasses, Galin's silence seemed to last forever. Rigid, he walked over to his son and held out a small, leather-bound book. "Here."

Golden embossed letters identified it as an ancient book—one most certainly forbidden. A lump rising in his throat, Tristan turned the book over in his hand. He wanted to speak, but the ache in his heart prevented the words from coming out.

"Try not to strain yourself and damage the work I've put into you."

Tristan ran his hand along the faded lettering on the spine. A lump rose in his throat as he slipped the book in his back pocket. "Thank you." Tears stung his eyes as he caught Galin's gaze. "Father, I..."

Galin held up a hand. "Don't." He looked like he glanced in the guards' direction. His eyes fell to the floor. "Let's go."

As they went outside, the guards were waiting with their shackles. Galin put a hand on Tristan's shoulder, pushing him past them. "Not in my house, Airman," he said stiffly, his hand remaining on Tristan until they were outside and in the waiting motorcar.

A crowd gathered outside the manor gates—mostly journalists eager to snap a photo or pen a story. They scattered when the car did not slow down. It was a silent drive. Everything passed through like a blur. People going about their day didn't bother giving the motorcar a second glance. How quickly one decision could turn life on its head.

Only guards were allowed on the prison platform, aside from those with direct authorization from the Governor. Today, only Minuet and Galin had such authorization.

Iron gates opened and closed, sealing the car in as it sped to where the sleek prison train waited. It would travel east until it reached the transfer station of Crescent Bay.

Train whistles cut through the still morning as they stepped out of the car. Galin's hand was still on his shoulder. He guided Tristan up the stairs to the wooden platform, where steam billowed out of the gray iron engine. From the opposite side, figures materialized out of the fog and Tristan stopped, taking a breath.

"Tristan!" The girl ran to him, throwing her arms around his waist, clinging to him with all her strength. His arms closed around her until he saw the Olbian squad posted by the open car doors, one of which walked toward them. His face must have betrayed his feelings, for Galin's grip tightened.

"Steady, boy," Galin said.

Zee shrank against Tristan on seeing Will, but Will did nothing but stare blankly, awaiting orders.

Minuet walked from the fog, looking tragically unbothered. "Take her to the car, Soldier," she ordered, to Tristan's dismay. She gave him a warning look and he let go of the girl.

"It will be alright, Zee. Just go with him," he pleaded. Zee nodded and followed Will, recoiling as he put his hand on her arm.

The three of them were alone now, except for the other Olbians flanking the train car. Tristan breathed in shakily as Minuet walked up to him. "Your hands," she said. He held them out, staring straight through her. She put cuffs on him, squeezing his hands before letting him go, her eyes letting a sorrowful look slip for just an instant.

Galin released his grip. Tristan turned to him one last time. So many things he should have said, but the only words he choked out were, "Goodbye, Father." He suspected no matter what happened, this was the last time they would see each other.

Galin gave him a slight nod before Minuet led him to the waiting train car.

"Do *not* tell *me* goodbye, Lord Highcourt. Not again," she said in an angry whisper. "I am expecting to see you again, alive and well, or Solomand Black will answer to me."

As Tristan stepped up and into the car, he grinned down at her. "Your wish is my command, My Lady." A slight smile passed her lips before he was yanked inside by the waiting guards, and the door rolled shut.

Rough hands shoved Tristan to the straw-covered floor on one end of the train. As he looked up at Will standing next to the cowering figure of Zee, the sickening feeling rose in him again.

The engine's whistle shattered the stillness as the wheels creaked and it inched forward, soon to speed up and hurdle through the desert to its eventual destination in the East; a world away. Minuet's contact had been wired a sizable payment. Though Minuet disliked the agent's reputation for being eccentric, she would follow instructions to the letter. Will had to find Solomand. He was the only chance Tristan had now.

Watching the rising trail of steam flow from the engine, Minuet felt like her heart was being torn apart. Did Galin feel the same? "Will you resume your research?" she asked. The train pulled away, its wheals screaming. Years of planning and sacrifice depended on what Galin did.

"I gave the Governor my word." His voice was listless as he fidgeted with his watch chain. "*Things* must end soon." His eyes met her for a second, a flash of fury in them. He inclined his head. "Lady." Fog swallowed him as he walked away. Minuet was left alone to listen until the last noise of the train on the rails passed from ear's reach.

Chapter 19

WILL

WILL KNEW ZEE was trembling. He could feel her next to him. Knees drawn up to her chest, her back pressed against the bolted walls of the train car by his side. A pain stabbed through his head and it was all he could do to maintain an expressionless vigil. As the train rattled out of the station, he issued an order in a low growl, "No one moves unless I say so."

"Yes, Sir!" the five other Olbians all replied at once.

Zee's golden eyes, wide beneath her uneven bangs, fixed on Tristan. He gave her an encouraging grin, holding a clutched hand to his chest. Sweat beaded on his forehead and his shoulders rose and fell with the unnatural rhythm of his breathing.

Will blinked, fighting down the urge to fixate on how it was his own fault. It was a long way to the Crescent Bay, and he had a job to do. Clear thinking was crucial. Hydra was the name of his contact in the Northland, but first he had to get there, preferably less outnumbered than he was. He assessed his companions' strength. Three were young, lacking experience—the others, a brother and sister, sported nasty scars speaking of past battles. Those would be the ones to watch.

The city transformed into a blur outside the window as the train's speed increased and the whistle sounded two short blasts. They were nearing the gate out of the city. In another flash of pain,

Will recalled he had come into the city this way; on the back of a train, along with Ivan. The throbbing in his head intensified as the memories broke through—painful stabs at his skull. They were out of the city now, racing through the red and brown streaked plains.

Will shifted his weight, leaning against the rigid metal of the train car for just a moment. Zee scrambled forward on her hands and knees toward Tristan. The scar-faced Olbian sprang forward, leaving her post by the door, seizing the girl by the hair and dragging her backward. Will hadn't expected his opportunity to come so quickly, but they were well outside of the city. A jolt reverberated through the car as the tracks transitioned into a bridge across the Red River. Rocks jutted from the riverbed, distorting the smooth water into a bed of knives.

The hardest part for Will was concealing the anger he felt when the girl cried out. In a flash, he had hurled open the door. Wind howled as the land below flew past, not yet at top speed. "Drop her." His voice rose over the noise. The woman complied, confusion on her face. Will seized her by the throat with one hand and hurled her out, her scream lost to the clack of the wheels on the shaking track. Zee in his arms, Tristan turned away. The female Olbian was already gone, smashed on the rocks far behind them.

The remaining four gave him questioning looks. Will slid the door shut and leaned against it, unexpressive. "She disobeyed my order."

The Olbian with the blue eyes glanced at Zee. "So did the girl."

Will kept his voice hard. "I do not give orders to prisoners."

The Olbian shrugged, and the others looked similarly disinterested. The explanation would seem reasonable to them. Orders came first.

Four to go. Will's hand rested on his rifle, resisting the urge to toy with the safety lever. There would likely be no such opportunity to get rid of the others until they reached the Crescent Bay. This did not bother him half as much as the look of shock on Tristan's face and Zee's quiet sobbing.

He distracted himself by imagining what he would do to Aleksei when he got his hands on him.

The prison train made quick work of the long trek, billowing at a steady pace. Light faded from the train car. They left mid-morning and had an ETA of early afternoon. Six hours later, the train slowed to a crawl. Will climbed up the ladder and opened the hatch to look out.

Desert melded into marshes now as they blazed forward, a bluish-gray glow shining on the horizon. Already the high-platforms and docks of the Crescent Bay were coming into view.

As he lowered himself into the car, he caught Zee's fearful eyes staring at him. The image of him holding her up out of the car to get a better view of the approaching Stratum Sea stabbed at his mind, the ache in his head bringing with it nausea. Will kept it hidden, so long as he stood perfectly still. The engine slowed to a stop and he motioning to the Olbian designated Echo-Three. "Tell the engineer to bring me the papers."

Echo-Three nodded and slid the door open.

Will moved to stand in front of the door as he waited for the engineer. The man was not long. He regarded Will and the others with particular discomfort and seemed all too eager to speed up their departure. Will shifted his rifle to his shoulder as he took the documents in his hand. He waved at the other guards, motioning for them to get the prisoners. Tristan, shoved along roughly by Tango-Five, gave Will a penetrating gaze, quickly averting his eyes when Will looked back. It would be like Tristan to suspect something.

It doesn't matter. Will took a breath of the sea air, following the others down the platform. They would soon be out of Aleksei's reach.

The Crescent Bay curved in a wide semi-circle where the Northeast Stratman Sea stretched streaks of pale blue beyond the horizon. Waves rolled in, lapping against the docks where cargo ships anchored, rocking with the churning water. Purple gulls screeched overhead, diving and swooping as they scavenged the white beach for crab and dead fish.

Wind smelled of fish and salt and was remorseless, sweeping across the Bay in great gusts. Sailors and dock workers glanced over the group without a second look as they made their way up the wooden ramp to the second level, where the airships docked.

There were few airships here, and they were all different from those common to the inner-Continent. Built for distance and efficiency, many combined sails with power units to take advantage of the sea breeze. His eyes were drawn to a black airship, sleek and battered. Nothing welcoming about it. This was the prison ship, Cerberus.

Will strode up to the man who leaned against the Cerberus. He was maybe five feet tall, wearing a captain's cap and greatcoat. Lined eyes looked up at Will, unflinching.

"You must be my passengers." Shivering at a gust of wind, he rubbed his hands together and looked at the ones behind Will. "*Krish amada.*" He cursed in Slav, shaking his head. "What'd this pair do? Rob a Coalition candy shop?"

"I am an escort." Will said, handing him the paperwork. "The prisoners' crimes are not my concern."

The pilot rolled his eyes as he thumbed through the papers. "Yeah, yeah. I know the drill, Olbian." He pointed to the open bay door of his airship. "Have your men put them in there." He folded up the papers and shoved them in his coat pocket. "I'm Captain Zayde. Don't suppose you have a name, though." He didn't wait for an answer. "Follow me. Got some papers for you to sign."

Captain Zayde led Will up the steps into the Cerberus's helm. He glanced sideways as the bay doors closed behind Zee and Tristan, then turned his attention back to the airship captain.

Maps and ashes from half-burned cigars were strewn across the copilot seat. Zayde went to a table where two bottles of liquor and a stack of papers sat and began shuffling the documents around until he found a brown parcel stamped with green wax. "Here you are." He handed it to Will and poured himself a glass of red liquor in the smudged glass.

"Going all the way, are you?" He took a drink, not waiting for an answer. "You must have pissed someone off."

"Why do you say that?" Will unfolded the brown scroll and bent over to sign it. He handed it back to Captain Zayde, who put it in his coat pocket. As he looked down at the pilot, the man took a cautious step back.

"I alternate runs to the Northland with a colleague of mine because twice in a row on that frozen block of ice would make any Fifth Continent man lose the will to live." He took another drink. "You'll see."

"How long will it take to get there?" Will asked.

"In a hurry to freeze, Olbian?"

Will stared back, his face an indiscernible mask.

Captain Zayde shuddered. "Great sense of humor." He slumped into his seat at the helm and began punching in coordinates, adjusting instruments. "My colleague and I have a bet over who can make one of you crack a smile first." He glanced up like he didn't believe this was possible for either of them to achieve. "Four days. If we don't run into trouble over the Sholcolm Tides." He sounded pessimistic, pausing before he continued. "Or a blizzard once we hit the mainland. And if you know anything about the North Continent, you'd know there's always a blizzard." He glanced up at Will. "I'd say, at best estimate, you'll be able to pass off your hardened criminals in a week's time. That good enough for ya?"

Will was only concerned about reaching the mainland, he did not intend to get as far as the destination. He gave the pilot a curt nod. Zayde pushed his cap back, yawning. He nodded toward the door at the back of the helm room. "You can reach your prisoners through there, Olbian. Enjoy the trip."

Chapter 20

TRISTAN

DON'T STRAIN YOURSELF. Galin's words echoed in Tristan's mind. He sank to the floor of the cargo bay as the mercenary pushed him inside the Cerberus. Lack of food and water combined with everything else made him too weak to stand any longer. Did Galin really think such a thing was possible, considering current circumstances?

Once the bay door was secured, the Olbians each guarded a door, taking out their rations and crouching down to eat, eyes looking up to check on the prisoners every few seconds.

As if we have anywhere to go. Tristan did not have the heart to laugh. His eyes shut, he rested his head against the ship's hard hull.

"Here." He opened his eyes at the familiar voice. Will held out an orange fruit and a small loaf of bread.

Tristan hesitated before taking it. Expressionless, Will turned to Zee, offering her the same, but the girl shuffled backward, turning away from him. Will handed them to Tristan instead, then took his own post by the door to the helm.

Tristan took a bite of the bread, eating as slowly as possible, aware of the hard look one of the Olbians was giving Will. Finally, the man asked, "Captain, why do you feed the prisoners?"

Will took a drink of water from his bottle, meeting the Olbian with blank glare. "I have my orders. That one," he pointed to

Tristan, "is weak. He must not die before we reach our destination. After that, they are no longer my concern."

The Olbian took a bite of jerky, chewed it slowly and swallowed. "What of the girl?"

Will did not visibly react. "He would have given her half of his share." When the man did not answer, he stood. His tone was pragmatic as his one eye stared at the one who spoke up—the other a pale orb scarred above and below. "Do you wish to challenge my leadership?"

Tristan's mouth went dry, and he swallowed the mouthful of bread with difficulty, eyes going from Will to the other man. A trained Olbian warrior would not question the actions of his commanding officer. Unless he suspected something was impeding his judgement. But if the man was doubting Will's ability to lead, he must have assessed it was a losing battle. "No, Commander." He went back to his meal.

Will sat back down, taking a bite of his dried meat like nothing had happened. From the corner of his eye, he seemed to watch the man who spoke up to him.

What have they done to your head? There was no data to determine what another administering of the brain-altering solution would do to a person. It couldn't be anything good. Tristan wished more than anything Minuet had not permitted him to be their escort. What would happen when her contact arrived? As dutiful as he was, Will would not go down without a fight, and Tristan had no wish to see him killed. He prayed it would not come to that.

Air grew colder the next few days the further inland they traveled. Their Olbian guards brought blankets and coats. He and Zee were both fed enough to keep hunger at bay. The men did not argue over this. But, after his break in duty, the Olbian who challenged Will did not return, and no one could find him. Will did his best to conceal a limp, but, judging by the remaining warrior's whispering in his absence, it was not unnoticed.

Chapter 21

WILL

FIVE DAYS INTO their journey and ice pellets battered on the hull of the Cerberus, forcing them on an alternate route. It was clear his men no longer trusted him. The longer Will delayed acting, the chance of his being found out increased. It was now or never.

Turbulence rocked the airship, knocking him against the wall as he climbed out of his bunk. The other two were either sleeping or pretending to be—either way, it did not matter. Leaving his armor on the floor, Will crept away and went to have a word with the Captain.

Captain Zayde cursed the weather when Will entered. "Not to worry your head. We'll still get your cargo where they need to go." He shivered as he unscrewed the top of a liquor bottle and took a swig. "Your friend made the right choice in jumping ship." He laughed, not knowing how right he was about the missing Olbian.

"Mm." Will grunted a response, staring at the navigation panel. The compass needled twitched left and right before settling on a direction. A red trail cut across the white outline of land moving further to the West. Will reached behind and shut the door to the helm, twisting the handle down to lock it.

Zayde spun around. Bloodshot eyes narrowed and alert. His hands were already on the radio, flipping a toggle which sent out a stream of beeps, lights flashing on corresponding dials. "I don't know what the hell you're up to, Olbian, but your friends out there warned me you've got some kind of defect." He adjusted the auto-pilot control. "I sent a transmission. The Grishtanburg militsya are tracking our approach. I don't want any trouble from you in the meantime." Dark liquid sloshed from the rim of the bottle, splattering on the floor. "I suggest you take a seat out there with your friends and wait until we land." He tapped a finger on Will's chest. *Mistake.*

Will had hoped he wouldn't have to kill Zayde. That didn't mean he would waste time mourning his loss, either. His eye still fixed on the Captain, he reached into his boot, pulling out a knife. "And here I was planning on helping you win that bet with your friend."

Zayde spread his hands, backing away from the blade.

"That was a joke," Will said, humorless.

Zayde smashed the bottle in his hand on the edge of the table, swinging the dripping jagged remains at Will's head. Will caught Zayd's wrist and twisted his arm back forcefully, slashing the unfortunate pilot's neck with his own weapon. Zayde flailed one arm, knocking the autopilot lever out of place before going limp.

Will slung the man's body over his shoulder and climbed up the escape hatch. Ice stung his eyes as wind howled past. He hefted Zayde over his shoulders and tossed him across the fuselage. With a thump, he bounced off, then slid, swallowed by the swirling white air.

As Will lowered himself back into the Cerberus, the airship tilted. Needles on the instruments spun into red zones, and the engines screamed.

That can't be good.

This swirl of ice and snow was something new. He fought with blood-smeared controls, trying to bring it back in alignment so autopilot could be engaged. A warning buzzer sounded through the cabin. The door busted in on its hinges. Two of the three Olbians charged in, knives drawn. Will let go of the controls. He feigned to the side, picking up his own dagger and thrusting it upward into the first man's chest. *Two to go.* This second one was more cautious, keeping his distance. The Cerberus crept into a nosedive. Empty liquor bottles crashed onto the floor, followed by an avalanche of papers. Will grabbed the hull to steady himself and the Olbian took his chance, moving to cut his throat, but catching him in the arm instead.

It took a moment for the sting to spread up his forearm and the man already had moved forward, gripping Will's arm where blood soaked through his uniform, the hidden knife on his gauntlets shooting forward into the leather armor covering his chest; he felt the tip prick his skin. Will grasped the man's wrist, jerking it away from his chest and twisting until it snapped.

Stifling a yell of pain, the man did not slow his attack, elbowing Will in the shoulder and shoving him against the control panel. Arms locked, they struggled around the cabin until Will's back was facing the door. Too late he realized what the Olbian was trying to do when he heard Tristan yell, "Look out!"

Will took the man with him, turning to see the other Olbian, Tristan on his back, his cuffed wrists slung over the man's neck. The mercenary slammed Tristan against the ship and jerked his arms from around his neck.

As Tristan fell to his knees, Will felt anger taking hold of him again. He slammed the first Olbian's head against the control panel, disabling him long enough to turn and slash the other man across the neck, turn back and stab him through the heart. Blood splattered across the instruments. The warning buzzed more frantically as he stood there, breathless. He dropped the knife and felt his way toward Tristan. He yanked him up by the shoulder. "Tristan? Are you alright?"

Tristan's head jerked up. "Will?" He looked like he didn't dare believe what he saw. "Is it really you?"

Will offered him a crooked attempt at a smile. "Yeah."

Tristan let out a breath, clutching his chest. "For how long?"

Will was at the controls, pulling back to draw the Cerberus out of its incline. "Since that day after..." He looked over his shoulder. "We don't have a lot of time."

Tristan, holding onto a shelf to keep himself from falling, slid his way to the control panel by Will as if he was suddenly awake. He punched on the altimeter. Something struck the window, cracking the glass and jarring the Cerberus. As they caught themselves from falling, Tristan and Will exchanged a startled look.

"I think that was the left stabilizer," Tristan said.

"You can guide it down, right?" Will was already climbing back toward the exit.

"Doubtful. But I can try to slow it from crashing as quickly," Tristan said.

"That'll do." Will was already out the door. The Cerberus could not recover from its plunge, which would mean they needed to abandon ship. Quickly. Will smashed the glass compartments and grabbed three parachutes on his way to the cargo bay for Zee. It was practically a climb as the Cerberus continued to tilt.

"Zee!" He called, catching sight of her, perching atop a bunk, trying not to fall.

Seeing Will, she yelled and tried to climb higher, even as she slid toward him. "Get away from me!" she screamed, balling her fists up and hitting him in the chest.

"Zee..." he said in a soft tone, not trying to stop her. "It's me." She wasn't listening. The engines let out a high-pitched screech that made his ears ring. "Sorry, Zee." He scooped her under his arm, grabbing hold of the fur coats against the wall. "You can hate me if you want, but I've got to get you out of here."

Careful not to slam her against the sides of the airship, he half slid, half stumbled his way back to the cabin. "Tristan!" Zee wriggled free. Will did not give her a chance to run away. Tossing the other coat and one parachute to Tristan. "Put this on." He shoved the coat in her arms.

"Zee, do what he says," Tristan told her sternly, buttoning up the coat and strapping the parachute on. Fear in her eyes, she did as he said, holding her arms out as he hurriedly helped her into a parachute. His hand paused on her head before cinching down the belt.

I'm sorry. There wasn't time for such an exchange. He took her hand and forced the parachute cord into her fingers. "I need you to do exactly as I say. Understand?"

After that, you can hate me all you want.

Tearfully, she nodded. "We're going to jump. Once you're out there, pull this cord." He folded her fingers over it and squeezed. "Once you land, I will find you and get you back to Tristan. Got it?"

The girl took a ragged breath and nodded again.

"Twelve hundred feet, Will!" Panic was on the edge of Tristan's voice. Will climbed up the ladder and kicked open the hatch.

"Let's go—out, Tris!" Will pushed Tristan ahead of him up the ladder, pulling Zee up alongside himself as he clambered up the rungs.

"Remember what I said," he yelled over the roar of the wind. She nodded, terrified, and he tossed her from the plummeting airship before propelling himself off.

Cold air rushed past, pressing and tearing as gravity dragged him down. Fingers frozen inside thin gloves, he struggled to reach the cord and yanked it. The parachute discharged, jarring him back with an unpleasant jolt, and slowed his fall to the frosted white ground below.

⚙

From her hiding place among the twisted, black trees, a woman watched the airship plunge from the sky like a shooting star arcing from its orbit.

"Right on time. Make a wish." She laughed and jumped to her feet, running under the weight of furs to locate the man in a red uniform falling to Northland tundra.

Chapter 22

WILL

FLAMES AND SMOKE shot into the cloudy night sky as the Cerberus smashed into the icy ground. Will landed with a heavy crunch in the snow and he unbuckled the parachute, staggering forward, fighting against the layers of snow. It fell all around him, noiseless white flurries, meeting the blanket that already draped the land. Black trees, twisted with the look of death, stretched out in an upward slope. Will leaned against the frozen bark of one as the cold took hold of him; his Olbian uniform was a death sentence in this harsh Northland climate. As he breathed in the frigid air, he felt like his lungs did not work properly, refusing to fully accept the sub-temperature oxygen.

His hand trembling, Will dug out his compass. They were only about two miles off the coordinates where the airship was supposed to land. His entire body was beginning to shake. Howling dogs shattered the silence. Will stiffened, recalling the pilot's transmission. If they were tracking the ship, their dogs could find any human in this place if they didn't freeze to death first.

He fought through the snow, sinking to his shins, cupping his hands to his mouth as he called for Zee and Tristan. His voice was hollow and out of place. As the howling grew more pronounced, he dared not do it again. Instead, he stumbled from tree to tree, searching for his friends.

Men shouting in Slavik mixed with the noise of the dogs, and Will crouched lower to the trees, realizing the absurdity of his actions. They could easily find him. The outline of trees blurred as he wandered in the direction he thought the other two were most likely to have landed. He slowed, limbs heavy, mind lethargic as he pressed on.

The girl's screams pierced the night, jarring him from the increasing drowsiness. Will pumped his frozen legs into a run. Shadows darted through the tree line up ahead. Something cold and metallic snapped against his legs, coiling and tightening in the passing of a second. Cold snow stung Will's skin as he fell face forward into the snow. Before he could see what it was to remove it, another object hit his wrist, coiling and binding him to a nearby tree.

Dead branches knocked together, dropping chunks of bark as he struggled to free himself. A cloak fell over him, and beneath its heavy warmth someone pressed against his back, clamping a gloved hand over his mouth as the Slavik voices neared.

He could hear Zee's yells, Tristan calmly coaxing her to do as they said. His heartbeat raced unpleasantly. As he twisted his hand against the biting wire wound on his wrist, a voice whispered in his ear through the grainy filter of a respirator. *"Be still. They have orders to kill everyone but those two."*

Will would not have cared, except he could not assess the situation properly, having never crossed paths with these Northland police. He could not help anyone if he was dead. Cursing to himself, he lay still.

Howls and voices drifted away with the roar of an engine revving and driving away until the only sound left was the steady pounding of his own heart and the restrained breathing. In a low growl of a voice, Will said, "If you want to live beyond this night, you'll cut this damned wire."

"Really? Because cutting a tiger lose isn't the smartest of choice where I come from." The fur cloak was thrown off. A figure dressed in white stood over him, holding a strange-looking gun. *"Ah, then again, what a tiger. Athena should've told me."* A hand moving to

the respirator. The figure pushed a button and pulled it over her head, knocking her fur-lined hood off. Short, caramel curls, high-lighted in purple and blue, fell just below her ears.

Will found his anger difficult to maintain. "Who is Athena?" He said, jerking at the tree and writhing against the burning cold of the snow.

The woman tossed her curls. Electric-blue lips pursed together at him as her head tilted backwards. "Oh, that's her codename. You might call her something else."

Codename? Will twisted his wrist again, then paused, taking a more direct look at the woman as he spoke. "Hydra?"

The women's eyes, which were a strange Turkish-blue, wid-ened as she gave him a broad grin. "Very good! You catch on quick, Cyclops."

Will gritted his teeth. Involuntary shivers came in waves. "Let. Me. Go. I have to get them back." Cold soaked through him like knives stabbing into his bones.

Slowly, a sad look on her face, Hydra shook her head. "Sorry, Cyclops. Athena told me if things went wrong I was to get you to the Black Recluse." She cast a carefree gaze at the night sky as snow continued to fall, sticking to her hair briefly before melting. "I'd say having to jettison from your airship right before it exploded…" she used her hand to mimic something falling to the ground, balling up her gloved hand and slamming it into her open palm, "qualifies as things going wrong."

Will glared at her. "Minuet." He gritted his teeth, letting his head fall back on the pillow and clamping his eye shut. Flecks of snow stung his face. Why the hell couldn't that damned Coalition Agent just let him do things his way? A torrent of emotion rose like the waters of a dam ready to burst free.

He could have saved them! It was an illogical thought; he knew this, as he lay shivering in the snow, unprepared and unable to deal with the harsh Northland from the start.

Zee. He'd promised her. Will's head pounded in that way that caused nausea to churn his stomach. "Hey, you alright, Cyclops?" The girl looked down at him, her eyes narrowed in a curiosity. Not so much a girl, she was really probably in her mid-twenties. She was supposed to help him?

He sat up, glaring at her. "Cut me free."

Hydra jumped back. "Love to, Tiger, but you've got to promise two things. First," she held up one finger, "you can't try to break my neck when your hand is free. Second, you can't go after them. Not yet. Athena's orders are very specific, and I've got a reputation to think of."

"Or what?" Will squared his shoulders, the cord cutting into his wrist as he twisted. "You leave me here to freeze?" His teeth chattered.

Hydra rolled her eyes. "Well, I'd prefer not to. That's terrible for business." Her lips pursed together as she paused, tapping her fingers on her arms as Will continued to shake. Letting out a huff, she kneeled down by his arm, her fingers working a device attached to the coil. She bit the fingers of her glove, pulling it off her hand and holding it in her teeth. Icy fingers touched his arm as she looked at him, still appearing doubtful.

"I won't go after them," Will mumbled. "Not yet." There was no point, anyway. He couldn't find his way here and was going to freeze to death soon if she didn't help him.

"Well, I'm glad to hear that." She fidgeted with the coil, and it came loose. Will rubbed the raw, red circle of his wrist where the metal and dug into his skin, staring at it as Hydra undid the one around his legs. It seemed like his lungs were working against him in the cold, refusing to let the frigid air in.

"Hey, Cyclops," Concern in her strange-colored eyes, Hydra took his head in her hands, looking at him like she was assessing the damage of something. "I've gotta get you somewhere warmer. This lightweight uniform may be good for the desert, but you couldn't have been less prepared for the Northland." She strapped a pair of infrared goggles to her head. He felt a cloak draped over his shoulders as she added closer to his ear. "That red color provides an exceptional target, too." She patted his back. "Let's go, Tiger."

Hydra dragged him to his feet, guiding him through the screen of white that surrounded them. She shoved him onto the seat of something like a motorbike, nudging him toward two handles as she straddled the seat behind him. Will's eye faced the ground. He saw her boot catch a throttle lever next to the vehicle's skis. A fan on the back whirred to life. "Hang on, Cyclops." His fingers throbbing and stiff, Will gripped the metal bars as the skimobile raised up and then shot across the snow. Bending his face against the biting wind, he felt Hydra pressing her body into his back.

Sailing across the snow, the snowmobile weaved through the trees. Hydra leaned to the side and Will thought he was going to fall off as one ski lifted and the whole thing tilted as they made a curve in the road he could not see. They jumped over a hill, and he felt his stomach rise to his throat. Hydra must have felt him tense, because she laughed in his ear. "What's wrong, Cyclops? This is one of the few fun things about this godforsaken snow globe!" The way she talked made it seem like this was all some kind of game to her. Or maybe it was the cold getting to him. Either way, he was not enjoying himself.

After an agonizing thirty minutes, the uphill climb of Hydra's bike came to a thankful end. Sliding sideways into a snow bluff, Hydra kicked her boot and the motor cut to a halt. She hopped off, moving the goggles to her forehead and squinting up at the sky. "I think it's coming to a head," she said, taking Will by the arm and dragging him off the vehicle. "Holy Tyr you feel like a block of ice!"

She reached into the wall of snow and there was a clicking noise; a door opened up and light poured onto the white ground. "Hurry up!" She shoved him inside and closed the door. Will glanced around and leaned against a glass window, the outside view buried under layers of the frozen white. It looked like a cabin, with one round exit leading to an even smaller chamber. He could see the control panel of an airship. The instruments looked different and had strange symbols and writing he didn't recognize.

"Here." Hydra handed him a mug. He took a drink, breathing in the warm air much more easily. She unbuckled the straps on his leather vest and pulled it off of him. "Get out of those wet things before you freeze to death." As she spoke, she was unzipping her white jumpsuit.

Will fell back, his eye widening. Hydra stepped out of her jumpsuit, tossing it aside and shaking her hair. She wore skintight, black pants and a white sleeveless shirt with leather straps over her shoulders; it rose above her midriff and had a defining neckline. "Ah, come on, Cyclops, don't be shy." She winked at Will and he knocked something off a shelf as he pressed against the wall to make space between them.

Hydra smiled at him in a flirtatious way, bending forward to unlace her boot while keeping eye contact with him.

"It's Will," he said in a hoarse voice.

Hydra sighed. "Alright, alright. I'll give you five minutes." She stepped into the other chamber, sliding a thin metal door shut behind her.

Will set the cup down, peeling off his rust-colored uniform pants to replace them with the ones Hydra had left for him. Feeling was returning to his fingers; they stung painfully as he undid his uniform coat and tossed it aside first, then his undershirt. While he was pulling on the long-sleeve wool shirt, he felt warm fingertips running up his spine. Will jumped back in alarm, pulling the shirt the rest of the way on.

Hydra laughed at him again. "What's wrong, Tiger? Don't you want me to warm you up? We could have some fun."

Will's eye fell to her revealing neckline, then jerked his gaze up again. Hydra smiled, taking a step closer as he pressed himself further against the wall. As her hand reached out, he grabbed it. "Stop!" Her advances made his heart race.

Will did not feel in control of himself as it was. Hydra made things worse. "Olbian's do not have... fun."

"Yeah, yeah." She waved her hand dismissively. "I know all about your training." She crossed her arms, shifting her weight to one side. "But you aren't like them anymore, are you?" She looked inquisitive now as she hopped up on a chair and curled her legs around the back of it. "I heard your pilot's radio call. He said your men thought you were defective."

Will eased himself to a cot by the cabin, remembering the unfortunate Captain Zayde. There was a map on the wall, with different colored tacks marking locations. "Where are we?" He ignored her question.

Hydra pulled her knees to her chest, rocking back and forth as she said in a cheery voice, "About two miles north of the Kiaggard Mountain range." She pointed to a red tack stuck in the biggest mountain, and a blue one just east of it. "That's Byorn Prison, where the militsya are taking your friends, and that," she tapped the blue marker, "is Chrobrough."

Byorn. The Bear. It was a top work camp in the Northland, where the worst criminals were mixed with petty thieves, all mining coal deep in the caverns beneath the prison. Most of it was sent to the neighboring town of Chroburough. Will leaned forward, pressing his head in his hands. "Do you know where Sol— the Black Recluse, I mean, is?"

Hydra feigned a pout. "What's wrong, Cyclops, don't like my company? And I thought we were hitting it off."

Will stared back at her, partly unsettled, partly confused. A shiver wracked his body. Hydra was already moving, as if sitting still might hurt her. "Actually, it would be near impossible for me to not know where your friends are. Not two days ago calls were all over the Ghost Channel of a foreign airship that fought its way off Grettos Port." She held up her fingers, counting; Will noticed each of her nails was painted a different color. "They counted... three, not including a pilot; a smart-mouthed man in a greatcoat, a Slav with a spider tattoo, and a redhead with a rifle. That sound about right?"

Damn, Sol. Not here too. His friend was not the most tactful of fugitives, but this seemed reckless even for him. "How long will it take us to reach them?" He asked Hydra, who was twisting a purple-streaked curl around her finger.

She shrugged her bare shoulders. "I have to find out where they're going first, and not before this storm passes, and you need to rest, anyway. You think your friend can avoid getting the militsya on his trail until then?"

That was the question on Will's mind. It was unlikely, actually.

Hydra's eyes widened, and she leaned close to him, the scent of cherry blossoms filling his nostrils. "At least it's not the Ice Wolves. Though they don't interfere in matters so close to Chroburough, unless they're paid well enough."

Aleksei. The Slavik's wolfish smile passed through his mind, and Will felt a redness rising to his vision, along with the pounding in his head. "Hey, you alright Cyclops?" Hydra's hand was on his neck. It was warm and oddly calming. His fingers tightened on hers for a moment before he removed her hand and backed away.

"My name is Will," he mumbled.

Chapter 23

Minuet

ON HER WAY to deliver the governor's morning report, Minuet stopped short of entering when she saw the door was cracked. LeFrost's voice was indignant and condescending. "What is the delay, Doctor Highcourt? You are supposed to be the best there is."

Minuet peeked inside to see Galin Highcourt standing in front of LeFrost's desk. His thumb and forefinger rubbing together. He cleared his throat. "It is proving difficult to replicate the findings. The fire destroyed much of my records."

LeFrost rudely cut him off. "It is a pity you did not raise your son to know his place in the world." There was a long silence before the Governor said sharply, "Fix this mess. You have three days."

There was no reply. "You are dismissed, Doctor." Galin came out, closing the door behind him.

Minuet had practically grown up in the Highcourt Manor. She recalled how she and Tristan were playing hide and seek in the parlor, and she knocked an expensive heirloom vase from its pedestal; Tristan had taken the blame. Galin looked then like he did now; like a dark looming storm cloud that may pass overhead with only thunder and the threat of rain, or explode into torrential downpours and lightning. He gave her a slight bow. "Lady."

Galin Highcourt was unlikely to put up with much more of LeFrost's needling. She went into the office.

"This lord of yours, how can you trust him, uh?" Aleksei was leaning back with a chair against the wall, his boots up on the edge of LeFrost's desk. He picked his nails with the bone-handled knife. "You think he is loyal to you, or this son of his?" His gaze raised to Minuet and he gave her a toothy grin that made her skin crawl. "You worry too much of this Tristan, anyway—what of this... Soloman Black, uh? It is time you stopped trusting his capture to amateurs." He grinned at her tauntingly and let his chair fall to the floor. LeFrost tried to speak, but Aleksei continued to talk, twirling the knife around his hand. "You come with me to Northland, uh? I teach you how we wolves hunt. We find this Captain Black of yours."

LeFrost shuffled through the papers on his desk, pretending to look bored as he waved his hand. "Out of the question. I have work to do here. The trade with Grishtanburg must go smoothly, and for that to happen, Highcourt must pull through with his job." He sighed, signing his signature with the flick of his wrist and shuffling through another pile of papers.

Aleksei looked up at Minuet. "The Lady can see to that, uh? And you can bring little girl home, I am sure she will be happy to see father who comes to rescue her from tough, Northland prison." He placed both hands on the desk and stooped over to get in the governor's face. "It would be a shame if anyone were to find out about the possibility you cannot deliver on promises you made about... certain weapons."

LeFrost cringed, leaning back. He tapped his pen rapidly on the desk. "I suppose making a trip abroad could not hurt."

Minuet couldn't believe what she was hearing. LeFrost was really going to let this bodyguard—this imposter—push him to go to the Northland.

"Lady St. Sebastian?" She realized LeFrost had been trying to talk to her.

"Yes, oh, sorry, Sir."

"Have my things packed and sent to the station. You have a handle on everything here, right?"

"Of course, Sir." She turned to leave. "Oh. Your report, Sir." She set the papers down on his desk and turned to leave, trying to walk as calmly as she could back to her office.

Aleksei was not supposed to go to the Northland. That was the whole point of sending Tristan away. She nodded to a passing guard, maintaining a cool outward appearance. Inside, she grew frantic. Suppressing the urge to run, she walked calmly down the cobbled path to the building where her office was. Inside, she closed the door slowly, hurried to lock it, and ran to the shelves behind her desk. She turned the knob, and a panel slid up, revealing her radio.

Maybe she could reach Hydra on the Ghost channel; the girl would warn Solomand for an additional fee. She sat down on a stool and began turning the dial, tuning it to the station that most radios would not go. Lights flashed red, then green on the control panel. Minuet flipped the toggle to activate the transmitter.

A silvery flash flew past her head, and a knife stuck through the casing for the amplifier. There was a fizzle and crack and Minuet jumped, her eyes fixed on the knife handle sticking from the radio interface.

"I do not blame you for trying." Aleksei's laugh was there suddenly, bending over her from behind as he jerked the knife from her radio. "But is not good for my plan, you see." From the corner of her eye, she could see that foxlike grin. A shiver ran up her spine as she felt his breath on her neck. "Do not cry, *voljenai (darling)*. I care not what happens to this Tristan of yours—he may yet live through this. Your governor is blind as well as fool not to see." He reached a hand toward her face, then drew it back.

"I cannot have you warning this Soloman Black, you see. It would ruin surprise I have planned for my old friend."

So that was it. He was after that Ice Wolf Solomand ran around with. Ivan.

Aleksei backed toward the door, putting a finger to his lips. "Will be our secret and maybe this Tristan comes back alive, uh?" He slid the knife in his belt and left.

Minuet stared in fury at the damaged radio, feeling light-headed. Hot, angry tears spilled from her eyes as she gripped the edge of her desk. She didn't really expect him to keep any kind of bargain, but his veiled promise meant he would ensure Tristan did not come back alive if she tried to warn him again. For the first time in a long time, Minuet St. Sebastian was forced to face the fact she was helpless to do anything.

Silent and shaking, she let the tears come, hoping that Solomand Black's dumb luck would help him as it always seemed to, just long enough for him to help Tristan, even if it meant she would never see him again.

Chapter 24

TRISTAN

MOONLIGHT SLIPPED IN and out of the clouds. The Northland patrol looked like a cross between men and machines—stalking through the forest with leashed hounds dragging them forward through snow drifts. Copper-tinged respirators accentuated the sound of their breath. Bulky clothes made of fur and canvas weighed them down. Beams from electric torches fell on Tristan, who was cutting himself free of the parachute. His eyes squinted away from the blinding light, and the knife fell from his fingers. The noise of rifles chambering rounds accompanied rasping shouts.

Tristan froze, raising his hands and shivering—air cutting through his coat like it was made of paper.

They kept a rifle on him as another man approached the girl lying tangled in the remnants of her parachute. Zee screamed and thrashed as they cut her free and kept her from running away.

A rifle jabbed into his back, and Tristan followed the guard to the giant steam-propelled sled. It was almost like a ship, but built to maneuver snow and ice rather than water. Sails shifted with the wind and steam rose from a boiler on the back of its engine. Tristan tripped as he walked up the steps to the deck, gripping the cold iron railing for support.

Shouting and endless barking followed as they shoved him into a dark hold. He caught a quick glimpse of the navigator engaging the engines before they shoved in Zee after him, and the two were closed into darkness. Her sobs bouncing off the walls, Zee gripped his hand. Her fingers shook in his.

"It'll be alright," Tristan whispered, wrapping his coat around her and trying to keep from shivering himself. Jarred around as the sled skis cut through the snow in an upward tilt, Tristan lost track of the time. At least they had shelter from the snow and ice outside. Drifting into a restless slumber, the engines grinding to a halt woke him with an aching dread.

His arm tightened around Zee as the hatch creaked open. "*End of the road, Otvali. Get out.*" One officer ordered in Slavik. His form shadowed against pale light, he motioned Tristan to climb up. As he gripped the bars to the ladder, a guard seized him roughly by the collar and dragged him the rest of the way up.

"Tristan!" Zee shrieked.

"It'll be alright." The reassurance in his voice sounded misplaced as the weight of his powerlessness set in.

"*Move, Otvali!*" The militsya shoved him off of the sled, using the derogatory slang Northlanders called foreigners.

It had stopped snowing. The sky was a grayish-blue as the sun rose over the mountains. White, frosted buildings half stuck out of the rock, the bottom of them sunk within the mountain like roots of a forest. Smoke drifted out of grated vents on the top three turrets; ice coated the sides.

Zee jumped as a dog barked next to her, her hand curled around Tristan's arm as they climbed up the snowy, stone steps. At the top was a door of iron bars and an unwelcoming sign of rusted metal with the prison's namesake punctuated by a bear's paw on either side; *Byorn.*

Boots sounded on the winding stone staircase leading deep into the mountain. Zee looked paler than usual. And Tristan did not think she was shaking because of the cold. He pulled her closer.

Stefan LeFrost, you bastard. Did the governor even have a clue to where he agreed to send his daughter? Or was he just a coward, unwilling to cross Aleksei? Whether LeFrost realized, it was clear to Tristan; Aleksei did not mean for them to leave this place. If her father gave a damn about the girl at all, which Tristan doubted, he had made a grave mistake.

Guards on the inside of the grate came out to greet the militsya. The leather armor across their chest and right shoulder was marked with a red bear's paw. At their belts, each wore two long, single-edged knives tucked in their belts; some had hatchets. Most had shaved heads, with tattoos scrawled behind their ears. Giving the militsya officers condescending looks, one asked if they were turning in the prisoners lost from the Cerberus. They had received a radio transmission, forwarded to them from the Chroburough militsya. Tristan had difficulty following their conversation. He stared at the open doorway, comparing it to the entrance of a tomb.

Gazes void of compassion slid over Zee and Tristan before they were both shoved inside by the guards. The door clanged shut, closing out the sound of the militsya's sled powering up. Faint golden flickering of electric lamps replaced the crisp light of dawn. One guard pushed them aside to walk in front, while the other followed. Their shadows slid down the uneven surface of the stone wall as they shuffled down the stairs. Every step made his limbs feel heavier. Tristan clung to Zee's hand. Dread crept over him like the icy chill of the air as he tried not to think about how helpless he really was to protect her here.

A cloud formed as he took a shaky breath. The temperature gradually changed the further into the cavern they went. Not warm by any means. It was at least milder than the surface. As they reached the bottom of the stairs, a guard unlocked another door and they were ushered down a dark staircase winding into the ground. Another set of locked doors.

Deeper.

Another set of stairs.

The guards were talking to one another about how the two of them were probably not going to last the night, unaware that Tristan spoke Slavik. *Like that's going to do me a lot of good here.* He tried not to hear the rest of what they were saying.

"Make sure they're alive, at least. The state of them isn't as important." The guards laughed darkly at one another.

Squeezing Zee's hand tighter, Tristan's breath hitched in his chest. He tried to focus on the layout of the building. At the bottom of the staircase they moved into another locked room, through another door and down a narrow hall which led into a larger room. Air was warmer here. A pot of water boiled on a stove in the corner. Guards stood around, sipping steaming mugs. Continuing with their conversations, they didn't bother to acknowledge the new prisoners.

The guard who accompanied them shoved a clipboard with papers into Tristan's chest. "Sign."

Tristan released Zee's hand and wiped the sweat from his fingers on the side of his pants. "I suppose I haven't much choice?" He took the clipboard and caught a pencil the man tossed in his direction. The flourished signature he left on the paper was not his name. Not that they would notice. Minuet always voiced how much she loved his handwriting. The guard took the clipboard and shoved a rolled-up blanket into his arms. It smelled like dust and mold.

A sudden vision of the lady laughing in his father's garden caught him off guard, drowning out the present circumstances for a moment. It had been many years since he'd seen her smile like that. A flame of hope flickered dimly in his soul. Maybe when all this was over, things could be different—what they might have been.

A rough hand on his shoulder brought him back to the present, forcing him from the guardroom and down a longer hall. Electric bulbs hung from the ceiling haphazardly, intermittently flickering and popping. Rooms, he assumed belonged to the guards, lined the left side, while the other was lined with steel pipes affixed to the wall with rusted brackets. Zee gasped, clinging to his arm as one of the pipes creaked, banging against the wall noisily as water was forced through it, carried throughout the prison. One arm clinging to her blanket, she pressed against him, nearly making him trip as they followed the guard.

Two more turns and they came to a much larger room. It was open and formed in the shape of an octagon. Many of the prisoners sat at tables, eating bowls of distasteful looking gruel. Others stood around, leaning against the wall or crouched in the corners. Some men, a few women, all the same—dirty, rugged, scarred, unkempt.

"Wait here for on duty foreman—he will be in charge of you." The guard said gruffly before leaving them.

"Thanks for the help," Tristan muttered, sliding his feet forward and keeping a protective hand on Zee. Who the hell was the foreman? Crossing the threshold into the common area seemed to awaken the other prisoners.

Small groups stood, some barefoot, some wearing shoes with holes in them. All had various lengths of unkempt hair, fresh cuts and scars. They eased closer, hungry eyes on the girl.

Shit. This was where he found out how strong he really was, or wasn't.

Keeping one eye on the approaching group, Tristan guided Zee to an empty corner. He assessed the other prisoners circling around him like vultures. Tristan took off his long coat and tossed it in the corner next to Zee. Vile, yellow-toothed grins jeered at him. They all saw thing; Tristan would be an easy target. He couldn't blame them.

A reel playing out in his head of all the times over the past ten years where he had so easily gotten in over his head and had to be rescued, usually by Solomand, sometimes Ivan, and in the worst cases, both. *Helpless.* All those years waiting to die and Solomand refusing to let him. A feeling he had choked down for so long finally rose. He balled his fists and took a step forward. He may not be as strong as any of these men, but his endurance had to count for something.

The first one came at him, and he ducked, much quicker than the man expected by the look on his face. *Hands up. Face guarded.*

Other men were gathering around now, and the ones lining the walls in the doorway of their cells. Their indiscernible shouts were like a low rumble.

Snarling, the man's stringy hair hung over his eyes as he threw himself forward. Tristan's fist caught him in the mouth and he hooked his foot under the man's feet. He fell back, spitting out a tooth as his head cracked. For a moment, there was no sound but the howling screams as the man pressed on his jaw, eyes watering. Then the entire room erupted with yelling. A sea of bodies pressing together all charged him at once.

Too many. Knocked down repeatedly by a barrage of five men, he forced himself up again and again.

A jolt of horror shot through him when he realized one of them had Zee. A fist hit his temple, and a ringing filled his ears. A square-jawed work foreman barreled through the crowd. With one giant hand, he seized the head of the man gripping the girl. As the prisoner let her go, the foreman bashed his head on the stone floor. Once. The man slumped forward, limp.

A blur of feet slowly backed away in the sudden quiet.

Do something!

Tristan struggled to push himself up as he saw the massive arm scoop Zee under it. His voice was deep and threatening. "*This girl is mine. And this... otvali.*" He glared down at Tristan before bending slightly to take hold of his arm and pull him from the ground. "*Do not touch him, either.*"

The other prisoners dispersed, keeping an exaggerated distance from the guard. Tristan couldn't blame them.

"*Don't strain yourself.*" His father's words echoed in his mind as his chest ached. *So much for that.* He knew that would not be an order he could follow, anyway. The foreman twisted his arm, shoving him from the room and down the hallway. Cracks on the stone floor spun in Tristan's vision, and he slumped against the wall once or twice before being prodded along by the foreman until they came to another cell block. With his free hand, the man fumbled with keys, unlocked the door and propelled Tristan inside.

"Let me go!" Zee shrieked as the door slammed shut. Her fists uselessly beating against the man's chest as she wriggled against his grasp. Tristan whirled around, swinging at the guard. The man's hand caught his fist. Tristan's knuckles cracked as the man's grip tightened. Then he found himself hurled up against the wall as the foreman tossed the girl onto a cot. Ignoring the pain in his hand,

Tristan sank to the floor as the guard spoke in a gravelly voice, heavily accented.

"I have questions for you, *Otvali.*" His hair was shaved close to his skull, and veins bulged from the side of his head. Thick eyebrows furrowed above his pale, marble-like eyes. His short beard was the mixed colors of wood and ash. The lines at the corners of his eyes became more pronounced when he spoke, giving him a fierce appearance.

Still dizzy, Tristan determined not to show the actual fear he felt. "And if I don't answer?" He breathed heavily.

In one step, the guard stood over Tristan, seized him by the collar, and dragged him to his feet. "I can break your head like walnut." Hand reaching for his boot, there was a familiar-looking ivory-bone handle; Tristan saw it before he felt the steel against his throat. There was a disturbing calmness in the guard's eyes. "You are from Lyonese. But your orders are signed by a man named Aleksei Yakoven. A Northman. Why?"

Tristan swallowed, feeling the blade cut into his skin. His pulse pounded like a drum in his ears. If this man was an assassin, it was possible he was in league with Aleksei. Was this what an animal felt when it was caught in a trap?

"*I would like to know the answer myself.*" Tristan spoke in Slavik.

"*You speak my language.*" The guard studied him for a moment. "*I asked you a question.*"

"*Why? Do you work for Aleksei?*" Tristan thought he already knew the answer. He was only asking to buy time. That was a mistake.

The guard's expression turned savage. His hand wound around Tristan's throat. "*Do not play with me, Otvali. Tell me why he sent you here.*"

Tristan gripped the Slavik's wrists as he was raised off the ground.

"Stop!" Zee jumped up and looked like she would run at the guard again. Tristan gave her a desperate look. "Stay out of this!" He rasped, then tore his gaze away from her to face his interrogator.

"He's looking for someone." He knew he had to tell the man something satisfactory or they would both be dead soon.

"Who?" The guard's hand tightened, then released slightly as Tristan gasped for air.

"A friend."

One eyebrow raised. *"What is friend's name?"*

Prying at the man's tattooed fingers, Tristan gasped out, "Ivan." He fell to the floor, coughing and rubbing his throat as the guard released him.

"Where. Is. Ivan?" He leaned over Tristan and pressed the knife to his neck.

Tristan swallowed against the steel. Blood trickled down his skin as it cut into him. *"I do not know."* Time with Solomand made him make another mistaken slip of the tongue. *"And even if I did, I would not tell you!"*

"No?" The guard's eyes hardened, and his glance shifted to Zee. Tristan felt the sting of the cut as the foreman drew his knife swiftly away from his neck. A dizzying rush rose to his head, threatening to drown out his vision. *"I swear I don't know where he is. Please."* His voice wavered, raising in desperation. *"Do not harm her."* Feeling like he would pass out, he dropped to his knees.

The guard sat back on his heels in front of him, the bone-handled dagger still in his hand. *"Are you sure you won't tell me where Ivan is?"*

Never. Tristan's eyes clamped shut. A horrible urgency to say something—anything to distract him from Zee forced him to speak. *"The girl has nothing to do with any of this."*

Surveying him with a cool look, the guard turned the knife over in his hands. *"Aleksei, he has way of making you answer questions, no?"*

Trying to keep himself from falling, Tristan leaned forward on his hands. *"Yes,"* he whispered. When he looked up to catch the guard's eyes, there was a flicker of emotion Tristan could have sworn was sympathy.

He slid the knife back in his boot and pulled Tristan to his feet. *"Don't worry. I am no friend of Aleksei."* He led Tristan to the cot where Zee was. *"I will help you here."*

"What?" A Cold sweat broke over Tristan. He was unsure if he should be relieved or worried.

The foreman frowned and handed Tristan a glass of water. *"Ivan was once friend of mine."* His hand briefly touched the black markings behind his ear meant to resemble the paw of a bear. "Aleksei. He will come. You are part of his game now."

"Game." Tristan choked on a swallow of water and the glass nearly slipped from his shaking hand.

The foreman took it from him and set it down. "I am Nikola. *Aleksei* did not count on me being here." His fists tightened when he said 'Aleksei.' *"This time—we turn the rules against him."*

Chapter 24

RAYN

CLOUDS MERGED IN a familiar pattern in the sky. It brought back the memory of another day long ago. Standing next to Solomand, the pressing in her mind felt more like an actual memory than an intrusive vision, like the ones she was used to. Her breath caught as she placed a hand on the glass, recalling a much younger version of the man next to her.

Long streaks of gray were spotted with towering mountains of white—a patch of clear sky made the illusive appearance as wind moved them on their way. Rain dripped from a solitary cloud in a way that seemed like its heart wasn't in it. Drops smattered on the stone, marking a fresh grave and stirring dust on the dry ground until everything settled—damp and resigned. Standing next to a figure now familiar to her, ten-year-old Solomand's voice wavered. "I'm not going with you!" Fists clenched at his sides, he turned a resentful look up at Lemuel Falcon.

Rayn glanced up at her father. Benjamin Ivers was not the same person who had been at odds with his friend years before. Whatever happened at Corcyra had pushed him to become something much more. He bit his lip as he stared at his friend, looking like he wanted to say something.

"Your parents would want you to spend time with your people," Lemuel said.

"*This is my home!*" Solomand snapped. His steel-blue eyes fell on the grave and his voice lowered to a hoarse whisper. "*My parents are gone.*"

Emotion stirred in Lemuel's eyes. He lifted his hand. It looked like he meant to put it around Sol at first. Instead, he adjusted his hat and said without sentiment "I'm sorry."

"*Sorry doesn't bring people back from the dead!*" Solomand yelled, and Rayn felt her eyes widen in shock.

"*Sol. That's enough.*" Rayn's father interrupted Solomand's outburst in a gentle but firm tone. "*You will go with Lemuel. It will honor their memory.*" He lay a reassuring hand on the boy's shoulder. "*You will always have a home in my house if you wish.*"

Wiping his eyes with the back of his hand, Solomand nodded. "Let's go get your things," Ben said. Before he led the boy away, he exchanged a long look with Lemuel. For an instant the mask seemed to drop from both men, and an unspoken conversation passed between them. No words were needed. It was written on their faces—sorrow, regret, gratefulness. Then it was over. Benjamin walked away, his hand on Solomand's shoulder. Lemuel stood alone at the grave of his friends; the ones he had asked Benjamin Ivers to look after. This is how it ended. His finger twisting the ring on his hand, he took a heavy breath.

Rayn crept up, slipping her fingers in his. Lemuel looked down, giving her a half-hearted smile as he squeezed her hand in return. Neither of them spoke.

The memory left an ache in Rayn's heart. She glanced at Solomand, wondering what it really was he had against Lemuel Falcon; but not enough to ask. Not yet.

"I hate this damned autopilot," he muttered, rolling tobacco in a paper.

"Why?"

"Too effective. I feel like I don't have a job." He leaned in to kiss her forehead.

"Thought your job was to make smartass comments." She Rolled up her sleeves as heat flushed her cheeks.

"Technically, yes, but Ivan has no sense of humor. I think he might actually cut my head off if I don't tone it down."

Rayn relaxed into the pilot's chair, tracing her fingers along the altimeter. She did not feel sick anymore. "What is with Ivan, anyway? He's taking this whole thing a little too seriously." She laughed nervously.

The scent of Kree tobacco filled her nose as Solomand rested his chin on the top of her head. Her stomach churned. "Honestly? Never thought I would say this in a sentence, but I think he's afraid."

"Why?"

Solomand looked at her with a face so filled with remorse and horror that she regretted asking. "Lots of reasons," he said.

Ivan was afraid; so was Solomand. For a moment, she wondered if she should tell him about the memories.

He walked to the window, rubbing the back of his neck. "I can just imagine Ivan delivering a baby out there. On the mountain. Single-handedly. Maybe he wasn't an assassin, after all. Ice... nurse?" He raised his eyes, nodding slightly.

Rayn laughed, rolling her eyes. "Don't be an idiot."

Sol grinned at her. "Honestly, though, can you imagine Ivan as a father?"

Rayn laughed again. "Can you imagine being his child? No one would *dare* so much as look at you the wrong way."

Solomand muttered in what was supposed to be Slavik, but was really a few curses mixed with gibberish. Mimicking Ivan's stern expression, he stooped over Rayn and gave her a kiss. Rayn's worries melted with her heart as his lips touched hers.

"Very amusing, *Captain*." Sol jerked upward when Ivan came into the cabin.

"Was it? I thought it was actually in poor taste and vow to never..."

Ivan crossed the room, giving Sol a hard stare.

"Alright. I can't lie to you like that." Solomand cleared his throat. "Not blatantly, anyway. Cigarette?" He dug the silver case out of his pocket and held it out.

Ivan took it from him, his grave expression unchanging. Rayn covered her mouth as she yawned and stood up. "Don't kill him, Ivan. He's kind of grown on me."

Solomand's shoulders slumped, and he pressed a hand against his heart. "Kind of? After all we've been through?"

Ivan lit a cigarette and handed the case back to Sol. He scratched his head of dark brown hair. Rayn recalled how he was nearly bald when they first met and looked near death. Now she could see why those who knew what he was would run away in fear. Though he didn't scare her.

Pushing herself on her tiptoes, she hooked an elbow on Ivan's shoulder, attempting to lean on him. "So, how many babies did you deliver?"

Ivan gave her a sideways glance and scowled. "I do not remember. You Fifth Continent Lyonese are coddled. We have no doctors out here, in wilderness."

Rayn laughed. "I'm only joking, Ivan. Let's hope you don't have to use those skills, uh?" His cheeks reddened as Solomand laughed at him this time.

Jank stroke in, holding a small metal device with a needle tip which looked like a pen. "Alright. I think I've worked it out. All you have to do is prick your finger, the blood goes inside and…" he went into an explanation.

"Enough, Jank," Solomand silenced him, unusually gruff. "We don't need to know how the damn thing works."

"Fine. You're welcome, by the way," Jank snapped and tossed it to Ivan before hurrying off.

"I think he doesn't like this airship either. Put together too well. Nothing to fix," Solomand said. He flicked at the instrument panel.

Ivan looked at Rayn. "Your hand." He shifted the cigarette to his mouth.

Rayn felt a sudden mix of startling excitement and dread.

I'm not pregnant.

Did she want to be? Trying to act nonchalant, she lay her open palm in Ivan's and waited for him to prick her finger. Blood beaded on her skin and slowly seeped into the clear side of the device.

A loud buzzer reverberated through the cabin. Cringing, Rayn covered her ears, smearing blood on the side of her face.

"What the hell is that noise?" Solomand flipped toggles and jerked at levers he probably shouldn't. "Would have been nice if Lemuel had left an operating manual!"

Rayn wiped the blood from her cheek, applying pressure to her finger. "What do you think Jank is reading?"

Solomand's jaw tightened. "I didn't know he was *reading* anything."

A woman's voice crackled over the radio. *"Dragonfly Three-Zero-Xray... can I speak to Captain Black?"*

Sol's mouth dropped open at the break from radio etiquette, and Ivan got to the radio before he could. "This is Dragonfly-Three-Zero-Xray, what is your call sign?"

"Call sign? Oh, you mean codename. Hydra. Who has the hunky Slavik accent?"

"What kind of moron uses proper names on an open channel?" Solomand grabbed the microphone from Ivan. "Who the hell is this? What do you want?"

"Ah, you must be the infamous Captain Black. I've got a delivery for you."

His face twisted in confusion, Solomand pressed on the mic, then let go of it. "What the hell's she talking about?" He spoke into the microphone. "What delivery?"

"I'm docking to your ship, don't alter course." A pause. *"Don't worry. I think you'll like it."*

The airship shuddered, and there was a thump. Solomand looked up, dropping the radio control. "What the hell..." he trailed off.

Rayn reached for her revolver. "You think she's trouble?"

"Hell yes."

There was a grating, sliding noise down the hull of the airship, and Sol jerked his head to Ivan. "Cargo bay," Ivan said. He and Sol both ran toward the door.

Rayn followed, revolver in hand, relieved he'd forgotten about the blood.

A flurry of snow and water pooled on the floor around two figures standing in the bay. One had her hand on the bottom rung of a ladder leading from an open air shaft; the other hunched on the floor next to her. The woman dusted herself off pulled her hood back. Purple-streaked curls fell below her ears. "Solomand Black, I presume," her gaze passed over Rayn and landed on Sol and, in a more intrusive way, slid up and down Ivan. "A Wolf."

Solomand leveled the muzzle of his sidearm at her head. "Introductions usually go two ways. Who the hell are you?" He glanced at the ladder, which none of them were aware of before now. "And how did you know where to get on board this airship?"

Giving the ladder a push so it retracted, the woman slapped her hand on the hull. "I know the people who built this airship." Her head tilted. "How do you not know the most basic thing about the craft you command?"

Solomand cocked the hammer on his pistol. "Name. Now."

"I told you my codename already. It's Hydra."

"You act like that's supposed to mean something to me. What the hell do you want? Docking onto someone's airship out of nowhere?"

There was something familiar about the woman's companion as he stooped, looking like he was trying to recover from their climb, broad-shouldered, short, dark hair. Rayn eased her thumb from the hammer of her gun.

Hydra took a step forward. "Now here I was, confident you'd be happy to see me." Her eyes dropped to the man. "Happy to see him, at least."

As the man raised his head, Rayn saw the eyepatch. "Will?" She gasped, spreading her arms as she stepped in front of Solomand's gun. "Sol, stop!"

"Rayn, what the hell?!" Solomand hurriedly lowered his gun.

Will pulled the hood off and scarf from his face. He was looking at Solomand now. "Hello, Sol."

Looking like he was seeing a ghost, Sol stared, his jaw tensing, eyes wide. Ivan drew his knife.

"How do we know it is really Will?"

Rayn's mouth hung open before she let out a shocked breath. "Ivan, what are you talking about?"

Sol put a hand on her shoulder and moved her aside. "He's right... they hit him with one of those damn darts." He swallowed hardly, cocking his hammer once more.

"You can't be serious." Rayn protested again.

A flicker of a smile ghosted on Will's face. "You're right to worry." He raised his arms—slowly, carefully. "For a while, I *was* gone."

"Don't worry." Hydra interrupted, waving her hand around like the situation bored her. "Athena went to great lengths to make sure I got him to you safe and sound. I don't think she'd have bothered if he was a run-of-the-mill Olbian."

Solomand squinted in confusion as his attention was drawn back to Hydra. "Who the *hell* is Athena?"

Arms still raised, Will slowly stood and the girl calling herself Hydra hung her arms around his neck. "That is a codename for, what was her name again?" She turned her eyes up at Will, batting long eyelashes.

"Minuet." Will shifted uncomfortably.

"Oh for... codename, *Athena*?" Sol angrily shoved the handgun back in his holster. "She would pick something pretentious like that—that mythological cow god would suit her better. Heather? Hippo?" He frowned, thinking, then snapped his fingers with a look of triumph. "Hathor."

Hydra let go of Will and clapped her hands. "Oh, very good. I didn't know you knew anything about mythology on the Fifth Continent. It's one of the forbidden texts, you know."

Solomand took a step back as she inched forward. "Yes, well, that's the one law Tristan was destined to break from the beginning of time. Always reading. I prefer a good technical manual for the mark II Alpha mini assault rifle."

Ivan gave him a long look. "You not read manual for anything."

"No. You really don't," Rayn said, crossing her arms.

Solomand frowned at both of them. "Don't need to. It's intuitive." He walked up to Will, trying his best to keep away from Hydra. Will tensed, lowering his arms.

"Sol…" He swallowed. "I have to tell you something."

Solomand turned pale. "What happened? Is Zee alright?"

Will pressed a hand against his head, closing his eye.

Solomand grabbed him by the shoulders. "Will, what's wrong? Tell me!"

"She's safe, for the moment." Will stared at the floor. "That's not what I wanted to tell you, though."

⊰✪⊱

"I'm sorry, Sol." Will buried his face in his hands.

Solomand looked like he'd been jarred from a bad dream. "Will, one of us would ever blame you for what some bastard did to you."

Swallowing with difficulty, Will shook his head. "I promised her I would find her and I couldn't do that either. I couldn't keep the militsya from getting to her and Tristan first."

"Zee and Tristan are here?! How? When?"

"Aleksei." Will said. "He convinced LeFrost to send Zee here, he's using her against him at this point."

"LeFrost." Solomand gritted his teeth together and ground the burning ember of his cigarette to indiscernible powder under his boot. "That piece of shit! After the show he made of wanting his daughter back."

"Tristan convinced Minuet to pull strings to send him here with Zee."

That was exactly the sort of thing Tristan would do. Solomand looked sick.

"*Minuet* seems to think all of you together have a better chance of busting them out of Byorn Prison than you would on the Fifth Continent," Hydra chimed in, again looking altogether too chipper.

"*Byorn Tutzale!*" Ivan burst out, jumping from his seat. "Has she lost her mind?"

Hydra clucked her tongue. "Temper, temper." She swagged her finger. "Anger can be attractive, though." She bit her bottom lip.

140

Ivan made a snarling noise before cutting his arm through the air and storming from the room.

Solomand looked like he just remembered she was there. "Excuse me." He raised his hand. "Where do you fit into all this, Harpy?"

Hydra laughed, tilting her head back. "Clever. You have a nickname for everyone, don't you?"

Solomand's jaw tightened. He looked like dealing with her was too much for his brain to handle. "I'm going to talk to Ivan," he rushed from the room, leaving Rayn to deal with the excessively chipper newcomer. Heat rose to her cheeks, and her stomach churned sharply.

"So." Hydra shifted her weight. "You must be the redheaded sniper that's been kneecapping port rats."

Rayn tasted bile. "I have to go throw up." She ran from the room.

Chapter 25

IVAN

IVAN'S REFLECTION STORMED alongside him down the corridor like an outraged ghost. Memories again. This time he let them come. Cathartic pain flared in his mind as different layers of his childhood peeled back. If he did not face it eventually, he would always be at the mercy of his desire to hide and forget. Things would have been far easier if he had died back then.

No. That was more cowardly than joining the Wolves. His mother and sisters would have been at the mercy of the village if that had happened. He recalled the fear in her eyes—the crying of his sisters.

"Mother, you have to go." Ivan spoke as if in a dream, telling her what happened. The man that got away—he would be back for him. There was no justice in this wilderness. Militsya did not care what happened to them. They left rural disputes to the Ice Wolves whose only sentence was death; they had time for nothing else.

His mother and fled into the woods with his sisters when the sound of approaching dogs carried through the forest. The man returned with ten more and Ivan stood alone between them and the path his family had taken. Ivan did not fight them this time.

Gripping him by the collar, the villagers dragged him three miles to the mountain's base where a man dressed all in white like a savage mountain ghost lead them into a cave. More men waited inside. They all had the same ivory-handled knife stuck in their belt. Massive wolves sat on the outskirts of the cavern. They were large enough for a man to ride, though any who tried such a thing would surely be torn apart. Baring their teeth, they growled and then let out a symphony of mournful howling as the strangers entered their lair.

The villagers shoved Ivan to the cold ground in front of a wooden chair where the Alpha sat, surveying the visitors with a dangerous stare. The one who attacked his sister spoke up. "We demand justice. This boy has broken the law."

Hand pulling at his chin, the Alpha's eyes passed over Ivan with boredom. He looked barely twenty—young for such a leader. "What did he do?" He scoffed. "Steal bread from baker?" A flicker of disgust crossed his face.

He leaned over to a man on his right with a bald head. "What do these village morons think I am, Iosif?" He leaned forward, locking his gaze with Ivan's and the boy felt his blood turn cold. "What crime did you commit?"

One of the other assassin's hand was on his shoulder, dragging him toward the Alpha. The grip tightened, and a voice snarled, "Answer him."

Ivan swallowed down the lump in his throat and raised his head. There was no regret in his heart. "Murder," he said, giving the man a hard stare, though inside his heart melted with fear.

The Alpha's white eyebrows raised. He leaned back. A knife blade pressed on Ivan's throat, cold and sharp. "You dare lie?"

"Rurik." The Alpha's voice was a low growl. "Let him go."

"You see. He admits it." The village men murmured as Ivan stared at the ground, his head swimming. Seconds slowed as his brief life passed before his mind.

"You know the law, finish him." This was the man who was going to lay his filthy hands on Lydia. Ivan's fingers balled tightly on the ground, wishing he could break his neck.

"Maybe I finish you, uh?" The wolf at the Alpha's side snarled viciously at the villager, as if in agreement. The Alpha scratched behind its ears, and it turned and licked the side of his head.

Ivan could hear the villagers easing away, back toward the cave entrance. The Alpha spoke again. "You do not tell me law. Get out before I feed you to Sasha, instead of boy." His hand stroked the wolf's massive head, and it whined, rubbing against its master. Ivan stared at the ground, feeling ill as he imagined those teeth ripping into him. The men practically tripped over one another in their hurry to retreat. They would see no blood spilled for their trouble that day.

It was quiet. Ivan waited for the order. The Alpha was going to have him thrown to the wolves. But the order didn't come. Only a question. "Who did you kill, boy?"

"Four men attacked my sisters." Heat flooded Ivan's face. He hated himself for not killing them all. His fists trembled with anger as he stared, unflinching, at the Alpha. "So I painted the snow red with their blood. Only... one got away. That was my mistake."

A sinister grin spread across the Alpha's face. "Three, uh?" He leaned back in his chair. "What is your name, boy?"

"Ivan S—"

The Alpha waved his hand dismissively. "Just Ivan. Whoever you were before, the villagers want dead. So dead you will be."

Looking back at the ground, Ivan's throat constricted. The wolves whining hungrily. The assassin that held him by the collar let go, shoving him toward the Alpha. "I am Aleksei. If you keep up with the pack, you can stay. Fall behind, and you die. Villagers can go to Byorn with their demands, uh. Sound good, Ivan?"

Ivan looked up to see the Alpha—Aleksei—giving him that same dangerous grin. Dizzying relief filled his head, realizing he wasn't meant to die tonight. He nodded at the Alpha. Anything sounded better than being torn to shreds by Sasha and the rest of the wolves.

Descended from his seat with long, careless steps, Aleksei gripped Ivan by the shoulder. His icy fingers burned through Ivan's thin shirt. "You learned your first lesson today, Ivan. Let no one get away." He flashed a toothy grin, throwing his head back in laughter. And that was that; he was now a member of the most formidable wolf pack in the Kiaggard Mountains.

Aleksei was a merciless leader, laughing at Ivan when he got cut up on an assignment, but applauding him more than anyone when the boy came away victorious. The first lesson he taught, Ivan never forgot. Shortly after he took him in, he pulled Ivan aside. "You killed for your sisters?" Ivan nodded. He would do it again. Aleksei's hand was on his shoulder. "You love them?" Something in the way he said it made Ivan's heart race, an alarm going off inside his head telling him to say no. "Yes." He said it anyway.

There was always darkness in Aleksei's eyes, but when he looked at Ivan, this time there was none of his usual amusement. "Hide them so well even you forget where they are." He glanced out across the mountains as snow fell like a lace curtain. "I tell you this because I like you, Ivan. Let no one be your weakness. One day, maybe you decide to cross me—they will die." The gravity in his voice fell like a hammer. A chill ran up Ivan's spine, knowing Aleksei would not hesitate to do what he said. He vowed no one would ever find his sisters, or his mother. No one ever did.

All these years later it still hurt to think of them, and Ivan wondered what sort of women Lydia and Nastya had grown into. But never so much that he dared to go to them. When he'd seen Aleksei in Corcyra, Ivan knew they were still safe. Had the Alpha any idea where his family was, they would have been hunted down already. Things he'd done as an assassin worked their way to the top of his mind, things he'd tried so hard to forget he nearly killed himself on furi. Even now, that hunger to drown his mistakes forever was still present like a faithful companion. Knowing Tristan and Zee were imprisoned in Byorn—an inescapable underground dungeon—only strengthened the hunger.

Coming to a stop by the stairwell, Ivan slammed his fist against the wall. As he did so, he noticed Solomand had caught up to him. He leaned over the railing, glancing uneasily down to the bottom deck.

Ivan let out a frustrated sigh. He was in no mood to dance around with a game of questions. "Byorn is no prison, Sol." His hand moved to his knife, then away from it again. "People go there to die."

Solomand shrugged. "We have to get them out somehow. How hard could it be?"

It was just like Sol to determine the result of something without weighing the difficulties. Ivan groaned, pressing the palm of his hand against his throbbing temple. "This not Corcyra. Byorn has one way in. People mostly leave in boxes. Aleksei." He shook his head. "He does not care about your governor, or whatever stupid scheme that man plans."

"Well, what the hell does he care about, then?"

Ivan gripped the railing next to Solomand, his knuckles whitening.

"Aleksei is coming for *me*. And anyone who he thinks I care for. And Will told you a little of how Aleksei deals with people." Beads of sweat trickled down the sides of his face. Why did he have to be so damned weak! Solomand watched him closely from the corner of his eye.

"You want to talk about it? They say it helps."

Ivan gritted his teeth. "Who is *they*?"

Solomand shrugged. "Know-it-all doctors. What do they know really, though?"

Taking a slow, pronounced breath, Ivan closed his eyes. "I do not want to *talk* about anything."

I want you to go away! He'd dug himself into this hole. It was only proper he found his own way out.

"I could tell you another story about smuggling illegal animals, which may or may not be true," Sol offered.

Glancing at Solomand with a hoarse laugh, Ivan backed away from the railing to rest against the hull. "Alright." He hadn't the strength to say no.

"Really?" Solomand worked a hand through his hair and looked deep in thought. "Sorry." He cleared his throat and paced in front of the stairs. "Give me a minute, will you? I didn't have anything prepared."

Ivan felt the racing of his heart slow. He crossed his arms. "Or better yet, how about a plan for breaking into prison?"

Solomand chewed on his lip. "Right." He raised a finger. "There was this lady with purple hair that wanted us to deliver a death lizard one time."

Chapter 26

SOLOMAND

SOLOMAND RIFLED THROUGH kitchen cabinets until he found the liquor supply stashed behind a bag of rice. A can fell over and rolled out as he reached behind to grab a bottle. "Damn." He groaned as it rolled across the floor, stooping as he scrambled to chase it down. He gave it an offended look as he tossed it back in the cabinet and shut the door. "Lyonese vodka." He eyed the peeling label with a lion on it before uncorking it and pouring himself a drink. Sitting in the dark, he drummed one hand on the table.

Zee. His hand gripped the glass. Lemuel assured him she would be alright. LeFrost was her father. One more thing the Falcon was wrong about. He gulped down a bitter swallow. His chest constrained, and he felt like the world was closing in on him from every side.

Just breathe, stupid useless lungs. Solomand lay his head on the table, trying to listen to his own advice.

At least there was some silver lining of good news; Tristan was alive. Their foolish plan had worked. Galin had saved his life. Even if he was in a prison Ivan seemed to think was impossible to break out of. He should know as well as the rest of them; impossible was more often than not an illusion.

As he took another swallow, there was an unpleasant nagging at the back of his mind. He was forgetting something important.

Hydra. Or, rather, Harpy. That must be it. She needed to leave. The clear liquor sloshed around in the glass as he swirled it, trying to dissolve the tortured look on Will's face. Like flood-water breaking through a levee, it all came crashing back, the old mixing with the new. Tristan, pale, stammering. "I... I couldn't save her." He hadn't been talking about Rayn, as Solomand thought at first. Life always had a way of cruelly forcing you to compare worsts. Your wife survived, yes—but; there was always a 'but.'

They hadn't known about the baby until then. His daughter. Each thought was like a knife stabbing and twisting in his lungs. Solomand didn't realize he was shaking until he felt the hand on his shoulder. He leapt to his feet, knocking the glass to the floor. "Rayn!" He breathed out slowly, watching as liquor dripped from the table, pooling on the floor.

"Are you alright?" She took his face in her hands.

Solomand pressed his head against hers, breathing in the scent of sandalwood from her hair. "I'm fine." His arms pulled her closer until he could feel her heart beating against him. A sensation of peace eased the tension threatening to take over as her arms tightened around his neck. Everything was fine.

And to think, he nearly let her go. "I love you." The words seemed inadequate. What he felt was more akin to '*I don't want to live without you.*'

Rayn ran her fingertips along the scar on his face. "I love you, too." Her smile was like a salve, numbing the aching parts of his soul. *What could she possibly see in me?*

Tracing the pattern of freckles on her face with the pad of his thumb, he kissed her forehead. "You know, Ivan's forgotten about earlier," he said, just remembering himself. He kissed her on the nose.

"I noticed." Her voice was a warm whisper. "So did you."

"Maybe." Solomand leaned in, his lips pressing into hers with a hungry, desperate need to be close. Warmth spread through his chest as her hands laced through his hair, pressing into him. Their lips melded, not battling for dominance, but ebbing and flowing like the battering waves of the sea. Invigorating, terrifying, all-encompassing. Breathless, he broke away and touched his fore-head to hers. It was astonishing how pleasant drowning could feel.

"Are you going to remind him?" Her head lay on his chest as her fingers toyed with his hair.

"I could think of other things I'd rather do." He whispered the words in her ear, and she shivered in his arms.

"Sol, maybe we should take this more seriously." She didn't pull away.

"I suppose…" Solomand sighed dramatically, giving her one last kiss on the top of the head as she ran her fingers down the sides of his face and arms to curl around his hands. He glanced at the clock. "A little late for it tonight, though. In which case…" He would have given her another kiss, but she cringed, holding her stomach.

"What's wrong?" Solomand's anxiety reminded him it had gone nowhere permanently as a swarm of 'what if?' questions swirled through his mind.

"It's nothing. I just feel…" She bit her lip, not wanting to admit it.

"Sick?"

Rayn nodded, fear spreading across her face.

"It'll be alright." He gave her what he hoped was a reassuring smile. "What do you need? A drink of water? Something to eat? The skull of your enemy?"

"Nothing," Rayn snapped, then looked sorry. "Take me to bed?"

"Anything." he stooped to swoop her into his arms.

"Sol, stop! Your shoulder." Annoyance flickered over her face. "Just walk with me?" Her fingers lingered in his for a moment before pulling free as she walked from the kitchen.

Solomand followed after, swooping his arm around her waist. As he pulled her against him, a pleasant tingle ran up his side.

The next morning, Solomand and Rayn went to the helm together. Rayn tied her hair into a messy ponytail as she walked. Solomand paused, holding his hand out. "After you." A smile played on her lips as she passed him. It faded quickly, and she brought a hand to her forehead, looking pale and tired.

Hydra stood on tiptoes, her face pressed close to the glass of the window as she pointed below. "That used to be a village. A local legend says the *Kirno Valk*—a black wolf—with blue eyes came down from the mountain and slaughtered everyone." Hydra sounded like she was talking about plans for dinner rather than a massacre. She shrugged one shoulder. "Probably just a myth, though." Sitting in a chair next to the control panel, she drew her knees up and spun around in the chair. "What do you think?" She leaned toward Ivan, catching his eye.

"What?" Ivan gave a start.

"Do you think it's true? The story. About the black wolf?" Hydra curled a lock of purple hair around her finger.

Ivan swallowed, a flicker of horror crossing his face. Solomand intervened before the harpy could prod whatever ghosts he was dealing with further.

"More *important* than some local legend," he strode to position himself in between Hydra and Ivan, glancing at his friend, "Can you set a course for Byorn?"

Giving Solomand a fleeting, grateful look, Ivan nodded.

"You mean Chroburough, right?" The Harpy spoke again.

Solomand's gaze shifted to her, annoyed by her chipper, know-it-all voice. "You don't actually plan to fly straight to the prison, right? Of course you don't, that'd be dense."

She rattled off a coordinate. "That will take you closer to the city." Her boots halted her clockwise rotation, then she pushed off to spin in the opposite direction.

Solomand gave Ivan a questioning look. "She is right." He sounded grudging.

"Thanks, Harpy. We'll take it from here." Solomand shooed her away with his hands. "I believe you've completed your mission. You can clear off now."

Hydra sprang from the chair, causing Solomand to give a start. Her sporadic movements were unnerving. Rocking back and forth on her heels, she shoved her hands in her coat pockets. "You sure you want me to? I can be helpful."

"You've done enough." Solomand muttered to himself. "Don't need your kind of help." He leaned over Ivan's shoulder as he produced the spherical Kree map from his pocket.

"Ah, come on, Captain. Let me show you." From the corner of his eye, Sol saw the fluid movement of her hand reaching for the gun strapped to her hip.

Throwing his coat back, he whirled around and drew his revolver. Will lunged for Hydra, who was aiming her strange-looking gun at his head. Before Will knocked her to the ground, Rayn stalked over and kicked the gun from her hand. It sailed over Ivan's head and clanged against the hull before falling.

There was a shocked expression on Hydra's face as she fell with Will's arms squeezed around her.

Hands on her hips, Rayn gave the disarmed Hydra a withering look. "Helpful like a migraine." She returned to her seat, drumming her fingers on the sides of her arms in an agitated manner.

Hydra wriggled under Will, then smirked up at him. "I was going to ask you to get off of me, but I kinda like it."

Will scrambled back, avoiding her gaze as he let her up. "You're no fun." She sat up, pouting.

Solomand was officially tired of Hydra's antics. "Don't you have another job to be getting to?" He glared at her, pressing a hand against his temple where slow throbbing had started.

"No." She sounded bored.

"Well, find some other way to make money. We can't give you any for your help, and I know how you freelance agents are." Unreliable, self-absorbed, treacherous. His mind went to The Falcon. Deep down, he knew it was an unfair comparison. When it came down to it, Lemuel, he was fairly certain, would be there if he needed him. He always had been in the past.

"Who said I wanted money?" Hydra cast a seductive glance toward Will.

"Oh, for the love of…" Sol dragged a hand down his face. "Plenty of employment opportunities for you then. Just not on my airship." Maybe hinting she was a prostitute would make her want to leave.

Hydra laughed at him. Infuriating! Nothing he said bothered her. She took a step toward him, then shifted a sideways glance to Rayn and must have thought better of trying her advances on him. Her curls fell across her face as she turned to Ivan.

Ivan held up a hand, giving her a single shake of his head.

Minuet would have stormed away by now. Solomand gave Will a meaningful look. "You deal with her." He hoped he would understand it to mean *'snap her neck when she isn't looking.'*

"You have plan once we get to Chroburough?" Ivan was cleaning the dirt from his fingernails with the tip of his dagger.

Solomand glanced at the changing landscape as the airship veered back toward the South. "Not really. Something will come to me, though."

Ivan frowned. "Is not smart, Sol. This seems too easy."

"Easy? The only thing more difficult than planning a prison break from the outside, is planning a prison break from the inside. Both require stealth I lack the capacity of pulling off in my current state." Stopping to breathe, he motioned to his still-healing shoulder.

A laugh made him turn his attention to the doorway where Jank stood. "As if *that* has anything to do with it."

"Don't you have something you're supposed to be doing?" Solomand was growing tired of smartass remarks—that was *his* department.

"No." Jank scratched his head. "I did it already."

Dread curled its fingers around Solomand's spine when he saw the look of remembrance registering on Ivan's face.

"Speaking of." He grabbed Solomand by the arm and dragged him from the room. "There is something I forgot."

Solomand gave Rayn a terrified look as she stood to follow them.

Chapter 27

TRISTAN

PRISONERS OF BYORN mined the coal, which provided fuel for the compound's boiler. They worked in a mine shaft below the prison.

Clanks of picks tearing into the rock was the only sound in the mine. Oil lamps burned as they worked, and there were no breaks until the flames went dark. Occasionally shouts from prisoners or the sound of guards barking orders carried over the racket of steel on rock. The smell of sweat and dirt filled Tristan's nose as he shakily swung his pick. His gaze shifted to Zee in between studying the layout of the compound. One swing. Then another. His exhaustion was maddening.

It shouldn't be this way. Blisters bubbled beneath the skin on his palms, and his fingers throbbed and ached.

When the whistle blew to signal a change in shift, he let the tool fall from his hands. As the new crew came in, they eyed the girl, muttering amongst themselves about what they would do to Tristan. One elbowed him roughly from his path. It was the same man who knocked him down the previous day. Tristan's eye was still bruised and puffy from the blow. Fingernails dug into his palms as he clenched his fingers into fists. If he had to fight again, he would.

The man quickly averted his eyes and took a pickaxe from the rack. A rough hand grabbed Tristan by the collar. It was Nikola.

"Come with me." He dragged Tristan back to his room. "Do not challenge prisoners." He glowered at him.

"Why not?" Tristan sank to the cot. He stared at his shaking hands—covered with black dust from the mine. Aching spasms shot up his back and arms.

Nikola gave him an appraising look before walking to a table on the far side of the room. He poured water from a stone pitcher into a tin mug and handed it to Tristan. "Better to not attract attention."

Stop shaking! Tristan wrapped both hands around the cup, drinking the water in gulps. "Thank you," he said, resting the empty cup on his knee. Zee sat next to him, leaning her head against the smooth stone of the wall.

Nikola let out a sigh. *"Keeping you alive will be harder than I thought."*

"Nobody asked you to, you know." Tristan felt instant regret for his snappish words. Using his shirt, he wiped sweat from his face. *"I'm sorry. I didn't mean... I am grateful for your help."*

Nikola handed them them pieces of dried meat and slices of leathery fruit. "Eat."

What he means is, you're not strong enough. Tristan thought as he slowly chewed the fruit, washing it from the roof of his mouth with water. Nikola was right. He glanced at Zee. "Are you alright?"

She chewed her food, listlessly staring at the wall. "I'm fine."

"Zee." He laid a hand on her shoulder.

"I'm fine." She pushed her silken black hair behind her ear, smearing the coal dust further across her face. It felt like a knife stuck in him, twisted by an unseen force. In a better world, Zee would have some time yet to be a child—innocent, trusting. But the world was far too cruel, and she had already learned this.

There was a hardness in her golden eyes as she glanced at him, but it was quickly gone. "LeFrost told me he was my father, that Sol had kidnapped me and now had no use for me," she blurted it out.

Solomand had never spoken of her father, ill or otherwise. Tristan wondered if this was a mistake now. "Do you want to know what the truth is?"

Zee's eyes flashed. "I already do. He's not my father, no matter what he says! Sol would never kidnap anyone, and he would never leave anyone behind. He will come. For both of us." She bit off another piece of meat and chewed angrily.

Nikola sat cross-legged on the floor, swiping the blade of his dagger along a sharpening stone. He glance up, frowning every so often.

Something was bothering him, and Tristan suspected it had something to do with Aleksei.

"How do you know Aleksei?" Tristan asked what he had wanted to for some time, and instantly regretted doing so.

Nikola's face darkened. His finger seemed to press the blade more heavily into the stone. "We were in same pack," he said grimly. "Ivan was, as well."

Tristan decided to push his luck. "Why is he after Ivan?" He set the cup down, rubbing a bruise on his forearm.

"Did he not tell you?" Nikola looked increasingly like he wished the sharpening stone was someone's throat.

"He never talked about his past." Tristan touched the tender skin just beneath his eye.

If anyone brought up the life Ivan left behind, a threatening energy surrounded him until his dark looks discouraged any further questions. Whatever mistakes haunted him were not important. Not then. Not now. He had proven his loyalty as a friend, and that is all that mattered. "I never asked."

Nikola bit the corner of his lip. "Aleksei...does not like to lose." He frowned in Zee's direction. "*The rest of us—Aleksei lost our loyalty when Ivan refused to obey him any longer.*" He dragged the blade over the stone once more. "*You saw how he likes to play with people?*"

Dried fruit and jerky mixed uncomfortably in Tristan's stomach. "Yes," he said, hoarsely.

"Is better for Wolves to have no family." Nikola's thick eyebrows drew together as his face twisted in a mix of rage and the ghost of sorrow. "Some of us did."

The silence of his pain echoed off the walls. "*I'm sorry,*" Tristan managed to say.

Nikola turned, the traces of anguish gone from his face. "*Ivan had sisters. Aleksei never found them.*" His troubling stare fixed on Zee. "I do not think that matters now."

Tristan was still processing the information about Ivan having siblings when he realized what Nikola meant. Dread intensified, like a chokehold on his chest. "When you said Aleksei was coming... that's what you meant, isn't it?"

Nikola nodded.

Tristan had wanted to believe they would be out of Aleksei's reach—Zee would be out of his reach. If he meant to use them as bate to lure Ivan into his grasp...

Mumbling a curse, his head sank in his hands. Solomand would come and Ivan with him. Aleksei meant for it to happen all along.

Nikola clapped him on the back, and Tristan thought for a moment he might have a spinal injury. "*Do not worry, Otvali.*"

Was he smiling? It was the grin of a fox who'd been hunting its prey—patient, relentless. "Aleksei is not the only one with plans for revenge."

Chapter 28

RAYN

THE CLOCK TICKED loudly on the wall in the kitchen. Rayn held her breath as Ivan pulled out the pregnancy test Jank had made. On the side where the clear tube was exposed, it had turned a pale bluish color. "Negative," Ivan said, setting it on the table.

"Negative meaning…" Rayn felt stupid for having to ask

"You are not pregnant. I will not lock you on ship if end up in fight again." He gave her a crooked grin.

"Oh, good." Rayn stared at the table as Ivan said something else to Solomand.

She had been worried at the possibility of bringing a child into this world. The timing was wrong. She wasn't ready. Ivan and Solomand's words were like the background noise of the engines.

I'm not really the mothering type. Her fingers traced the metal top of the counter as the unfamiliar feeling of crushing disappointment settled over her.

"Rayn."

"Hm?" She looked up, realizing Ivan was talking to her.

He laid his hands on her shoulders. "I am sorry. For being overprotective. But, if anything were to happen…" Relief flooded his eyes. "I would never forgive myself."

"It's alright, Ivan." Rayn forced a smile, wishing she felt the same relief he did.

Giving her a curt nod, he left. Another wave of emotion swept over her, and she bit her lip as it quivered.

"Everything alright?" Solomand hugged her from behind.

She swallowed back tears. *What is wrong with me?* She tried to nod, furiously wiping away the dampness gathering in her eyes.

"Hey." Solomand took her by the shoulders and moved to stand in front of her. "What's wrong?"

"Nothing." She pulled away from him. "I don't know. I guess I'm just relieved. I don't think I'd be a good mother, anyway."

Solomand raised his eyebrows. "Rayn." The way he half-whispered her name made her heart skip a beat. His steel-blue gaze bore into her as he took her face in his hands. "Don't be ridiculous. You *will be* the most fantastic mother one day." His thumb wiped away the tear rolling down her cheek.

Her lip trembling, Rayn let him pull her into the warmth of his chest. He kissed her on the top of the head. "A bit like Ivan, maybe. A little less terrifying," he said playfully.

Rayn laughed, wiping her eyes as she pulled back to look at him. Solomand reached out, his fingers running down the strands of hair hanging loose around her shoulders. He tucked it behind her ear. "Did you want to be?"

"No." Rayn looked away, rubbing her arm. It would complicate things. A child had no place among a band of fugitives set on a course to attempt a prison-break.

Why do I feel this way, then? Would it have been a boy or a girl? With the likeness of Solomand, or herself? Shaking her head, she faked another smile. "Ivan was right to be worried about it. Maybe when we're not risking our lives trying to break into a prison. Or similar endeavors."

Solomand's fingers wound around hers and he gave her a smile, which said she was not fooling him. The sadness in his eyes made her think she might cry again. He pulling her into his chest. "When this is over, we'll find a place where no one will bother us. Somewhere having a family isn't such a crazy idea."

Rayn pushed herself up on her toes to loop her arm around his neck. "Are you sure that's what you want?" She ran her hand along the neck of his collar. There was a lump in her throat.

"Mrs. Black," Solomand chided. He took her chin in his hand, tilting her head back. "I have what I want." There was a flutter in her heart as he pressed his fingers into her back, closing what space remained between them. "Anything else is cream in the coffee."

Eyes half-closed, Rayn looked up at him with a more genuine smile. "You don't put cream in your coffee, Sol."

A tingle ran up her spine as his breath brushed against her ear. "That doesn't mean I wouldn't like it."

Maybe it was Solomand that caused the weakness in her stomach.

Chapter 29

SOLOMAND

I DON'T THINK I'd be a good mother. The disappointment in Rayn's eyes felt like a knife twisting in Solomand's chest. How could she think that? Hands laced behind his head, he stared at the ceiling of the cabin. The same thoughts he had gone to sleep with persistently plagued him at this early hour. Rayn slept next to him. Her leg hooked across his as she curled further into the blanket. His eyes watched the rise and fall of her chest—the rhythm of her breathing quieted the growing storm of tension.

The Dragonfly hit a patch of turbulence, and Rayn shifted her leg away from her, pulling it further under the blanket. Her hair fell over her face. It reminded him of the reddish hue the leaves took in fall on Lyonese. Memories of that night gripped him again—feelings like his heart was fractured in a million pieces. Rubbing his fingers nervously, he sat up, taking care not to wake her as he planted his feet on the ground. It had been a girl last time. His daughter.

Somewhere in the sea of emotions, he searched for the relief he should have felt. Ivan was right. This was not the time or place for children. But no matter how he sifted through his mind to find it, it wasn't there. Hope had been resurrected with the possibility of a second chance—hope he didn't realize he needed.

For a moment, the room faded. He traveled back in time to a night where starlight was dim. Rayn was not lying next to him but

161

in Ivan's arms, covered in blood and debris. This was one of the few times he ever saw fear in his friend's eyes.

Forcing a shaky breath, he stood, pulling his boots on, and slipped out of the cabin. It was about time to get up, anyway. Running a hand through his disheveled hair, he stopped short of walking into the kitchen. There was a light on, and a grating female voice met his ear. Scowling, he tucked his shirt in and walked through the open door. Will sat at the table looking uncomfortable as Hydra chattered at him.

"You still here, Harpy?" Solomand pulled a mug out of the cabinet and slammed the door shut. "Didn't I tell you to deal with her?" His eyes narrowed at Will.

Will swallowed. "You were not specific on the details of how specifically to deal with her."

Solomand grunted, eyeing her with distaste. "Don't you have somewhere to be?" Coffee spilled over the brim of his cup as he poured it and roughly banged the pot back on the stove.

She shook her head, eyes far too bright. "Still no jobs, and you all seem like such fun."

"Really." Solomand blew on the steam roiling over his cup as he brought it to his lips. "We may be a lot of things, Harpy. Fun isn't one of them. Maybe you should consider my other suggestion." He took a sip, cursing to himself as it burned the tip of his tongue.

Hydra positioned herself in Will's lap, causing him to stiffen with a shocked expression. "I'm a one-man girl now."

For the love of all things... Solomand gave her a doubtful glance. "Not if it's that man."

"What's wrong, Captain Black? Jealous?" Her lips brushed against Will's cheek, and Solomand couldn't tell if the look in Will's eye was a desperate plea for help or not.

He leaned back against the counter and gave her a hard stare. "What is it you really want, Harpy?"

She traced the tips of her fingers along Will's neck. "You are very cynical."

"Out with it." He took another sip of the scalding coffee.

"Well, Will has mentioned you might know a mutual acquaintance. The Falcon."

Solomand raised an eye. "*Mutual* acquaintance?"

"Yes. We went on a date once, him and me. We met on the Sholcolm Tides."

She spoke convincingly.

"Have you call him The Falcon, does he?"

"Why, yes, as a matter of fact. I think he likes it." She kicked her legs out in front of her and slid from Will's lap.

Solomand stared at her, unblinking. "You must be on narcotics if you think I'm going to believe that line of shit."

She replied with a syrupy smile that said she was hiding something.

"What do you want with him, anyway?" Sol asked.

"He has some research which would open doors for me," she said. "Only..." she curled a strand of hair around her finger, feigning an innocent look. "I forgot where he told me I could find him."

Solomand rolled his eyes. "He doesn't tell anyone where he can be found. Ever." Which was rather annoying as Solomand needed him to help decipher that cursed Kree map. "What makes you think I know where to find him?" He blew on the coffee again. Steam dampened his face.

"Will said you have a history. Few people can claim they know The Falcon, aside from me and you, I mean." There was that irritating smile.

Even if he had known, there was no way he would reveal Lemuel's location; to her or anyone else. Some men you did not push your luck with. Lemuel Falcon was one of them.

"I have no idea where he is, or how to find him. So, if that's what you want, you are still out of luck. In which case, you can clear off." He headed for the door.

"Don't be silly, Captain." She brought her hand to her forehead, giving him a one fingered salute.

He glared at her before stomping away, muttering loudly about pathological liars. Coffee sloshed over the side of his cup, splattering on the floor.

Ivan turned the radio dials, cycling through the channels. Still nothing from Minuet. Unless her idea of helping them was of dropping that annoying girl in their lap. Ivan glanced up as Sol walked into the helm. He leaned back in the chair, dropping his hands in his lap. "Do you have plan yet for when we get to Byorn Prison?"

No, actually. Solomand sat down, glimpsing his reflection in the sheen of the control panel. *Do I really look that bad?* "Oh, you know, just the usual." Rubbing at the circles under his eyes, he took another swig of coffee. Ivan's gray eyes narrowed into a stony stare, and Sol gave him a sarcastic smile. "Alright." He scooted to the edge of the controls and set his cup down. "The plan is not to die. Or get caught. Or horribly maimed." It was depressing that most of his plans centered on this.

"No shit, *lochek*." Ivan shook his head and went back to the radio.

Chapter 30

IVAN

"*Y*OU NO TALK, uh? Hey, Kirno Valk." *Aleksei's cool gaze snapped to Ivan. If a wolf could have grinned, it might have looked like that. "We do this the hard way." He motioned for Ivan to go through with his part.*

The man's face was like all the others; a pale blur. Ivan did not remember any of them. But the eyes were hard to get out of his mind. Feelings locked deep down inside some dark corner of his soul, along with the little voice that would have told him to hesitate or draw his blade away from the boy's neck altogether. He was only thirteen. But the voice was quiet, staying where it belonged. No one defied Aleksei's orders.

It would all be over soon, anyway. They usually said whatever Aleksei wanted them to as soon as the screaming started.

Staring at snow-capped mountain tops and black, twisted trees below. Soon they would be close to Byorn. All Ivan could envision was Tristan and Zee's eyes, both the same color of fear. His forehead pressed up against the glass of the window. Deep, pressing hunger gnawed at him. A voice, cold and overpowering, screamed at him. *If they knew what you have done,—they would have nothing to do with you.*

He tried to focus on his breath, closing his eyes to shut out the words. But they were right. *I would have nothing to do with me, either.* A tremor ran through his hand, tapping on the coolness of the glass.

"Ivan?"

Ivan jerked his head away from the window. The sympathy and worry in Solomand's eyes was infuriating.

"Yes?" He heard himself snap.

Solomand held up his hands defensively, but he did not leave. He took a step forward.

Shame burning in his chest, Ivan opened his mouth to speak, then closed it. He sank to the ground, his heart hammering like he'd just ran miles through the mountains—something he used to do regularly. *I'm sorry.* He could not make himself speak.

Solomand sat down cross-legged next to him and held out a lit cigarette. Ivan took it without a word. They sat smoking in silence as the world passed below through a filter of gray and white patches of cloud.

"Any idea of a plan?" Solomand acted as if nothing was wrong. "You know this Aleksei better than anyone."

Kirno Valk. Ivan could see Aleksei's stupid laughing face when he gave him that name. It was a joke. Inhaling the rest of the cigarette in one breath, he hid his trembling hand at his side. There was only one plan that would work, and Solomand would never agree to it.

He would if he knew the person you really are. Sorrow and bitterness coiled within him. Maybe the voice was right.

Solomand's gaze narrowed as he watched Ivan, always more perceptive than he ever let on.

"Sol," Ivan closed his eyes. "There is something you should know about Aleksei. And me." He forced himself to lock his gaze with Solomand's. "I have done... terrible things for him."

"Ah." Solomand sighed. "And here I was thinking you were going to tell me his secret weakness was being doused with saltwater or something riveting like that."

"I am serious, Sol. I do not know what you think an Ice Wolf does, but..." he swallowed with difficulty. "There are many things I want to forget... long before I met you."

Solomand held a hand up. "Stop. I think I know where you're going with this. And you should know me well enough to know it's not going to work. Ivan, I don't give a damn what you were before I met you. What you are to me now, is a friend. You're one of us." There was a rare, somber look on his face. "Nothing you ever did, or say now, is going to change that. Never. So, unless your plan involves dousing this Aleksei bastard in sunlight or staking him in the heart,"

"Sol." Ivan's hands clenched into fists. As grateful as he was for Solomand's loyalty, it would never do. There was only one thing Aleksei wanted. "You know what I need to do."

"Sorry, Ice Man." Solomand pulled his revolver out of the holster and clicked the cylinder one chamber at a time. "You and me, neither of us deal with this sort of thing rationally."

Ivan did not threaten to rip off his head for calling him Ice Man this time. He glared sideways at Solomand. "Is stupid for any of you to go anywhere near Aleksei."

Solomand put his revolver away. "Since when have you known me to do things that you wouldn't call stupid? Besides, what am I supposed to do, drop you into the snow and retreat a safe distance until he finishes you?"

Ivan cracked a grin then. "He will not finish me—not this time."

"Really? Because last time, if I remember correctly, you didn't fair too well."

"*Suiti (shut up), lochek.* He took me by surprise." Ivan scowled.

"That's an excuse I would make."

Ivan reached out and punched him in the shoulder and Solomand doubled over with a groan, muttering, "least it wasn't the one I got stabbed in—owe!" he scrambled away after Ivan gripped his injured shoulder. "Damnit, Ice Man. What the hell is wrong with you?"

Ivan stood, adjusting his coat. "Sorry."

"You are not—and trying to make me hate you won't work either, if that's what your game is."

"You would know if I want you to hate me." He grabbed Solomand and pulled his shirt collar aside to check his injury.

"Owe! Watch it! Miss your calling as one of those village healers, did you?"

Ivan raised an eye. "You cry like baby. Come to infirmary. I will fix it."

Solomand pulled free, still rubbing his shoulder. "Fine. But you can get Jank to look at it. I'm going to the helm."

Ivan rolled his eyes. "Whatever you say, *Captain*." He went down into the depths of the engine room where Jank had taken to hiding. The engineer was bent over his sketchbook. When Ivan said his name, he jumped, jerking his head upright.

"Solomand wants you to look at his shoulder."

Jank rolled his eyes, snapping the book shut. "Why me? Am I the sodding airship medic all of a sudden?"

Ivan gave him a look which would have silenced anyone but Solomand. Jank cleared his throat. "Alright, I'm coming." He walked over to a shelf lined with disordered tools and grabbed the handle of a medical kit. It slung open as he lifted it, and the contents spilled over the grease-stained floor.

"Shit." Jank kneeled down, picking up bandages and ointment packets and throwing them back into the metal box. Ivan took a knee to help. There was a small, clear vile with reddish powder in it. Jank saw it and snatched it up, uttering another curse. "Oh… no."

"What?"

Jank licked his lips nervously. "Well, uh. This was supposed to go with that test you had me make. It's no big deal, though, it just affects what color is shown depending on the chemical reaction insi—"

"What do you mean, *lochek*?" Ivan's relief at one of their endless problems was dissipating.

Jank scooted an arm's length away from Ivan. "It means it wouldn't turn red like it's supposed to, that's all."

"What color would it turn?"

Jank swallowed. "What color did it turn?"

Ivan stood up and Jank jumped to his feet, looking ready to climb the reactor out of reach. "Blue."

Pale, Jank muttered in a quiet voice. "If it was negative, it would have been colorless."

An alarm buzzer sounded through the intercom, and Solomand's voice came over. "*Looks like we're about to reach Chroburough. Standby for landing. That's an awful lot of trees in the way... Will, get up here!*"

Chapter 31

Tristan

TRAYS OF FOOD clanged on the tables in the cafeteria. Voices of prisoners echoed across the walls of the octagonal shaped cavern. Tristan stirred a spoon around the bowl of colorless broth. Zee sat next to him, methodically drinking the substance, with her eyes constantly shifting around the room. Coal dust embedded under his fingernails and in the pores of his fingers. He adjusted his elbow on the metal face of the table, and his chest and arm muscles responded with a series of aching pangs. Letting the spoon fall from his fingers, he leaned his head in his hand.

"What's wrong?" Zee elbowed him in the side.

"Not hungry," Tristan mumbled. Nausea that comes from not eating too little, too late coiled around his stomach.

"Really, Tris?" Zee crossed her arms, leaning back on the bench. "If I said that, you'd force me to eat, anyway."

Another wave of aches roiled through Tristan as he sighed and twisted his head to look at the girl. "Touché."

"What?" Zee's brows knitted together.

"Oh, never mind." He straightened his back and reached out to grab the spoon. Hands slammed on the table, rattling the trays and spilling the soup over the sides of his bowl. Zee jumped, gasping as she eased closer. Tristan raised a cool gaze to see Deyan, the man who picked a fight with him the first day they arrived. Leering down at them, he leaned further forward. Tristan struggled not to recoil at the man's unpleasant scent.

"*The Wolf will not always be around to protect the pair of you.*" Deyan's sunken eyes darted around the room, as if to verify Nikola was not present. His lips curled into a sneer directed at Zee. "*And when he tires of the girl, she will be mine.*" He reached a filthy hand toward her.

Swallowing down exhaustion, Tristan sprang to his feet. Fingers gripping his food tray, he slung it and its contents against the man's head. "*I don't need Nikola to protect either of us.*" Tristan said. The swift movement caused his temple to throb.

Deyan yelled, stumbling back and clutching the side of his face as soup dripped through his hair and down his face. Snarling, his hands curled, and he charged for Tristan. Zee jumped up, slamming her own tray against the other side of Deyan's head before he could get closer. "Back off, pond scum!" Her insult echoed off the walls. The rest of the room had gone silent. Keeping his eye on the injured Deyan, Tristan glimpsed her from the corner of his eye. When had she gotten this tall? And her hair, usually no longer than her ears, reached her slim shoulders.

Tristan slid his hand in front of Zee, pushing her behind him as Deyan jerked his head up, roaring as he moved to run at them. He stopped short, horror flooding his eyes as they moved to the doorway at their back.

The rest of the prisoners on Nikola's crew scattered, scraping benches on the floor as they hurried from the room. Tristan turned to see the foreman, his glare like a spear stabbing into Deyan. "*You wish to fight me?*"

Deyan's entire body flinched. "*N-no, Foreman.*" He held his hands up, feet sliding backward as if putting distance between him and Nikola would help his situation.

"*It looks like you do.*" Nikola's voice was a low rumble, like thunder before the flash of lightning.

Licking his lips, Deyan shook his head vigorously.

"*If it happens again, I will give you what you wish for.*"

Deyan wiped soup from the side of his face and nodded, cowering.

Nikola's glance passed from Zee to Tristan. "You two. Come with me."

Tristan wiped his hands on the side of his pants before trudging along with Nikola back to his quarters. The foreman locked the door, turned around and leaned against it. "Bad news."

"Bad news as compared to what, pray tell." Unable to ignore the dizzying feeling any longer, Tristan sank to the cot.

"We received message—governor from Fifth Continent on his way."

"What?" Tristan touched a hand to the persistent throb in his temple. Why would LeFrost be coming here? Not that it mattered. What was more important was who would accompany him.

Aleksei. And that would mean…

He jumped to his feet, instantly regretting his quick movement. "Nikola, we have to get her out of here!" Stars blurred his vision.

"Not just her." Nikola took two steps forward. With one hand on Tristan's shoulder, he pushed him back onto the cot. "*You do not look so well.*"

Tristan found a glass of water forced into his hands and reluctantly took a sip.

"Getting out of Byorn, not so easy." Nikola dragged a stool next to the bed and lowered himself to sit. "Makes it good place for hiding." Was that shame in his eyes?

Why could nothing ever go the way it needed to? This was all for nothing. Coming here did no good to escape Aleksei. He would use them both in some twisted game to get revenge on Ivan. Tristan's heart hammered out of control. He took another quick drink before setting the cup on the floor. "What do you propose we do then?"

Nikola rubbed the top of his head. "I have had long time to think of such things."

"Are you saying you have a plan?" Why could he not keep the skeptical tone from his words?

Nikola smoothed his beard, then hooked his hands on the top of his leather vest. "Of sorts." Worried lines formed around his eyes. "There are risks."

There were always risks. "Tell me."

With a reluctant breath, Nikola drew his knife and scraped the tip along the dark stones of the floor, carving a light outline; a crude map of the prison. "There may be another way out." He tapped the tip of his knife on the mine entrance. "There are abandoned tunnels further in mine. I think it is old way to surface."

"Think?" Already this was sounding less like an actual plan.

Scowling, Nikola arched an eyebrow. "I do not know for certain. But I believe enough to try it myself. Now that time is right." He turned the knife over in his hand and scratched his head. "If I am right, we still have bigger problem."

Life was an endless chain of progressively larger problems. Tristan swallowed down a helpless laugh. "Just one?"

Nikola's brow furrowed. He must not approve of the dry humor. "We cannot simply disappear from our shift. I will be missed. So will two of you."

Pieces of a puzzle pulled together in his mind. "We need a distraction."

"More than that." Nikola's finger tapped on the room adjacent to the mine entrance, which housed the boiler to the prison. "We need to cut guards off from chasing us. Easiest way to do that is blow boiler during our shift."

Tristan felt his insides tighten. The foreman had more of a plan than he thought. "That would do it." He breathed out slowly. A vision of fire, fractured pipes and crumbling rock swirled in his mind.

Nikola continued with his details about overloading the boiler with coal, shutting off the relief valve and escaping into the tunnels while blood and piles of bodies presented themselves in Tristan's mind. His foot slipped, knocking the glass to its side. Water puddled under his shoe. Its color darkened on the stones as he stared at it. How many other prisoners were on Nikola's crew? They would be cut off from escaping. Tristan saw only one way of dealing with that. And what of any guards caught in the proximity to the boiler?

"How many will we have to kill?"

Nikola twisted his head, a confused look on his face. "What does *that* matter?"

Tristan bit the corner of his lip, his fingers drumming on his knees. "A great deal, actually."

Grunting, Nikola stood, using his foot to shove the stool aside. "No stomach for death, Otvali?"

Inwardly, Tristan cringed. How much death was he directly or indirectly responsible for?

"I would prefer to minimize it." His eyes were drawn back to the pool of water. So much like blood, and yet so different; one was life-giving, the other was life lost.

Nikola threw his hands up. "No one is good here—including me." He slammed a hand on his chest.

His gaze bore into Tristan's, daring him to contradict this belief. "*I did not wait all this time to die like rats in trap, waiting to be eaten by the one who set it!*" The vein in his neck bulged. Eyes flicking to the girl, his voice softened a little. "I am only concerned for us. Death is certain for you if we do not try to escape."

Maybe not. Solomand was coming.

When did you become a man who waited for others to rescue you? He glanced at Zee, his eyes closing for a moment as he wrestled with the wrongness of it all and wishing for an end to the cycle of blood and death. Would he ever be able to escape it?

Taking a determined breath, Tristan opened his eyes and met Nikola's hard gaze. "Alright."

"Really?" Nikola looked doubtful.

Tristan picked the cup up from the floor and handed it to the foreman. "*I promised to keep her safe. That is what I will do.*"

Nikola laid a heavy hand on Tristan's shoulder. "*I think we understand each other a little.*"

Trading others' lives for his own was not something Tristan could have agreed to—not even men like Deyan. But for Zee? Well, that was different. That's what he told himself, anyway. "What do you need me to do?"

His finger grazing against the makeshift map again. "Someone will need to stuff the boiler with coal and turn off relief valve. I will distract guard long enough."

"I'll do it." Zee lifted her head, a fiery determination in her eyes.

"No!" Tristan objected at the same time Nikola nodded at her. "No," he said again. "I will."

Jumping to her feet, Zee lifted a hand in frustration. "Why not? I can *do* this, Tristan."

Tristan shook his head slowly. The girl rolled her eyes, uttering an annoyed noise.

"Let her," Nikola spoke.

"What?" Tristan held a hand to his chest to stave off the throbbing pang. He glared at the Northman. "*You stay out of this.*"

He wondered if Nikola would grow angry at this slight. Worse, he was positively unbothered. Tristan may as well have been a mosquito buzzing in his ear. "*And who will be responsible for her if you are no longer around?*" He waited for a moment, then added. "*Even fox kittens know how to take care of themselves here. Let her learn.*"

He was right; realizing it felt like a punch in the chest. "Alright." Tristan gave Nikola a brief nod, unable to shake the guilt taking hold within him. What if something happened to her? No matter whether it was true, the blame would be his alone to bear. Closing his eyes for an instant, he prayed he would not end up with such a burden; not for his sake, but for the girl's.

Exhaling heavily, he let his hand fall from his chest to rest on his knee. "Nikola, d*o you have any paper I could have? There is something I need to do.*" Before we go to our probable deaths.

Nikola opened the drawer of his dresser and dug out a bundle of blank pages. He handed them to Tristan, along with a pen.

That night, he sat close to the bars of the cell to see better with the yellow light from the hall as he wrote. Zee was already asleep, curled inside the blanket, facing the wall.

If things went wrong, as they were apt to do, there would be no words left unsaid. One letter was addressed to his father, one to the lady he left behind, and one to those who had become his family.

Chapter 32

SOLOMAND

THIS AIRSHIP WAS a damned nuisance. Probably why Lemuel handed it over to them. When it was off autopilot, it was far too touchy. Needles spun to red, and a metallic voice echoed through the airship.

Warning. Entering critical lack of control.

Solomand raised his head, holding onto the controls as the airship pitched from side to side. "First time that's happened." He gripped the lip of the control panel to keep from falling over. "Why the hell hasn't anybody thought up an autopilot that lands the damned things?! That's the difficult part."

Will ran in, somehow maintaining his balance amid the swaying of the airship. "About time." Solomand's fingers slid from the control panel as Will took over. He toppled to the floor, skidding away from the controls.

"They say flying is in one's blood." Will glanced at Sol for a split second. "What happened?"

"Is that a joke? From you?" For a moment, the airship leveled off and Solomand rolled over to his back, breathing with relief. "I take after my mother's side of the family."

"Do you really?" Hydra stood over him, hands on her hips.

"Great." Solomand sat up. Relief at seeing Will turned to annoyance. "Why do you always turn up? Like a damned virus—never wanted and always at a bad time."

Hydra did not have time to answer him. The airship dropped with a suddenness that made them both rise from the floor—her more gracefully than he did. Will regained control as they both fell back to the ground. Solomand slammed painfully onto the metal and was reminded of all the minor bruises, scrapes and injuries from the previous months. Clawing himself upright, he glimpsed the rapidly approaching stretch of black twisted trees against a backdrop of white snowbanks.

The drab gray of the metal floor was all he could see. From there, he could not see the rapidly approaching tree line, black twisted branches against a backdrop of white snowbanks. The airship clipped the top of one of the black oaks. Air knocked from his lungs from the jarring impact, Solomand felt suffocated as they crashed and slid across the icy ground, coming to an uncomfortably fast halt.

Everything hurt. Was this what getting old felt like? Will looked down on him, worry lines formed on his face. It took Solomand a moment to realize he was speaking his name. "I think you've knocked him silly," Hydra said, eyes narrowing and her head tilting so her pinkish-blonde curls touched her bare shoulder.

What the hell was that gasping sound? *Oh. It's me.* Solomand tried to sit up, failing his first two attempts. "What the hell, Will?" He pressed a hand to the growing lump on his head. "You've lost your touch."

Will looked dejected. "Sorry, Sol. This airship is not the same as the Osprey."

Solomand gave him a grudging look. "Will, you could fly a sailboat. It's that damned Harpy messing with your head." He glared up at her, resentful as she laughed in an insufferably good-natured manner.

Windows were white from snow pressed up against them. "Where the hell are we, anyway?" He did not resist when Will helped him up.

Hydra slid her sleeve up and looked at a circular device strapped to her wrist by a leather cuff. "We're twenty klicks south of Byorn." Numbers scrolled across the screen as she punched buttons. "In the Amezwal Forest." She looked up. "Not the greatest place to land. If there is anyone out there, they'll be the types that belong in Byorn."

"Naturally." Solomand steadied himself on the back of the seat, then started for the door. "I'm going to go scouting the area for shifty, Byorn prison types."

"I can come with—"

"I'm taking Rayn with me on this one," Sol uttered hurriedly. "You can assess the airship's damage."

Hydra shrugged. "Suit yourself, Captain."

"Are you sure you don't want me to go?" Will looked worried again.

"No. Thanks." Solomand gave him a regretful smile and went to find Rayn.

$$\dashv\bigcirc\vdash$$

Hopefully the frigid air would help clear his mind. Rayn walked next to him, her rifle at the ready. Her breath clouded in front of her face. The red in her hair intensified against the white of the snowy forest.

Their boots crunched in the fresh snowfall as they trailed through the black trees. Birds dug through the frosted ground for food, flying away without a sound as they walked past. It was a stoic, uncomfortable silence, like all life in the forest had a knife at its neck and a hand clamped over its mouth.

Solomand hated the deathly hush of the place. He whistled a few off-tune notes. "Solomand. Keep quiet." Rayn hissed.

"I'm trying to lighten the mood." Solomand whispered back, turning his head against a gust of bitterly icy wind that cut through him. He uttered a curse in Kree, shivering.

"What's wrong? Cursing in Slavik not going to cut it any-more?" Rayn raised an eyebrow.

"Not in this damned cold!" He took a few steps back to where she was. "Doesn't it bother you?"

"Yes. It's miserable." She spoke through chattering teeth.

"Well… you know." Solomand slipped an arm around her waist. "We could dig ourselves a nice spot to warm up in." He gave her a devilish grin.

"Really, Sol?" Rayn rolled her eyes.

"Why not?"

Her mouth opened for a moment as she raised her eyebrows. "You can't be serious."

He wasn't, but he hadn't won a smile yet. "Can't I be?" He leaned closer, his lips hovering over hers. Heat traveled through his body like a bolt of lightning as their mouths pressed together. For a moment, time pleasantly ceased to move forward.

"What's with you?" She pulled away, balancing her rifle in the crook of her arm as she shoved him with her other hand. There was a lightheartedness in her eyes. It reminded him of when they were younger, experiencing fleeting moments of normalcy. To see that light in her eyes every day would warm him more than any fire could.

"We are supposed to be checking the area." Both hands settled on her and she brought it further into her shoulder.

"For what?" Solomand glanced at the empty forest. "Snow?" His arm hooked around her as he rested his neck on her shoulder. "I believe that we are." He kissed her neck. "All alone."

"Sol." She shrugged him away. "Stop!"

"You're no fun." He pulled her close, giving her a kiss on the forehead before letting her go.

There was a flush of red on her cheeks. "Check the ridge." She nodded to the top of the tree line. "I'll cover you."

"Anything for you." Solomand gave her a crooked grin and limped up the snowbank at a swift pace. Wind blew up the snow in waves, and the white mountains rose in the distance, climbing up the horizon like unnaturally stacked rocks. Solomand shivered, shrinking back into his coat. "Snow, what a surprise." He started walking back down the hill.

Rayn lowered her rifle to her side. "Well, at least we know we're alone now." Her eyes caught his, and she quirked a smile. "That is *not* an invitation."

Solomand was trying to think up a clever response when his eyes caught movement in the trees. The white ground shifted and blurred. He realized too late it was a wolf—alarmingly large and pure white. Fear, colder than the air, coiled a hand around his throat as the beast tore through the snow straight at Rayn. At the sound of heavy panting, Rayn whirled around. The wolf bared its teeth and snapped at her arm as she threw it up to ward the animal off.

"Rayn!"

She fell under the animal's weight, yelling out in pain. Solomand jerked out his pistol, taking aim at the wolf's shoulder. It was a clean shot, echoing across the landscape. Blood splattered sickeningly bright on the frozen ground. The wolf jerked in response, letting out a growl as its teeth clamped tighter. Rayn let out another yell, gritting her teeth as she beat the animal over the head with her rifle. Solomand took aim again. But the wolf's head was too close to Rayn for comfort. "Shit." He ran forward, bashing the animal in the throat until it released its teeth. Solomand pulled her back across the snow, positioning himself between her and the animal. Its pale eyes fixed on him. Blood matted its fur, splattering on the ground as it snorted. Pawing at the snow, it raised its blood-stained snout upwards, letting out a mournful howl.

"Solomand—get down!" Ivan was running from the airship. Solomand couldn't bring himself to move, though. There was more howling in the distance. Ivan's knife flew past and stuck in the wolf's head. The animal collapsed, its howl silenced. Ivan was there, pulling his knife from the animals' neck and cleaning his blade before returning it to his boot. "It has called pack—they will come now." Ivan scooped Rayn into his arms while Solomand stood there, dazed, unable to move.

"Sol—we have to get back to airship!" Ivan yelled at him. Solomand nodded, forcing himself to follow. It wasn't really him moving. This was all a horrible dream.

"My rifle!" Rayn was reaching for the gun as she grimaced in pain.

Ivan was already running toward the airship, holding her to him like she weighed nothing. Solomand picked up the gun; it was still wet with blood—it soaked through his gloves, sticky and warm. There was more howling now, coming from the ridge.

"Sol—*tranjiye*—run! Now!" Ivan yelled over his shoulder. Solomand looked up to see four more of the massive wolves starting down the hill.

He raised Rayn's rifle to his shoulder and fired a shot at one of them before turning and running after Ivan. The animals yapped back and forth to each other, making it sound like there were ten instead of four. Solomand struggled to run in the thick snow, cursing to himself all the way. *Just a little further.* Ivan was already at the airship, dashing into the open bay doors. Kicking up mounds of snow, his toes frozen, Sol hurried to catch up, clambering into the cargo bay, whirled around and flipped the toggle to close the doors. Nothing happened. The wolves kept coming, moving faster.

"Work, damn you!" Solomand gnashed his teeth, flipping the toggle at least twenty times (exactly what Jank had warned him not to do). He pounded on the panel with his fists, breathing out resolutely. Nothing happened. He whirled around, raising Rayn's rifle to his shoulder.

The first shot hit the front wolf directly in the shoulder. It snarled at him and kept coming. Solomand's hands shook as he reloaded and emptied the remaining rounds into the wolves. A grinding noise sounded and lights flashed on the panel. The door slid shut as the wolves slammed into it, howling and clawing.

Solomand stood there, staring at the puddles of melting snow beneath his feet. "Those things are…" His heart pounded wildly in his ears as he searched for an adequate word to describe the beasts.

"Monsters?" Ivan offered. "Yes. He was busy cutting Rayn's shredded sleeve from her arm; her coat already lay next to her as she leaned against a supply crate. Pale and startled, she glanced down at her arm, then squeezed her eyes shut.

Why didn't you do anything?! It happened too fast for him to react. But that was no excuse.. Rayn cursed as Ivan cleaned the injury; large puncture marks oozed blood. "Sorry," Ivan said. He gave Solomand a worried sideways glance. Sol kept waiting for Ivan to say this was all Solomand's fault, that he should have waited; but the lecture did not come.

"Well—looks like you found something out there after all." Hydra stepped inside and Solomand jerked his head up.

"Out!" He stormed toward her, pointing at the door. "Now. Or I'll throw your ass out to keep the wolves company!"

Hydra jumped back. Eyes wide with shock, she slunk away. Solomand went back to watching Ivan from the corner of his eye, not wanting to see how bad the bite was.

"Sol." His chest tightened when Ivan said his name, looking up with a calm, gray stare. "I need your help."

Solomand swallowed his feelings and knelt down. "Squeeze her arm to make blood come out."

"What?" Sol gasped.

"To help wash out infection. Do it." Ivan grabbed Sol by the wrist and moved his hand to Rayn's exposed arm. Solomand cringed, his fingers trembling as his grip tightened. Rayn's skin was slick with blood. Applying more pressure, he turned away as more blood poured out onto his hands. He kept his eyes locked on hers, trying to fight back the nausea.

Rayn grimaced, gasping out, "You look like you're going to be—sick."

"What is wrong with you, *lochek*? You are green." Ivan moved Sol gently out of the way, dousing Rayn's arm with another splash of antiseptic before wrapping it in gauze.

Gritting her teeth, Rayn turned to him. "Say something—stupid."

Solomand's mouth was dry. "Sorry. Are you calling me stupid, or you want me to say something stupid?" He undid the top button of his coat with shaking fingers, realized they were still damp with blood, and dropped them.

Rayn gave him a half-hearted smile. "Pick one."

Why did she want him to talk? For once, he did not feel like it. "Ok..." Ivan motioned for him to hold the gauze in place. His mind was blank. "The mountains are rather beautiful off in the distance... fancy settling down here?"

Rayn shook her head.

"Done." Ivan sat back on his heels.

Solomand let out a shaky breath, reaching for a rag to wipe his hands on. "Well. That wasn't so bad, huh?" The words were hollow.

Ivan frowned. "Wolf bites have danger of infection. We must watch closely."

Rayn winced, wiping sweaty hair from her face. "So we watch it." She shrugged, not taking it as seriously as Ivan wanted her to; Solomand could tell by the look on his face.

He looked away from her. "There is something else you need to know."

"What?" She frowned with worry.

Ivan cleaned his hands on a towel before balling it up and tossing it in the pile of blood-stained swabs and shreds of clothing. "Jank made stupid mistake."

Solomand finished unbuttoning his coat and slipped it off. "Ivan. You're going to have to be specific as to what you're talking about."

Ivan looked uncomfortably at Rayn and cleared his throat. "Blood test he make, it was wrong."

Solomand struggled to remember what Ivan was talking about. Ivan looked from Rayn to him like they should understand the severity of this. "The test he made... it was positive."

Positive? It took Solomand a moment before the implications all came crashing, crystal clear. He looked at Rayn, his eyes widening. "You mean we're... she's..." All the reasons this was not a good time were dwarfed for a moment in a warm rush of excitement.

Rayn's hand went to her mouth. There were tears in her eyes. Solomand looked up at Ivan. "Are you sure this isn't some mistake?" Sol asked.

"No mistake." Ivan crossed his arms, the trace of a smile forming on his face. "Congratulations—despite *circumstances*." He glanced down at Rayn, his grim look returning. "Now maybe you understand. Is too dangerous for you to leave this airship." He lifted her from the ground and started up the stairs.

Chapter 33

TRISTAN

A SHRILL WHISTLE blasted through the prison block, signaling the break of dawn. Those who were on the morning shift had little time to roll out of their bunks and collect their meager rations before reporting to the mine for duty. The lock on the rusted panel of the cell door clicked open. Tristan and Zee stepped into the hall and made their way to join the rest of Nikola's crew. How many days had they been there? How many days did they have left?

Nikola gripped his shoulder from behind. "Tristan, a word." It was strange to hear his name spoken. Nikola dragged him into the shadows. One hand came to rest on the wall over Tristan's head. "We must leave. Today."

"What?" A jolt fired through Tristan's heart. "But, Nikola, we are not ready!"

I am not ready. There was no *we* about it.

A man and a woman shuffled past, and Nikola's hand lowered to grip Tristan by the collar and shove him against the wall, uttering Slavik threats. The two quickened their steps, hurrying to be past Nikola and his ill temper. "Sorry." He released Tristan, giving him an apologetic punch on the arm before turning grim. "They are coming."

No. "Already?" Tristan rubbed his shoulder, contemplating what damage would have been done if the big Northman hit him in earnest.

"The dungeon master. He told me to watch you two. That you would be released to custody of important visitor soon." Nikola scowled, his fingers curling into a fist. "There is more. Other guards talk of airship crashing in the Amezwal forest. Something has stirred wolves there."

Tristan's heartbeat quickened, first with hope, followed by a sharp, stabbing dread. This is what Aleksei wanted. Tristan felt a sinking, sick feeling, wishing that Solomand, Ivan, and the others were far from this place. Aleksei meant to kill them all. But this time, Tristan would not be the one waiting while the others worked to save him. This time would be different. "Alright." He said hoarsely. "What do you want me to do?"

"For now, join the others." Nikola nodded down the hall. "I will speak with you soon." He strode purposefully in the opposite direction, disappearing around a corridor as other prisoners continued to straggle out of their cells. Fear clenching his heart, Tristan followed them, Zee at his side.

In the cafeteria, as the others sat shoveling gray, tasteless porridge into their mouths, Tristan calculated the negligible odds that they would survive the next twenty-four hours. The clank of spoons on bowls and muffled conversations blended together—an echoing murmur in the background. How many of them would be dead when their plan was executed? A bone floated to the top of the gruel and he pushed it to the edge of the bowl. None of these prisoners looked like they were here by accident. Why did it have to plague his conscience so?

"Otvali." A hand clamped on his shoulder. The spoon fell from Tristan's fingers as he jumped. "Eat." Nikola frowned at his tray of untouched food. "You need your strength." He left, walking up and down the rows of tables, giving the other prisoners intimidating looks.

"Strength," Tristan muttered. He took a bite of a stale slice of bread, washing it down with a gulp of water; the rest, he slid into his coat pocket.

A whistle sounded, and Nikola started yelling orders for them to move out. Clearing their trays, Tristan and Zee made sure they were the last to file from the room. Steam escaped from a shoddy fitting in the aged pipes on the wall with a sinister hiss as they passed. Sidestepping, Tristan's heart leaped within his chest, pounding with overtaxing rapidness.

"Tris? You ok?" Zee nudged him with her elbow.

Probably not. Tristan momentarily smiled down at her. "I'm fine. Let's go." He guided her down the dark hall toward their uncertain fate, wishing he had the faith in their escape plan that she obviously did.

Heat compounded the scent of sweat and coal dust as they crossed the threshold to the boiler room. Prisoners from the previous shift stumbled past; listless—slick with sweat and covered in grime. They were all marked with the same exhaustion, resigned to the fate of their endless toil in the depths of the mountain. Would he look the same if they stayed long enough?

Nikola pointed a finger at Zee, barking an order for her to tend the boiler. Without hesitation, she scrambled to wrap her hands with strips of cloth to prevent blisters as she took her place on the mound of coal. Fire reflected in her eyes as she hurled shovelful after shovelful of the black fuel into the furnace.

I can't leave her alone. What if things went wrong? Anxiety claimed more ground as he paused on the first step, looking back and forth from the dark mouth of the mine to the girl.

"*Move!*" Nikola yelled at him in Slavik, shoving him roughly from behind. Tristan tripped down the steps and would have fallen the entire way if Nikola had not grabbed his arm and held him an inch from the ground before yanking him back up. Air turned cold as they reached the heart of the mine—the heat and light from the boiler room like a distant star in a black sky.

The others had already set down their lanterns. A chorus of metal picks chipping away at the coal carried throughout the cavern. Nikola's grip tightened on Tristan's arm as he eased him against the wall. "Stay out of my way," he hissed, drawing his knife. "We have ten minutes before patrol returns," he whispered and edged past Tristan.

Tristan's pulse ratcheted up another level. Ten minutes before the guards would see Zee doing what she shouldn't be. It was such a brief span of time. Light from lamps across the uneven surface of the walls silhouetted shapes of men as they sank into the rhythm of swinging in their quest to survive another day in Byorn. If they only knew, their sentence was at an end.

A flash of light reflected off the steel blade of Nikola's knife like a bolt of lightning. Tristan's hand left the comfort of the wall as he crept forward. His foot found a dip in the ground and he fell onto his knees. Hands catching the rough surface, he brought his head up. The cavern grew darker as the lamps dimmed, one by one. A muffled cry followed annoyed shouting. Two shadows connected for a moment on the wall. Their struggle was over in an instant. The smaller framed man slid from the larger one's grip and disappeared as his attacker slunk away.

Fumbling forward, Tristan's knees and hands scraped against the rock surface. The noise of men working diminished. Nikola was not wasting any time. When Tristan dared to glance up again, he saw the foreman not far away; his arms were around one man's neck and his back was toward Tristan. Behind Nikola, a familiar figure inched forward, a jagged rock in his raised hand; Deyan.

Nikola, look out! The words would not force their way from his throat. Without thinking, Tristan jumped to his feet, picking up a fallen pickaxe as he charged forward, swinging the flat end of the tool. It met the side of Deyan's head with a gut-wrenching *thwack!* Teetering to the side, Deyan fell back, swearing.

Letting the body of the man in his arms slump to the ground, Nikola spun around. Deyan was struggling to stand. A knife flew from Nikola's hand, burying itself in Deyan's heart. He fell back and went still.

Panting, Tristan let the tool slip from his fingers. It clattered to the ground as he stared, light-headed and sick, at the gruesome scene before him.

Nikola gave Tristan an appraising look as he retrieved his knife, wiping the blood from it on Deyan's own shirt before returning it to his boot. "Good work... *for someone who does not stomach death.*" He clapped a hand on Tristan's shoulder, glancing at the lifeless prisoner. "*It seems I am in debt to you.*"

Gulping, Tristan could not tear his eyes from the expanding stain on Deyan's shirt. He swayed slightly and leaned on the nearest wall for support. "*We will call it even,*" he replied.

Nikola bent over and turned the flame up on a lamp, making it easier to see the carnage. "Wait here. I will get girl." Nikola dashed back up the stairs, moving faster than Tristan thought a man of his size should be able to.

A metallic smell filled the cool air, one he wished he was not familiar with. Breaking into a sweat, Tristan loosened his collar, leaning one hand on the wall. A shiver passed over his damp skin.

Breathe. It was ironic he should again practice the mantra that once was a daily, desperate prayer for more time. One more day, one more week, another year—it was never enough.

The shadows of the lamp danced across the trail of bodies scattered around the room. Where was Nikola? Tristan took a shaky breath, focusing his eyes on the stairs—and only the stairs. He should have returned with Zee by now. The pounding of blood in his ears felt like the urgent countdown of a stopwatch. *One minute.* His hand went to his breast pocket, where in ordinary circumstances his watch would be. Counting down the passing seconds in his head, he made his way to back to the stairwell, stepping over fallen tools, a body and blood-stained rocks. Trembling, he peered up into the boiler room. An inviting heat poured from the doorway. There was no noise of shoveling coal. No voices—nothing.

"Damn it all!" Tristan seized the rotting wooden rail with one hand as he cleared the steps two at a time. His legs ached and his lungs were fit to burst when he reached the top.

"Tristan!" Zee whipped her head up to look at him as she struggled to pull a lever behind the boiler. "I can't get it to move!" With her entire body, she strained to make the relief valve move, to no avail. In the doorway leading to the hall, Nikola grappled with another guard.

Rushing forward, Tristan seized the rusted metal and threw all his strength into making the valve move. It gave with a grating screech. Steam hissed from a gap in the cracked seal. Nikola raised his voice. "I told you to wait, *Otvali*." His hands twisted and there was a sickening crack as the guard's neck broke. He heaved the man's limp form down the stairs to the mine. Voices shouted down the hall.

"Go!" Nikola motioned Zee and Tristan ahead of him.

Adrenalin pumping through his body, Tristan flew down the stairs and jumped over the dead guard at the bottom. *What's one more dead body?* It was a painful thought, and nausea hit him sharply as it entered his mind. "Quickly!" Nikola shoved a lamp into his hand. "Follow me."

Zee gripped his arm, pulling him along. Clambering over stacks of rocks, they followed Nikola into the darker edge of the cavern and along a faint path winding away from the center of the mine. Deafening noise from the explosion reverberated through the cavern. The ground shook. Rocks and debris rained down behind them. Glancing over his shoulder, Tristan saw the last traces of light from the prison blocked completely as the ceiling continued to cave in.

That's it then. For good or worse, there was no turning back.

Chapter 34

RAYN

A QUEASY LIGHTHEADEDNESS spread from Rayn's throat, toying with the rhythm of her breath. Was it residual effects from the wolf bite or Ivan telling her she was going to have a child? Either way, she remembered something else. It was a memory clear enough she didn't wonder if it were only a dream or merely the work of her imagination.

A tall man with broad-shoulders gripped her small, five-year-old hand in his. Birds dove around the canopy of trees in a clear blue sky and waves crashed nearby. The man with the falcon on his shoulder spoke in a quiet tone—days before they had been shouting, she remembered. "Ben." He ran a hand through Smokey-black hair. "I am sorry for losing my temper."

Ben—her father—nodded, his hand tightening around hers. "I deserved it."

Lemuel hesitated, his gaze falling as his head bowed. "I—I know I don't deserve to ask anything of you."

Ben's face twisted into a crooked scowl. "Lemuel. This is me you're talking to. Ask it."

Lemuel's eyes raised. "In Corcyra, there is a boy." He looked at Rayn and worried lines formed on his brow. "He and his parents, they mean a great deal to me." He spoke in a hoarse whisper. Like this was a secret only the two of them should ever know.

191

Ben let go of Rayn's hand. "You want me to look out for them."

The falcon on Lemuel's shoulder careened its head and took to the sky with a screech. Eyeing it as it sailed above the trees, Lemuel did not respond. His thumb rubbed at the ring on his right finger and his eyes squeezed shut. "Yes." It was obvious he did not want to say it. "Only, it is too much to ask. It could comprom—"

"Shit on that, Lemuel! Those damned Morai have gotten to you." Ben tapped the side of his head. "Of course I will do it. Whatever it is. I've made mistakes and we haven't always gotten along. But all the same, we're friends—you remember what friends are, don't you?"

Lemuel slipped his hand in the pocket of his coat, staring wistfully in the distance. "Not really."

Ben laughed. "I'll have to remind you then." He ruffled Rayn's hair. "Come on, Sunbird. So long, Lemuel."

The next thing Rayn knew, she was in her bed. Solomand was there. "About time you woke up. I sent Ivan for some water."

She sat up. There was a brightness along with concern in the steely blue of his eyes that wasn't there before. Rayn couldn't help but smile at him. "Lucky it was my right arm that bastard tried to bite off." The memory fresh in her mind. Should she tell him about it?

Solomand paled. "For the love of god, Rayn, don't joke about it. Especially around Ivan. No humor whatsoever."

Rayn suddenly remembered Ivan's promise. *You will not leave this airship.* She kicked off the blankets, swinging her legs over the side of the bed. For now, Lemuel Falcon was forgotten. "I feel fine, Sol." She said sharply. "I'm not a damn invalid."

Solomand shifted closer to her. He took her gently by the shoulders. "I know that, Rayn. Ivan is right, though," he said softly.

Rayn pulled away, hiding the pain in her arm as she got up. So what if they were right? They weren't going to lock her on this airship, while the rest of them went out to face the wolves, Aleksei, and everything else. She would show them both; she didn't need looking after.

-≼○≽-

In the cabin, Hydra held the speaker of her radio to her ear, turning the knob, listening and looking like her mind was a million miles away. Will was not there; he must have slipped away to get a break from her constant harassment. Ivan's back straightened in the chair he sat in and he stood up. "You should be resting." He looked meaningfully at the bandaged arm she held to her side.

Rayn sighed dramatically. "It's not like I'm going to die."

Ivan's jaw clenched. "I do not exaggerate."

"I'm getting a lot of interesting chatter from Byorn's radio channel." Hydra spoke up.

"Such as?" Solomand came into the room, looking like he hated having to ask her this. "And is this public knowledge? How did you get on their radio?"

She shrugged. "Freelance agents know how to tap into all the other channels, even if they're blocked. Just one of our many talents." She glanced around, probably looking for Will, but returned to her radio in disappointment when she realized he wasn't there.

"Anyway, there are some exciting goings on over there. Some kind of explosion happened on the inside. There was a cave-in." She chewed on her lip. "How unfortunate, and they are expecting an important foreign visitor from the Fifth Continent—a governor from the sound of it—any day now."

A chill ran up Rayn's spine. Stefan LeFrost. It had to be. So close, after everything he had done to them? Coming here would be his last mistake if she had anything to do with it.

"Anyone dead?" Rayn asked.

"Some." Hydra shrugged. "Apparently, an entire crew got buried in the mine. They seem to be arguing about the missing foreman. Apparently he was an Ice Wolf. And two of the prisoners on his crew were going to be turned over to these visitors."

"It couldn't be Aleksei?" Rayn felt herself leaning and reached for a chair. Sol guided her to sit before she fell.

"No." Ivan's frown deepened. "If explosion was intentional, maybe they found a way out. This foreman probably helped them. Did they say his name?"

Hydra shook her head.

"We have to go out there," Solomand said.

Rayn went to cross her arms, then remembered about the wolf bite. She glared at Sol. *I'm not staying behind.* Not this time. "If we know he's out there, why don't you let me take a position in the hills and pick him off. It would make everything a hell of a lot easier."

Ivan's chiding look fell to her arm. "Out of question."

Rayn rolled her eyes, knowing he was going to say that. "Let Sol do it then. He's not as good of a shot as me, but it's worth a try."

"No." Ivan shook his head.

"Why not?" Rayn and Sol both asked.

"Don't tell me you think it wouldn't be fair," Sol added.

Giving Sol a look like he said the most maddeningly stupid thing he'd ever heard, Ivan shook his head. "I do not give damn about *fair*. If there were even slim chance of success, I would say go ahead. Unfortunately, Aleksei is not idiot. These hills are dangerous and you do not know them like I do. Or Aleksei. He would not put himself in a vulnerable position."

Solomand ran a hand along the back of his neck, looking defeated. "Alright. We'll go first thing in the morning." He looked at Ivan. "Whenever the expert says it's safest."

Ivan raised an eye. "Is never safe."

Chapter 35

TRISTAN

CAVE WALLS NARROWED, pressing in as Zee and Tristan followed Nikola deeper into the mountain. It seemed a lonely place for a tomb; no grass or flowers to entice a passing bird to keep you company while you slept. Tristan's fingertips trailed along the coarse rock as he thought of his father's garden. *If I could see the sun shine just once more.* He laughed to himself, recalling how many times he went to bed with the same prayer on his lips, only to wake up the next day and long for death to take away the pain.

Fingers tightening around the handle of the lamp, he kept moving. The walls came together sharply, forming a dark doorway. Nikola came to a stop. He bent down and picked up two packs that sat at the entrance. He handed the smaller one to Zee. Tristan raised an eyebrow. "You're prepared, aren't you?"

"I told you." Nikola slung the heavier pack on his shoulder. "I think of this for long time. I knew Aleksei would come back, eventually." He frowned. "I swore he would not find me so easily."

"No," Tristan murmured as Nikola stepped into the passage. "I don't think he would."

Zee didn't hesitate to follow their guide into the darkness. Holding his breath, Tristan went after her. Rocks grazed his arms on either side when the walls drew together. The sound of his own breathing and the scraping of their shoes on the ground was almost maddening.

As they advanced deep into the passage, their lamps slowly burned the last traces of oil. Nikola talked to Zee—asking her if she knew how to use a knife.

"Not really. Not for fighting," she said. Tristan kept close to the sound of her voice, feeling his way through the darkness.

"Did Ivan not teach you how to fight?"

"No. Ivan wasn't around much."

"Oh."

Tristan focused on the sound of their voices, pictured what their faces looked like.

"*Otvali? Talk to me.*" Nikola called in Slavik.

"*D-don't feel like t-talking.*" Tristan's teeth chattered. His legs were stiff, chilled to the bone, hands aching from cold.

"Don't worry. It can't be much further." Nikola sounded optimistic to hear Tristan's voice.

"Wh-what's to w-worry about?" Shivering, Tristan rubbed his arms and leaned against the wall. *Only a moment.* When was the last time he drank? A rapid heartbeat and dry throat suggested it had been too long.

Need to keep moving. Thoughts bounced around his head, sluggish and unfinished. How far away were his companions? Plodding forward with one hand on the wall, he listened for their footsteps. A stiffness settled in his neck, and he stopped again. Was that the sound of movement, or merely a ringing in his ears?

"Tristan!" Zee's voice carried through the tunnel. Her fingers wound around his arm. "We made it! Nikola found the way out!" Her words spilled out, breathless and excited.

"Really?" Tristan's own voice sounded like a croak.

"Come on!" She tugged at his arm, pulling him along with her. He tried to keep pace with the girl's rapid steps, but knew she was slowing to meet his own lethargic pace. Shouldn't they have found Nikola by now?

"Come on—it's this way!" Zee was dragging him up a pile of rocks. His vision blurring, Tristan would have fallen on his face if it weren't for Nikola grabbing him and roughly hoisting him the rest of the way.

Cold air hit him like a punch in the chest and he dropped to his knees, hands burning from cold as they rested in snow. Nikola draped a coat over him and pushed a flask of water to his lips. "Don't die now, Otvali."

Tristan took the flask from Nikola and thirstily drank. The water soothing his parched throat and calming his pulse. He gasped for air in between drinks. "I suppose that would be ill timing, wouldn't it?"

Light from the two moons glistened on snow-covered hills, making it look like they stood on a mountain made of diamonds. Below, the dark trees stretched to the sky, dotted with endless stars in a backdrop of perfectly blended hues of blue and black. It was not sunshine, but it was breathtakingly beautiful. Another reprieve. The overwhelming sensation of thankfulness filled his heart as his eyes squeezed shut. In that moment, he did not feel like life was an endless cascade of missteps fated to end in misery. At that moment, he did not feel so alone.

"*Otvali?*" Nikola gave him a worried look. "I said we need to find shelter. Quickly. Unless you wish to die?"

"No." Tristan gave the foreman a weak smile. "I suppose I don't." In fact, he wished very much to live.

Nikola frowned as a fierce wind cut across the mountain. "I think it best to stay in cave this night." He fixed a worried look on Tristan again. "When daylight comes will be safer to make our way off the mountain." Taking Tristan by the arm, he lowered him back into the opening of the cavern. Zee scurried down at his side and they moved down the pile of rocks before Nikola dropped to join them.

The moonlight was too faint to see, but they could hear Nikola fumbling in his pack and tearing what sounded like paper. Sparks flew off a flint as he worked to light a fire close to the exit. Flames took to the twisted paper, curling the edges and working to light a small pile of coal. When it was burning to his satisfaction, Nikola motioned Tristan to come closer. The warmth felt like heaven. All three held their hands over the flames, soaking in the heat. "We will not freeze tonight, at least." Nikola gave Tristan another worried glance. He may as well have said he thought Tristan was going to keel over at any moment.

I'd probably think the same in his shoes. After eating a meal of dried fruit and jerky, he lay curled up in the coat Nikola gave him. Shivering soon subsided, and he fell asleep listening to the wind howl overhead.

When he woke up, the fire had died to embers and Nikola was gone. Rubbing his eyes, Tristan sat up, letting the coat fall from him. He slipped his arms into the sleeves as he stood.

A large man, dressed in a hooded white coat, dropped into the cavern. Just waking, Zee's eyes shot open. Her screams echoed through the cave as she scrambled to her feet. With a gloved hand, Nikola pulled the hood from his head. There was a sadness in his brown eyes as he looked at her. "*Gera djeya (little girl).*" He spoke to her in a pained tone. "I am *not* Aleksei."

Zee nodded, furiously wiping a tear from the corner of her eye. His face hardening once again, Nikola turned to Tristan. "We will make our way to Chroburough. Here." He gave them both woolen shirts, pants, and a pair of boots. "You will need these."

Tristan held the clothes up, raising an eyebrow. "Where did you get these?"

"Not important. Put them on."

"If you say so…" Tristan exchanged a doubtful look with Zee as he removed both the coats he wore. Zee retreated into the tunnel to change. "Why Chroburough?" Tristan asked as he slipped into the layers of clothing.

"Will be harder for Aleksei to find any of us in Chroburough." Nikola pulled three apples from his pack. He tossed one to Tristan and one to Zee as she emerged from the tunnel.

Tristan turned the red fruit around in his hand before taking a bite from it. An uneasy feeling settled in his stomach with the fruit. It felt like they were running away. He kept this thought to himself. For now, following Nikola's lead was the best they had at survival.

They finished their meager breakfast and went out into the bitter cold of the northern mountain to meet the sun.

Sun played off the brilliant white. Faint outlines of the moons could still be seen in the blue of the sky as they traveled down the mountain and skirted the edge of the forest that bordered the way to Chroburough. Twisted black branches housed birds, chirping warnings to their children as the stranger's passed. It differed greatly from the green lands of Lyonese, but beautiful in its own way. Tristan admired the way the trees contrasted against the paleness of the country until he saw a color that had no natural place there. Freezing in place, he reached out and grabbed Zee.

Up ahead lay wreckage of a vehicle like the sled the militsya had brought them in to Byorn. It was a mangled heap in a thicket of thorns. He would not have noticed it at all were it not for the red spatter on the ground.

Nikola saw it, too. "Wait here." Knife in hand, he crept forward to investigate. When Nikola came back, he did not look happy. "Militsya. Their throats have been slit."

"Do you think it was...?" Tristan's hand tightened on Zee's arm before he realized it. He released his hold.

"Aleksei?" Nikola slid his knife into his belt forcefully, glaring across the forest like a wolf might jump at him. "Yes. I do."

Not here already! Tristan felt his heart pound at an unhealthy pace. "Why would he kill them?"

"Wolves do not get along with militsya, or guards of Byorn usually. *We* are only law in wilderness." He swept his hand wide. "Anyone else we see as imposters." His eyes moved to Zee, and the furrow in his brow deepened. "*But more than that, Aleksei enjoys killing. If you have not realized that by now.*"

Zee's eyes flashed at Nikola. "You are saying something you don't think I should hear. Aren't you?"

"Zee. That's enough," Tristan said gently.

"I'm not some stupid kid who can't see what's going on in front of my nose." Her voice raised.

Nikola made a noise that might have been a laugh. "Little girl is right." The corner of his mouth twitched into something like a smile. "You are right. But I do not try to keep things from you. Sometimes is easier for me to speak in my own tongue. Understand?"

The girl nodded, her eyes dropping. "I'm sorry," she mumbled.

Stooping, Nikola laid a hand on her shoulder. "Don't be. Your spirit will keep you alive in this country." He turned his attention back to the forest. "We should not keep on this path."

"What do we do then?" Tristan hated not having a plan to work with. He curled his toes inside his boots to make the blood flow.

"We travel further up mountain. Will make the trip take longer, but is safest way."

As they left the forest's edge to take the higher road, the uneasy feeling grew inside Tristan. Aleksei would arrive at Byorn soon, if he hadn't already. When he did not locate his prize, he would no doubt take a keen interest in the downed airship the guards would surely tell him about. He would find Solomand and the others.

What am I doing? Guilt grew heavier with every step Tristan took across the snow. Glancing over his shoulder at Zee, he quickened his steps to catch up with the foreman.

"*Nikola.*" He started the conversation in Slav.

"*Yes?*" Nikola gave Tristan a sideways glance.

"*I need you to do something for me.*"

"*What is it, Otvali?*"

Hands deep in his pockets, Tristan fought to keep from shivering. "*At nightfall, I am leaving. Take the girl to Chroburough—get her far away from Aleksei.*"

Nikola jerked his head to look at Tristan. "*Where do you plan on going?*"

"*Aleksei will not follow either of you when he finds me.*" Tristan felt the cold recede as the fire of determination worked its way through his veins.

Falling back into step, Nikola relaxed his shoulders. "*You want to die?*"

"*No. But I'll do what I must.*" Running away and leaving Solomand to face whatever came next was not something he could ever live with doing. If Zee was safe, that was all he cared about. All those years his friends centered their life on keeping him safe when it would have been much easier to their well-being to abandon him. They could have left Lyonese long ago if it were not for him. Now that he'd decided, all doubt was gone. This was the right thing to do. He gave Nikola a wan smile. "*They are my friends. I will face whatever they do.*"

"*Tristan…*" The sadness that slipped out from time to time entered Nikola's eyes again. "*You can't beat him.*"

"*I know.*" His gaze met with Nikola, resolute, unblinking. "*But I can make sure he never harms her again.*"

Nikola looked like he was thinking. At length, he nodded. "*Aleksei will never find the girl. I promise you this. Hiding is what I am good at.*" He fixed a vacant stare on the ground in front of him.

"*Thank you.*" Tristan breathed in relief. "*I am in your debt.*"

"*No. No one owes me any debts.*" Nikola chewed his bottom lip. He reached into his boot and withdrew his curved dagger. "*You have the heart of Wolf. Take this with you.*" He held it out, handle first. "*It belonged to a friend. And now, I give it to you… a friend.*"

Taking the knife, Tristan's jaw tightened. "Thank you."

Nikola gripped his hand once before they walked on in silence.

Solomand. I'm sorry. Tristan glanced down into the shadowy trees, looking like hands twisted toward the sky, hoping that his friend would understand.

Chapter 36

WILL

WILL SAT ON the bed in his cabin, methodically twirling an unlit cigarette through his fingers. Here was the only place he seemed able to avoid Hydra. She confused him. He wanted to be around her and far away from her at the same time. His mind quickly went to Aleksei. If he was out there in the snow, Will was going to find him and tear off his head. Clenching his fingers, he crushed the fragile paper of the cigarette within his fist as if it were Aleksei's head.

"Hiding from your devoted harpy?" Solomand walked in.

"Captain." Will moved to stand.

"Don't give me that shit, Will. It's *Sol*." Solomand looked injured. "And don't get up."

"I'm sorry." Will sat back down.

"And *don't* say you're sorry." Solomand sank to the bed next to him and exhaled heavily. He brought his hands up to cradle his head. "Listen, Will…" Solomand massaged his temple. "I have a favor to ask."

Will let the remnants of crushed cigarette fall through his fingers into a pile on the floor. "Sol, you know I'd do anything you ask me."

"Yes. I know." Solomand stood and paced the length of the small cabin. "That's the problem." He threw an arm up in frustration. "I don't want you to do anything because you think you owe it to me. You don't owe me anything. I don't want you to do anything because I asked you to. You don't want to do it, then say no."

Will raised his gaze to meet his friend and maintained what he hoped was an earnest look. "Alright." It felt bad to lie. Barring anything outrageous, Will couldn't say no to Solomand. They both knew it.

"You know about Rayn."

Will suspected what Solomand was going to ask. "Yes." He pushed the flecks of tobacco around with the toe of his boot.

"She's not going to listen, you know. Impossibly stubborn! She'll go out there with us no matter what I, or anyone else says." He drummed his fingers repeatedly on the side of his leg, biting his lip as he looked up guiltily. "She can't go out there, Will."

"You want me to make sure she stays on the airship," Will said. Solomand was taking too long to get to the point.

"I know how you feel about this Slavik bastard." Solomand rubbed at his forehead. He looked tired—older, like the stress of everything had caught up to him; always wanting to fix everything, even what he hadn't broken.

Will glanced up at the ceiling. Sol probably didn't know just how badly he wanted to snap Aleksei's neck. He wanted to say no. "Alright, Sol. I'll keep her on the airship." Visions of revenge dwindled to disappointment.

"Thank you." Solomand breathed in relief. His grateful tone made Will's rising resentment dissipate. "Do you want to get something to eat? Better than your own cooking."

Will cracked a smile. "No, I would rather stay here for a while."

"Ah, you are hiding from the harpy then." Solomand paused, his hand on the door.

"Something like that."

"Alright." Solomand gave him a somber look. "But next time, I won't take any excuse. Deal?"

Will gave the captain a nod. "Deal, Sol."

Solomand looked doubtful, but he left. Will watched the lever to the door lock into place and paced the cabin slowly. His cigarette remains scattered into the cracks of the steel floor plating.

His thoughts turned to Zee again. It relieved him to delay seeing her. He was a coward—a coward who had no place here anymore. How could he face her again when he'd let her down—twice? For the first time, Will thought of the future and whether his path lay elsewhere.

⚶

The morning came too soon. Two moons hung in the pale sky over the shadowed forest. Ivan and Solomand stood at the bay, dressed in layers and heavy boots. Solomand had a rifle slung over his shoulder; one of Rayn's. He looked up at Will and held a finger to his lips as he and Ivan slipped out. She should have known better than to trust either of them to wait. Ivan had told her he would not let her off the airship.

When she came into the bay, she still looked pale, realization on her face as she saw Will leaning against the door. "You can't keep me in here!" she yelled.

A knot tied itself in Will's stomach. "I'm sorry, Rayn." He caught her in his arms as she tried to push past. "I promised," he whispered hoarsely. She gave up fighting him far too easily. Through her long-sleeves he felt the heat of her skin.

An angry tear rolled down the side of her face. "Solomand is a damn idiot if he thinks I'm going to forgive him for this," she muttered. A shiver ran through her, and he felt her consign more of her weight to his arms. Looking up to catch Hydra's gaze on the stairwell, Will scooped Rayn in his arms and carried her back to her room.

Hydra unwrapped the bandage on Rayn's arm. Having her there was a relief. She was calm and precise, not teasing him, but relaying things as matters of facts. It is what he needed, especially when he saw the telltale signs of infection in the bite marks.

"It's not bad, though. After some strong antibiotics, you'll be knocking Solomand and your Wolf friend on their asses for tricking you," Hydra chirped as she finished dressing the wound and wrapping a fresh bandage around it.

Rayn glared at her but did not reply. Her face red, she fell asleep muttering. "They're not the only ones who will be knocked on their asses."

Hydra laughed. "Your friend is quite the spitfire." She pushed her curls from her face. "She'll be resting for a while, though." She jiggled a bottle of sleep medicine and gestured to the cup of water Rayn drank from moments ago.

Will glanced at her from across the bed. "Hydra?"

"Hmm?"

"Thank you."

She smiled crookedly that was genuine, not fake like her usual one. She leaned across the bed and kissed him on the cheek. Her fingertips grazed the side of his face. "Don't mention it Cyclops."

Chapter 37

RAYN

WILL WAS SITTING at her bedside when Rayn woke up. Her head throbbed with annoying persistence. Lying in bed here, injured and half aware of what was going on, seemed a familiar feeling. The walls of the airship cabin turned into pale wood planks. For a moment, the old feeling of not knowing who she was returned. Something was wrong, but she couldn't place what it was. She was back at Port Ashbury, the place Sol had sent her to be safe as the war took a turn for the worse. Her memories were gone, and she had nothing but a name and a mysterious visitor.

⚙

Birds sang outside an open window and, instead of Will, someone else sat in a chair beside her bed. His elbow was propped on a nightstand as his head slumped forward into his hand. Thick, black tattoo bands wrapped around his wrists and up his arms, disappearing beneath his rolled-up sleeves. Lemuel Falcon.

He did not change much in her memories. His black hair and beard had grayed slightly and there were more lines on his face; otherwise, he was the same. With eyes half-closed, the thumb of his left hand toyed with the silver band on his ring finger.

Rayn hadn't remembered who he was then, but was too weak to care. "I'm sorry, Rayn." His voice was hoarse. "This is all my fault. I should never have asked your father for anything." He did not realize she could hear him.

Rayn started to close her eyes and slip back into unconsciousness when the door opened. A figure strode in. She could make out the bottom of a long crimson coat. At her bedside, Lemuel did not react. "To what do I owe the pleasure of your company, Alaric?"

"Falcon." The man's voice faltered. "You waste your time here when you have a mission to complete."

Lemuel's head raised. Menace crept into his voice. "What do you know of wasted time?"

Alaric spoke again, his voice placating. "I know the girl is important to you. I will do my best to keep Fyodor from finding out."

The chair scraped on the floor as Lemuel stood, blocking Alaric from Rayn's view. "Why bother doing me any favors? I'm just another outkast. Same as her—and everyone else."

A thick silence filled the room, followed by Alaric, who sounded surer of himself this time. "I will keep Fyodor from knowing. But you must return to your mission on Argos. If not, I'm afraid…" His voice lowered. "Fyodor knows about the boy."

"I see. So you're bringing him into this, at last."

"I am sorry. My vote was not for this, but you know what will happen if you do not return to your assignment."

"I know," Lemuel snapped. "I was planning on leaving tonight, anyway."

"Splendid." Alaric sounded relieved. "Oh, one more thing. The girl. You must tie up any lose ends with her."

"Lose ends?"

"She is Ivers' daughter—her implant. The homing device which can locate your base, you must remove it."

"Oh." Lemuel was less caustic this time.

"It is merely precautionary."

"As your leaving should be." Lemuel's voice was more tired than threatening.

"Farewell, Falcon." Alaric's voice was sympathetic. "I will keep my word."

"And I will think no more of you for doing so. Condescending Moirai kuang." Rayn was the only one to hear his insult. Alaric was already gone.

Lemuel's hand was on her wrist. The cold edge of a knife touched her skin. Rayn stirred, and the knife withdrew, her skin undamaged. "To hell with your lose ends." He slammed the knife on the nightstand. The smell of ink and gun oil swept through the room as he slipped into a long black coat. "I have to go. But I will be back when time allows. Stay strong, Sunbird." There was pain in his voice as he laid a hand on her forehead. "God knows what the boy will do if he loses you too."

⚙

Panic ceased Rayn as she sat straight up. Once that one memory worked its way through, it was like the breaking of a dam. Everything came back to her all at once—like a raging torrent, overwhelming and threatening to drag her so far down she might drown.

Sunbird. That is what her father called her when she was small. The bird's red plumage was not unlike the color of her own hair. She was five, then—running and exploring the forest and listening to the waves crashing on the distant beach. She found a nest with bright red eggs on the ground and was crying. Her father had been away then, and it was Lemuel who took the nest from her and placed it back in the tree.

"But it's not in the same spot. Do you think the mother will come back?" Rayn remembered asking.

"Of course she will. A sunbird can always find its way home." Lemuel scooped her in his arms. "And a mother will always find her young."

Rayn sniffled, rubbing the tears from her eyes. "Really?"

"Really." Lemuel gave her a sideways smile. Laying her head on his shoulder, she remembered feeling as safe as she would in her own father's arms. Benjamin Ivers.

208

She already knew what happened to him—LeFrost tricked him and Solomand into a negotiation meeting which ended with Benjamin being beaten to death.

Tears stung her eyes. Remembering hurt more than she thought it would. A face entered her mind; Stefan LeFrost. What was it he had told her? *There are losses on both sides of any war.* As if *he* wasn't responsible for ripping her family apart! Anger far stronger than any fever took over every ounce of will she had.

She glanced at Will. His arms crossed and his chin resting against his chest in the chair. Ever the dutiful soldier guarding her like he no doubt promised. It wasn't his fault.

Solomand, you ass! Rayn felt a stab of guilt for what she was about to do.

Laying back down, she flung her hand out, tipping over the jug of water on the nightstand. It clattered to the floor, and Will jumped.

"Is everything alright?"

Rayn shut her eyes, murmuring weakly for water, adding a cough for effect.

"Just a moment." Will jumped up and rushed from the room, as she knew he would.

When the door closed, she kicked off the blankets. The pain killers kept her arm from bothering her as she hurriedly slipped into cold weather clothes and grabbed her revolver.

Sorry, Will. She tiptoed out the door and down the hall. Once she was sure he could not hear her, she jumped over the railing and down the stairs and into the cargo bay.

Her hand was on the panel when a voice sounded from behind. "Going somewhere?"

Rayn whirled around to see Hydra, one hand on her hip, a chiding look on her face. "I don't think Cyclops knows you're trying to skip out on him. Does he?"

Rayn raised the revolver. If she shot the pest Hydra, it would complicate matters. She shoved the revolver in her holster. "He doesn't need to know. This is something I need to do." She slipped gloves on her hands. "You understand, I'm sure."

"I do." Hydra's reply shocked Rayn. She gave her a quick two-fingered salute, turned, and sauntered up the stairs.

Rayn flipped the toggle switch on the control panel. It wouldn't take long for Will to figure out she ran away, whether Hydra told him or not. And Jank would stick his nose in as soon as he heard someone fooling with the door. She would not give either of them time to stop her.

Cold air swept over her as the door slid open. Rayn made sure it closed and ran away from the warmth of the airship bay into the forest.

Wind stung her face as she ran—first following the trail Ivan and Sol left, then veering away from their path into the forest. It would do no good to overtake them. Sol and Ivan would both overreact and try to send her back. That would not happen.

Bending her head to hide her face, she leaned into the wind, eyes stinging. Black branches snagged at her coat, offsetting the white landscape.

LeFrost was out here. Somewhere. Last time she had not remembered what he took from her. Benjamin Ivers had only been a name. Recalling his laugh and the way he carried her on his shoulders made him more than that now. He taught her how to fix guns and showed her some things were worth risking everything to stand up for. All that mattered now was the man responsible for his cruel and unnecessary murder was going to pay.

Chapter 38

WILL

WILL HURRIED DOWN the hall, back to Rayn's room with a glass of water in hand.

"What's the rush, Cyclops?" Hydra threw an arm around his neck, causing the water to slosh over the top of the glass.

The understanding they seemed to be coming to fizzled as molten anger rolled through Will. He peeled her hand from around him. "I'm busy."

"Oh, come on, you're too serious." Hydra jumped in front of Rayn's closed door, looking up at him, batting her eyelashes.

"Move." Will pushed her aside and opened the door. "I don't have time for your games. I'm trying to help my friend..." His voice trailed off as his eyes fell on the empty bed and he immediately searched the corner table where Rayn's revolver should have been. It was gone. "You knew." His hand tightened on the half-empty glass. "Why?" Hydra backed up as he took a threatening step toward her. "She could die out there and it will be because of you, so you're going to tell me why you thought helping her leave was a good idea?"

Hydra looked up at him with a cool nonchalance. "Rayn knows what she's doing. You've no right to keep her locked up like she can't take care of herself. She'll be fi—"

Will hurled the glass of water against the wall. Hydra jumped at the sound of it shattering. She shrank away, arms reaching for a weapon as he came closer.

Fear flickered in her violet eyes as she tried to extend the distance between them. Her back found the wall and her shoulders relaxed as her hands hung at her sides. "Will, I'm sorry." Her eyes narrowed into a sincerity he doubted was real. "You underestimate your friend," she said in a small voice. Her trembling lip may have been an act, but it still made Will's temper subside. He could not bear being the one responsible for anyone's terror. Even if she deserved it. With a quick step, he walked outside the room before turning to look at her. "I think Sol is right. It's time you left."

Hydra's mouth dropped open and her eyes widened. "Will, wait!"

There was no more time for letting her play with his emotions. Will hurried to find Rayn before it was too late.

Hydra was on his heels. "I did it because I would want someone to do the same for me, OK?" She had to take three steps for every one of his to keep up. "I wouldn't want to be locked behind when I could perfectly handle myself—and Rayn is no different. Why won't you just look at me?" She maneuvered herself in front of him, forcing him to stop.

Will frowned. "Rayn is strong. But she is injured. And not thinking. You are still wasting my time. If she dies…"

"I'm sorry!" She burst out again, putting a hand on his chest.

Taking her by the shoulders, Will moved her out of his way. "I don't care what you are."

As he slipped on his coat and walked out into the frigid air, Hydra ran after him. "Wait! I can help you find her." The wind jostled her curls before she pulled her hood up.

Will followed the trail of footprints leading from the airship. "Why do you care?" He wished she would go away.

"Because you do." He felt the warmth of her hand slip around his neck as she jumped up to press her lips to his, pulling him into her forcefully. She gave him a crooked smile before running ahead of him.

Will stared after her in stunned silence. When he gathered himself enough to hurry after her, he was not as angry as he wanted to be.

A thick sheet of clouds rolling in from the North cut the morning sunlight short. The First flecks of snow felt like ice raining down on Will's face. Flurries quickly turned into a blinding sheet of heavy, white flakes falling from the sky, covering the trail he and Hydra followed. A sinking feeling weighed him down. He could not even see Hydra through the snowstorm. How was he supposed to find Rayn?

"Will." Like a ghost slipping in and out of the shadows, Hydra was suddenly at his elbow. "The trail breaks off here. We should split up. How about you go left and I take the right?" Her hand dropped to squeeze his gloved fingers.

Will nodded, squinting to see the faint line of depressions winding through the trees. Sunlight pierced through the clouds in random streaks as the snow slowed as quickly as it had started. As Hydra veered off into the twisted, black trees, Will ran, hoping it was Rayn he would find at the end of his searching.

Icy air burned his lungs, and the returning sun did nothing to warm him against the short bursts of wind tearing across the land. Rayn could not have gotten that far ahead. Panic swirled inside him like snow in the wind as thoughts of wolves and marauders lurking in the forest urged him to move faster.

Instead of a single woman making her way through the Northland with an oversized revolver, two figures materialized into view. Will quickly recognized Solomand and Ivan. Every step he took felt heavier until the two of them finally looked back as he reached them and stood, the dismayed feeling rooting him in place.

Tugging the scarf from his face, Sol exchanged a concerned look with Ivan. "Let me guess."

"I'm sorry, Sol." Will panted, clutching his aching side. "Was hoping to catch up with her—other trail went that way." He gestured in the direction Hydra had darted.

Worried lines formed on Solomand's brow as he groaned, looking in the direction Will indicated. "Damn it all, Rayn! Why do you have to be so stubborn?"

"No different from you. Is perfect match, I think." Ivan glowered beneath the hood of white leather. "Both need watching," he grumbled.

"And when exactly was it you appointed yourself as my babysitter?" Shivering, Solomand set his rifle down to readjust his scarf. "I don't need you always telling me—"

Ivan's arm shot out, shoving Sol forcefully. He lost his balance and flew forward, landing face-first in the fresh snow. As he pushed himself up, sputtering and slinging curses, Ivan yanked him back to his feet without the slightest acknowledgement.

"I will go find Rayn. You two will only slow me down." Ivan stared into the black forest before giving the two of them a severe look. "If you find Aleksei, be careful."

Will felt the anger from earlier rising once again upon hearing the name of the Slavik assassin. He gritted his teeth and nodded, hoping they did meet him.

Retrieving his rifle from the snow, Solomand gripped it in his hands. "You too," he said in a toneless voice.

Ivan disappeared into the forest, melding into the landscape like an actual wolf might.

Chapter 39

RAYN

RAYN WOVE HER way through the twisted black trees. Imagining revenge was easy. All the right words, the proper amount of displayed terror from the culprit, and everything ended in the satisfaction of a smoking barrel. Real life, however, was messier than any plan could account for.

When she saw the figure slumped against a knotty tree next to a mech sled, she wondered if it really was LeFrost. Taking a few steps further, she saw his golden eyes; the same ones as his daughter.

Another step forward. The cold of the snow melted away as anger quickened her heart. The gray of his beard reminded her even more of what he had taken. Her father never had the chance to grow old—to know his grandchild.

A tiny voice asked the question; where was his bodyguard? Rayn scanned the surrounding hills and trees, her eyes narrowing. There was no sign of the Ice Wolf. Hiding behind a tree from a one-armed woman didn't really seem Aleksei's style, from what she knew of him. What motives possessed him to abandon the groveling governor behind, she could not guess. It was of no concern to her.

Throwing her coat open, she reached across her body with her left hand and drew her revolver. The crack of the shot broke the silence of the frozen dawn. LeFrost's shoulder snapped back, and he jerked, falling against the metal side of the sled, crying out in pain.

"Damn," she muttered, lowering her hand. If she had been using her right hand, she wouldn't have missed his heart.

Fear plastered on his face, LeFrost searched until his eyes fell on her. One hand pressed to the shoulder of his white coat where a red stain was spreading. In his other hand she saw a silver-plated derringer—much like the one Minuet carried around.

"Governor, LeFrost. Where is your bodyguard?" Rayn glanced up as a flock of birds alighted with warning cries.

"The Ice Wolf? He left me here." His voice wavered.

Rayn laughed. How far the man behind the curtain had fallen. Her finger hovered on the trigger.

LeFrost's look of confusion infuriated her. Her hand trembled as she cocked the hammer of her handgun and walked forward.

She moved her head so the hood of her coat fell back, letting her red hair cascade down her shoulders. "You don't even remember who I am." She let out a sharp breath. "It's alright. I didn't remember a lot of things the last time we met." She took another step forward and pointed the revolver at his head. "But I remember now."

"Wait!" LeFrost gasped, faltering forward as he spread his arms in front of him.

"Don't come any closer," she ordered, eyeing the gun in his hand.

Removing his finger from the trigger, LeFrost froze, stammering, "I remember you—Rayn Ivers—your father was..."

"Beaten to death." Her head tilted to the side. "By order of you."

With the look of a panicked animal, LeFrost slowly moved to aim his derringer at her, still holding his injured shoulder with the other. "It does not have to be this way. We can both walk away. I can offer you and your friends a pardon."

A hollow laugh escaped Rayn's lips. "Who said I wanted one? Oh, and my name isn't Ivers anymore. It's Black." Steadying her arm from shaking, she took aim.

Fire flashed from the muzzle of the derringer as LeFrost pulled the trigger. Rayn's shot rang half a second later. The echos of the gunfire lingered through the hills. The force of the bullet knocked LeFrost further back, but he was alive. Something had thrown her aim off even more. It must have been the force of what hit her.

Staggering, she looked down at the red stain soaking her side.

"See what you've done now?" There was fear in LeFrost's eyes as he fumbled with quivering hands to reload the derringer. "We could have both walked away. Now…" He raised his arm. "Neither of us will."

"Rayn!" Ivan's voice startled her. Before LeFrost got off another shot, a knife stuck into his chest. His hands clasped it before he fell back, coughing and gasping for air until he at last grew still and lifeless eyes stared at the sky.

After all this time. LeFrost was gone. The man who hunted them for so long was lying alone in the icy wilderness of Hyperborea. It all seemed so sudden; anticlimactic, almost. Rayn let out a breath of premature relief.

The revolver fell from her hand onto the red-splattered snow, and she looked down at the blood seeping from her side.

What have I done? Gripped with a sudden terror that her decision to hunt down LeFrost had cost the life of her second child, she shook. A wave of fear forced her to her knees. Howling carried over the ridge. When Rayn turned her head to look, she saw them prowling over the hill. It looked like the snow was moving as wolves loped from tree to tree.

A hand was on her shoulder, easing her onto her back. "Ivan…" Rayn whispered his name, locking her horrified gaze with his.

"Be still." Ivan drew a smaller knife from his boot and sliced two long strips off his coat.

Cold felt like it was seeping into her bones. "But, the wolves." Her breathing grew more rapid.

"*Tishinal.*" Ivan spoke sternly before holding a finger to his lips. "Ignore them." His hand moved to look at the bullet wound in her side. "Is just a graze. But, Rayn… I have to stop the bleeding—fast." He talked while he cut the fingers off one of his gloves.

Rayn gritted her teeth and looked away. Ivan gave her an apologetic look. "*Izvinjase*," he said, then as if he forgot she didn't understand him, he added quickly, "sorry." He opened her coat and pulled her shirt up to expose the wound.

Using the fingers of his gloves and the strips of his coat, Ivan pressed into the wound and wrapped it tightly. Gritting her teeth, Rayn clamped her eyes shut as tears escaped her eyes. "Do not scream." Ivan squeezed her shoulder.

"Need any help?"

Rayn opened her eyes on hearing the overly chipper voice. Hydra stood there, her colored hair blowing in the breeze, hands shoved in her pockets. Ivan barely glanced at her. His attention was on the approaching pack of wolves.

"There are too many." Ivan frowned, rising to one knee.

Rayn dared to glance around and realized the massive animals had formed a circle around them. She counted at least ten. Their teeth bared, the animals growled as they crept closer. Her heart sank. There was no way of escaping.

Ivan gestured to Hydra to get her attention. "Can you drive that?" He nodded toward the sled.

"Of course I can—I can drive anything."

Ivan scooped Rayn up in his arms and darted up the steps to the top of the vehicle. "This pack overturn sled to stop us. They will not let everyone escape." He set Rayn down, turning to Hydra as she followed him to the top of the sled. "Get her back to airship." His eyes turned to daggers, and he said something else in Slav. Whatever it was, the confident look on the girl's face slipped. She nodded, a flicker of fear in her eyes. "Don't worry. I'll get her back."

No.

Rayn suddenly realized what Ivan intended to do as he surveyed the approaching pack with a determined look.

"Ivan, no!" Rayn reached up, seizing his wrist. A surge of pain ran from her bite-wound up the rest of her arm, but she ignored it, tightening her grip. "You'll die!"

Ivan peeled off her hands and held her by the shoulders, crouching down to look in her eyes. "If I stay, we *all* die." He pulled her into a swift hug.

"Go!" He yelled at Hydra and leaped from the sled.

As the engine roared to life, Rayn's frantic pleading was lost. There was no way Ivan could survive ten of those wolves, and by the look he had given her, she knew he did not expect to. Standing over LeFrost's body, he stooped to jerk the knife from the dead man's chest, then turning to meet the two wolves lunging for him with bared teeth.

If she could have moved, she would have jumped off to go help him. Instead, she turned on Hydra. "Go back!" The wind stung her face as the sled raced across the snow. "He'll die if we don't help him!"

Hydra turned her gaze for just a moment, regret in her eyes. "I can't." Her voice raised above the sound of the roaring engine. "There's nothing we can do, anyway. Not against that many wolves."

Cold washing over her, Rayn bit her lip. Ivan was going to die, and it was all because of her. Her shoulders shook as she collapsed forward, sobbing.

Chapter 40

TRISTAN

THE COLD SEEPED into Tristan's bones and stayed there, refusing to leave. Tristan shivered, taking a sip of water from the flask Nikola had given him. There was dried meat left in his pocket, but he wasn't hungry. His fingers were stiff and hard to bend, even in thick woolen gloves. Faint light glowed across the hills and line of woods that stretched out below as night gave way to dawn. Zee would be waking up now. She would not be happy to discover his absence, but Nikola had given him his word she would be safe. That was enough. Tristan almost forgot about everything that weighed on his shoulders as the dawn unfolded. "This. It's almost worth the cold."

It was not a strenuous hike down the mountains. Hardly packed snow crunched beneath his boots. Tristan had time to think. He was grateful for the air that filled his lungs without effort, the sting of the air on his face—for everything.

He breathed in, pushing the hood back from his head as the sun warmed his face. He closed his eyes for a brief moment, then looked upward. *Thank you.* He said this to the Krishtaren god his father would not approve of.

He did not have to wait long on his walk toward Byorn before he saw the man approaching. His white coat whipped behind him in the wind as he swaggered down the trail of snow. The Wolf grinned at him. "You have spirit, Tristan Highcourt. *Not like that otvali, Frost, uh?*" He spoke in Slavik, then laughed.

"*Where is LeFrost?*" Tristan didn't really care what had happened to the governor of Corcyra, but if it would delay Aleksei in his hunt, he would have asked anything.

"*Your governor?*" Aleksei sounded surprised at the question. "*The wolves will soon have him. He was no longer useful to me.*" He grinned. "*I have come to check on his charming little girl. Where is she?*"

Tristan drew the knife Nikola had given him from his boot. "*You will never see her again.*"

Aleksei's gaze fell to the dagger. "Ah, so you have help in Byorn, uh? I wonder who that was. You tell me, perhaps, then you tell me where girl is?"

Tristan glared at him. "*Never.*"

Aleksei shrugged, peering behind Tristan. "Ah, is too bad. You know, funny thing about our snow here. It never lies to us." He cracked his knuckles. "*Little girl will be mine soon enough. Ivan has been very foolish—collecting weakness.*"

The tracks! Tristan tried to hide his mounting fear. How could he have been so stupid? Aleksei could easily find his way to Nikola and Zee. He had to stop him somehow.

Tristan took a step forward, scowling at the Wolf. "*Why do you need the girl when I am in front of you?*" He swallowed, taking a fighting stance. He spoke in a calm, decisive voice. "*I will be no one's weakness. You will fight me. That is fair.*" It wouldn't be enough. But that hardly mattered.

Aleksei threw his head back in laughter. "*Oh no, Otvali. I will fight you, but it will not be fair. Not for you.*" He ran forward, his knives reflecting the sun like a muzzle flash from a fired gun.

Chapter 41

SOLOMAND

AT LEAST THEY were in no danger of freezing to death at the pace they kept. The thought was little comfort to Solomand as they tramped across the rise and fall of the landscape. It may have been hours, or only minutes, when they heard a scuffling sound beyond a dip in the snow-covered hills of the forest. Solomand looked at Will, and they both ran to see what made the noise.

On the edge of the forest, two men fought. One, a small-framed blonde and a taller man dressed in the clothes of an Ice Wolf. The smaller man was clearly outmatched.

Tristan. Was that really him? It was not the same man on the verge of death he had last seen. All thoughts of the cold left him as he and Will ran closer. He shouldered the rifle, taking aim at Aleksei. As his finger hovered on the trigger, Aleksei looked up and moved closer, wrenching the knife from Tristan's hand and dragging him in front of Solomand's aim.

"Damn!" Solomand lowered the rifle, clicking the safety forward.

Aleksei turned his pale eyes on them, beaming with delight. He twisted Tristan's arm behind his back so he could not move. "Well, well. If it isn't lonely soldier." He greeted Will. "Who are you taking orders from now, I wonder?" He laughed.

"No one." Will's hands formed fists at his side. "Let him go."

Tristan grimaced as Aleksei yanked his head up. "You want him too, uh?" He looked disappointed, shaking his head. "I already have plans that do not involve you, *Otvali*." A smile flashed across his face. "But you can join in fun."

Sun shimmered on his blade as he raised his hand and sliced the back of Tristan's ankle before shoving him to the ground.

Will snapped off a tree-limb and dashed forward, crashing into the knife-wielding Slav.

Shoot the bastard! Even as he thought it, he knew it was too risky. He could hit Will. Solomand felt useless as he watched them fight. He hated that feeling. It worked its way from his feet and spread through his veins with a petrifying terror that kept him from moving. The white landscape blurred with their movements, forcing him to look away. A startling pool of red jarred his vision back to normal.

Tristan lay on the ground, clutching the wound on his ankle. Solomand dropped to his knees and crawled forward with the rifle still in his hand. Hopefully Will could keep Aleksei busy enough not to take notice of him.

"Shit," he said when he finally reached Tristan and saw the deep gash running the length of his Achilles tendon. Blood still gushed out onto the snow.

"Good to see you too, Sol." Tristan grinned at him.

Solomand tugged off his scarf and wrapped it around Tristan's ankle, tying it tight. "It's good to see *you*. Not such great circumstances."

Tristan's smile was distant and his momentary silence heightened Solomand's worry. "Listen, Sol, I have something to tell you." He licked his lips, eyes closed as he still clutched at his injury.

"No," Sol said firmly, pointing a finger at Tristan's face. "Don't tell me anything. Do it later."

He could tell by the somber look on his friend's face what he would have said.

There may not be a later.

Solomand rose from his knee and chambered a round in his rifle. "Tell me later," he repeated.

Chapter 42

IVAN

HE HAD NOT wanted to die here. Not like this—with Aleksei still lurking in the Northland. Ivan needed to put an end to his madness. He plunged his knife up through the jaw of the wolf lunging for him, piercing its brain before freeing his blade to meet another. No one survived a pack of hungry wolves such as these. He slashed at another one, but it dodged the tip of his blade and he felt teeth sink into his shoulder.

"*Get off!*" Dropping and rolling out of the animal's grip, he kicked it in the mouth. It yelped, then snarled, edging closer. There were more of them now, snapping and howling as the Alpha looked on in the distance. For every slash Ivan gave them, they returned it with a nip of their teeth or claw.

Another round of howling on the ridge signaled more of the wolves were coming to join the pack. Backing himself against a tree, Ivan eyed the animals prowling closer as he took into account the bite and claw marks they had already inflicted. The Alpha—proud and unworried, looked like Aleksei's pet, Sasha, which made Ivan hate it all the more.

It was irrational, but he yelled out in Slavik at the wolf, anyway. "*Why don't you kill me yourself, Zohpai!*" Lowering his head, he dashed forward at the closest wolf, determined to cut a path to the Alpha and kill it if it was the last thing he did.

"*Ivan!*"

Ivan looked up to see a man on the top of the ridge, dressed the same as he was. Another wolf appeared at the man's side. Its coat was midnight black.

"Ruslin?" It couldn't be. Surely he would be long dead by now. But the wolf's eyes were clear blue, looking out from black hair fringed with gray. The other Alpha let out a howl and his pack ceased their attack, focusing on the other wolf at the top of the ridge.

Black wolf pups were cast out from the litter. There was no place for those who did not blend in with the color of the white, snowy landscape. When choosing his wolf, Ivan had defied his mentor for the first time. There was something about the pup's eyes that made Ivan want him and no other. It amused Aleksei. He let Ivan keep the pup, but forever after called him *Kirno Valk* (black wolf). It was a joke. But no one else thought it funny. They knew the Black Wolf was twice as deadly as any white one, and its master was just as dangerous.

When Ivan left the Continent, he should have killed Ruslin, like was customary. But he couldn't bring himself to do it. He never imagined he'd live this long on his own, though.

Ruslin let out a low howl, his eyes fixed on Ivan. More wolves joined him and stood, waiting for his signal. Some were gray, some white, some black. The black wolf had not only survived on his own; he was the Alpha of his own pack.

Ruslin threw his snout to the sky and howled. Snow tore up under his paws as he charged down the hill, his pack at his heels. Abandoning Ivan, the white alpha ran forward to meet the charging alpha.

Half-sliding, half running down the ridge, the other man circled to avoid the clashing wolves and made his way to Ivan. As he grew closer, Ivan recognized scars and features of a friend he thought was long dead.

"Niko!" Ivan lowered his knife. Hard bark dug into his back as he fell against the nearest tree, exhausted, yet too on-edge to be relieved by the sight of his old friend.

"You looked like you could use a little help." Nikola gave him an appraising look.

Ivan glanced down at his white clothes, splotched with red-stained puncture marks across his arms and legs and tears from claws across his back. Pain slowly stabbed at him now that he was not fighting. Breathing heavily, he shoved the bloody knife in his boot, not bothering to clean it. *"My friends. You helped them escape from Byorn?"*

Nikola crouched down, looking over Ivan's injuries. He always had a habit of being overly cautious if the odds were against him. *"I did. And do not thank me for it."* He put his hand on Ivan's bloodied shoulder and Ivan winced. *"How bad is it?"* he asked.

"I've been worse off." It was not a lie. Ivan rolled his eyes as Nikola's stare hardened. *"Help me up."* He held up his hand, and Nikola pulled him to his feet. He staggered a few steps before finding his balance. *"Are they safe?"*

Nikola's frown deepened. *"The girl is fine. Tristan was last time I saw him. But he went off to find Aleksei on his own and told me to take girl far away."*

That was exactly like Tristan. Ivan groaned. *"Why does everyone make stupid decisions?"*

Nikola scowled, reaching out an arm to steady Ivan. *"It was brave. And noble."*

"Bah." Ivan gritted his teeth, waving off Niko's aid. Every step revealed new pain. How much blood had he lost? *"Brave and noble, yes. That does not make it any less stupid. We are dealing with wolves."* He gestured in the direction of the animals, now ignoring the two men as they fought ferociously amongst themselves.

Niko's words were heavy with accusation. *"He killed them all, you know."*

Ivan stopped walking. Reaching a shaking hand to lean on the nearest tree, he turned to look at his old friend. The disappointment in Niko's eyes made him hate himself. Nikola wanted him to challenge Aleksei back then. Fight him. Kill him. Become the new Alpha. Ivan had the heart for none of those things.

"Sushinka?"

Wind whipped through the trees, knocking branches together, mournfully whistling as it stirred up gusts of snow. He could see her now; braided brown hair against pale skin and eyes a mix of dark crimson and rosewood; they were unlike any color he'd ever seen. Sushinka never let her guard down. Except with him.

"*She was able to get away for a while. But... you know how he is,*" Nikola said.

"*Yes.*" Ivan held his glove up and stared at the tips of his fingers where blood was half-dried, half-frozen. A warm smile flashed in his memory—Sushinka reserved it only for him. Aleksei would kill everyone that meant anything to you. A part of him wished the Alpha had killed him when the villagers had requested it.

"*I'm sorry.*" Nikola's hand was on his shoulder. "*I saw her when she returned. She said to give you a message when I saw you.*"

"*What message?*" Ivan grasped at anything to stifle the images of death he dealt by Aleksei's order.

"*She left something for you on the coast—in a town called Ramshorn. Look for a man named Kryllen.*"

Ivan doubted he would ever make it out of this forest, let alone to Ramshorn.

Aleksei. If it was his last act on this earth, he would wipe that smirk from the man's face.

"*I am sorry. I was wrong to leave. But I could not face him then.*" Ivan exhaled sharply and set out at an uneven walk back where he had left Sol and Will. "*I have to find him.*"

"*And you can face him now?*" Niko raised his voice in exasperation. "*You are in pain and already losing blood. How do you plan to win?*"

Ivan whirled to face Nikola. He glanced down at the obvious wounds on his body and shrugged. "*This. This is not pain, Niko. I may not live to fight another day...*" He glanced at the wolves as Ruslin let out a victory howl, standing over the body of the white alpha. "*But neither will Aleksei.*" He turned and set off in a slow run, ignoring the aching, the limp warning him to slow.

"*I will come with you then.*" Nikola called as he ran to catch up. "*You will not have to fight him alone.*"

Giving his old friend a sideways glance, Ivan said, *"There are not good odds with this fight. You never were one for bad odds."*

"No." Nikola looked away, shame in his eyes. *"But I do not care so much now. Only that Aleksei is dead at the end of it."*

Chapter 43

SOLOMAND

IT WAS NEVER a good time to take the shot. The rifle pulled into his shoulder. Solomand's hand never stopped shaking. Will got in a few jabs with his branch and managed to dodge Aleksei's blade, for the most part. But he was too close to the assassin, and Sol did not trust his own aim.

Taking the upper hand of the fight, Aleksei kicked Will's foot out from under him and twisted the stick from Will's hand as he fell. Touching a hand to the red mark on the side of his head where Will struck him, he let out a laugh and pressed the splintered edge of the wood on Will's throat, circling him with wide steps.

"*Hey, lochek!*" Sol walked toward him, gun raised. "Why don't you hold still so I can shoot you?"

Turning his head, Aleksei grinned at Sol, then yanked Will from the ground. "I do not think you wish to hit your friend or you would have already taken a shot."

"No shit." Solomand snapped, his finger twitching over the trigger.

Aleksei's attention turned to the forest behind them, and his eyes widened with delight.

"*Kirno Valk!*" He hurled the stick to one side and Will to the other, spreading his arms like he was welcoming an old friend.

Solomand kept his distance from Aleksei as jogged up to Will. "You alright?"

"Yeah." Will wiped blood from his lip and nodded at Ivan. "He doesn't look alright, though."

Bloody splotches and tears marred his white coat. Still, the murderous glare he had fixed on Aleksei as he limped forward was enough to make Sol afraid of him.

"I look for your sisters." Aleksei twirled the knives in his hands. "You are the only one who took my words to heart. I never find them. But now," his grin widened as his gaze raked over Tristan, Sol, Will, and came to rest on Ivan. "I not need to, uh?"

"*Zohpai!*" Ivan's knife was in his hand.

"Ah, *Damechey*. After everything we go through together, you choose these *Otvali* over me?" Aleksei looked disappointed. "Your new friends must not know who you really are—why don't you tell them why the villagers whisper in the shadows about you *Kirno Valk*, the Black Wolf." He laughed again, his head tilting. "They may not think so much of you then, uh? These Lyonese—they have no taste for violence."

"*Shut up*," Ivan yelled.

Solomand thought about what Ivan had told him, in that reserved, frightening way. *There is something you should know about me and Aleksei.*

"Ivan," he called. "Remember what I said. It doesn't matter."

Aleksei clucked sympathetically. "Should have taken lesson like you did with sisters, Black Wolf. You cannot save them all. You will have to choose." He dashed forward, jerking Tristan from the ground before anyone could reach him. His gaze came to rest on Solomand, and he smiled. Twisting Tristan's head to face Sol, the Alpha raised his blade, grin widening as sun caught the steel.

Tristan's gaze met Solomand's and an apologetic smile crossed his face—like any of this was his fault! Solomand wanted to yell out, but words stuck in his throat. Tristan's eyes widened as the blade stuck into his back, and Aleksei kicked him forward into the snow. Solomand dropped his rifle and ran without thinking. Aleksei was coming toward him now, but Solomand could not bring himself to move.

Ivan flew past, catching Aleksei's blade with his own, and the two of them fought a few feet from where Tristan lay. To Solomand, they may as well have been on another planet. He rolled Tristan over and tore open his coat. Blood already soaked through his shirt. Solomand ripped off his coat sleeve to use as a bandage.

"Sol, stop." Tristan held his hand up, grabbing Solomand's wrist. Color was draining from his face. It was no use. Solomand knew it in the back of his head, but was not prepared to accept it. There was always a way out. There had to be. "Looks like I strayed too far from home again, eh?" Tristan lay his head back on the snow, grinning—of all the fool things to do. "Don't look at me like that, Sol. We've been through this a hundred times, anyway. Lots of practice."

Tristan had been on the verge of death for years. Solomand never accepted it then, either. He gripped Tristan's wrist, feeling his friend's pulse slow.

His eyes slowly closing, Tristan said, "Tell me some good news, will you."

"Rayn is going to have a baby." Solomand felt like he would choke on the words.

"Really?" Tristan's eyes opened. "Who is the lucky father?"

Tears stinging his eyes, Sol laughed. Looking satisfied, Tristan added, his voice slowing as his breath grew more pronounced. "That is fantastic. If it is a boy, name him after me."

Solomand gripped his friend's hand now, as if that would somehow keep him from leaving—keep his heart still beating with life. "I would have done that, anyway." His voice cracked.

Tristan grinned in the way he used to right before he joked about his own death. "If it's a girl... name her Minuet."

Sol forced a smile, but his humor was gone. "Not even for you, Swank."

Tristan's shoulders shook in a silent laugh. "Solomand Black... I'm glad to have known you."

"Don't say that." Sol felt suffocated.

Tristan gave him a hope-filled smile. "Don't worry, Sol. We'll meet again."

His eyes shut for the last time, and his arm went limp. "Tell my father... I'm sorry, will you? And tell Minuet... oh never mind. She knows."

Chapter

IVAN 44

ALEKSEI'S BLADE SLIT Ivan's cheek, and a fleeting stream of warmth trickled down the side of his face. He jumped back, panting.

"*You've grown soft, Kirno Valk.*" Aleksei said, trying to work his way to Sol and Tristan were. Ivan charged forward, ducking as Aleksei swung his blade and catching him in the mouth with his balled fist. He may die here, but Aleksei would get nowhere near his friends.

Laughing, Aleksei wiped the blood from his cracked lip. "*Is no good, Ivan. You should have run away again. Like you did last time. Maybe if you not refuse to fight me then, not so many would have to die.*" His grin was the same as the one he would give Ivan when they worked together. He knew what he was trying to do, but he couldn't help but let the anger take him. Damn him! Aleksei was right. Ivan should have fought him then. At the time, he still viewed Aleksei as the man who spared his life. He did not want to kill him. Now, he had no such reservation.

Aleksei slipped to the side and caught Ivan's wrist, knocking the knife from his hand and cracking his arm at the elbow before driving a small blade into his shoulder. As Aleksei kicked Ivan in the leg, a splitting pain shot up from his shin through his knee.

Ivan fell to his knee, jerking the knife from his shoulder as Aleksei stood over him, opening his arms. He didn't even look like

233

he'd broken a sweat. "Don't make me kill you now, Ivan. Not yet. Our fun is just starting!"

Ivan spit on Aleksei's white boots, struggling to his feet. Blood dripped to the ground from his arm, and he could barely support his weight on the leg Aleksei had kicked.

Aleksei laughed, crossing his arms. "You can barely stand, *Kirno Valk*. What do you plan on doing to me?"

Arrogant bastard. He always was over confident. Ivan spread his hands and motioned for Aleksei to come at him. "Move and you will find out."

Aleksei drew a small dagger from his boot and hurled it at him. Ivan caught it and threw it back in a swift movement. It stuck in Aleksei's side and he looked down, mildly surprised, then back to Ivan. His eyes narrowed. "I guess I underestimated you." He pulled the blade from his side and threw it so it stuck deep into the truck of a tree. The sound of wings beating filled the air as a flock of birds vacated the swaying limbs.

Biting his lip, a dangerous look entered Aleksei's eyes. *"But I only do so once, Ivan."*

"Don't you remember what you taught me?" Ivan's fingers scraped the snow as he picked up his knife with his left hand, as his right arm hung limp at his side. *"One mistake is too many."*

There was a howl from the ridge, and they both looked up. Nikola made his way down the hill with Ruslin at his side.

The amusement melted from Aleksei's face. *"Nikola."* Lines formed at his eyes. *"Another coward who ran away."* His eyes glanced over the mark of a Byorn prison guard behind Nikola's ear and laughed, shaking his head. "Very clever to hide for so long." He moved his arm and Nikola drew his knife at the same time Ivan raised his.

Aleksei laughed, crossing his arms as he looked from one to the other. "You know, Ivan. I was saving him for last." He nodded at Nikola. "He was almost as clever as you. But not before it was too late for his sister." He ran a finger along the dull edge of his knife blade.

Face twisted in anguish, Nikola moved like he was going to tear off Aleksei's head.

"Wait." Ivan held up his hand. Nikola stopped, his chest heaving, hand poised to strike. Ivan stepped in front of Nikola. "*You're right*," he told Aleksei. "*I should have fought you. Now you get your wish.*"

Aleksei shook his head, pretending to look sorry. "*If only you saw reason sooner, not so many would be dead.*"

He threw his stupid head back in laughter that was short-lived. Knife handle still gripped in his hand, Ivan cracked Aleksei in the face with his knuckles. Aleksei staggered back before charging at him. With an angry snarl, the black wolf leaped at Aleksei, causing him to jump back.

"*Ruslin, no!*" At Ivan's command, the wolf sat down, pawing at the snow and whimpering.

Ivan twirled the knife around in his hand and pointed the blade at Aleksei. He did not need the help of a wolf to beat the Alpha. With the help of a friend, he had battled his own demons. And won. Aleksei was not stronger than that unyielding hunger that lived in his soul like a sleeping snake. He was stronger than he used to be; wiser. Aleksei always wanted him to take on the mantle of the wolves. If that is what he wanted, so be it. Ivan would be the one to end his madness, and no one else.

He clashed into Aleksei, beating him back, no matter how many times he felt the knife tear into his skin. Driving him further and further across the snow until they were on the forest's edge. Gritting his teeth, Ivan sliced at Aleksei's wrist, knocking his knife out of reach and using his elbow to force him into a tree—the same tree Aleksei's dagger was buried in.

In stunned silence, Aleksei held up his arms, distancing himself from the knifepoint aiming at his face. "Are you going to kill me, Ivan?" His chuckle lacked the usual confidence. "After everything I've done for you. If it were not for me, you'd be a dead child—another ghost to this land."

Ivan slowly removed his arm from Aleksei's chest, being careful to keep his attention on the knife in his hand. "You hunted my family." He transferred the knife to the hand of his injured hand. "Used me." He saw the calculating glint in Aleksei's eyes as he quickly glanced at Ivan's injured arm.

"Turned me into an animal." Ivan brought his other hand to rest on the trunk of the tree, next to the knife. "That was *your* mistake." His fingers coiled around the handle. "You should have killed me back then."

Aleksei smirked. "You talk more like Alpha now than ever. We pass judgment—hold life and death in our hands. Or at least—I do." He brought his knee up, kicking the knife from Ivan's hand.

Ivan jerked the knife from the tree. With one slice of his hand, he slashed the blade across Aleksei's throat. The Alpha's hands went to his neck, staring at Ivan with wide, disbelieving eyes.

Ivan stepped back, breathing heavily. "No, Aleksei. The god of the dead can pass judgement. I merely send you to his arms."

Ivan turned away as Aleksei slumped to the ground and finally grew silent. Ivan fell to his knees. Something cold touched his forehead, and he jerked his head up. The black wolf was face to face with him.

Hand trembling, Ivan reached out and lay a hand on Ruslin's head.

A hand gripped his shoulder. "Ivan."

"*Niko.*" Ivan hadn't the strength to raise his head. All the pain and exhaustion crashed into him at once. Nikola's face blurred in front of him.

"*You are badly wounded.*" Nikola pulled him to his feet. Ivan leaned against his friend without resisting his help this time.

"Are you alright?" Will walked over, holding a ball of torn cloth against a cut on his cheek.

"I'm fine." Ivan said. His hand felt cold and damp inside his gloves. He yanked them off and tossed them aside.

"*Shall I bring girl now?*" Nikola asked.

"Zee?" Ivan cringed as he took in the gory scene of blood and tattered remains. "Take her to the airship."

Nikola nodded. He transferred Ivan's weight to Will and left. Turning his attention to where Solomand knelt over Tristan, Ivan felt a sinking feeling. He knew with sickening certainty that it was too late for one of them.

Chapter 45

SOLOMAND

TRISTAN COULD HAVE been sleeping. There were many times he looked like this before, when he was ill. But this time, he wouldn't be waking up. It was this pointed fact that Solomand's mind refused to wrap around. After all this time and struggle, their journey together had come to a shockingly swift end, here in this frigid wilderness so far from where it began.

Blood, already frozen, seemed wrong in this sea of white that engulfed them. Solomand Black had lost many people he loved; his parents, the man who took him in afterwards, a child he never got the chance to know, and his wife. Rayn was the exception to the others. She had found her way back. Tristan though... Solomand felt directly responsible for. It was curious how having your heart torn open never felt the same. The pain was always different each time it happened.

Solomand's tears were silent, freezing on the side of his face. Shivering involuntarily from the cold, he was not aware of the fighting of the Hyperborea assassins behind him, or of anything else beyond the harrowing noise the emptiness of one life lost made.

When Ivan lay a hand on his shoulder, Solomand did not acknowledge him. "Sol, you will freeze here. We have to go." His voice was quiet. He sounded wary.

Solomand's teeth chattered as he spoke almost against his will. "I'm not leaving him—not like this." The thought of the wolves coming down over that ridge stirred gruesome possibilities. His eyes clamped shut as Ivan dragged him to his feet.

Solomand looked at his friend for the first time, realizing he was covered in blood himself, and his left arm hung limp at his side. He remembered Aleksei running for him and Ivan rushing past to meet him, to protect Solomand. If he had not reacted so quickly, Sol would likely be dead too. Once again, he owed Ivan his life. "We will not leave him," Ivan said, glancing to Will.

"*Ruslin, dachi* (come)." A monstrous black wolf approached at Ivan's call. If Sol could have felt anything, it would have been terror at the site of the animal. Ivan lay a hand on the animal's head and spoke to it in Slavik.

Solomand did not remember much about their trek back to the airship. Only that Will carried Tristan and Ivan walked with one arm over the wolf, and the sun playing on the glistening ground was much too cheerful. It was the longest walk he ever took.

Chapter 46

Rayn

RAYN SHIVERED UNDER a pile of blankets. She'd allowed Hydra to help her dress the knife wound. Afterwards she told her to leave, with a colorful choice in words. It had been hours. Ivan couldn't be gone! Taking out her anger and sadness on Hydra was easy to do, but she blamed herself.

If only I hadn't been so stupid! After everything LeFrost took from her and Sol, revenge was too enticing. Another memory hit her so hard her head throbbed from the pain of it. What seemed like a lifetime ago, someone close to her thought the same.

Water pooled on the cobblestones of an alleyway. Two people reflected in the murky water. They didn't know she listened.

"Listen to the wisdom of your people—your mother's people." Lemuel Falcon spoke words she didn't understand—it was the language of the Kree. "Do not seek revenge," he repeated in Common. "It will not be worth it."

"What do you know about such things?" A much younger Solomand snapped.

There was a heavy silence, and Rayn could almost see the familiar grave look in Lemuel's dark eyes when he finally spoke in a gravelly tone. "More than I care to, Boy."

Lemuel was hiding something. Rayn traced the lines on her wrist, wondering how the tracking device in her could find The Falcon. Was that even a good idea?

The door opened, and she looked up. Hydra peeked in, all the laughter in her eyes gone. "They're back," she murmured, her hand still on the door.

Rayn threw off the blanket.

"Maybe you should stay..." Hydra trailed off as Rayn gave her a withering look. Without bothering to put anything on her feet, she shuffled out of the room. At the top of the staircase her heart jumped in her throat when she saw Ivan, then plummeted when she realized Tristan lay on the floor as a menacing-looking Slav draped a blanket over him.

No.

Light rose to her vision, Rayn felt herself begin to fall forward. It was Will that dashed up the stairs and caught her before she toppled to the cargo bay floor. Hot tears came to her eyes as she pressed her head into Will's chest.

Hydra's voice sounded next to them, strangely quiet and hollow. "Will, I... I'm sorry."

Retreating footstep was the last thing Rayn remembered as Will carried her back to her room.

Chapter 47

MINUET

'STEFAN LEFROST: DECEASED. Tristan Highcourt... Deceased.'

Minuet stared at the message from Hydra for the longest time. It was the first one she had received since her radio was repaired. If only it were still broken. Hydra's primary aim was to return Tristan to her. It had always been a long shot, but to hear those words fractured the wall she'd carefully built up for years. More clicking as the machine tapped out another message. Minuet eyed the coil of paper. *'Please advise.'*

Minuet did not know how to answer. Holding up such an impossible hope was a dangerous thing. The unbearable weight of it fell around her now.

All the words he'd written in letters. A smile that would dismiss the idea of anything being impossible. He couldn't be gone. Minuet stared at the machine.

'I am sorry.' There was a pause before the next message. *'They did everything they could.'*

They would have done nothing less. Solomand, in particular. Now that there was nothing stopping her from using any information at her disposal to be rid of him, she found her hatred fell flat. Solomand wasn't her enemy anymore. He never had been.

No tears came to Minuet's eyes. There were things that needed to be done first. As she read over Hydra's next messages, her mind processed the bits of intelligence. She sent a final job offer to the freelance agent and waited. The machine ticked away, typing out Hydra's reply. *'Accepted.'*

So that was it. Minuet did not bother to destroy the messages before leaving her office and the governor's compound for the quieter streets of Corcyra. The sun was dimming and stars scatters across the sky, bright beacons in the gray. Residents walked down Main Street with their dogs and small children, laughing, smiling. Feeling less herself than ever, Minuet glimpsed them with increasing disgust, first with their insufferable cheeriness, then with herself as she walked mechanically down the manicured iron fence to Highcourt Manor.

There was no need to knock or inform the staff of her presence. In a daze, she reached Galin's lab. He looked up from his microscope, took in her appearance, and frowned.

Minuet leaned on the doorframe. "Sir, I…"

Galin took off his glasses and pinched the bridge of his nose. "He's gone."

Minuet managed a nod, numbness taking over. Galin flipped his research book closed and walked to the wall, where he pressed a switch on the silver intercom system in the wall. "Fineas?"

"Yes, Lord Highcourt." The butler's voice crackled through the speaker.

Galin gave Minuet a sideways glance. "Dismiss the staff. Ensure they are out of the manor in the next twenty minutes."

"Yes, Sir."

Galin slipped his coat on. "Minuet…" He gave her a sad, half-hearted smile. "You should leave."

A fragment of rationality left in her wanted to tell him to not act rashly, but it was too late for that. They both knew it. She left the house and the halls where she'd played hide and seek as a child, searching for the boy with eyes like the summer sky. Everywhere she looked, she saw a part of him. It hurt knowing neither of them would ever see these halls again. Minuet knew what Galin meant to do.

Warm air and the scent of flowers were unfairly pleasant. Minuet walked through the garden, leaving the gate open, and continued down the street with no destination in mind.

It was nearly half an hour later when sirens blared in the distance. A fire engine raced past and people jumped out of the road. Pillars of smoke and flame blazed like a beacon as Highcourt Manor burned. Minuet sank to the ground and sobbed.

Under the light of the waning moons, she didn't realize she'd gone to the border wall separating the inner-city from The Mud district. No one would disturb her here, as years' worth of sorrow spilled out uncontrollably. A hand touched her shoulder, and she looked up, eyes blurry with tears.

Galin looked at her sadly before sitting at her side. Minuet collapsed into his arms and buried her head in his shoulder.

Chapter 48

SOLOMAND

THERE WAS A cave in the Kirragard Mountains Ivan knew of. They planned to bury Tristan there in the morning. The night before, Solomand didn't bother going to bed. Walking the halls like a ghost, he toyed with his lighter—listening to the smooth sound of metal scraping on the flint inside as he opened it and closed it repeatedly.

Stepping inside the helm, it surprised him to see Jank sitting on the floor; the radio was laid out in front of him in pieces. The engineer glanced up as Solomand's shadow invaded his space. "Hey, Sol." He rubbed at his eyebrow, leaving traces of oil on his forehead.

Solomand slipped a hand in his pocket, nodding at the dismantled radio. "What's wrong with it?"

Jank slid a coiled wire inside the brass case. "Not a damn thing." He picked up his wrench and twisted a bolt in place.

"Can't sleep, either, eh?"

"Not really." One shoulder slumped, Jank pushed a black knob back into place in the front panel.

"I'll leave you to it, then." Solomand tapped a hand on the doorframe before retreating to the windowed hall. Jank obviously was in no mood to talk, and neither was Solomand.

Running one hand along the clear window panes, he went back to playing with his lighter. The spark reflecting in the glass reminded him of the campfire outside of his uncle's camp. Resting his hand on the wall, he stared out into the darkness. He imagined he was at that fire now.

Flames danced in the wind. Tall grass stirred throughout the valley. A thousand fireflies alternated their yellow and green flashes along the banks of the stream. Solomand shut his eyes. He could hear the owl hooting in the forest and crows crying back and forth to each other.

"Sol?" Rayn's voice was a whisper. Her arm slipped around him from behind.

Opening his eyes, Solomand slipped the lighter in his pocket and closed his arms around her. Staring at the moons half-concealed by tree branches, he found it in himself to speak.

"You remember that night when you went to my uncle's camp?" He brushed her hair behind her ear, his finger stroking her ear.

"Yes."

"There is a legend among the Kree. I think they told it around the fire that night." He rocked back and forth, his arms tightening around her as he repeated the words. "Those who turn their backs on their people, no longer have the spirit of life. Death will be their companion."

"Oh, Sol." Rayn pulled back, her green eyes glaring at him reproachfully. "You don't believe that, do you?"

Solomand let out a joyless chuckle. "Grandfather told it to me when my parents died. Lemuel made *certain* I didn't believe it."

He recalled the look in Lemuel's eyes when he rebuked the old man's words. His hand gripped Solomand's shoulders. A torrent of emotion spilled through as he made Sol repeat that he controlled his own destiny and not some superstitious story. What was more terrifying was the raging sea of passion below the surface of Lemuel's gaze. It was the first time Solomand was ever frightened of anyone. He did not want to be the one that broke the levy and unleashed whatever Lemuel Falcon was capable of.

Solomand shrugged, letting go of Rayn. "I never thought of it again, really. Until now."

Rayn leaned her head against him. "Sol. Do not take such blame onto your shoulders. He wouldn't want you to."

Solomand sighed. "I know. I just wish…" He swallowed with difficulty. "I wish I could have made things different." Looking back on the trail of death that followed him since his youth, it was difficult to dismiss the Kree legend, even if he knew it was bullshit.

What would Lemuel have done differently? He used to believe the mysterious Falcon was capable of anything. Not anymore.

Solomand curled his fingers around Rayn's hand and held on like she was the only thing between him and falling over the edge of a cliff. "I don't want to say goodbye." An ache spread from his heart, throbbed painfully in his chest. How many hours did he have left?

Rayn answered in a whisper thick with emotion. "Me either."

⊰◯⊱

There was a shelf of rock inside the cave. They packed snow around him—sealing it. As they walked back into the snow, the sun shone down. Its brightness did not ward off the bitter cold that raked over Solomand. He glanced at the entrance where ice crystals frosted along the rocks in layers. Lemuel had shown him what they looked like under a microscope once. Each one was unique and intricate beyond imagination. When light hit them just right, a kaleidoscope of colors erupted across their surface. It was amazing something that looked so unassuming at face value, contained endless complexity and beauty. Tristan would like that.

He turned, blinking against the sun as Nikola buried the blade of his knife deep into the shelf of ice over the cave's entrance; it was the burial token of an Ice Wolf—a warning to let the one who lay here rest in peace or call down the wrath of his pack.

Their collective breath forming a frigid cloud. Zee slipped her hand in Solomand's; a single tear rolled down her cheek. Her fever barely broken, Rayn leaned against him. Silence hung thick in the air until he spoke words he never wanted to say.

"Tristan Jude Highcourt was one of the best men any of us will ever hope to know. He was selfless. Fearless. Loyal. The best friend anyone could ever have." His hands tingled with cold from entombing his friend in snow. Memories of Tristan flashed in front of him; from the moment they met until he breathed his last. "Some of his last words were, we will all meet again one day, when our own journeys come to an end." His voice cracked, and he cleared his throat. "We all know, Tristan was always right. So, I don't think goodbye is appropriate." He glanced back into the mouth of the cave—blinded by daylight now. The empty feeling in his heart widened like an opening chasm. "Until next time." His arm tightened around Rayn. There was a half-hearted murmur of "until next time." from the others.

Jank pulled a piece of paper from his coat pocket and tossed it in the air. As the wind took it, it fell against the cave's opening; it was a drawing—Tristan holding the hand of a little girl; Solomand and Rayn's child. Giving Solomand a sorrowful look, he shoved his hands in his pockets and started back toward the airship.

That was it. The biting cold on the walk back to the airship was welcoming. Thankfully, no one spoke. Solomand held Rayn close with one hand, casting a wary glance at Ivan. His friend still didn't put a lot of weight on his leg, limping with one arm over the fearsome black wolf. Normally, Solomand would have objected to the frightful animal anywhere near him. But he didn't have the strength to protest or even make a sarcastic remark.

When they arrived back at the airship, Hydra was waiting in the docking bay. She moved to Will and laced her gloved hand in his. Will didn't seem so uncomfortable with it. Solomand peeled off his jumpsuit and sat on the nearest crate. Absently, he drew the letters from the pocket of his greatcoat and ran his finger along their edge. The paper cut his thumb, and he stared at the line of blood until he realized Ivan was repeating his name. "Hmm?" He glanced up.

"Do you wish to post those?" Ivan slid to the floor with difficulty, his hand on the head of the wolf. It stared at Solomand with uncomfortably expressive eyes, and he turned away.

"No," he replied.

"By falcon then?" Rayn asked from her seat next to him.

Unfounded rage flashed through him like a bolt of searing lightning. "Not a falcon—never again!" He shoved the letters back in his pocket. *You should have been here.*

Rayn looked taken aback as he continued. "I will deliver them by hand. It is the only way." There were at least a dozen other ways, all more practical. But Solomand would not send Tristan's letter to Galin Highcourt. Much as he did not care for the man, he deserved to receive his son's last words in person, and from the man who was responsible.

Ivan ran a hand through his hair, his eyes scrunching shut. "You wish to return to Lyonese?" He sighed tiredly, not saying what a stupid idea it was.

Sol reached a hand to Rayn, and she came to him, frowning. "You cannot come with me." His eyes moved to her stomach, hoping she would listen; if not for him, then for their child. "Please," he pleaded.

Rayn's lip trembled, and she pulled her hand away. "Fine." Anger rolled off of her.

"I will stay with, Rayn," Ivan said. He winced as he massaged his leg.

"I don't need you to," she snapped.

Ivan raised an eyebrow at her. "I know. But you are better company than Sol."

Rayn's anger faded. "I'm sorry, Ivan." She sighed, splaying her fingers and resting her head in her hands.

Hydra cleared her throat. "I can take you to Corcyra on my ship. It's much faster, and you could be in and out without many people knowing."

Reaching a hand in his pocket, Solomand dug out his lighter. "And what do you have to gain from this?"

Hydra shrugged. "Athena asked me to offer it, actually."

"Ah. So you're to deliver us to the new acting governor of Corcyra, are you? Does she know?" Minuet probably had a firing squad ready and waiting.

Hydra's head tilted to the side. "She knows. But it isn't like that."

Rayn's eyes narrowed. "Why should we trust you?"

Hydra gave her a wry smile. "I wouldn't trust me if I were you. But Athena is only paying me to *offer* you a ride there and back again. You are free to take the opportunity or not. Believe me, I would rather see you alive than captured. You have connections that your friend *Minuet* does not."

Lemuel. So she was still hoping he could arrange a meeting. But she couldn't be more wrong. The Falcon was conveniently unreachable when he was needed most, leaving the pawns to fight it out while he did god knows what. Solomand's hand tightened on the lighter. Lemuel never seemed to turn up until it was too late to be of any good.

This wasn't entirely true. After his parents died, Lemuel came every season to take him to the valley where the Kree camped. When Rayn was gravely injured, Lemuel came. He took her to a safe place. After Benjamin's death, he was there; always when Sol needed him most. Maybe that is why it bothered him that The Falcon was absent now.

So help me, when we meet again, Lemuel... This time he would get an explanation. One way or another.

"Alright," he broke from his musings as he gave Hydra an answer. "We'll go with you."

Chapter 48

RAYN

MOONLIGHT PLAYED ON the snow and made the trees look like silvery ash. Rayn shrank into the blanket around her shoulders as the air froze in front of her. Stars glistened in the black backdrop of sky, swirling in patterns and hues from purple to green.

Rayn held her breath. Lemuel Falcon was out there somewhere. One day, she would tell Sol everything she remembered. For now, it was best to wait. After Sol's outburst, what would he do if they came face to face with The Falcon?

It was strange to think months ago she had the same reservations about the man Sol did. But the Lemuel she remembered was different—less sure of himself, younger, more vulnerable. And he cared for Sol in a way it was clear he never wanted Sol to be aware of.

Telling Sol everything felt like it would somehow betray Lemuel. Keeping it to herself was best. But she still wanted to talk to Lemuel herself. There were questions she had that only he could answer, and there was one person she knew who could get in touch with him.

She took in the look of the downed Dragonfly. Its sleek black steel had a long scrape across the nose from trees it had come in contact with. There were nicks and marks from bullets in the steel plating from their run-ins at various ports where they'd attracted the wrong attention. In a way, it resembled all of them—tore the hell up on the outside, but it would keep flying.

Rayn went into the docking bay and peered in the engine room as she passed. Jank was on his knees, rattling tools and working to loosen the bolt on something else that did not need fixing. She tiptoed past and went up the spiral stairs step by step, all the way to the third deck. Bulbs glowed behind wire-mesh light fixtures, turning on automatically as she passed them.

Past the helm, Hydra was staying in a room close to Will. It was easy to find. Rayn twisted the handle and pushed open the door. Fully clothed, down to her boots, Hydra lay on a bunk with a gun in one hand, something that looked like a communication device in the other.

"Hydra." Rayn nudged the bed with her boot. "Wake up."

At first, Hydra nearly jumped out of her bed, gun in hand. When she saw it was Rayn, she dropped the rectangular device in her hand and covered a yawn. "What is it?"

"I need you to send a message for me."

"To who?" She rubbed her eyes.

Rayn tugged the blanked over her shoulders. "The Falcon."

"What?!" Hydra combed fingers through her curls and shook her hair.

"I know you can." Rayn narrowed her eyes.

Hydra shrugged, swinging her legs over the edge of the bunk. "Sure, I can send a message. And he'll probably see it. But he'll never answer, you know." She tossed the pistol onto her bunk.

"I don't need him to answer."

Shrugging, Hydra picked up the communicator and pulled out a metal antenna. "Alright then. What's the message?"

Chapter 49

SOLOMAND

HYDRA'S RAPTOR WAITED for them to leave. Solomand stared at it with reservation. How the hell did the thing stay up? The fuselage was the shape of a dragonfly's body, made of metal plates fitted together like a mosaic of gray and black. At the nose, the windows were a row of glass tiles connected to form the window. The wings resembled the wings and tail of a bat, or dragon from ancient lore; they were constructed of a lightweight material woven into a flexible framing, like the skeletal structure of a hawk. An engine was mounted on either side of the fuselage, below the wings. Two wheels at the front and one at the back formed retractable landing gear.

"Don't worry." Hydra hopped from the cockpit and lovingly patted the side of the machine. "She sails a lot better than that thing of yours does."

Solomand pulled out his cigarette case, giving the Raptor another appraisal. "If you say so…"

"Sol!" He turned to see Zee running toward him. "Sol, I don't want you to go!" Her golden eyes glistening with tears. He took her face in his hands and touched her forehead to his.

"Zee. I'm sorry. You have to stay here."

"No! I'm tired of people telling me to stay behind and trying to keep me safe from anything, and then they don't come back!"

She yelled, jerking out of his grasp. "So don't tell me to stay here because it's safer, because I don't care if it is!"

"Zee." Solomand took her by the shoulders. "I will come back. I swear it."

Her gaze moved to Will, and Solomand took her by the chin. "And Will. He will come back with me. Do you trust me?"

Brushing back tears, she nodded. Sol ran a hand through her hair. "It will be alright now, you'll see." He hugged her again, then turned to Hydra. "When can you leave?"

She swallowed, looking curiously distressed. "Whenever you are ready, Captain Black."

I will never be ready for this. Solomand put the letters into his pocket. He gave Rayn a lingering kiss. "We'll be back."

"You better be." Her cool fingers slipped from his cheek.

Will and Solomand boarded the sketchy airship, waving from the window as it took off with disturbing movements, like a bird taking off. Airships weren't meant to fly like sodding herons! Solomand retreated from the window, shielding his eyes until they leveled off.

As Hydra piloted the ship, Will and Solomand sat in the cramped compartment together. Under other circumstances, Sol would have found Will's stooped posture comical. Shuffling a deck of cards repeatedly, the Olbian was quiet, in a stoic way that worried Sol. He suspected it in the way Will grew increasingly distant from all of them and spent more time with the delusional code-named girl; he meant to leave.

Sitting across from his friend, Solomand cleared his throat. "Look, I'm not impressed with your choice in women, but I..." he bit his lip before finishing "I wasn't impressed with Tristan's choice either." That was supposed to go somewhere witty, but he found he didn't have it in him.

Sighing, he pulled the knife from his pocket and picked at his fingernails with the tip of the blade. "What I'm trying to say is, I understand if you want to leave. But I don't want you to. Not for the wrong reasons, anyway."

His hands till shuffling the cards, Will glanced up. "You mean for the wrong person?"

Sol rolled his eyes. "No, asshole, I meant—"

"Sol. It was a joke." Will gave him a dispirited half-smile.

"Ah. You doing jokes now? About damn time. All it took was what, six years?"

"And a second dose of a chemical weapon. Apparently." Will tapped the deck of cards on the palm of his hands, aligning them all in a neat stack. "Sol, I know what you're trying to say. It's not like that."

Solomand moved on to his other hand, scraping the knife point at dirt that wasn't there. "Alright. As long as you're not leaving because you think I, or someone else, wants you to."

Will looked away then. "I know you don't." There was a troubled look in his eyes when he looked at Solomand again. "I need to find my own way."

Solomand didn't like it, but he understood. "Alright," he said again. "Do me a favor before you leave?"

"Anything for you, Captain." Will said, his smile more genuine.

"Tell Zee goodbye before you go."

Will took a shaky breath and shuffled the cards again. "I will."

Solomand put his knife away. "And you thought I wanted you to strong-arm Rayn again, didn't you?"

Will managed an actual laugh then. "I should have said anything but that."

Solomand chuckled, rubbing the back of his neck. "Glad to see you finally developed a sense of humor. All too late, uh?"

Will started dealing out the cards between Sol and himself. "It's never too late to learn something new. Maybe you could learn how to fly one day."

"Ha-ha." Solomand raised an eye. "Now you're just being an ass."

Will shrugged. "Learned that from you."

Solomand collected his cards. "Careful, Olbian. Your friend in there can't help you while she's flying."

Will looked amused. "It's ok to say you missed me Sol."

Solomand lit a cigarette. "Fine. I missed our long, in-depth conversations. Just didn't want to say anything and make your girlfriend in there jealous."

Will grinned. "I'll miss our long talks, Captain."

Sol was quiet now, his shoulders slumping as he let the smoke curl over his lips. All desire to be witty vanishing. "Me too, Will. Me too."

⊰✺⊱

As Hydra's Raptor touched down, it jarred Solomand awake. He jumped up, banging his head on the ceiling. "Owe. Damn small, good-for-nothing ship!"

"Welcome to the lovely city of Corcyra—twelfth in consumption of fire bolts." Unbuckling herself, she slid into the cabin, sidling up to Will as she went to open the hatch.

"And how are we going to go unnoticed in this... thing?" Solomand made a sweeping motion with his hand.

"It's night." Hydra shrugged. "And we're invisible."

Solomand glanced at Will, then back to Hydra. "Where did you say you were from again?"

Her head tilted to the side. "I didn't. You should ask your friend, The Falcon, when you see him. He has interesting theories on the subject."

Solomand followed her out, scoffing. "Sure. I'll add it to the list of things to ask Lemuel," he mumbled.

"What was that?" she looked over her shoulder.

"Nothing, I..." he stopped, twisting his head to look at the obviously visible Raptor. "It's not invisible."

Hydra folded her arms, shifting her weight to one side. "Isn't it?"

With a roll of his eyes, Solomand decided to ignore her. Arguing with pathological liars was a waste of time. As soon as the warm air hit his face, he looked up at the sky and took a pronounced breath. He stooped down and scooped up a handful of dirt. "Land that isn't frozen!" He let it run through his fingers, savoring the dusty, grainy feel of it.

"Captain."

Sol glanced up as Will nodded toward a familiar iron fence—the barrier that blocked out Tristan's world from his own. They were in The Mud district. A woman leaned casually against the bars, dressed in a more conservative outfit than Solomand had ever seen her in; a plain, gray suit like the one the former governor used to wear, though it looked more flattering on her. Her hair was plated to the side of her neck.

Solomand froze as she walked forward, moonlight lighting her fair face and dark hair. She looked almost amiable as she nodded in acknowledgement. "Solomand Black." She turned to Will. "Good to see you are yourself again."

Will bowed his head.

Solomand swallowed as he dusted the dirt from his hands. "Minuet." Face to face with her, he found all his animosity dissolved. "You've changed your uniform."

Minuet glanced down, smoothing her skirt. "Yes. The Coalition has elected me governor since the report of LeFrost's untimely demise."

"Really? Well, I suppose I should congratulate you."

Opportunist. He tried to find something wrong with this, but didn't have the spirit.

"Yes, well. It doesn't mean I can offer you a pardon."

"Naturally." That was the last thing he wanted.

Her eye raised. "But I won't be actively pursuing you. The people have grown tired of LeFrost's petty waste of resources on personal revenge." There was something different about her as she fell quiet. "Walk with me."

Solomand lit a cigarette and slipped a hand in his pocket, feeling for the letters as he strolled rigidly next to Minuet along the fence-line.

He had braced himself for a deserved accusation of being responsible for Tristan's death, so it came as a shock when Minuet finally spoke. "Hydra tells me you are going to have a child."

Solomand stopped walking for a moment, then started again, matching her unhurried pace. "Yes," he said cautiously, wondering why Hydra thought this information was worth divulging to Minuet St. Sebastian. And what did she intend to do with it?

"Don't you think it would be wise for Rayn to consult a doctor after, you know, the accident?"

Solomand's eyes narrowed. The tip of his cigarette glistened as he inhaled. She was right. But there were also few options for fugitives. LeFrost had seen to that. "Why do you care all of a sudden?" He could not keep the annoyance out of his voice. All these years they had made no secret of the fact they did not like each other. Tristan is what kept both of them from doing each other in. Now that he was gone, there was no need for any pretense.

Minuet stopped, looking sharply at him. "Because *he* would."

"That has nothing to do with you." He couldn't help feeling it.

Minuet's eyes misted over as she glanced up at the sky. "I know." She seemed genuinely at peace, which was itself unnerving. "There is someone who might help you, discreetly."

Solomand's chest tightened. "No."

Lacing her hands behind her back, Minuet sighed in exasperation. "Unreasonable as ever, I see."

Solomand finished his cigarette and dropped it on the ground. "Did you have something you wanted to ask me, Minuet?" He crushed the smoldering tobacco under his heel, ignoring her tone.

"Yes, as a matter of fact. I have a favor to ask."

Solomand shoved his hands in his pockets, gazing up at the sky, waiting and dreading. Whatever it was, he couldn't very well say no to her.

"Galin Highcourt would like to see you."

"Where can I find him?" he asked, leaving out the fact he meant to go see Galin, anyway.

"In the old meeting house." She nodded toward the abandoned town.

"Here?"

She gave him a disheartened smile and turned to go. "Think about what I said, will you? For Rayn's sake."

Solomand swallowed. "Minuet, wait." He pulled the letter from his pocket and held it out to her.

Her eyes brightened for a moment, then shimmered with tears as she took it. "Thank you," she whispered.

Solomand cleared his throat, not liking the pity he was feeling for her. "Farewell, Lady St. Sebastian. Or should I say, Governor?"

She smiled and raised a hand. "I like the sound of that. Goodbye, Solomand Black." There was a finality in the way she spoke that was oddly bittersweet.

Chapter 50

Solomand

I NEED TO DO this alone. Not so much because he was brave, but because he was afraid.

"Stay with your Harpy, will you," Solomand spoke to Will with what he hoped was a commanding tone. He needn't have bothered. Nobody listened to him unless they damn well wanted to. He could tell Will was about to protest, and resorted to pleading. "Please, Will? I'll be fine."

Will frowned. "Alright, Sol," he said, reluctantly.

Galin's hate was sure to have deepened. Solomand didn't blame him either. Pacing the street, he passed the ramshackle building a half-dozen times, eyeing the light on the window.

I should have just posted the damn letters. He twirled the chain of his medallion around his finger again and again. Crickets chirped in the background and a night bird trilled from the top of the building. How he'd missed the sounds of life! The scent of grass and dirt—even the humidity that hung in the air.

God above, just get it over with!

Talking to himself was a bad sign that he needed to act fast. With every step, he took a slow breath in, then one out. Tension in his chest decompressed slightly, and he forced himself to walk up to the door. As he raised his hand to knock, it opened.

Galin gave him an appraising look. "If I did not know better, Solomand Black, I would think you were afraid of me."

"Sir." Solomand gulped, lowering his hand.

"Sir?" Galin scoffed. "Formalities do not really suit you, Solomand." He shut the door as Sol stepped inside. His apparent lack of venom was, if possible, worse than anything Solomand had expected.

Get it over with, Highcourt! Fidgeting with the medallion, he scanned the room, breathing in the aroma of charred wood and brewing tea.

The surgeon adjusted his glasses and placed a silver surgeon's tool into an open black case. "I wondered if you would come," he said quietly.

Solomand's throat constricted, and he cleared it, forcing himself to speak. "I had something to deliver to you." There was a tremor in his hand as he drew out Tristan's letter and held it out at a distance, irrationally afraid to come any closer.

Galin looked at the bloodstained envelope for a long moment before taking it. "An airship would have delivered this just as well, you know."

Solomand drew himself up and took a shaky breath. "No, Sir. It would not do." It would have been cowardly. "He wanted me to tell you he was..." He paused, looking at the scuffed toes of his boots. "He was sorry."

An uncomfortable silence passed between them. "Did he say anything else?"

Sol studied the pattern of grain in the floorboards, clinging to a fragment of self-control. "Only that we would meet again."

Galin took off his glasses, pulling on his chin. "Yes," he said, softly. "I expect we will."

Solomand felt light-headed. Only months ago, Galin would not have hesitated to point out the fact that he'd killed his son. Why not now? There was something on his mind, though. Solomand prayed he would get it over with so this dreaded meeting could end and they could part ways. When Galin finally spoke, it was worse than anything he imagined.

"What happened to Tristan was not your fault. He chose his own path, one which has made me immensely proud. Though it took me far too long to realize. I wanted to thank you for helping him find his way and showing him what a true friend really is."

Solomand sank into a chair, burying his face in his hands. There was nothing he could say to this. A telling-off would have been easier to hear.

Galin was placing things into his bag again. "Minuet tells me Rayn is going to have a child."

She didn't! Of all the—Solomand raised his head, but didn't answer right away. Galin spoke again. "I need to leave the Continent. There is nothing left for me here. I was wondering if you would give me a ride?"

Swallowing with difficulty, Solomand stood. "Where do you want to go?"

"Argos." Galin snapped an open suitcase shut.

Argos. The Second Continent, land of the Firebolt Catchers and red deserts. And, less-appealing, the Slave traders. Solomand wondered why a man like Galin Highcourt would ever wish to go to a wild and savage place like Argos. "If it isn't too far out of your way," Galin said, his voice changing to a more tactful tone. "I can only offer you my services as a doctor for payment, I'm afraid."

Solomand's voice was hoarse when he spoke. "I can ask nothing of you."

"I thought I was the one asking *you* for something. Namely, passage to Argos. And if there happens to be work for me on the way, well, it would be against my conscience to let it go undone." There was a lordly edge in the man's tone as he slipped on his coat, daring Solomand to oppose him. In other circumstance, Solomand would have told him where he could put his demands.

"Why?" Solomand snapped. A dozen insults entered his mind in reflex reaction to the man's tone. He did not like a pig-headed swank telling him what he was or wasn't going to do.

Galin's lips formed a satisfied smirk, like he was betting on this reaction. Solomand's face burned with shame. *You idiot.* "I'm sorry. I didn't mean… I would be grateful."

Placing a hat on his head, Galin put one bag under his arm and held the other in his hand. "And yet, you would never have asked for it." He smiled, looking at Solomand with curiosity. "Perhaps we have more in common than you think."

There was a time when Solomand would have denied this vehemently. Now he merely opened the door for Galin, avoiding his eyes. "Why Argos?" Changing the subject was his usual strategy.

Galin blew out the lamp on the table as he stepped out into the night. "Why not?"

Chapter 51

IVAN

IVAN LIMPED TO the infirmary. He probably should have used a cane to walk, but stubbornness was a hard habit to break. The door was cracked open. Jank was talking to someone and there was a clanging and clattering of things being moved. Ivan pushed open the door with the toe of his boot and leaned in the doorway, relying on it a little too much for support.

Zee was bringing medical supplies from the tarnished metal cabinets on the wall. Jank laid them out on the stainless steel table, organizing and writing on a piece of paper. He glanced up at Ivan and stuck the pencil behind his ear. "You look…" He cleared his throat.

"Like shit?" Ivan took a rocky step forward. "You can say it. I am in no position to tear off your head." His fingers lingered on the support of the wall as long as possible.

"Here." Jank dropped the paper, stepped from behind the table, and brought Ivan a chair from along the wall. He set it down by Ivan, then jumped back with a frightened yell, colliding with the table. Scalpels, gauze, and jars of medicine clattered to the floor.

Ivan twisted his head to see Ruslin stood in the infirmary doorway. Lowering himself carefully into the chair, he raised an eyebrow at Jank. "He will not tear your head off either."

"Yeah right!" Jank scoffed.

As if to prove himself, Ruslin padded across the room to where Zee stood, sniffing the air. His nose touched the nape of her neck. Zee held her hand out, and the wolf licked her fingers, yawned, and lay at her feet. "I don't know why you're so scared of him." She took a roll of gauze from the cabinet and tossed it to Jank.

"Oh, I don't know." Jank put the gauze on the table and began scooping up the fallen items. "Maybe because he's as big a sodding *horse* and has more teeth than an airship engine gearbox!"

Ivan shook his head as he unwound the bandage wrapped around his hand. Pain shot through his elbow and he flinched, sucking in a sharp breath.

"Here." Jank looked at him through narrowed eyes as he sorted through the glass bottles for one half-filled with white pain pills. He twisted the cap to open it.

It was the last bottle. "No." He held up a hand. "I don't want them."

Pain was useful. It kept other things at bay.

Jank hesitated before capping the bottle and tossing it back on the table. "If you say so." He gathered a handful of bandages and a jar of ointment. "At least let me help you, then."

Ivan relaxed with a nod. Jank gave Ruslin nervous glances as he helped Ivan change the bandages on his many injuries and set his arm better. "You sure you don't want something for the pain?" Jank folded his arms and leaned back against the table.

Slipping his arm through a sling, Ivan cleared his mind of distraction. Every ache and throb and sting spread through his body, entangling with the deeper wounds in his soul. Did he want it to go away? Yes.

He stood. "Give it to Rayn."

Jank's eyes widened, and he held his hands out in front of his chest. "*You* give it to her. I'm not going near her with the mood she's in." He thumbed a finger at Ruslin. "I'm more scared of her than that damned killing machine of yours!"

"Fine." Ivan took the bottle from Jank, shoved it from his pocket, and shuffled from the room. Ruslin trailed after him.

The door to Rayn and Solomand's quarters was open. She sat cross-legged on the bunk, rifle components laid out in an organized fashion. Pale, her hair hung around her face and her injured arm was still in a sling. "Before you ask again, I'm fine." She sounded annoyed. Wiping oil from the bolt of the rifle, it fell from her hands and banged on the floor. Sighing angrily, Rayn fell back against the pillow.

Ivan made his way to the table by her bed. Dipping his hand in his pocket, his hand closed around the bottle of pain pills, tightening for a moment before he took it from his pocket and set it down. He picked up the bolt and laid it on the bed as he sat down. "It's too damn cold here." She held out her arm, presumably realizing he would not leave until she let him check it.

"You get used to it." Ivan unwrapped her bandages with one arm, as his other one was too painful to move. "How do you feel?"

"I feel like shit."

"So do I." Ivan cracked a grin. "At least we both tell truth now."

Rayn pulled her arm back against her chest. "Where's your wolf friend?"

"Ruslin?" Ivan raised an eyebrow. "You wish to see him?" After nearly having her arm torn off by the white wolf, he didn't think she would want nothing to do with the old Alpha.

"Yeah," she said. Ivan let out a low whistle. Ruslin had been laying in the hall just outside the door. He walked into the room, stiffly like an old man, and up to Ivan, ears erect. He lay his hand on Ivan's knee and Rayn reached out her hand to stroke his head. Unafraid, as ever.

"He's beautiful," she said nonchalantly, like she was talking about a harmless kitten.

Ivan rubbed the back of his neck. "Not first word I would use to describe a *wolf.*" Menacing, deadly, lethal; those were all better choices.

"So what's keeping him from killing me, then?" She kept stroking his head, and the wolf moved its muzzle closer to her, his eyes closing slightly.

Ivan shrugged. "He can sense if I don't like someone, I think. But even then, he waits for me to tell him to attack. Unless I am in trouble, then he will not wait." It was hard to describe the bond between the assassins and their wolves.

"That would come in handy." Rayn scratched the wolf's ear. "Where can I get my own?"

"In mountains. You have to kill mother to get one, too."

"Oh." Her face fell. "Seems kind of… brutal."

"Is brutal country. Is only way you will ever get hands on a pup without dying," Ivan said.

"I'll pass." Rayn winced. "Even though I already had a name picked out."

Ivan was amused. "What name?" he asked.

"Solomand."

Ivan laughed, shaking his head as he stood, shifting the brunt of his weight to one leg. "I'll leave you alone now. Do you need anything?"

Rayn glanced down at the rifle pieces strewn around her legs. "No."

"You wish Ruslin to stay?"

She shook her head. "I wouldn't want him to forget you like me and tear my arm the rest of the way off."

Ivan's eyes narrowed, and he gave her a crooked grin. "That is something Sol would say."

Rayn's eyes clenched shut. "Fine. I want him to stay."

Ivan lay a hand on Ruslin's head. "*Chechnye*, you almost make me want to go get you your own *leid valk. Ruslin, stani.*" The wolf closed his eyes and curled up by the bedside obediently.

Ivan left them like that, leaning on the wall all the way to the helm room as he limped. His leg was getting worse, not better. He sank to the floor, leaning against the glass and glancing out at the forest.

"*Kirno Valk.*" Niko's voice was nostalgic as he walked in, towering over Ivan.

Ivan flinched. "*Don't call me that.*"

Nikola's laugh was like a low growl. "*You will not claim your role as Alpha?*"

"*No. I never wanted to be a Wolf. You know this.*"

Nikola stooped to tighten his bootlaces. "*I know.*"

"*What about you? Will you return to the life of an assassin?*"

Nikola shook his head. "*No, Ivan. I will return to Byorn. I've had enough of such a life.*"

Recalling Aleksei's words about Nikola's sister, guilt swept over Ivan once more. "*I am sorry for what you lost. If I could change it—*"

Nikola held up his hand dismissively. "*Don't. We all know how volatile Aleksei was, especially toward the end. We played with fire in a world of ice and snow. The end was inevitable.*"

Ivan adjusted his leg, cringing. "*I know. But still.*"

An annoyed look flashed across Nikola's face. "*Forget the past, Ivan. You wish to make things right in your mind? Go to Ramshorn. Find whatever Sushinka left for you. She said it was important.*"

"*Important?*" Ivan wondered what she could have meant. "*She did not say what it was?*"

Nikola shook his head. "*Only that it would be with an Obojin, the man I told you about earlier—Kryllen.*"

"*An Obojin?*" Ivan was more than a little surprised that Sushinka would have any dealings with anyone from the raider tribes. Aside from the Ice Wolves, there was no one on the North Continent more feared or hated. They were seafarers, called the Crimson Eye by some, because of their eyes, which were a deep-ruby color. Not much else was known about them. They came in their ships and raided coastal villages, killing all, or mostly, everyone, and disappearing again into the ocean waves. They were wild looking and usually wore paint on their faces.

"*Ivan. I promised her I would have you go there.*" Nikola must have seen the reservation creeping into Ivan's thoughts.

"*I will go.*"

"*Good. Then it is time for me to go.*" Nikola looked satisfied.

"*I wish you luck.*"

"*And you.*" Nikola looked sad as he gripped Ivan's hand. "*Farewell, Brother.*"

Chapter 52

SOLOMAND

GALIN WAS ASLEEP, and Will was at the controls of the Raptor. Solomand eyed Hydra. She sat across from her, painting her toenails different colors. "Can I help you?" Her head tilted to the side, curls sliding over one eye.

Solomand glanced out the window, then brought his view quickly back inside the machine. There was too much about her not to trust.

You could help me. He thought to himself, running a finger along the window frame. If she told Will he couldn't go with her... tempting as it was, he couldn't do it.

"What interest do you really have in him?" He nodded toward the cabin.

Hydra's hand slipped forward and green paint smeared on the front of her toe. Setting the bottle down, she blotted at the polish with a rag. "I have no idea what you could possibly mean—"

"Oh, cut the act, whatever your name is." Solomand sighed in exasperation. "He means to leave with you and I need to know."

It sounded a little ridiculous. Will was a grown man—an Olbian warrior. But more importantly, he was like a brother.

Hydra let a look of surprise slip, then a shimmer of joy glistened in her eyes before her mask of carefree nonchalance returned. Biting her bottom lip, she gave him a studying look. "You're worried about him."

Solomand drummed fingers on the side of his arm. "He is my friend."

And I don't want to lose another one.

Hydra planted her bare feet on the ground, sitting up straight. "Solomand Black, I would never do anything that would lead your friend to harm."

Solomand kept his doubt to himself. Smiling, as if she knew he would not believe her, Hydra added, "I wouldn't want to ruin any chance at a future meeting with The Falcon, would I?"

"Bah!" Where the hell was Lemuel, anyway? It was unfair to be mad at him, but Solomand couldn't help himself. "You two have more in common than you know," he muttered. A vindictive voice inside him half-wished he knew where The Falcon was so he could tell the girl.

Hydra laughed. "I doubt that very much. Anyway, you should probably know Hydra is not my actual name."

"You don't say?"

"I know. Shocking. It's Filomena."

"No, it isn't." Solomand sighed. "But it doesn't matter. The Falcon has more than one name, too."

"You know his name, don't you?" she looked interested. "Will said you had a history, I think it's more than that."

Solomand remained stone-faced. Whatever she suspected, he would say nothing that would lead her, or anyone else, closer to Lemuel—no matter how mad he may be.

Hydra looked thoughtful. "You're protecting him."

Solomand hated how everything was a statement with her. "Don't worry. However dangerous you think I may be, I need his help."

So did I. The bitterness left a bad taste in his mouth, and Solomand wanted to drop the subject of Lemuel altogether. "We will discuss it next time we meet. Deal?"

Hydra tilted her head, holding a hand out with a grin. "Deal." Her grip was firm. For the first time, he thought she might be sincere.

-¤O¤-

The first thing he noticed when they landed was the snow was cleared away from the Dragonfly. Scuffed up, but no worse for wear. The airship was ready for takeoff. The only damage appeared to be the barrel on the aft gunner station was irreparably bent. That didn't matter, though. They were unlikely to be engaged in any airship battles. At least that's what he hoped.

"Stupid, endless gloom." Grumbling to himself about the cold, Solomand zipped up his jacket and stepped outside, skating across compacted snow.

Ivan stepped out of the Dragonfly docking bay, his arm in a sling. He leaned against the hull, the black wolf at his side; the others were behind him. When Ivan saw Galin Highcourt, he gave Solomand a questioning look. "He's coming with us," Sol said, glancing uncomfortably at Ruslin. "He's still here, I see. Still harmless?"

Ivan looked at him like he was stupid. "He is only harmless if I want him to be, *Lochek.*"

Solomand spared him a grin and went to Rayn. He wrapped his arms around her. "Missed you." He kissed her. "Ivan take good care of you?"

Her one-armed embrace was stronger than he expected. "Yeah. Less a traitor than you are." She breathed out a relieved sigh and whispered in his ear, "I'm glad you're back." She drew back, her eyes searching. "Sol, what's wrong?" Sick at heart, Solomand glanced over at Will; he looked unsure of himself as he walked over and Rayn's face fell.

"I... I've come to say goodbye." Will glanced back at Hydra, who watched on from the proximity of her Raptor.

Rayn pulled free of Solomand and went to Will's open arms. Solomand stuffed his hands in his pockets, watching as Jank disappeared into the airship to avoid another goodbye; they weren't really his thing.

As Rayn pulled away from Will, he looked like he wanted to run away, as Zee came up to him.

"Zee." He stuck his hands in his pockets.

"You're leaving?" There was a bewilderment in her voice.

"Yes."

"But I don't want you to go," she whispered, tears welling up in her eyes.

For the first time Solomand remembered, he saw Will fighting back tears as he pulled the girl into his arms. "I'm sorry." His voice was a whisper. He ripped the insignia off his Olbian uniform coat and handed it to her. "I'll be back, Zee. I promise.

Solomand looked away, wondering if the girl believed Will. Would she believe anyone else ever again? When Will finally broke free from her, she ran back to the airship, furiously wiping tears from her eyes.

Solomand wanted to run to her, to tell her it would be alright. But it wouldn't be enough. He held out his hand to Will, remembering when they first met as enemies on a bloody field of battle.

"Don't be a stranger. I know that Harpy of yours can find us if she really wants to."

Will jerked Solomand's arm forward, pulling him into an embrace. "I'll see you, Sol."

He walked away to the waiting Hydra and boarded the Raptor.

Solomand remained outside in the oppressing cold as everyone except Ivan returned to the airship. He lit a cigarette, feeling unusually morose as he glanced at Ivan. "Where's your friend, anyway?"

"Nikola? He is gone to Chroburough," Ivan replied.

Solomand was afraid to ask. Tristan was gone; now Will. The Olbian they might see again, but Ivan? This was his home. If he chose to say, Solomand doubted they would ever see each other again.

"I expect you'll be following him then?" Flicking ashes into the snow, he tried to make it sound like he didn't care.

Ivan's eyes narrowed. "Do you want to be rid of me?"

"No!" Solomand burst out. "It's just, you only left because of Aleksei, now he's gone, so I assumed…"

Ivan's hand was on the wolf's head, and he stared into the trees. "I have no place here anymore."

So that was it then. Solomand's spirits sank. "I understand." He flicked his cigarette away and watched the snow put it out almost instantly. "Owe!" he yelled as Ivan smacked him on the back of the head.

"No, *lochek*. I mean here." Ivan motioned to the forest. "In Northland." He spoke with a half-smile.

"Oh." Solomand contained his relief. "But what about your family?"

Ivan shook his head. "To them, I am dead. It is best that it stays that way. My mother would rather that be the case than find out I am Wolf." His face hardened like it always did when Ivan was done speaking of his past.

As silence settled over them, Solomand wanted to say he was glad Ivan was sticking around. Ivan already knew, though. They turned and walked up the ramp to the docking bay.

His hand resting on the wolf (probably for support) Ivan asked, "Are you in hurry to leave for Argos?"

"Not particularly." Ivan opened the bay door. "Why?"

Ivan glanced through the twisted trees toward the mountains. "There is something I must do before I leave Northland."

Chapter 53

IVAN

NAVIGATING ALONG THE southern coast of Hyperborea took around four months. It would have taken less time had they not needed to stop due to storms, or for supplies and equipment. These stops took longer each time, as Ivan prevented Sol from repeating their first mistake of leaving a well-documented path for others to follow them. Galin Highcourt came in handy. He spoke the language; he was more than willing to accompany Ivan out into the skyports and proved himself a shrewd businessman.

When they finally arrived at the fishing village, Ivan would let no one go with him but Solomand. He still wasn't sure if Sushinka had laid a clever trap for him. She was, after all, furious at him for leaving.

Ramshorn was the town off the coast Nikola had said to go to. The name of the town meant Road's End. Ivan thought it was appropriate. Framed by cliffs to the East, which formed a semi-circle at its back. This was the most temperate climate on the whole Northern Continent. There was no snow here when they arrived, but a bracing wind swept in from the sea as great waves of treacherously cold water crashed on the pebbled beaches and threatened to tear the schooners from the docks.

Having ditched his heavier clothes for his greatcoat, Solomand cursed the cold, turning up his collar. "Of all the times you could have taken Galin instead of me," he muttered.

The cold didn't bother Ivan. "Only reason I take Galin instead of you before is because he is not so volatile. Better for doing business. You are better in fight."

"Expecting one here?" Solomand looked wary.

Ivan shrugged. "Perhaps." They walked down the curved path into the village. He told Ruslin to wait where he could not be seen. A black wolf would bring more attention than they needed.

An old man with rough hands wound a rope around the peer, fastening a fishing boat in place. A boy of around fifteen helped him, keeping the slack in as the water threatened to pull the craft out to water. On the peer at their feet sat a basket of freshly caught fish.

Ivan walked up to him, his boots clambering on the weathered planks of the walkway. "*Epralsitei (excuse me)*," he spoke in Slavik. The man gave him a suspicious look, his weathered face lined and apprehensive. "*I am looking for a man named Kryllen.*"

The boy's round eyes grew wider, looking at his elder companion with fear. The old man uttered a curse and looked away, finishing his knot in a hurry. Ivan was not surprised. Obojin evoked this reaction, and anyone looking for one would be mistrusted.

"*I was told I could find him in Ramshorn.*" He pressed the man further, standing in his way as he tried to leave.

Scowling, the fisherman ordered the boy to grab their catch, but Ivan's hard stare made him speak. "*Not in town—not his kind.*" He tried to move past again.

Ivan held his hand out, pressing it into the man's chest. "Where?" he growled.

"*By the Sea. In an old cabin,*" the fisherman relented, grudgingly. As Ivan removed his hand he cursed again, "D*evil take you both. And the crimson eye!*"

Ivan glared at the old man as he hurried away, the boy giving him nervous looks over his shoulder. "Same to you, *steir shleroff.*"

"Old fool, huh?" Solomand was trying, unsuccessfully, to light a cigarette against the endless gusts of wind. "What's his problem?"

Ivan scowled. "It was probably my mention of this Kryllen."

"Ah. What was that about the Crimson Eye?" He tried one more time to light his cigarette, but the wind tore it from his mouth. Making an aggravated noise, he followed Ivan as they followed the faded path which led from town toward the cliffs by the sea.

"Obojin," Ivan answered. "They are raiders, mostly. A strange people. Many people believe they are devils. Stupid rumors." He gave Sol a sideways glance as they walked. "When did you learn new words?"

"Caught that, did you? I pay more attention than people may assume." Solomand kicked a rock from the path. "Obojin, huh? I think Lemuel tried to tell me about them during one of his attempts to tutor me. It was boring, and I never paid much attention."

They were nearing the end of the trail and a small cabin came into view, near to the water's edge. There was a dock that went out into the sea, but no boat was tied to it. A pile of firewood was stacked in front, and smoke curled from the chimney. Ivan stopped, pondered the possibility of a trap. He whistled for Ruslin and waited for the wolf to appear.

"You think this might be a setup?" Solomand toyed with his lighter, absentmindedly watching the sparks as the wind blew them out at each strike.

"Anything is possible."

When Ruslin reached his side, he told the wolf to stay, and crept forward. The noise of their boots on the rocky path was masked by the roar of the waves. "So, you think this Kryllen is going to throw the door open and axe us in the head? Should I wait outside in case, so I can shoot him if he gets a swing at you?"

Ivan rolled his eyes. He started to say that was just the sort of thing he would expect of Solomand when something struck him in the temple. Moving a hand to his head, he searched for where the object had come from.

"Shit, Ivan. Are you alright?" Solomand's eyes were wide. "You're bleeding like hell!"

Ivan drew his hand away from his head and looked at the blood dripping from his fingers, dazed. "Look out." Solomand shoved him to the ground as a rock sailed by his head, barely missing. It came from behind the pile of wood.

"Go away, *otvalis*!" It was a girl's voice that yelled at them.

He and Solomand exchanged a surprised look. A girl of about seven, or maybe eight, barefoot and dressed in a white leather dress with matching armbands, stalked from her hiding place. Hands on her hips, she stood in the middle of the path, staring them down with savage gray eyes.

Her brown hair was long and wild. A stripe of red and black paint ran the length of her face just below her eyes. His mouth hanging open, and a look of disbelief on his face, Solomand pulled Ivan to his feet. Ivan wiped the blood from his still-bleeding head.

He lunged forward, taking the girl by surprise as he grabbed her by the arm. "Do I *look* like *otvali* to you, little girl?"

"Let me go!" she fumed, twisting and yanking her arm. "My father will come—then you'll be sorry!"

"We came to see your father, *ea daeval* (she-devil)—owe!" He let go as she kicked him viciously in the leg that had barely healed. She sprinted toward the cabin. "Come back here!" Holding the side of his leg, he didn't so much run as limp after her.

As he rounded the corner of the cabin, his eyes widened. The girl brought the machete in her hands down on a rope connected to a machine formed from twine, pulleys, and small trees. The blade sliced through the rope, and a log hurdled toward him. Ivan ducked, and it flew over his head, slamming into Solomand, who did not move from its path quickly enough.

Crying out, Solomand fell heavily on the ground, cursing in Kree. He sat up, tilting his head back as blood streamed from his nose. "That's it. I'm waiting here."

"I told you to leave, *otvali*!" The girl yelled, raising her machete over her head, small hands grasped firmly around the handle.

Ivan looked from Solomand to her, feeling increasingly out of control of the situation.

"I think she's serious." Solomand dabbed at his nose. "You sure whatever this Kryllen has of yours is worth it?" Solomand struggled to his feet, then leaned against the cabin, eyeing the girl like at any minute she would do something that might kill both of them.

Ivan's face darkened, and he pointed at the girl. "Enough, *ea daivol*! You should not play with knives!"

The girl's small nose wrinkled as she yelled defiantly, "I am *not* playing." She ran at him.

This is ridiculous! She is just a child. Ivan let her come. She sliced his hand before he wrenched the blade from her grasp and pinned her arms to her sides.

"Get your hands off of me!" she spoke through her teeth, squirming and kicking.

Ivan's grip tightened. "I think not, *ea daevol*. We will wait until your father, Kryllen, gets here."

"Kryllen is *not* my father," she snapped. "My father is an even stronger warrior. When he comes, you will be sorry."

Ivan raised an eye. "You said that already, *ea daevol*."

The girl's eyes flashed. "That is *not* my name!"

"And *otvali* is not mine." Ivan's voice raised, and he lifted her off the ground.

The girl stopped fighting for a moment, her small chest rising and falling rapidly as she seethed, refusing to look at him. With a sigh, he decided to make peace with her. He sat her down, but kept his hands on her shoulders. "My friend and I will wait for Kryllen. But, if you tell me your name, I will tell you mine, uh?"

The girl glared back silently. "Fine. *Ea daevol* it is."

She took a deep breath. "My. Name. Is Micha Simenov," she snarled.

Simenov! Ivan's grip loosened in his shock and the girl jerked free of his grip, retreating to the dock where she proceeded to hurl pebbles in their general direction.

"Uh, Ivan. You alright?" Solomand pulled Ivan out of the line of fire more than once before he asked. Rocks bounced off the cabin's edge as they hid behind it.

Ivan sank to the ground. "Cigarette?" He held out a hand to Sol, who lit one for both of them.

Simenov? It couldn't be. He let the smoke fill his lungs.

Something of yours. Sushinka said nothing to him. *Something important.* He dragged a hand down the side of his head, smearing fresh blood from the cut on his hand.

Solomand looked worried as he squatted down. "Look, I know you made a promise to Nikola, but I think you've honored that by coming here. I mean, he never mentioned anything about a demon-possessed child, did he?"

"No." His voice was hollow. "He did not." Nikola probably had no idea. Pressing a hand against his head, he stared far-off, inhaling his cigarette in one breath.

"*Ea daevol!*" Ivan called. The rocks momentarily stopped as Micha Simenov listened and waited. "When will your father be here?"

"I'm not telling *you otvali!*" The rocks continued to fly past their heads, knocking against the logs of the cabin.

Ivan took a shaky breath, catching Solomand's studious and somewhat worried gaze. "If her father isn't an Obojin, he must be a hell of a…" his voice trailed off and he transferred the cigarette to his hand. "Ivan. You and Sushinka. Were you two ever…" he waved his hand, searching for the right words. "An item."

Giving him his best annoyed look, Ivan said everything he needed to by not answering.

Solomand's hand went to his mouth. "Simenov. That's your surname, isn't it?" Without waiting for an answer he stood, "Oh god above. Just like that, everything makes perfect sense. I never took you for that type. Got anymore hellcats stashed along the coast I should know about?"

"*Shut up, asshole.*" Ivan glared at him, dabbing at his throbbing head. "And, no. It was only ever Sushinka. If I'd have known, I would have…"

Would have what? Come for her? It would have brought Aleksei straight there. God knows he is the last person who needed to know of her existence. Ivan leaned over, feeling ill at this discovery. "Maybe is just name Sushinka told her to use."

Solomand smirked, shaking his head. "Oh no. That girl is *exactly* how imagined a child of yours would be."

"A savage?" Ivan scowled.

Solomand looked pensive as he pulled on his beard. "Something like that—owe!" his head rolled to the side as one of Micha's rocks finally found its mark.

That's it! Ivan let out a low whistle as he stood and dragged Solomand behind the cabin. "*Ea daevol*, Micha!" He called, hoping the girl would stop throwing stones for a moment. She did, and he dashed around the back of the cabin with Ruslin at his side.

The sight of the huge black wolf startled the girl. Her hand drew back with a stone in it, but she froze, eyes widened as they fixed on Ruslin. A moment was all he needed. Ivan tackled her to the ground as gently as he could. Dragging her up, he took the rock and hurled it into an oncoming wave.

Micha's eyes were still on Ruslin. He seemed to have shocked her into a calmer state for the moment, but Ivan didn't trust her to not run away. "Now you listen to me!" Her eyes, full of anger and fierceness, shifted to him. He saw himself in that moment. "Where is Kryllen?" he demanded.

"At sea." She did not sound particularly upset that her guardian was absent.

"He left you alone?"

"I can take care of myself, *otvali*."

Ivan eyed the blood which still seeped from his hand, feeling light-headed. "I don't doubt that, *ea daevol*."

"Besides." Micha's lips pursed together. "My father will be here any day, and—"

"*Tishinal* (silence)!" Ivan raised his voice. Feeling like he might pass out, he took a knee, meeting her gaze. "Have you ever seen your father?"

Micha looked indignant. "No."

"Then how will you know who he is? Eh?"

"He is a warrior from the mountains." Her eyes moved to Ruslin again.

"An Ice Wolf, you mean. There are many of those."

Her lips twisted into a scowl. Ivan nodded to Ruslin. "He is an ice wolf. Mine. An old friend." Speaking to her made him strangely uncomfortable. He felt like he would pass out again, and his grip loosened. She tried to pull free, but he stopped her. "Uh-uh." He pulled her back. "I didn't tell you my name yet."

She did not look like she wanted to hear it, but Ivan didn't care. "I am Ivan Simenov," he said sternly.

Micha's eyes flashed, and he felt her stiffen. "*You're* Ivan Simenov? *You're* my father?"

Ivan nodded. "So it would seem. Disappointed, *ea daevol*?" He grabbed her and threw her over his shoulder. "I'm sure it won't be the last thing you are disappointed about."

"Wait!" She pounded her fists on his back.

Ivan looked at Solomand. "We will not wait for Kryllen. Probably he did not plan on coming back."

"You know, I think you're right. Doubt he'll be shedding any tears." Solomand nodded, looking at Ivan like he held a venomous reptile. He kept his distance. "Sure about this, are you? I think the wolf is less dangerous."

He knew Solomand was only joking, but he had a point. He had never felt such a strange mix of doubt and conviction. Giving Solomand a weak grin in answer, he started down the path, away from the cabin.

"I wish you luck," Sol grimaced. "You're going to need it."

"So will you, *lochek*." Ivan let out a laugh as Solomand turned a shade paler.

Chapter 54

THREE MONTHS LATER.

WHEN THEY REACHED Argos, a storm hurling a wall of red sand forced the airship down in the northern desert, just on the other side of the electrical storm belt. This was when the child of Rayn and Solomand entered the world of Roanoke.

Pacing the hall endlessly, Solomand watched lightning send fracturing bolts of light through the haze of sand outside. At least it wasn't ice and snow bombarding them. He found his way to the kitchen where a light was on and the smell of fresh coffee wafted. Ivan sat at the counter, cutting slices off a loaf of bread. Solomand strode around the kitchen several times, eyeing the clock on the wall. Despite the doctor's assurance that she would be fine, he was terrified.

Ivan sat at the table and took a drink from his cup, his composure giving way to an annoyed stare. "Sit down, Sol." He spoke between bites. "You're giving me headache."

The airship creaked under the force of the wind. Solomand's heart lurched as the lights flickered off and then on again. He sat down across from Ivan, fingers drumming the table, while his knee bounced.

Ivan shook his head. "Why do you worry, anyway? Is nothing to being father."

"Oh, is that so?" Solomand folded his arms over his chest, retorting, "So glad you're here to guide me, wise one."

The last he saw of Micha, she was sleeping in the storage room, curled into the side of the black wolf. There were stripes of red and black on her face; Ivan could not get her to stop painting herself. Even in sleep, she looked like an untamed creature—ready to jump up and attack. He shuddered. "I don't envy you, my friend. Wait until she's older."

Ivan took another sip of coffee. "Careful. Or you end up in same boat with me. Zee is older than Micha."

"Ha!"

His soul shrank back as his mind veered down a path where Zee and Micha were both the same—running through the desert together. It was not a pleasant thought.

"Solomand."

Sol sprang to his feet when Galin stuck his head in the door. Unrolling his sleeves, the doctor looked amused.

"H-how is she? Is everything alright?" Sol's words spilled out over each other.

"They are both fine." The words barely out of Galin's mouth, Solomand bolted from the room and all the way to the infirmary.

On the other side of the door, a baby was crying; loud and clear. Heart in his throat, Solomand burst through the door.

Rayn looked tired, but her smile was the brightest thing he had ever seen. In her arms was a tiny bundle, pink arms stretching upward. His child.

Solomand's hand covered his mouth as tears came to his eyes. Ivan shoved him forward, and he staggered over to the bedside. Still smiling, Rayn held the bundle out and he took it, petrified.

"A perfectly healthy baby boy." Galin sounded satisfied.

The boy stopped crying, grasping a tiny hand around Sol's finger. The pain and loss were pushed back to somewhere for later—eclipsed by the moment of their child's arrival. Cradling the baby close to his chest, he was terrified and proud all at once. He opened his mouth with a yawn and nestled a hand against his face.

Solomand looked at Rayn, unable to keep from smiling.

"Congratulations," Ivan beamed at him. "What will you name him?"

The boy who would be named after the three men who had taught him the most important things he ever could have known. His own father, who taught some beliefs are worth dying for; Rayn's father, who taught him some things are worth fighting for; and the last—that friendship and loyalty were both.

"Jude Tristan Benjamin Silas Black." He looked up at Galin, then held the child out to him.

Galin smiled, cradling the baby in his arms. "A good name."

⚙

Some weeks later, Solomand sat on a stool in front of the airship, working with Ivan to fashion snares from spare wire he had found in a box in the engine room. Galin walked outside, squinting across the horizon. His sleeves were rolled up and his shirt hung loose. The dry heat of the Argos desert was different from the warm weather of Lyonese.

"Ah. I've been looking for you." Galin strode up to Solomand, cleaning sand from his glasses on the side of his pants.

Biting his lip, Solomand held the wire in a loop as Ivan clamped a metal bracket to hold it in place. "Oh? What can I help you with?" He said.

"Rayn and Jude are doing well. All of your injuries are taken care of. It is time I went on to my final destination."

Solomand put his finger through the snare and pulled it tight to test it before tossing it to the ground and grabbing another strip of wire. "Where is that, Doctor Highcourt?" "A city called New Ankhor, where legend has it there is a library of forbidden books from the old world." He stared off into the distance before giving Solomand a tired smile. "The only way into New Ankhor is by train. I will make the rest of the journey alone."

"The hell you will." Solomand stood abruptly. "You know what's out there once you run into people?" He gestured across the horizon, wire still in hand. "*Slavers, Doctor* Highcourt. You know what kind of target being a doctor makes you?"

Galin may think he would be fine here, but he did not understand how out of league he was. Solomand had run into Argos
Slave traders before on Lyonese. They were brutal cutthroats.

"You've brought me far enough," Galin said wistfully as they
watched the sun set beyond the desert plain. Lightning flashed in
the distance in a line across the entire sky. "The next skyport we
come to, I will take my leave."

"No, Sir." Solomand could not bear the thought of Tristan's father coming to harm when he could prevent it. "That will not do."

"You cannot very well prevent me from walking away, boy."
There was a hint of that old pretension in the way the surgeon
spoke.

"I won't take you to any damned skyport, though," Solomand
said with stubborn resolve.

"You do not owe me anything, Solomand Black," Galin said,
his air of superiority growing.

"It's not about that." It was more than a feeling of responsi-
bility, though he wouldn't say it. Even in Galin's better than thou
attitude that hovered below the surface, Sol had grown to enjoy
having him around. "Let us see you to the city, at least."

The angry-eyed Micha interrupted Galin's response. She
dashed up to Solomand. "Captain!" Sol whirled around, taking a
step away from the girl. Ivan had told her to call him captain as a
joke, and she would not disobey him.

"What's wrong, Micha?"

Balled fists on her hips, Micha said indignantly, "Zee took my
knife."

"She nearly cut my hand off with it," Zee called. Solomand
looked up to see she was perched on the top of the airship.

"I did not." Micha stomped her foot.

Solomand looked from one girl to the other, feeling increasingly out of control of the situation. As the girls continued to argue, he looked at Galin. "Be honest. Is this why you want to leave?
It is, isn't it?"

Galin laughed as Ivan stood and smacked Micha across the back of the head, ending the argument. "*Ea daevol*, stop being bully."

Micha's mouth curled into a scornful pout as she looked up at him, crossing her arms. "Strength is *not* being a bully. Kryllen said—"

"I do not give *myerdaish* what Kryllen say." Ivan looked down at the girl, brow furrowing in annoyance. "*I* am your father. Now, you listen to me." He pointed to the bay doors. "Go. And stop playing with knives!"

Micha stomped away, scowling.

Looking amused, Galin said, "You know, I think maybe it is better that I travel with you. Just until I reach New Ankhor. It is only a matter of time before those two end up severely harming each other."

"Ah, yes." Solomand stroked the stubble on his chin. "I would be very grateful if you did."

"And once we reach the city, where will you go?" Galin's question took him aback.

Tir Eadon. Blue skies and a river cutting through fields of green; Solomand recalled his mother's painting and the place where he would no longer have to run from anyone; none of them would. It was not merely a legend; he knew because he had the map. The only problem was, he needed Lemuel to get it to work. It always came back to Lemuel. Always out of reach. What if he couldn't find him this time?

Solomand shrugged. "Stick around Argos. Maybe Miramet." he said, truthfully. "We'll have to find some way to make a living. Smuggling won't really do anymore."

"No. I suppose it won't." Galin glanced at Rayn as she came outside, cradling Jude in her arms. Jank followed her, a wrench in his hand. He stopped, jaw tightening as he stared at the wire in Sol's hand.

"Where did you get that?"

Solomand looked down and hurriedly tossed the wire into the pile of snares. "What?"

"You *know* what, Sol. The damn wire in your hand. Have you been messing in my toolbox again?"

Solomand shrugged, raising his arms up and playing innocent. "Now, why would I do a thing like that, Jank?"

The boy was about to go on a tirade about people misplacing his tools when a gust of wind swept across the desert, throwing sand in their faces. When it settled, a torn, dirty poster skittered across the ground, landing at Jank's feet. He stooped to pick it up. "Wanted; Firebolt catcher. No experience necessary. Unrivaled compensation…"

Solomand scoffed. "Unrivaled. That's because you won't live to collect it. Firebolt catchers have the shortest life expectancy on Argos—maybe the whole planet."

Jank turned the paper over, making an irritated noise. "The rest is missing." His eyes narrowed in the distance. "It must have come from Miramet." Miramet was the closest city, about an hour's walk. There was a disturbing note of interest in his voice that made Solomand pause.

"Jank?" Solomand raised an eyebrow. "You can't be serious."

"About what?" Jank absently folded the mangled poster. "We should go to Miramet soon, you know. Good a place as any to find work—and we'll need to you know."

It was a sound argument. Solomand would have dismissed his initial horrified reaction at the glittering in the boy's eyes had Jank not taken care to slide the folded poster in the pocket of his grease-stained jumpsuit before going about his work repairing the landing gear.

He's not a boy anymore, you idiot. When he first met Jank, he was a jumpy, scrawny fifteen-year-old delivered to the doorstep of Benjamin Ivers by none other than Lemuel Falcon. He'd changed since then. So had Solomand. They all had.

Ivan, brooding and explosive, confronted the ghosts of his past; and won. Even if they came back to haunt him, he would win again because Solomand and the others would not let him fight alone.

Will had found a new path. It was necessary to find your own way, but Solomand hoped they would see each other again one day. Rayn? He stole a look at her then, hair blowing in the wind, baby in her arms. Green eyes turned to look at him and his heart pounded wildly as if it were the first time they'd met all over again.

After everything she'd been through, she fell in love with him; not once, but twice. Some people would call that luck. The Kree would say he was blessed. He glanced up at the darkening sky and the endless pattern of stars looking down on them.

As Jude let out a soft cry, Rayn walked over. "What's the matter? Did Mama make you cry?" Solomand took the boy from Rayn, laying him gently over his shoulder and bouncing him.

Rayn punched him in the shoulder. "No, but I'll make you cry." At the sound of Solomand's laughter, her annoyed expression melted into a smile. After all the heartache he'd endured throughout his life, it was hard to accept such happiness was possible.

As Rayn slipped her arm around his waist, he recalled words Tristan said once. He wore that same confident smile on his face he went to death with. *Life will always be difficult. We will always do battle with pain and death and suffering. There's one way to beat it, though. By stealing.*

A sunset. A kiss. The company of a friend. Life can be made of moments of joy, if that's what we wish.

Solomand let the air fill his lungs, his hand tightening on Jude as the baby's heart beat rapidly against his chest in the rhythm of new life. He looked down at Rayn; the way the stars reflected in her eyes made it look like they were depthless windows. "I love you."

Rayn's lips turned up in a crooked grin. "What do you want?" Then, laughing, she moved her hands around his neck. "I love you, too."

As their lips connected, a current of energy rushed through Solomand. It was deeper than a kiss. Their souls felt entangled. If he chose to believe in the existence of fate, it was this; that they were meant to be—rebelling against a cruel world together by pilfering moments of happiness.

I could get used to being a thief.

Epilogue

L EMUEL HAD BEEN away for too long. He staggered into his cabin, loss weighing heavily on his shoulders. This last assignment was dangerous, and the death of his contact stung more than usual. The Moirai made sure their assignments kept him busy as of late. It was no doubt because of his interference in Corcyra. There were always consequences to interfering. All the same, it distanced him from crossing that dangerous line. For so long, he had worked to protect the person who meant the most to him. Once the step was taken, there would be no undoing it.

On his workbench, the machine, which was part radio, part stenographer, spit out endless coils of paper; decoded messages he'd programed it to record. Information was invaluable in his trade and he needed to at least keep up a pretense of needing such devices to record it.

Mirage screeched from her perch on the window, blue wings silver in the light from the moon. Craning her head at Lemuel, she took flight. A gust of wind scattering more papers on the dusty planks of the floor.

Lemuel eyed the rolled up scrolls of paper the falcon had delivered; messages from Solomand. The boy, as he always thought of Jessamine Black's son, was infinitely unreasonable. Never mind that his overseers, as he always thought of the Moirai, refused to let him get away. Solomand only saw one piece of a puzzle and would never understand. Lemuel meant to keep it that way.

The firebolt core dwindled with long and short flickers as Lemuel sifted through the radio messages, skimming them half-interested. There was one without a source designation.

The troublesome girl from Valhalla. It was a conversation between her and the Lyonese government agent, Athena. As he read it, his spirits sank, and he wished he'd never found the damned thing.

Tristan Highcourt was dead. Lemuel's hand tightened on the edge of the paper as he stared at the message, regret welling up.

He crumpled it into a ball and tossed it in a darkened corner by his bunk.

Always too late. That's what Solomand told him once. The first time was after Silas and Jessamine's funeral, the second was the loss of Solomand's child.

"You never show up until someone dies." That was after Rayn's father was executed. Solomand could not know the grief each one of those deaths caused him—nor the untold energy of keeping that secret from others and the Boy.

It was all my fault. Decisions one by one fell in his mind, toppled like dominos in some twisted game of fate which ended in a pile of dead bodies. Lemuel only cared about the corpses with names.

He should have never asked Benjamin to get involved. Then after, when his friend pleaded with him to help fund his rebellion, Lemuel agreed, but only after Silas and Jessamine were murdered. He knew better. Anger got the better of him. That had ended in sickening tragedy.

Alaric never brought it up, but he suspected the Moirai knew. They always knew. Fyodor probably thought it would keep him from making rash decisions, but it was proving difficult to stop.

Lemuel picked up a fogged bottle of Argos brandy and bit off the cork before taking a long gulp. It burned all the way down to his stomach. It occurred to him he only drank it when someone died.

I'll need another bottle soon. As his eyes scanned over the messages, he did a double take, coughing as the liquor went down the wrong way. It was a message from Rayn.

How much did she remember? Would leaving her implant be something he should regret? It always seemed to go wrong when he ignored their orders.

The door swung open on creaking hinges as he trudged outside, bottle still in hand. Stars glistened in the blackened sky over the island. A warm wind stirred the trees and bushes around his cabin. *Tristan Highcourt.* There was no end to his regret that they tied his hands in that matter. "It would have been interfering," he muttered bitterly, then raised his voice, yelling over the chorus of insects. "Isn't that right?"

"Well, damn you and your rules!" The bottle of brandy smashed in an explosion of glass against the nearest tree. Mirage's mournful cry echoed the feeling deep within his soul.

ACKNOWLEDGEMENTS

Being a writer often feels like serving a life sentence for terrible crimes in a past life. I would like to thank my fellow cursed human friends for helping push me along, Mel and Leu. Judah, Elizabeth and everyone else who read it when it was much worse off. Without your support, these pages would have made a lovely fire for roasting s'mores. If you have any complaints as a reader, you know who to take it up with...

ABOUT THE AUTHOR

Anna: mom, wife, animal-lover, sometimes poses as an artist; wielder of sarcasm and sharp objects; cursed, but doing her best.

www.ingramcontent.com/pod-product-compliance
Lightning Source LLC
Chambersburg PA
CBHW031700170626
46808CB00005B/1539